THE CARPET CIPHER

The Agency of the Ancient Lost and Found, Book 1. A Phoebe McCabe Mystery Thriller

JANE THORNLEY

River Flow Press

PROLOGUE

Venice, February 2019

How long had it been since she had last ventured into the Venetian streets at night—five years, ten? Too long ago, in any event, and to do so tonight of all nights, when the carnival finale was in full swing and the revelry would reach a raucous pitch, seemed foolish even for her. How she detested the noise, the crowds, even the fierce and gilded costumes that would press against her in the dark like fevered dreams. To stay home by the fire with a book and a glass of wine seemed far preferable. Still, it must be done. After tonight she would lay one matter to rest and possibly see the conclusion of another, much older mystery.

She opened the front door, hesitating briefly before leaving the safety of her palazzo and plunging into the throng, her velvet coat wrapped tightly around her to ward away the spring chill. As expected, the young people were outdoing each other with fantastic finery. Gone were the days when only the time traveler mode of long gowns and medieval costumes ruled, though plenty of those still roamed the streets. Now creative interlopers had arrived with glittery fairy wings, and was that a chicken? Yes, a chicken, complete with an enormous egg tucked under one false wing! She stifled a laugh.

Her own mask, on the other hand, was demure by comparison, a lovely sun/moon creation she had had especially made for another carnival long ago when she had been a young woman, her whole life stretching ahead. Then, the duality of light and dark had been no more than a playful game. As on that evening, she also wore the cape worked in deep blue velvet stenciled in gold stars with Mariano Fortuny's distinctive flair. Now, that subtle silken loveliness seemed to sink like a poor cousin against the surrounding sequins and gaudy trappings.

Never mind, she told herself, the man she was to meet would appreciate it for what it was: a testament to artisan beauty in a world that had long lost sight of what does not scream for attention. That she would reunite with the one with whom she had first worn the ensemble was a fitting end to their long torturous relationship. Though they had not seen one another for many decades, she prayed that he had finally forgiven her long enough to help her now. He of all people would know the significance of what she had discovered.

But first, she must resolve the other matter. There was to be no meeting at her family's weaving studio, on that point she was firm. The call had come just moments before she left the villa and her first response had been to refuse the request, but then she reconsidered. The matter could not be avoided forever and perhaps could be dealt with fairly. Her counteroffer was generous. She would make the meeting brief, citing her other appointment to excuse her haste, and hopefully the ugly matter would be laid to rest at last.

The chosen rendezvous was tucked away from the street in a corner she had reason to believe would be suitably private, close to the canal but not in the midst of the celebrations. She slipped through the press of merrymakers. At least they were good-natured and she could only hope that the person she was to meet would be in a similar mood, or at least open to compromise.

She passed a market stall now caged for the night and turned a corner to where the winter storms had damaged the street so that temporary planking now bridged the narrow side canal. Behind the repair works, tucked against the side door of an ancient church with steps leading to the canal, the meeting place offered privacy.

It was surprisingly dark, much darker than she had anticipated. Fool. Why hadn't she thought this out more carefully? Two, maybe three shapes detached themselves from the dark clot of shadows against the church door, one of them immediately recognizable, and at once she knew she had miscalculated. There would be no easy resolution, after all.

1

The man staring at me had been dead for over two thousand years yet still made a better companion than some of the men I'd known.

"Phoebe?"

I tore myself away from the bust to see Serena, my gallery manager and friend, arriving on my stair landing office carrying a mug of tea. The shop was closed for renovation but she had been busy storing our rare textiles while workmen banged away downstairs. Baker and Mermaid was in the midst of a metamorphosis from textile gallery to undercover art retrieval and repatriation center that we jokingly referred to as the Agency of the Ancient Lost and Found.

"So, this is what I've discovered so far," I began. "Our Roman here is a probable mid-first century A.D. funerary piece discerned because of the dark earthen encrustation on the back of the head. Dr. Rudolph confirms that assessment but has no idea where the piece might have come from. We ran it through Interpol's database but nothing." My specialty was actually textiles but no one can afford to be too narrowly focused in the art and artifact retrieval business. "Anyway, there's no trace of anything matching this description missing from any of the museums so I'm guessing it's from a looted grave."

"Phoebe."

I stopped and stared at her. "Serena?"

"You sit up here all day and many hours in the evening and work, work, work. It is not healthy." She passed the boxes of books and personal belongings ready for storage and scanned the piles for a place to set the tea. "We thought you could use some cheering up." It took a moment to clear a spot on my desk. "There, see? Chocolate helps." A small wafer of very expensive Swiss chocolate was slid in beside the piled papers.

"Help what?" I could always use chocolate and tea, of course. That was a given. "Okay, so I'll take a break."

I pushed away from the desk and reached for the tea.

"Phoebe."

I looked up.

"You must snap out of this. You seem depressed, in the doldrums—is that the right word? Max agrees." Serena's English had much improved over the years but the Italian roots still tangled with her syntax.

"I'm not in the doldrums, I'm working—a considerably more productive state of mind altogether. Besides, there's so much to do."

Everybody had plunged into a fury of activity readying Baker and Mermaid for its dual existence. We had recently acquired a haul including three paintings, the Roman sculpture, and an assortment of other museum-quality artifacts as yet unclaimed or even identified, and that was only the beginning. Our colleague, Nicolina Vanvitelli, had a similar cache housed in Rome.

And in case you thought, as I once did, that there are well-financed government departments in the world with the sole purpose of handling the retrieval and return of stolen art and artifacts, forget it. What exists remains underfinanced, overworked, and shackled with cross-border red tape. Interpol's divisions on the theft and illicit traffic in works of art, cultural property, and antiquities accept all the help they can get, providing we work closely with the multiple affiliated organizations involved.

"You do not have to work all the time," Serena was saying. "We think you are depressed."

"Depressed—are you kidding me?"

"You have much to be depressed about, I understand this. There is no shame in admitting it." Serena was squeezing my shoulder as if testing a grapefruit for ripeness.

In summary, I had just sent my brother and only living relative to prison, ended a romance (actually, I sent Interpol after him, which is probably the same thing), and outmaneuvered a friend to the point where we were no longer speaking. I didn't blame myself for any of this, you understand. I had simply experienced a three-incident pileup at the moral crossroads of life and finally taken the high road amid the wreckage. For the record, the high road has to be the loneliest damn path on the planet.

"I would never feel ashamed admitting that I had any kind of mental health issue had I one but, in fact, my mood is more on the triumphant side."

It's true that for months all I did was work, primarily categorizing and classifying the art and artifacts and working closely with Britain's Interpol Works of Art Unit coordinator, Sam Walker. By hiding deep inside the minutiae of classification and research, I didn't have to examine too closely the yawning hollows in my life. That was not what I term depression but recalibration.

I stared at my desk and frowned. "I'm not sure I like the idea of you and Max discussing me behind my back."

"Then we'll carry on the conversation in front of you, darlin'," my godfather boomed as he marched up the stairs.

I sighed. A delegation. Max Baker had gifted me half of the rare textile gallery, Baker and Mermaid, but it was I who mostly bore responsibility for branching off into this new initiative.

Standing over me now, he was as debonaire and handsome as ever at seventy-five. "You really do need to snap out of this."

"I don't require snapping out of anything." I gazed up at him. We'd had this conversation before, multiple times.

"Really? You've barely left the building in weeks. Besides, you can't continue to sit here while they tear up the stairs."

That was true, especially since my open-plan Perplex office landing was essentially *on* the stairs. Soon we would have three levels, including a high-tech work space in the basement plus an enhanced gallery area on the main floor with my flat above caught up in the transformation. The basement art repatriation center was something entirely new. In two days or less, I literally would have no place to sleep.

"Are you going to come stay with me or not?"

A month spent under the same roof as Max wouldn't be unbearable but it didn't strike me as the best scenario, either. I had yet to make a decision. For some reason, decisions had become so monumental that I preferred to wait until they went away.

"Maybe," I said, gazing through the transparent stairs at the chaos below. Stacks of lumber littered the ground floor and none of our extraordinary carpets remained visible—all in storage. Part of me quavered at losing the view of those rare textiles on a daily basis, since each of them had comforted my beleaguered heart on more than one occasion.

"Nicolina says that you've barely communicated since she returned to Rome. She's sent messages and says you text only a few words back," Max continued.

I blinked at him, realizing I'd missed part of the conversation. "Pardon?"

"Nicolina, she says you are incommunicado," Serena added.

A little self-defense was in order. "Texting is hardly the safest way to communicate in our line of work. Who trusts encryption these days? By the way, is 'incommunicado' Italian or Spanish?" I lifted my head. "I often wondered."

"*Phoebe,*" Max said, tapping the desk. "I, too, am wrestling with the loss of Noel. I finally reconnected with my son only to lose him again, but I'm confident that he'll eventually find us. He always does."

"He can find you, if he wants, but he can leave me out if it. It's over," I said with more asperity than I'd intended.

"I don't believe that for a moment," Max said.

Why did people keep saying that as if I didn't know my own mind? "Believe it. Either we're together or we're not and he chose not, at least not any time before I turn sixty-five."

"He chose not to go to jail. Surely you can understand that?" Max was shoving his thick gray mane away from his forehead, a sure sign of agitation. It made my heart ache to think that he'd once dreamed of the three of us as some kind of weird semi-criminal family.

"It's totally his right to remain a hunted criminal all his life and equally my right not to join him. The moment he made his choice, it was over and, frankly, sending Interpol after him probably tipped the scales." I stared into space. "As for Toby, I sent my dear brother to prison to save his life. Maybe someday he'll even forgive me in time."

"You think three years a long time, then presto—" Serena snapped her fingers "—it is gone."

"Do you know what you really want in life, darlin'?" Max asked. He had to be watching *Oprah* reruns again.

"Yes," I said with enough assurance to surprise even me. "I want to retrieve stolen art and antiquities and return them to their original owners, thus preserving as much of history as possible for future generations." Okay, so that sounded stilted but I loved history and art with enough passion, to make everything else bearable.

A sadness gathered like clouds in Max's blue eyes. "Anyway, you need to take a break. While the shop is closed and renovations under way, it's a prime time for you to get out of Dodge."

"I have a feeling you already have a suggested location."

"Go to Italy to visit Nicolina," said Serena, jumping in with a flourish to land the trump card. "You always love Italy and Italians, yes?"

I nodded. "But who goes to Italy in February?" I caught the exchange of glances and knew the significance: *she's really in a bad way.* People of sound mind knew that any time was the perfect time for visiting Italy apparently.

"Nicolina, she needs you in Rome now. So much work to do, she says, but there are other matters that need your attention," Serena said. "She would not share the details on the phone but it all seems very urgent."

"She has Seraphina to help her," I pointed out. Seraphina was Nicolina's über assistant. Everybody in this line of work had talented, armed assistants seconding as bodyguards and I had just recently acquired one of my own.

"But she says she needs *you*, Phoebe."

"I suppose she needs my help in sorting through all the loot we brought back." After all, we brought home about fifteen crates from my brother's hoard—all that we could carry to the plane actually—leaving the remains for Noel to steal.

So far, we hadn't seen Nicolina's share and the topic was hardly safe for electronic communication of any kind. I did need to visit and soon.

Max was looming over me, hands on my shoulders doing the papa-bear thing, which I detested but totally lacked the energy to protest. "You must go to her, Phoebe."

"Yes, all right," I said flatly, talking to the top button of the vintage velvet waistcoat. Serena had given it to him for Christmas one year and I'd never seen him wear it until now. What else had I been missing? "I'll join her in a few weeks."

"Now, before your apartment is out of bounds," Max said.

"I suppose."

"She needs you, Phoebe, as in immediately," Serena added. "She made that clear."

I shrugged.

"There's been a death in her circle apparently," Max added.

I gazed up him. "What does that have to do with me?"

"A good friend, Maria Contini, passed and Nicolina says she needs your moral support and expertise."

COUNTESS NICOLINA VANVITELLI NEEDING MY SUPPORT, MORAL OR otherwise, was hard to get my head around. Needing my expertise was something else again. I didn't consider myself an expert so much as possessing good instincts with occasional jolts of pure intuition. My undergraduate degree in art history combined with a passion for textiles didn't hurt, but more than anything, I had a good eye and good instincts.

"Apparently Maria Contini has passed away suddenly," I said, standing in the downstairs demolition zone talking to Penelope Williams known as Peaches who happened to be my new bodyguard.

"Nicolina mentioned her to me once," I told her. "She has—or *had*—a fabulous textile collection of Fortuny and Renaissance textiles. Maybe she needs me to help with those?" Technically, Nicolina, Peaches, Max, and I were partners in this ancient lost and found initiative.

"That makes sense, doesn't it? I mean you're the expert in that fabric stuff." Peaches was definitely more hardware than soft wear. A curvy, toned, six-foot-one-inch-tall engineer by training, commando by inclination, she never could see the value in anything soft. Her current construction supervisor role with us was as close as she'd come to gainful employment in her field of study.

I gazed up, way up. "Textiles, not 'fabric,' Peaches. Anyway, I'm going."

"Whatever. I get that people collect all kinds of weird shit that would never float my boat. When are you leaving?"

"Tonight."

"Need a bodyguard?"

"Why would I? Anyway, you have to keep the construction team on track."

"Well, hell, sure. I'll keep these dudes whipped into shape."

"I know you will. Just remember that we can't afford to lose more construction guys."

"Right, Phoebe. Don't worry about a ting." And sometimes she slipped into what I called Jamaicanese. She stood studying me, outfitted in black spandex topped by a leather jacket, an ensemble which would have reduced most women to an ill-packaged mess of athlete-meets-biker-momma. On her, it was simply Amazonian. "Anyway, I'm glad you're getting away. Probably the sooner, the better." She shook her cornrows and picked up a piece of marble tile from a pile. "See this? You hardly pay attention to any of the renovations."

I mumbled: "I've been busy."

"Translation: uninterested—I get it. So listen up: we're laying this on the lower level, which will have a modern vibe—clean and antiseptic like a time laboratory instead of this whisper-rich thing you got going on up here. You're going to miss your colors, I know, and I totally sympathize with you, girl, but you're going to love it. You'll see. When you get back, we'll be that much closer to spectacular."

"I believe it." But I didn't really. Too much change in too short a time. I gazed around the gallery, or what was left of it. I'd seen the drawings for the new space but it was challenging to imagine this gutted shell as anything but what it wasn't—my beloved carpet and rare textile gallery.

"I know that everyone has the renos in hand." I turned toward her. "Are you all right here?"

Peaches looked at me hard. "Of course I'm all right here. Like you said,

I have work to do. I told Mom and Dad that I'd come see them in Jamaica in a few weeks, anyway—have to get my work visa straightened out."

I smiled. "Fabulous. I'm so glad you're part of the team."

She frowned. "Did you really just say that?"

"Forget I ever uttered the phrase. I think I'm in worse shape than I thought."

"That's what I've been trying to tell you."

And then the doorbell rang.

"Who's that? We're not even open." Peaches strode though the debris to our paper-covered glass storefront and unlocked the door to Agent Sam Walker, who nodded a greeting and stepped in.

"Sam, what a surprise. We haven't seen you in, what, two days?" I said.

"I think actually that it was more like one," Peaches said.

Sam grinned in that lopsided way of his that sent his scar chasing his eyebrow halfway up his hairline. It was a singularly arresting face in a bald man that I'd grown to like but not in any romantic sense. "I just dropped in to have a word."

I stepped forward. "About?"

Peaches swung away to yell at one of the drywallers as Sam led me over to the far corner. "I was talking this morning to my Italian colleague who informs me that a very valuable painting has been stolen from a palazzo in Venice under mysterious circumstances."

"Are you putting me on the case or something?" The *or something* bit was critical since so far Interpol had happily allowed us to do the cataloging and database checking of the pieces we'd retrieved but had yet to assign us to a proper case. We were, after all, not trained police officers or even detectives.

"Not exactly," he said.

"I knew it: always the bridesmaid, never the bride."

He quirked a smile. "We appreciate your efforts in all respects, Phoebe, but our reason for approaching you now is because you may have an inside lead that could prove valuable. The painting in question belonged to a very good friend of Nicolina Vanvitelli, a friend who died that same night as the theft."

"It wouldn't happen to be Maria Contini, would it?"

"How do you know that?"

At that moment my cell vibrated. I pulled the phone from my pocket and read the text from Nicolina:

Phoebe, we must change plans. Meet me at the airport in Roma. We must proceed to Venice at once. I have arranged the flight. Nicolina

"Ah," said Sam, peering over my shoulder. "Ah, so her majesty speaks. Excellent. Go and snoop around but keep me informed this time."

❧ 2 ❧

I should have asked *where* exactly in the Rome airport I was to meet Nicolina. Why did I think I could just arrive in a metropolitan hub and suddenly the obvious meeting spot would appear like a mirage?

Apparently I was not supposed to do the finding but wait to be found. Once I got that into my head, it took less than five minutes.

"Phoebe!"

I turned to see Nicolina's assistant, Seraphina, shoving a man aside in order to commandeer my arm. *"Scusa,"* she said without giving him a second glance while to me she added: "We must hurry."

She attempted to take control of both my roller suitcase and my tapestry bag but I refused to relinquish the latter despite its weight. After a moment of tugging, she shot me an irritated look and gripped the roller while jerking her head to follow her. "The plane, it takes off in twenty minutes."

Small and fierce, Seraphina was not easy to warm up to. In fact, at times I found her unnerving the way one might a bad-tempered terrier that perpetually bares its teeth.

I followed along, expecting to endure yet another laborious security screening. Instead, we were whisked off to an alternative corridor and through a more streamlined system, emerging several moments later in a private waiting room. I knew without asking that Countess Vanvitelli, aka Nicolina, had pulled the gilded strings again and that we were likely taking her friend's private plane.

I looked around the small lounge with only time enough to see Nicolina sweeping down to embrace me.

"Phoebe! I missed you, and you would not properly answer my texts. How I worried, but things will be better between us now, yes?" Air kisses followed along with a gracious Italian hug, which I liken to halfway between a bow and a benediction.

I stepped back, admiring her sleek merlot-toned leather pantsuit and the flawless everything of my tall Italian friend. The fact that her reddened eyes almost matched the hue of her ensemble hardly spoiled the effect. "I hope so. I'm sorry for being incommunicado, Nicolina, but I've been preoccupied."

"There is nothing to forgive," she said with a wave of her hand. "You are here now and that is all that matters. What's going on?"

"Oh, Phoebe, such a difficult matter. Maria Contini has died suddenly. We were childhood friends, our families very close. It was only the day before yesterday when we spoke and now she is gone, and robbed, too." She dabbed her eyes with a handkerchief. "I cannot believe it. Something is wrong, very wrong. There are too many odd occurrences that I do not think I can wade through by myself—too emotional. I need your support."

Since when? I wondered. "And you have it. Was she killed during a robbery?"

"Yes and no. Both events happened on the same night, the last night of Carnevale."

I planned to wait until she told me about the painting. "How and where exactly did it happen?"

"Nothing makes sense. She was a quiet woman—a recluse, you say in English—and no longer even attended the festivities, and yet she left the villa by herself that night and ended up dead the same time that her prized painting was stolen."

"Really? I'm so sorry, Nicolina," I said, grasping her hands. "This is horrible. To lose a friend under such traumatic circumstances."

Her eyes might be swollen but they held such a glint of determination that only a fool would think it was due to grief alone. "Whoever did this will pay. No one harms my friend and gets away with it, no one."

I nodded. "We'll find out the truth."

"Poor Maria, she did not deserve to die like this!" She tugged her hands from mine and began to sob.

"Died in what fashion exactly?"

"I don't know!"

"Was the painting stolen from her villa?"

Nicolina shook her head and turned away. "We must talk more of this later. For now I must pull myself together." Then she turned back to me and smiled sadly. "I wish you had known her. You would have loved her. She adored textiles as you do and had gathered many fine pieces over the years, including her late grandmama's Fortunies."

"Look, I hate to grill you but could you tell me if the police believe Maria's death was accidental or if there were signs of violence? Where was she found and who found her?" I never bought into the one-question-at-a-time school of thought and, not surprisingly, my law background was already kicking in.

A loudspeaker announced that boarding would begin immediately.

"Maybe just answer the first question," I called over the announcement.

"Later. We must board now," she called back. "We go." She linked arms with mine as we followed Seraphina, who now carried four carry-on bags plus a grudge that I wouldn't let her make it five. Together we marched up to passport control. "We will speak later on the plane," Nicolina assured me.

But later was late coming, considering that I was enveloped in an effusive welcome by Fabio, our steward, followed by a hearty handshake from Otty, the pilot. This was the private plane owned by Nicolina's mysterious friend and we had all been together before.

Naturally, there was much to catch up on plus many treats to sample along with nonstop service of strong Italian coffee equivalent to jet fuel. I sank back in the plush leather seats and attempted to enjoy the short flight but I was getting very caffeinated very fast.

"So, do we have another priceless artwork to return to its rightful owner?" Fabio asked as he offered us a tray of biscotti. A touch of turbulence caused him to take a step back, pirouette, and quickly regroup. The man had acrobatic grace partnered with an equally showstopping sense of style, today in his uniform of a pale blue vest and matching pants. Apparently he had tried to dress his partner, Otty, in something similar but the captain preferred a more traditional look.

"Another?" I asked, turning to Nicolina.

"Well, there was Naples—" Fabio said before catching Nicolina's expression.

"We are coming to Venice to discover who murdered my friend," Nicolina said in her contessa tone.

"Oh, dear. How dreadful. So sorry for your loss," Fabio said, shooting me a quick look and promptly pivoting around to head back to the galley.

I kept my attention fixed on Nicolina. "Have you returned a painting already, Nicolina, without the necessary arrangements through Interpol?" The question was hardly irrelevant but maybe a tad insensitive given the gravitas of the moment.

She waved her hand. "Just one. This I told Max. It was a private matter, a piece stolen from a friend and returned to him in Naples. The provenance trail was clear. I did explain this to Max."

"You did?" I knew that I'd been distracted lately but I couldn't believe that I'd missed something so important. "And does Interpol know?"

"Interpol!" she scoffed. "They are every day in my villa, asking questions, poking around. They will not leave me alone. Forget Interpol. I am more concerned about you, dear friend." She leaned over to touch my hand. "I have spoken to Max many times while, Phoebe, you have been—" she fished for the perfect word "—unavailable. Yes, you have been unavailable. Did he not say?"

"Perhaps he did."

"You have not been yourself," she hurried on. "This I understand. Noel and your brother—all very difficult. I know this after my problems with my family. Do you remember?"

How could I forget? A grandfather who locked her grandmother away, parents killed by the Camorra, a husband who tried to steal her fortune, the overbearing brother who believed being male made him automatically head of the family, possibly the universe... "I remember very well."

"So, you know that I understand how one must heal by being strong and busy with purpose," she continued. "You have had two big blows and have been very, very busy."

"Actually, I counted three," I said, "not that losing Rupert's friendship is considered a blow by most."

"Rupert," Nicolina said with another note of impatience. "He or his manservant are never far away but stay out of sight like rodents, yes? Back to you: work helps much better than thinking too hard on our losses. I will help you move on, as they say, and you will help me. Now I have a loss of my dearest friend and I must discover what really happened to heal my grief. Keeping occupied is the only way. Together we help each other. I know you do not shrink from such things. Strong women help each other."

I sat back. It struck me as odd that she wanted my help in solving Maria's murder and odder still that Sam Walker had requested that I become involved. Clearly the police didn't trust Nicolina any more than I did. "I will do what I can, of course."

She nodded and smiled sadly. "We will solve this together now. Dear Maria, I cannot believe that she is gone."

I took another gulp of coffee. "I'm sorry, Nicolina. Losing a friend is so difficult. Where exactly in Venice we are staying?"

Nicolina gazed out the window, now nothing but a scud of dark as we began to descend. "I had thought at first of the Danieli but then knew that it would be best if we stayed at Maria's, as much as I will find it unbearable. She would want this and I have much work to do there, though the police will be coming and going. I always stayed with her when I visit Venice so why not now when I have business to attend and the police wish to speak with me? Maria's housekeeper, Zara, is distraught—she has worked for Maria for decades—but she has readied the rooms at my request."

"Did Maria have children, maybe a husband or siblings?" I asked.

"No family. Maria was an only child and never married, though she was engaged long ago. I was like her sister. She often called me her *sorellina*, her little sister." Nicolina subsided into her thoughts while I tried to muster mine.

I had so many questions but, once again, I was diving blindly into a situation and needed to figure things out on my feet. You'd think I'd get used to this by now but somehow I never could.

Fabio darted into the cabin to remove our cups and check that all the safety boxes where ticked before landing. "Just sit back now and relax," he said. "Otty says that we are in a holding pattern for a few minutes but as soon as we get clearance we'll be landing pronto."

I peered out the window, gazing far down at ribbons of light followed by dark expanses. I had never flown into Venice before, my string of one-day visits occurring back in my twenties while doing the budget thing around Europe. Venice had always been a day-long bus tour, the most recent out of Bologna, and remembered as a flash of mental postcards—St. Mark's Square, the Doge's Palace—along with tourist-infested streets and watery byways. I'd loved every moment and always left hungry for more.

And this visit was supposed to in some way help my own dark night of the soul? Venice as the site of sudden death did not a happy pill make. But this wasn't about me. This was about helping Nicolina. Still, an intense sense of foreboding had overtaken me and I was one of those people who took these things seriously.

As we flew over the black lagoon on our descent, the uneasy sense of about to land on water intensified as I strained to see the runway lights. I had a sudden thought and looked across the aisle. "Nicolina, what did you mean by having business to attend to and that the police wanted to speak to you?"

She pulled herself out of her thoughts and sighed. "Did I not mention that I am the executor of Maria's will as well as her main beneficiary?"

❧ 3 ❧

I had flown into many airports but never one that required waiting for a boat on a dark rainy night. Naturally Seraphina had everything in hand and soon we were ushered to a private speedboat for a brief zip across the lagoon.

Lagoons should be turquoise, tropical, and warm, not inky dark, layered in mystery, and scented like the breath of time. That was Venice for you, always a mystery, no matter how often you approached her. She had once grown rich and gilded from trade centuries ago, and though that luster still glowed beneath layers of age, it now felt tenuous. Venice: you could never say you'd been there no matter how many times you had. She would always be the most unknowable city on earth.

As if the city had already cast a pall, my companions remained sober and disinclined to talk, not that conversation was even possible over the roar of the boat engine. There were so many things I needed to know. Of course, Nicolina had just suffered a loss and here I was about to intrude upon a house of mourning and as what—a detective, a purveyor of moral support, an observer? The whole thing made me edgy.

After a few minutes, I escaped the noisy silence to duck outside where I could feel the wind and rain in my face. I pulled up my rain jacket's hood and hunched down to watch Venice approach. I needed time with my thoughts. That Nicolina was Maria Contini's executor was a relationship I hadn't anticipated. What else about this situation had I yet to learn? Again, my own fault for not doing due diligence and insisting on answers before taking the leap.

Ahead, Venice appeared as a mirage—lights strung out over a reflective darkness whipped by rain. I held my breath as the boat skimmed past tall shuttered villas looming down over the water, and glimpsed the golden domes of St. Mark's Basilica just seconds before we sped into one of the main arteries—the Grand Canal, I realized—awash with light from the multitude of lamps and windows like some kind of ancient, dignified playground.

Stands of gondolas rocked at their moorings, a tour boat churned the wake beside us, and I glimpsed people dashing somewhere with their umbrellas popped on either side of the canal. When we sped under the Rialto Bridge, I could only gaze up as if I was seeing Venice for the very first time, overwhelmed by the impact of history and the city's unique kind of magic.

I wanted to call to Nicolina to share this moment, to see Venice as I did at that very instant, but how pointless was that? My friend struggled with grief while I tried to emerge from my own losses. A veil of loneliness came over me that set my mood adrift. If only I could visit Venice with somebody I loved—with Noel, maybe—as if that would ever happen. I had cast away the man of my heart, and if that heart was broken as a result, that, too, was my own damn fault for falling for a man like him. Color my mood self-recrimination.

The boat darted into a smaller tributary and the driver immediately throttled the engine back to a sedate putter. Now the slosh of water against stone accompanied the sounds of the boat as we snaked our way deeper into the city's heart. We passed under many bridges and slipped past multiple tiny *campi*, their rain-washed cobbles deserted. Once I looked up to see a man on a balcony gazing down as he smoked a cigarette. He lifted his hand to acknowledge me but the boat had turned into another artery before I could wave back.

Traveling anywhere in Venice with its watery streets and myriad *porti* felt like a journey of mythic proportions and always delivered you to some place unexpected even if it was your intended destination. Whatever I was expecting of Maria Contini's doorstep, it wasn't a narrow ledge tucked around a corner of a tiny canal with only a battered and algae-scummed hunk of timber for a door. No knob, no latch, not even a bell to ring. At least there was a light blazing blearily down on us from a motion lamp fixed to the wall above.

The driver grappled for one of the steel docking rings to secure the prow while I clambered to the stern to tie the rope around the other. He was calling something to me in Italian that I couldn't grasp—maybe *thanks for not being merely decorative* or *you know boats,* sì? I didn't require a translator to do the obvious. I'd been around boats most of my life.

Soon Seraphina appeared and the Italian truly grew intense as she began dispensing instructions, I'm guessing, while the driver argued back. That gave me time to look way up to where the dark wall of the villa loomed overhead. This was not my first experience with a looming Italian villa, but I had to admit, Venice did them best. If structures were faces, this one was totally inscrutable with closed eyes under long arched lids and a dark countenance. The arched windows indicated Islamic influences, meaning the building must date from at least the 1500s.

And then suddenly one lid flew open as a woman unlatched a shutter and called down. Seraphina responded and more debating ensued. Then Nicolina appeared, the hood of her coat flung over her head. "Zara wishes us to use the front door but the driver, he says that is not possible tonight," she told me. "There is construction in the front of the canal. We must enter through the cantina."

Cantina, I knew, did not translate into *café* in Italian but *cellar,* which meant we were to enter through Venice's idea of a basement, something which would horrify most hosts and certainly Zara, judging from her tone. In the case of Venice, a cellar was likely the villa's first-floor back door.

The moldy wooden door creaked open and the driver began to unload the luggage and try to help the ladies, though both Seraphina and I refused his proffered hand. I leaped over the stoop on my own steam whereas Seraphina insisted on helping with the bags. Nicolina, however, waited for assistance with her usual grace.

That left me standing alone in a damp cavernous space peering into the darkness lit by a single overhead bulb. A small motorboat sat on tracks pointed toward the now-open door, ready to be pushed into the canal when needed. These bottom floors also seconded as boathouses. This one had to be at the bottom of a very large footprint, by the looks of the capacious space.

I detected two more narrow boats propped on stilts way back in the shadows—very old by the glimpse of an ornate lantern peeking out from under one tarp. The area was also a repository for things stored for centuries with odd shapes clustered on stands in the shadows or hung from hooks on the damp walls. Repeated floods had those hooks positioned five or six feet above floor level to escape the jagged green line that seemed to chase the objects up the walls. The scent of motor oil, diesel, and damp was overpowering but brought me back to my childhood.

I had just caught the gaze of an elaborate mask covered in clear plastic when Nicolina came up and touched my arm. "Phoebe, come. Zara awaits upstairs."

I traipsed up behind her, Seraphina bringing up the rear. Masks on the walls watched our progress like a row of bizarre spectators frozen in shock. It was a relief to step into the villa proper where a small, dark-skinned woman with graying hair scraped into a bun waited for us in the shadows. Nicolina made the introductions and the woman shook my hand and shot me a perfunctory smile.

"I'm so sorry for your loss," I said.

She turned to Seraphina for a translation and nodded when it came but soon forgot about me the moment she enveloped Seraphina in an expansive embrace amid a battery of Italian. We were then ushered down a dark hall into a large high-ceilinged room and asked to sit.

The salon was like the reception rooms of all Italian villas I had known and yet different. This one had the same high-ceiling grandeur of Nicolina's residences and yet a pervading sense of loss clung to the walls along with the richest array of disintegrating textiles I had ever seen. Though the clear outline of a missing frame was visible over the fireplace, I was too distracted by the surroundings to focus there.

Threadbare brocades and velvets covered every shabby chair and settee, their deep Prussian blues and golds still rich in the lamp and firelight. It was as if the entire room was paved in fabric and jeweled colors. My eyes traveled around the space touching every glossy inch, marveling at the silk-covered walls, the kilim cushions, and magnificent patterned Persian carpets spread underfoot.

Nicolina spoke softly. "It is as I told you, Phoebe. Maria celebrated textiles as if they were dear friends, much like you do. It was in her blood, you understand. I will explain later. Please be patient for Zara speaks no English and I will translate when I am able."

I nodded, relieved not to be expected to speak, especially since my gaze had focused on a framed piece of damask on the far wall—very old, I guessed. Fabric treated with as much veneration as art met with my approval, though conservation didn't seem to be a consideration here.

While I studied every detail within my range of vision, Seraphina sat beside Zara while Nicolina and I sat on the opposite side on a flaking velvet and gilt wood settee. The Italian flowed, intense and emotional. I gathered that Nicolina and Seraphina were asking questions of Zara until, at one point, the housekeeper disappeared and returned with a tray of wine.

Forgoing the wine, I continued sipping water, absorbed in studying the edge of a rare carpet when suddenly I caught the change in Zara's tone. I pulled my attention back to my companions and noted that Maria's assistant now appeared to be answering Nicolina and Seraphina's questions as if every word had to be pried out of her. Her replies escaped her slight frame in bursts, one moment sitting silent with her lips pursed and the next responding with an artillery of short, terse sentences.

Nicolina asked her something that caused Zara to jump up from her chair with a cry and dash from the room, Seraphina following after.

"What was that about?" I asked, turning to Nicolina.

She sighed. "Maria's death has been very traumatic for her. She does not wish to speak of it to me any longer."

"But surely she must?"

"Yes, I agree she must, but not tonight. Today the police have questioned her over and over again and she is weary. This I understand. Seraphina will take care of her while we talk and enjoy our vin Santo. They have been friends since I first began bringing Seraphina here years ago."

Nicolina attempted to pour me a glass of her beloved sweet wine but I shook my head. Her eyebrows rose. "Phoebe, I hope you do not refuse the wine because of what happened in Amalfi? I only drugged you because of the need to keep you safe and—"

I waved away the notion. "It's not because of that, Nicolina, though it's true that I'll never look at Santo quite the same way again. It's just that I don't do well with wine in general and I have had too much coffee tonight already."

"Then you need the wine to help you relax, yes? Here, I will pour you a glass and you will drink or not, as you wish." She poured a goblet of the deep maroon drink and set it beside my water glass before sipping deeply of her own.

"Zara must have told you something about what happened?" I pressed.

"But of course. She said that Maria, for whom she has worked for nearly thirty years, had seemed troubled over these many weeks. She does not know why as Maria would not confide—they were not as close as I am to Seraphina, not as a confidantes, you understand. Their relationship was more formal."

As if I could ever understand the relationship between an employer and a long-serving employee/servant. Serena was more my friend than gallery manager so that didn't count.

Nicolina continued. "It had something to do with money, she believed. Over the years, the household has become increasingly poor and Maria had been worried. I noticed an edge in her tone when we spoke on the phone days ago but I thought it because she was feeling—how do you say?—under the weather. She never mentioned an illness to me or to Zara. She was very energetic, very spry, as the English say. Zara thinks she was very worried about something."

"How old was she?"

"Sixty-two."

"Oh, young, then."

"Exactly. Yet the police suggested that Maria may have tripped and fallen into the canal that evening as if she was clumsy or drunk. That was not Maria."

"Maria was found in the canal?" I almost choked on my water.

"She was found in the Cannaregio, yes. Apparently there were no signs of struggle."

I followed her gaze to the ceiling-high brocade drapes I had been admiring earlier, which I now realized must shield equally tall shutters that looked out over the main canal. "They think she drowned?"

"The autopsy is not yet complete. There are many events during that last night of Carnevale—the grand finale, the water parades, the revelry," Nicolina said, pouring herself more wine. "Maria did not feel up to taking part, Zara says. She said she would stay home and watch the water parade from her balcony and yet she did go out. Nobody knows why. Perhaps she stepped out to a café or restaurant, though they would be very busy that night, and Maria did not take big meals in the evening anymore. Or perhaps she decided not to miss the excitement, after all."

"But didn't she say where she was going to anyone?"

"There was no one here to tell, only Zara, who always spends Carnevale with her niece in Mestra. All the other staff had been let go years ago, including Zara's brother. Had Maria wanted her to stay, she would have but she insisted that Zara go. In the old days, there would be parties that Maria would host or attend but not for many years. She now lived a quiet life and yet..." She gazed down at her glass, deep in thought.

"And yet...?"

"And yet she went out."

"But maybe she decided to join the festivities, after all?" I offered.

"Perhaps, but this does not fit with how anxious she had been lately. Zara says that she suddenly became very concerned about the painting one day last week. The painting had hung in the same place for centuries—in her bedroom, and there had once been one over there, which is the one she sold months ago." She glanced toward the vacant spot over the fireplace. "But last week she received a phone call. She would not say who from but immediately insisted that they crate up the last painting and store it down the street in the family vault."

There was a family vault. I fixed on the rectangle of lighter peachy silk wall covering over the mantel. "So, the remaining painting was stolen from this vault and not from here?"

"Yes. Did I not say? I apologize. Yes, the painting was stolen from the vault down the canal on the same night that Maria was found dead. The vault had been breached by explosives. The police say that the thieves must have used the fireworks and all the noise outside to hide the sounds.

All very clever, really—the excitement, the masks, everyone running in costumes—how easy it made it for them to steal."

"But who knew that the painting was even there?"

Nicolina turned her red-rimmed eyes to me. "Zara, Seraphina, me, possibly one other."

"That's all?"

"I do not think she widely announced that she was the owner of such valuable art but many knew about the warehouse. It was once the establishment for her family's weaving business, now closed, and some of the ancestors once lived on the top floors. Maria resisted pressure to sell the building and planned to turn it into a museum to the weavers one day. It was a dream she clung to, though she had no idea how to finance it." She paused, gazing to the empty space above the fireplace. "She loved it there. She felt in touch with her ancestors as her family has had a weaving studio in that location since the fifteenth century. I will take you there soon."

"And the vault?"

"She called it the *banca*. It was there that one of the earliest Continis built a large vault that has served as the family bank for centuries. The Continis have jokingly called it the *banca* since then, though I suppose in the fifteenth century it truly was their bank. That is the way things were done in those days, yes? It has always been very safe. Maria had tried to keep the security features updated as did her father and his father before him down through time—cameras, sensors, everything—but it is difficult. So expensive. I offered to help her fund an update once but she wouldn't hear of it. That is where she had the painting taken just days before the robbery. It seemed so safe to her but Seraphina had checked it out on our last visit and thought the security full of holes, as they say."

"So it wasn't secure?"

"No, it was not and, in the end, neither was Maria. Zara says that it is almost as if Maria had a premonition—is that the correct word?—that the painting was in danger. There have been other times when she has stored her art there—when she traveled, when there were floods—it was not so strange. What was strange is that she would make the request after this phone call and that she would die on the same night that the painting was stolen."

"I don't believe in coincidences," I said, still gazing at the empty wall.

"I do not, either."

"If we find the thieves we may also find out Maria's killer or, at the very least, discover why she died."

"Yes."

I sighed, suddenly needing a swig of vino but still resisting. "Who discovered Maria was missing?"

"Zara arrived home late the next morning and found her gone. She called the police and the search began. She was found early yesterday morning...floating...in the canal."

Nicolina lowered her glass and quietly wept while I sat imagining the scene. How awful it must have been to arrive home and discover that someone you presumably cared for or looked after was gone—all the searching, the fear, the sense of pending loss...

And yet what if Zara wasn't as devoted as she appeared? "Did the police check Zara's alibi?" I whispered.

"I'm sure they would but it will not be so hard to prove that she was with her family." She sniffed. "I do not believe that she would do this thing. Why now when she'd have worked for her for years?"

"In any case, we need to find out who Maria was speaking to when she suddenly decided to hide that painting."

"Yes, I have already put Seraphina on the task. We will know very soon."

"And what about Maria's will? Are there other beneficiaries?"

She turned to me then, fixing me with her beautiful swollen eyes. "Of course. I know every detail and now it is time you did, too."

I gazed back, waiting. "Why are you hesitating, Nicolina? Is it complicated?"

She sighed and looked away. "Everything is complicated, is it not true? Parts of the will are not so difficult: Maria has left a sizable bequest to Zara, which she discussed with me. She will not have to work ever again."

"That makes sense," I agreed.

She nodded. "Other than that, I have been left the villa and the weaving studio and all of the contents, including the painting."

"Is this why you're hesitating? To me, that makes sense, too. Didn't you say that she had no family?"

"No immediate family, no, certainly no one who she would trust. I refused at first but she pressed me to agree. She wanted to entrust the studio to someone she knew would renovate it as she would and not just sell it to the highest bidder, as her cousin wished to do. And then there is this villa. Villas in Venice are—" she tossed her hands upward "—worth a fortune. This cousin once remarked that Maria should sell up and retire someplace less difficult. She would, if it were hers, but Maria would never leave. She said that Venice's canals were like blood in her veins."

"All right, so you are the major beneficiary and Maria was right to trust you with the largess."

"She also made me promise to follow through with establishing her weaving museum. I will do all these things, of course. The cousin will not contest the will." She shrugged. "I have spoken to her and she has no interest."

"Well, that's good. I know that you will honor Maria's wishes and your friendship." I studied her for a moment. "But why do I get the feeling that there's something else you're not telling me, something you don't want to tell me?"

She turned to me again. "You will not like this, Phoebe."

"Not like what—why would any of this be something that I would dislike in any way?"

"Because there was once another beneficiary in the will whom Maria had removed years ago. To him she had originally bequeathed both paintings because he loved them when she loved him. Love can make a strong woman weak."

"Don't I know it. And she removed this man from her will long ago, you say, and now the last painting has been stolen? That makes him a possible suspect. Is this what you want to tell me?"

"Yes. The man is her former fiancé but she did not tell him that she had removed him from the will, or at least, not that I know of. I believe he found out recently."

I sat back against the cushions and clasped my hands as if to fortify myself. "And I know him, don't I? That's why you're hesitating. All right, out with it, Nicolina. Who is our prime suspect?"

"Rupert Fox."

4

Sir Rupert Fox and I had been friends for years starting from when he and his driver/bodyguard, Evan Barrows rescued me from a spot of trouble. That he was a probable top-drawer pilferer of ancient artifacts was something I had long suspected but couldn't prove. Somehow he managed to fly under Interpol's radar. His London antiquities shop, Carpe Diem, appeared to do a thriving business in rare and arcane artifacts. In any case, for all the years I'd known him he'd only ever mentioned one love, that of his late wife, Mabel.

"Maria Contini and Rupert Fox were engaged?" We were standing on the stairs as Nicolina took me on a flash tour of the villa. I couldn't quite process any of it. In fact, I could hardly focus on the all the treasures she was showing me, for that matter.

"Yes, I said this before, Phoebe. They were secretly engaged almost forty years ago—long before he'd met Mabel and when they were both very young. This is how I first met him, too."

"But how, where?"

"He was in Italy with his father to purchase antiques."

"You mean that his father was an antiques dealer, too?"

"Yes. He owned the same shop Rupert has today."

"But I always thought Rupert acquired Carpe Diem as a front for his art-foraging ways. I had no idea he had inherited it. He's always had that to-the-manor-born thing going on so I thought he was a blue blood."

"Blue blood?" Nicolina gazed at me uncomprehendingly. "Oh, yes, I see: you think he was always wealthy, but before he married Mabel, he was not rich."

"And 'collecting'—" I put the word in air quotes "—art and artifacts has clearly contributed to making him richer even after marrying into money. Okay, so he and his father came here to the villa..."

"And I was there visiting Maria with my grandpapa at the time. Now I will continue my tour *and* my story also, so do be patient, Phoebe. Come."

I followed her up the next two flights. "I'm trying to be patient but you've delivered a couple of info bombs here. I never knew any of this about Rupert."

On the top floor, I paused to gaze through a round window that looked down onto a wide canal blurring with rain and lights—the Cannaregio. So, the way we came in was the back alley, so to speak.

"Why would you? A man does not tell everyone that he was jilted. Do come." I glanced up and hastily joined her.

"He was left standing at the altar?"

"Not exactly but almost," she continued. "It was all very painful for them both. I was never to speak of it to either Maria or Rupert again and, for a time, I never did."

She stopped by a glossy wooden door and slowly turned the brass knob. "We are here," she whispered. Touching my arm, she led me inside and closed the door softly before flicking on a switch. The room suddenly bloomed into a rich tapestry of color.

If a bedroom could be a museum of extraordinary textiles, this was it. At the foot of a four-poster bed swathed with deep blue velvet brocade stood a mannequin in a Fortuny evening ensemble. I'd recognize that style anywhere—the elegant gold-stenciled black silk velvet coat hanging in deep lustrous folds over a pleated silk Delphos gown. Those gowns were Fortuny's signature creation, a masterpiece of pleating designed to drape the female form in a way that enhanced both woman and textile. Even in modern times, no one had quite been able to duplicate the sublime sinuous fusion of color, handiwork, pleating, and design that composed those wonders.

"Oh!" I took a step forward, stopped, and pressed my hands to my mouth. "Oh."

"She could not part with any of them. The Fortunies she rotated from her closet to these stands. Some were her grandmother's, others she collected. There are more there and there."

I wrenched my gaze away from the black-and-gold to fasten it on the deep pomegranate, gold-embossed gown with the transparent pleated overtunic, which stood on another mannequin directly under an orb of light. From there, my gaze went traveling across the room to another illu-minated design, this one a deep apricot pleated velvet seemingly etched in gold vining tendrils with one sleeve parted along the seam to reveal the pleated peach silk gown beneath.

The effect was mesmerizing, akin to fairy tale loosened upon a pre-Raphael dreamscape. "This is one of my favorite decorative periods. The organic flow of color and design, the dynamic movement of shapes and forms. But they should be in a conservation room away from the damp."

"Yes, I know. Come." Nicolina led me across the room and through another door where an enormous glass-enclosed closet opened up on either side. I recognized temperature and moisture-controlled storage shelves and hangers of the most sophisticated nature holding length upon length of fabric as well as boxes and trunks. "This had been her greatest expense—the careful conservation of these treasures so important to her. She would keep her gowns here but would bring a few into her room 'to breathe,' she called it. They were like her friends, her loves. She imagined them one day displayed in similar storage areas in her dream museum down the street along with samples of all the textiles her family made across the centuries. She loved them all. How she loved them!" Her voice caught.

"I'm so sorry, Nicolina."

A pair of slipper chairs sat companionably against one wall beside a low marble table holding a stack of books and a decanter of wine. A single painted crystal glass—I guessed early seventeenth century—sat nearby where I imagined Maria sipping vino while admiring her treasures. A halogen light shone down onto an empty rectangle of silk on the wall over a low marble table. Nicolina indicated for me to take a seat.

"And this was where the last painting originally hung?" I asked.

"Yes, her favorite, and it was once willed to Rupert also. I have photographs. They have never been published or shown in any gallery despite general knowledge that the Continis owned them." She picked up a large leather folder from the table and passed it to me. "The one on the left is the one she sold two months ago."

I opened the portfolio to find a rendering of the artwork on each side of the book-like holder. Once again my breath caught; yet again I succumbed to the glory of brilliant color but something else besides.

Not surprisingly considering the period, one painting was ecclesiastical, an annunciation rendering of incredible detail depicting an angel dressed in velvet trimmed with silk arriving at an open door to witness Mary receiving the seed of God, which appeared like a lightning bolt from the sky. But it was not the Immaculate Conception that interested me so much as the rich textiles revealed through the open portal. A carpet, definitely Anatolian from the late fifteenth century, blew in the breeze from a balcony above in a rich pattern of ochre and reds rendered with such precision that I could attribute it to the region without difficulty. A second textile covered a mantel behind the Virgin. That one I recognized as an Anatolian animal carpet. My mouth went dry. I looked up. "She sold a Crivelli?"

"Yes, Carlo Crivelli painted it in 1487. It broke her heart to let it go but for financial reasons she had no choice."

My gaze swept over to the second painting, which showed a gathering of richly dressed citizens wearing varying shades of silks and velvets celebrating what I assumed to be an engagement or a wedding in a church. An unusual prayer rug warmed the marble under the bride's feet while the family members stood on a carpet design I did not recognize but which almost looked Berber. That, too, was painted in such detail that I could almost feel the nap enough to know it was probably silk. "A Bartolo —seriously?"

"Of course you know your art. Yes, that is Domenico di Bartolo's *Marriage of the Merchant's Daughter* painted in 1441, the one that was stolen. Maria loved both paintings so, as much because of the textiles as the subject matter. She said that those very robes in the Bartolo—you see how the bride's gown features that feathered scroll design?—came from her family's very own fifteenth century silk looms. They sent their textiles far and wide as Venice had an active trade in luxury textiles at the time and that design was unique to the house."

I stared at her. "She believed that this painting illustrates her family's own fabrics?"

"Yes. They may have been painted from life."

"That's incredible provenance."

"Yes, it is."

"Bartolo's known for his frescoes, of course, but he painted other mediums. And the carpets? It can't be a coincidence that both paintings feature carpets prominently, or prominently to me. There are only a few Renaissance artists known for using carpets in such exquisite detail and these two are among them. But I don't recognize the design of this larger version where the wedding party is standing."

"Yes, it has always been an enigma."

My gaze returned to the photo. "The Bartolo carpets are an odd mix of symbology. It's very unusual for Renaissance painters to use Berber carpets in their work. They were usually purely Anatolian or Chinese. There isn't anything purely one thing or another in any of the symbols here."

"I knew you would notice. That painting was very special, as you can see, not just by a renowned Renaissance artist but perhaps linked to her family by the bride's gown. Imagine the value? Imagine how disappointed Rupert was at having them both slip away from his fingers again and again?" That steely look had returned, chasing away the vulnerability of sorrow I had witnessed seconds before.

I cleared my throat, fixing for a moment on the shy look the bride was casting her fiancé and his ardent gaze in return. That, too, was odd. "I can see how Rupert and Maria would have had lots in common but I'm sure the loss of his love hit him far stronger than the loss of these paintings, despite their value. Why did they break up?"

"I was still a young girl and watched the affair from the wall, as they say. Maria and he were very much in love, or so I thought." She sat with her hands clasped in her lap, staring straight ahead.

"But not enough to keep them together?"

"That is a romantic view, one that we Italians have celebrated in art since the being of time, but there are so many other kinds of love that tear at us, is that not so? I am no longer convinced that love conquers all—or, at least, not the romantic kind." Her gaze found my face again. "Do you believe that Noel did not love you enough to go to prison so you could be together?"

Where'd that come from? I met her eyes. "I believe he loves his freedom more," I replied carefully, "and I, in turn, love myself enough not to choose to continue living in a way that makes me unhappy."

I must have passed some kind of test because she rewarded me with a sad smile. "This is good that you stand up for yourself when it is all so difficult. That is what we women must do."

Were we speaking of me or Nicolina? "Back to Maria and Rupert," I said gently. "Did Maria choose another love over what she may have felt for Rupert, is this what you're saying?"

She nodded. "Maria's father was much like my grandpapa—very overbearing. His rule was the law and he believed family and bloodlines sacred. When he discovered the secret engagement, he went wild, threatening to have Rupert shot and Maria cast off from the family."

"A bit extreme, wasn't it?"

Nicolina regarded me sternly. "This is Italy."

"Of course. Sorry."

"Her father would not permit her to marry a penniless antiques dealer, you understand, or to sully the bloodline. Rupert begged her to elope with him but she refused. In the end, she chose the love of family over romance. It is equally powerful, is it not? To give up one for the other, so difficult. I have tried it and did not fare well."

"Poor Rupert."

"Poor Rupert? Well, yes, perhaps poor Rupert. Maria made her choice to remain a Contini and Papa Contini chased him out of town. In Venice, such things were easy in those days. It is a very small place still. Rupert never forgave Maria and Maria never forgave herself."

"That's tragic." I sighed. "So, Maria gave him up for money."

"Not money," Nicolina said, fiercely shaking her head, "but *family*. It was not being penniless that tortured her so much as it was being separated from her mama and papa, from her inheritance here in Venice, and the history that flowed in her veins—her blood, you know? To never live in this house again, to never touch and breathe among these velvets, to perhaps never again walk these halls—that she could not bear."

"So in refusing to marry him, she kept all this."

"Yes, these paintings that she promised to give Rupert as a wedding gift at first she decided to give him still—a very big sacrifice, you understand."

I really didn't like where this was going. "So obviously something happened to change her mind again."

Nicolina nodded. "This time, her mother. Though the paintings were Maria's by right—willed to her by her maternal grandmother—her mother raged against her for taking them from the family. She said that to rip them from the Continis was like cutting off her limbs and letting her very own mother bleed to death—chop, chop! Her mama was very dramatic. How they argued! And then Signora Contini had a heart attack right in the middle of their argument and died that very night."

"No, that's terrible!" Like a bad soap opera made worse by reality. Sometimes life is more bizarre than fiction, I swear.

"Yes, horrendous. These rooms have known so much sorrow. Maria blamed herself for her mother's death as well as for her father's heartbreak, and for hurting Rupert also. I told her over and over that she was not to blame, that she tried only to do the right thing by all, but sometimes there is no way we can please everyone, yes?"

"Yes, I mean, no: sometimes there is no one right way and you can't please everyone. So poor Maria rescinded her promise to Rupert once again because she believed she had no choice? How awful for her and for Rupert, too. I'm sure he didn't take any of this well."

"No." She said the word with short, bullet-like emphasis. "At first, he left the country—was chased from Italy, in truth. I did not reconnect with him until many years later, but when I did, I asked him about the broken promises. He was still very bitter."

"About losing his love, you mean, or losing the paintings?"

She turned to face me and I was struck by the rigidity of her jaw, how her mouth formed one hard line.

"Nicolina?"

"With Rupert, how would you know? I did not. I still do not. I only know that when he wants something, he goes after it."

"He would feel very wronged—who wouldn't?" I looked away—my turn to stare at the wall. Maybe Rupert would have felt very hurt and angry at first but I'd never known him to hold a grudge. Or at least I hoped not, since I had yet to mend the rift between us.

We sat in silence for a moment, deep in our own thoughts, and then I couldn't take it any longer. My mouth opened and I uttered the one thing neither one of us wanted to say: "And now the painting is missing and Maria is dead under mysterious circumstances and you think that Rupert may be responsible."

"Yes."

"Nicolina, no. Rupert may be a conniving little low-life weasel in Saville Row tailoring but he's a good man—sometimes—and no murderer."

Nicolina was on her feet in an instant towering over me with that hard light in her eyes. "You do not know him, Phoebe. I have known him off and on all my life and believe he is capable of anything. What he will not do himself, he makes his ex-MI6 man do for him. You know this. You know he is very dangerous—both of them are very dangerous."

"I know him, too, but differently from you. We have been friends for years. To kill a former love just to acquire a painting? No, never!" The words hung before me as if solidifying midair.

"People have killed for less."

She held my gaze.

"Yes, they have," I said after a moment. "Well, okay, I do know that people have killed for much less and that Rupert never fails to miss a trick." And how well I knew it. Hadn't I been there for the attempted Raphael heist, the Etruscan debacle, the Goddess hunt? "But murder, no. That I can't accept."

"Accept what you will, Phoebe, but I will tell you this: we have learned that a phone call was made to the house the night Maria left the villa and met her death. Should we discover evidence that places Rupert on or near the site of Maria's death on that day, I swear he is a dead man. I will kill him myself."

5

icolina was definitely capable of killing somebody. Hadn't I witnessed her impressive markswomanship when she gunned down a hit man on the streets of Rome? Still, killing an assassin was one thing, executing a friend something else again. Could she do it, *would* she do it?

I stood in the center of my room after Nicolina had taken me there, oblivious to the carvings, the inlaid furniture, the silken brocades, the tiny perfect Venetian canal landscape in greens and blues on the wall, even the folder of paintings on the table. For a moment I even forgot to breathe. Rupert could be a swine—that I knew too well—yet he had also saved my life upon occasion, even though it was often he who had put me in danger in the first place. And Evan, his "driver," that powerful and talented right-hand man, had I ever seen him kill? Never.

Nobody was black or white. Rupert was a man capable of great generosity while simultaneously attempting to steal something from under my nose. He'd saved my life at least once. Our relationship was complex. We'd become close even though I wanted to throttle him more times than I could remember. He lied, he cheated, and he stole, but I believed his heart was still bigger than his greed. I cared about him and for Nicolina, too. Where did that leave me?

True, Rupert wasn't speaking to me at the moment but only because I had outwitted him for once. At some point he was bound to get over his pique, providing he lived that long. Yes, he had the formidable and enigmatic Evan to protect him, but I was convinced that Seraphina might be equally dangerous in her own way and Italy was her territory, after all.

I strode to the window and opened the shutters a crack. Down below on Venice's liquid street, the rain had stopped and the canal had taken on a shimmery glow. Rupert was out there somewhere. For once, I wished I still had the special phone Evan had rigged for our private communications, even if those calls tended to come with an array of special features like detonating devices and tracking chips. Evan was a techno-wiz and endlessly inventive with app creation. Now I just wanted to find out their side of the Maria story, warn them, perhaps. And would that betray Nicolina's confidence? Maybe that didn't matter. What really mattered was the truth.

I took the folder of paintings and opened them under a lamp, studying every detail until my eyes hurt. So many elements that didn't add up, especially in the Bartolo, which was atypical for this artist of the Sienese School. In all my years of art and textile study, never had I seen a painting like this. I had once studied Domenico di Bartolo with interest because his use of textiles had been extraordinary. Though he had worked primarily in Siena, he was also believed to have traveled to Florence, and now apparently to Venice also. This was a commission, as they all were. His *Marriage of the Foundlings* drew striking similarities to the Contini piece and I wondered if he had been commissioned to do this one based on his fame there. I pulled away and rubbed my eyes. Nothing to do now but let it brew in my subconscious for a while.

I scanned the room, my eyes landing on my suitcase. Along with my battered carpetbag, which traveled with me everywhere, I had brought an equally beat-up roller. That's all. I tended to travel light and yet somehow a smaller Vuitton carry-on now sat beside them like an interloper. Not my bag or my style but by now I knew Nicolina's tendency to give me things I didn't know I needed or necessarily want. Whatever lay inside that bag was probably way above my budget, or deadly, or both.

Reluctantly, I lifted the bag onto the inlaid bench—mosaic, probably late fifteenth century—popped the lock, and stared down at mounds of folded tissue paper. A familiar tingle hit my spine. Anything of a textile nature did that to me and I recognized carefully tended fabric when I saw it. Unwrapping the contents revealed a long black silk dress, a velvet hooded cloak, black stockings, tall leather boots, and a short black leather jacket in the biker style, all from an Italian couture house I didn't recognize. I stared. Was I to masquerade as Little Black Riding Hood now? Maybe a Jane Eyre dominatrix? Baffled, I let the silken folds drop to the bed. Since I was wearing jeans, black trainers, and a green turtleneck to pick up the colors in my kelp garden wrap, presumably I was not dressed for elegance, whatever the occasion.

The jacket, however, was something else again. Nicolina knew my history with outerwear, considering I had stuffed a bloody postcard inside my last leather jacket and then dunked the thing in Jamaica's Rio Grande. Perhaps she offered this one as a replacement gift?

I left the clothes strewn across the bed and turned away. Then I had a thought. Returning to the carry-on, I reached inside, felt along the lower edges, and found what I sought. My fingers sprung what I knew to be the mechanism that hid an X-ray-shielded false bottom and soon I was pulling out a handy little Magnum pistol and several rounds of ammunition, the perfect accessory for a woman who travels apparently. Pack it right below your toothbrush, yes, ma'am.

Well, damn. I stared at the thing. Nicolina and her guns. She always carried them and expected me to, too, as much as I rebelled against the idea on principle. However, principle had taken a bit of a hit in the past few years to the point where I had taken firearm lessons with a former policewoman along with a side of martial arts training. Though I objected to violence, that didn't mean I planned on being a victim anytime soon. I took the thing and carefully set it down beside me on the bed. I'd leave the extra ammunition where it was for now.

Next, I whipped off a text in code to Max: *Here in Venice. Weather mixed. Nicolina says hi.* Max would get the point: something was going down in Venice and it wasn't the weather. Besides, Nicolina would never say hi.

I checked the time: 10:15 in the UK. Max would either be watching the news or tucked into bed, his phone left downstairs on the kitchen counter as usual. He never took to sleeping with his devices. No one I knew seemed to have quite the same relationship in bed with their phone as I did. That said a lot about my lack of sleeping companions. In any case, I wouldn't hear from him tonight.

Sighing, I gazed around. Obviously I needed to knit, my sleeping pill of choice and as soothing to me as hot chocolate and a lullaby. I was far too buzzed to sleep and yet the villa had gone quiet as if everyone had retired early. Now I wished I'd taken Nicolina up on her nighttime vino offer since wine inevitably made me sleepy, but no decanter and glasses had been made available. Apparently I was lucky to have access to water, which presumably I could fetch from the en suite bathroom.

So it was to my sedative of choice that I turned. I took my carpetbag and pulled out my beloved Melancholy wrap with its comforting lengths of green and mahogany silk that I had added only the night before. Oh, how lovely. Yes, this would do.

For a few moments the feel of the yarn in my fingers soothed me and I was ready to happily dive into those stitches until sleep tugged away. Or so I thought. The moment I thrust my hand in my bag to retrieve the second needle, my comfort was replaced by a stab of panic: I could not locate that familiar stick of polished wood! Alarmed, I emptied the bag onto the bed and pawed through the balls and skeins, my overnight kit, the change of undies and extra sweater, but came up empty. Absolutely no second needle. Somehow it had slipped from my bag and was gone.

My sense of loss was as powerful as it was ridiculous. I felt agitated the way one might when they realize a critical prescription had run out and some dreadful symptom was about to inflict itself. I stood up and began pacing the room, seized by the knowledge that, without knitting, I would probably obsess over Rupert and Nicolina until my body collapsed in a shaking heap. I needed vino, badly needed vino. I could honestly say that, without knitting, I could be driven to drink.

Pushing the door open a crack, I peered into the hall. Everything was dark and quiet. Presumably Nicolina had retired to mourn in private while Seraphina was either comforting her friend or asleep. Or something. What did it matter? I wasn't doing anything clandestine, unless locating a glass of nighttime vino was considered socially unacceptable in an Italian household, which I strongly doubted.

Still, no lights were left on downstairs, which meant I must use my phone light for navigation purposes. I padded downstairs as quietly as I could with the intention of heading straight for the salon where I had last seen the decanter. The place was much larger than I thought—room after room branched out on either side of the long hall but most rooms appeared to be locked. Working from memory, I proceeded down the long dark hall trying doors until I reached a room on the right-hand side where I was certain Zara had delivered us hours before. The door opened easily and I beamed my light toward the low table. Empty. Someone, presumably Zara, had tidied up after we'd gone upstairs.

Now what? I wasn't an ordinary guest in a hotel but an interloper in a house of mourning. I'd go straight for the kitchen and pour my own wine. I headed toward where I assumed a kitchen would be in a Venetian villa— somewhere at the back of the house—and I was right. As soon as I shoved open the tall wooden door, my phone light caught the gleam of chrome and porcelain. I was about to flick on the light switch when I caught a sound coming from below.

For a moment, I just stood listening. There was no way in hell anyone should be down in the cantina this time of night when the residents had retired for the evening and the place was dark. No, this was not right.

Retracing my steps, I bounded upstairs to my bedroom and knocked on all three of the doors. "Nicolina, Seraphina, Zara, get up! There's someone downstairs in the cantina!"

I expected a flurry of doors to fly open or, at the very least, a cry of alarm. Nothing. "Hello?" I tried again.

Finally, a door squeaked open at the end of the hall followed by a light switching on, and there was Zara wrapped in a long mauve robe stomping toward me as if she wanted to shake out my molars.

I took a step back. "Where's Nicolina and Seraphina?"

Stopping a foot away, she asked me something in Italian to which I shrugged. Turning, she marched up to one of the doors and knocked on the oak imperiously. "Contessa Vanvitelli?" No answer.

In a moment, she was storming inside the room, me at her heels. Not only was there no Nicolina, but her bed hadn't been slept in.

Zara swung around and pushed past me out the hall across to another door where she repeated the process. No Seraphina, either. Standing in the middle of the elegant room, Zara peppered me with a battery of Italian.

"*Excusi*, me no speak Italian." The things we say when stressed. "But there's someone down in the basement—the cantina. *Comprendo?* Maybe Nicolina and Seraphina? We must look!"

She stared at me. *"Cantina?"*

"Downstairs!" I pointed downward and stamped my foot for effect.

Realization dawned. Zara straightened her bony shoulders and hurried off down the stairs without another word. I hesitated only long enough to return to my room and grab the gun.

I was shoving my feet into my sneakers as I climbed down the stairs, my phone in one pocket, the gun in the other. In seconds, I was at the top of the kitchen steps.

"Zara?" I called down. The light was on and I heard something like a grunt below. Holding the gun, I followed her down. Zara was standing beneath the overhead light, hands on her hips, glaring straight at the closed canal door.

Seeing me, she pointed at the tracks leading from inside the door straight through toward the canal. I got the picture: someone had taken the small speedboat, that someone probably being Seraphina and Nicolina.

Zara glared balefully at the gun, which I hastily lowered, at which point she assaulted me with angry Italian. *"Hanno preso il motoscafo!"*

"Well, don't blame me," I shot back. "I'm as in the dark as you. Is there another *motoscafo*? I'll even take a regular *scafo*."

Zara shook her head furiously. *"No motoscafo e non stai prendendo la gondola!"*

I wasn't certain exactly what she was saying but I got the gist: no boat for me, not even a gondola. I pocketed the gun and dashed back up the stairs all the way to my room to grab the new jacket, suddenly fuming. Nicolina and Seraphina had taken off on some midnight assignation and left me behind stranded like an extra overnight bag?

What was worse is that I knew it had something to do with Rupert. I had defended him to Nicolina, clearly didn't believe that he had anything to do with Maria's death, and now my deadly countess would do what she felt necessary with or without me. That was just all wrong, grief or no.

I bounded back downstairs and straight down the hall to slide the bolts on the grand front door while Zara scurried behind me, barking in Italian. A beeping had begun as a little red light flashed from the panel on the wall.

"I'm going out one way or the other," I told her. "You'd best deactivate the alarm unless you want the Venetian *polizia* here in a nanosecond."

Zara tapped the code onto the panel and the beeping promptly stopped. I swung open the door. *"Dove credit di andare?"* she asked as I stepped out.

Of course I didn't know what she said but I took a guess. "I'm not sure when I'll be back. Don't wait up."

❦ 6 ❧

I had no idea where I was going, only that I had to move. Remaining locked in that villa of sorrows while my friends went off on some dubious excursion without me stuck felt so wrong. At the very least, a walk might burn off enough caffeine-fueled energy to allow me to sleep. Maybe, if I was extraordinarily lucky, I might even glimpse Seraphina and Nicolina zipping by in the *motoscafo*.

Despite the lateness of the hour, Venice was not sleeping. Though the villas along the Cannaregio were shuttered for the night, the restaurants and bars still percolated with activity. In fact, after I had navigated the barricaded edge of the canal that had apparently been damaged in a recent storm, I found myself striding along a wide brightly lit cement walkway that was clearly still open for business.

On the left, gondolas could be seen resting among a forest of mooring poles while a handful of diners lingered inside their plastic-screened restaurant patios huddled up to outdoor gas heaters. I envied them their cozy company, the laughter rising up over the tinkling glasses. In truth, I also envied them their pastas and grilled fish, dishes I could only imagine by their scent. I was starving.

Nicolina had said that the warehouse lay farther down the street, but without a number or any other identifying features, I couldn't determine which was which at first. That is until I saw an armed carabiniere, an officer of the national guard, a kind of militarized police force that co-policed Italy with two other organizations, standing outside a nondescript door. Above loomed a large terra-cotta-painted building featuring rows of pointed arched windows reminiscent of Eastern influences. The building looked simultaneously welcoming and imposing and the uniformed officer did not look friendly. In fact, he looked quite out of sorts. I strolled by slowly, studying the warehouse.

"Move along, miss. This is a crime site," the officer barked in English. It was goading to be recognized as a tourist so easily. Picking up my pace, I strode quickly past.

It had stopped raining and, though still chilly, the air smelled fresh and watery. With a sudden ping of excitement, it occurred to me that I was actually in Venice, *Venice*. And that I was alone, which was exhilarating because it meant that no compromise was necessary, that I could go where I wanted, walk anywhere I pleased—be a random voyager, in other words. As my younger self, I had been leashed by a tour group and had never felt prepared enough to stroll a city alone at night.

Now I had a suite of skills at my disposal including martial arts and firearm skills. How I resented all those years when I'd felt restricted because cities were presumed unsafe for women in a way that didn't hold true for men. Considering what I had been through in the past five years and that I was armed and probably dangerous, fearing the ordinary criminal wasn't in the picture. I could defend myself against pickpockets, rapists, robbers, and the like, so cities at night no longer frightened me. In fact, I almost dared anyone to try anything.

Besides, the stalkers who had once dodged my heels had presumably lost interest now that Toby was locked up and I had broken up with Noel, not that we had ever really been together. It was as if the underground communication channels had informed the black market that I was no longer a person of interest. How long would it take for everyone to figure out that my friends and I sat on a fortune of rescued art? Until then, I flew under the radar, or so I hoped. I may as well enjoy it while it lasted.

The lively canal boulevard retreated into the distance the farther I walked. Enticing little alleyways beckoned me on and I took the path less traveled every time. Long dimly lit passageways hemmed in by looming buildings hundreds of years old suited my mood. I loved the mysterious atmosphere, the sense of treading in the footfalls of thousands of souls that had gone before me combined with that haunted hush that descends upon very old places at night. It was almost like walking among ghosts, a sense one rarely experiences when in the company of others.

Shop windows illuminated old bookstores, souvenir shops, and mask vendors, all closed for the night. The city still bore the tawdry remains of revelry as if Venice was just too exhausted after the Carnevale to wash off her face paint. I'd see streamers floating in puddles, a glittery mask hanging on a doorknob, and everywhere the sense of festive aftermath, from the ragged paper signs announcing past events, to the streamers and iridescent confetti plastered onto the damp cobbles.

Occasional groups of four or five pedestrians passed by me in full medieval regalia complete with sparkly masks as if nobody had told them that the Carnevale was over. Lost in time like Venice herself. One man dressed like a fifteenth century courtier poked his face into mine and said something in winy Italian while his companion pulled him away laughing.

Strollers of the more sedate variety squeezed past me in the alleyways, too—lovers arm in arm, a young man marching purposefully with his hands in his pockets, head down. I'd turn a corner and find myself sweeping over a tiny bridge, picture-postcard views of a sleeping canal on either side that left me enchanted, totally in the moment. I felt I could walk forever, stepping over and around this ancient city with its twinkling lights and watery byways while its foundations of ancient logs moldered away deep in the lagoon beneath my feet.

Of course, history always kept me company, a ponderous but fascinating companion. I knew how Venice was built as a refuge against invading marauders and constructed in the lagoon by logs plunged deep into the cold mud, wooden foundations that remained preserved for centuries. Amazing to think that this miraculous floating city was actually sinking by the minute and not because of rotting foundations, though there were signs of that, too, but because the rising sea levels threatened to swamp the ancient streets.

Lulled by the up and down of bridges, the twisting alleys and tiny *campi*, my mind traveled along its own windy path. After a bit, I left thoughts of history behind and focused on my own small universe. Look how far I'd come from the days when I wanted so desperately to please everyone that I could be lured unwittingly into danger time and time again. *If you don't know what you stand for, you'll fall for anything.* That saying certainly applied to me.

These days, I dove into trouble with eyes wide open. What I had to gain far exceeded what I had to lose, to my way of thinking—my life and those I cared about aside. Now I knew what I stood for and was willing to fight for it: protect the world's art legacy for future generations and prevent the priceless from slipping into the hands of the criminal few. And spread the love for textiles while I was at it. Yes, I'd protect my friends and loved ones, too—yes, I would—even if they didn't want me to. Toby came to mind since he hardly wanted to be incarcerated in order to get clean.

I crossed another bridge and caught sight of lovers kissing deeply in the shadows and an ambush of dismay hit me so hard I almost gasped aloud. I carried on across a deserted little *campo* toward a medieval well, and sat down on a stone bench, suddenly heartsick. So much for bravado. Bravado was a rogue wave of emotion at the best of times. Look at me now: I'd given up love in lieu of principle. Wasn't I grand? This new kick-ass Phoebe had handed over her brother and cut the heartstrings to the man she loved. I felt the hole in my heart as deep as the grave and it didn't matter that a moral choice influenced both acts.

What would I do if Noel were to appear over that little bridge right then? He had ambushed me at unexpected moments before. How I longed to see him and how I didn't—the conundrum of heartbreak.

I stood up. Yes, I sent my brother to prison for a reason, and if Noel seriously wanted to turn his life around and spend some good years with me, he could have taken a stand that night in Jamaica. But he didn't. He didn't want to turn his life around, not in the legal sense. Instead, he ran. That's not what I wanted in a man. I wanted a partner, a lover, a companion, not to mention somebody I could see more often than once or twice a year. I was tired of runners. Enough.

My backbone fortified, I continued my walk more resolved with every step but still oblivious to where I was going. Rupert and Evan were somewhere in this ancient city and by now they'd know I was here, too. Maybe they were even following me.

I swung around to gaze as another twisting alleyway disappeared into the shadows. Footsteps echoed behind me, stopping when I stopped, pausing when I paused. I had been so lost in thought I hadn't noticed until now. Who knew how long I'd been followed? Noel, maybe? My breath caught and I waited. And waited.

Not Noel. He'd approach. My spine tingled. Well, hell. Just when I thought no one cared what I was up to...but then again, maybe the mute stone walls, the narrow alleyways, the shadows, ghosts, and mists were wearing on me. Maybe my true stalker was my own conscience. I checked my watch: 11:05.

Turning away, I carried on down another alley, around and over and into and out, listening to the footsteps echoing out of sight behind walls and on the other side of bridges. Now I knew the stalker was real and it wasn't Noel. Maybe whoever it was had been keeping me company the whole time. The Accademia Bridge came and went in a burst of bright lights, bars, and clusters of people in masks. I turned, hoping to catch a glimpse of my stalker in the crowd but it was impossible.

Fog began wafting in from the lagoon, thick and atmospheric, and now I had arrived on the other side of Venice. All the mysteries set in the city rose into my imagination unbidden: *Don't Look Now*, every single Donna Leon book...

Hell. Stop that, Phoebe. I kept on walking and listening, thinking that I would find a dead end and wait for my stalker to arrive. That's what children were advised to do with monsters chasing them in their dreams—face them—and that's what I'd do, too. Only I was prepared to tackle my monster if necessary. I released the safety catch on the pistol in my pocket and kept on walking.

Two more small bridges came and went, each of which looked exactly like the other. I reached a dark body of water where the fog was so thick that lights across the canal could barely penetrate the gloom, where overhead streetlights pushed damp halos through the mist. Behind me stood the imposing domed church illuminated by spotlights that I recognized as the church of Santa Maria della Salute, consecrated in 1681 as a votive from the people of Venice following the devastation of the plague. Why did I have to recall all this historical minutiae at times like this? The plague church. Like I needed that. I turned and waited.

Before me lay the Grand Canal and across the water St. Mark's Square shrouded in fog, which may as well be a million miles away. I had walked across the whole of Venice, which also meant I'd have to walk the whole way back. I stepped onto the pier toward the deserted platform of a vaporetto depot. This late at night, I could be waiting for the next ride for a long time. Forget that. And what was worse, my pursuer did not step out of the alleyway to introduce himself.

I waited and waited and so, apparently, did he or she. Okay, so if my stalker wouldn't come to me, I'd just meet them en route.

Thus began a frustrating interlude of me trying to retrace my steps over these same two little bridges to get back toward the Accademia Bridge from whence I'd come. Somehow I'd end up right back at the foot of the Salute having gone in one big circle. I rubbed my eyes, obviously far more tired than I thought. I tried again with exactly the same result and still those echoing footsteps on my heels.

What was I doing, taking a left when I should have gone right? Was my stalker hanging back in the shadows laughing at me while I lost myself over and over again? I felt a presence standing deep in the shadows somewhere. Once more I turned the corner following the side of the church until I reached the first bridge, and once again the second bridge led me to a passage between two buildings and straight back to the Salute.

"Who are you and what do you want?" I called out. Of course no one answered.

The fog was thickening, I was tiring of the game, and at last I pulled out my cell phone. My plan was to activate the GPS and find my way out of the maze but instead I found myself reading a text from Nicolina:

Phoebe, where are you?

I typed back: *At Salute pier. Where are you?*

We are at the villa, of course. Stay there. We will come get you. It will take at least fifteen minutes.

Great, fifteen more minutes of fog, shadow, and my unseen companion. Why not? I strode across the concrete to wait by the edge of the pier, looking down into the dark water. "If you're still watching me, the least you could do is step out and hold a conversation." Nothing.

Five minutes longer, I looked up to the sound of a speedboat approaching. Nicolina already? I stepped closer to the edge and waited.

A single figure manning a small speedboat approached, throttling the engine as the craft put-putted up to the wharf. It took me a moment to realize that the man wore a cape and a black mask, *Phantom of the Opera*–style. I was so not in the mood for this.

Fingering the gun in my pocket, I stepped forward. "Ahoy. Who goes there?"

7

"**G**ood evening, madam," the figure called up with a grin that I found both encouraging and unsettling, under the circumstances. "I have come to offer you a lift, rather like an Uber Vaporetto."

My breath caught. I recognized that deep voice. "An Uberetto? Well, this is a surprise. A lift to where, may I ask?" I called down.

"Wherever you wish, madam. I am at your service."

"At my service, really—in a mask and a cape?"

The man shrugged and smiled. "When in Venice…"

It didn't matter, since I was extraordinarily glad to see this man no matter what his get-up.

"Were you just stalking me?" I asked. But being in two places at once was impossible even for him.

"Absolutely not. Was someone following you?" he asked, alarm in his voice.

"Someone was but refused to reveal himself in order to be properly introduced."

"How rude."

"I thought so." I accepted his gloved hand and allowed him to guide me into the craft as if I couldn't get my own self into a boat and drive the thing, too. He knew it, I knew it, but I took a seat in the prow facing my driver with my hands clasped between my knees. "Seriously, Evan, what's up with the mask?"

"Venice is a city of subterfuge, madam, especially now. Where would you like me to deliver you?"

"Away from here as fast as this *motoscafo* can take us. Nicolina and Seraphina are gunning their way toward me now and I'm sure you don't want that encounter. Take me to Rupert."

"Sir Rupert?" he called over the engine noise as we churned away from the pier. "Sir Rupert does not expect you this evening, madam. He's indisposed. We only wished to ensure your safety."

Bizarre that something that once drove me to distraction—being tailed by Rupert Fox and his multitalented right-hand man—should now cause me so much relief. "My convenience was more the issue here than my safety but thanks, anyway. Rupert is indisposed, really? Does he require his pajamas pressed or something? Well, you can take me to see him, anyway. Please call him to say I'm coming over and that's that. This can't wait."

"As you wish, madam."

"And stop with the 'madam' stuff, will you? You know my name." I'd lost count of the number of times I'd made that request but it never made a whit of difference. Apparently Evan was hardwired to call me "madam." If James Bond had been pressed into active service as a dogsbody following his stint with Her Majesty's Secret Service, it would be Evan.

While he spoke rapidly into his cell phone and steered with his other hand, I pulled out my phone and texted Nicolina: *Ride not needed. I have another lift. Will be back in a couple of hours. Sorry for the inconvenience. Don't wait up.*

When I looked again, I realized that Evan had darted the boat into one of the smaller canals on this side of the Accademia and for the first time I wondered exactly where Rupert was staying—not at one of the luxe hotels along the Grand Canal, as I had expected. No, we were winding deeper into this side of Venice's watery maze, the boat slowing down to a sedate putter after several twists and turns as we threaded between mostly residential buildings.

Soon Evan cut the engine and we floated for a few moments on the watery darkness. Had I not known him better, I would have thought he planned to slit my throat and toss my body into the canal—the perfect setting—but I'd always trusted this man with my life. Around us, Renaissance buildings with tall shuttered windows loomed down like long dark faces with their eyes closed. See no evil...

I was about to ask him what was up when he said: "Madam, what have you brought with you from the villa?"

I looked down at my new jacket and patted the pocket to indicate the gun.

He nodded at me and held out his hand.

Without a word, I shrugged off the jacket and passed it over, watching as he ran his phone up and down every seam until the device beeped. In a flash, he pulled a pocket knife from his jacket, slit the jacket's lining, and tugged out a shiny coin-like object, which he promptly tossed in the canal. Next, he studied my phone, turned it off, and returned it to the jacket pocket and proceeded to investigate the gun. That, too, had some kind of tracking device secreted on its barrel. Once it was dropped into the water, the jacket was returned and he held out his hand again.

I passed over my carpetbag this time and watched as he performed the same test over each seam, finding another device tucked into the lining.

"Well, damn. Seraphina. I've got to get better at looking for those things." I sighed. "They probably already know where I am."

"No matter." Then he pointed to what I thought was a black blanket folded beside another bundle at my feet. "There is a rain cape in that package, which you may find useful. Please put it on."

Though it wasn't raining, the mist was thick enough to dampen everything. I opened the package and unfolded a plastic rain cape, which I donned, pulling the hood up so as to give my hair less excuse to frizz.

"You will also find a mask in the other bag. Please put that on, too."

"Seriously? Carnevale is over, Evan. Am I going to a masquerade or something? I know Rupert loves his balls but this hardly seemed the time, though admittedly the place couldn't be more perfect."

I was rewarded by a small smile. "Not quite, madam. The mask is for your protection. Should you be interrogated as to Sir Rupert's location, you will truthfully be unable to provide directions."

"So it's not a mask so much as a blindfold?" I pulled something stiff and cumbersome from the bag. Holding it up to the meager light, I stared aghast at a hood to which was affixed empty eye sockets and a long beak-like extension like a grisly comic-book bird. I recognized it immediately. This kind of bizarre mask was once worn by physicians in the Middle Ages who stuffed the beak with potpourri in the hope that the herbs would protect them against pestilence. "The plague doctor? Are you kidding me?"

"I assure you I am not," he said. "This is the only thing I had on hand, and though not technically a blindfold, there's a very slim chance that you will be able to identify our route while wearing it. Sir Rupert feels that even though you might swear not to reveal our hideout, you are, he says, 'an abysmal liar.'"

"His fault for raising the bar so high. Is he hiding out, then?"

"The mask, please, madam."

Rupert was in hiding. Did I blame him? Thoughts of Nicolina and the stalwart Seraphina peppering me with questions I might not want to answer clinched it. I dropped the thing over my head and stared out into the muffled silence. True enough, I could barely see more than misty shadows through the eyeholes. "I just want to say that floating through the Venetian canals dressed as a plague doctor with a masked bandito at the helm of a *motoscafo* is not how I thought tonight would end." There was a mouth hole under the beak so presumably he caught the gist but he said nothing in return, or at least nothing I could hear.

In moments the boat lurched forward and we were on our way again, me caught in some kind of strange, sense-deprived limbo as we zipped along. With nothing left to do but think, it occurred to me that I knew the man at the helm only by his first name until recently. Though I'd spent many hours in his company, mostly in heightened situations, he remained a total enigma. That he had once been an MI6 agent was common knowledge, how he ended up as Sir Rupert Fox's right-hand man was not. He was amazingly skilled at multiple things, from cooking to finagling technological devices to performing improbable feats at short notice. Yet he appeared to live a solitary life attached to Rupert's side. Why would a man with Evan's talents be content to work for another, except for the obvious —money and adventure? And yet, there was something about him that made me think that there had to be more to the story. There always was.

I felt a tap on my beak. "Hold on, madam," he called.

All thoughts were jolted away when I heard the engine throttle to full as the boat hit open water. I stared ahead at nothing as we zoomed through the chop toward some undisclosed destination. I managed to catch glimpses of lights stacked off to the right. Skyscrapers? No, cruise ships! We had to be following the cruise pier on the right-hand side, which meant that we must be on the broad Giudecca Canal. Hell, did I want to know even that much?

Not that it mattered. Soon we were turning back into the canals, I guessed, judging by the multiple abrupt turns and the occasional echoes of the boat's engine under bridges. After only a minute of that, I was totally disorientated. Once I caught a whiff of blossoms—cherry or maybe apple —leaving me with the impression that we had passed a garden, but otherwise I may as well be a million miles elsewhere. Eventually and at last, the engine was abruptly cut and the boat coasted a few yards forward.

"Are we here yet?" I whispered

"Yes, madam. Directly. Best to be silent."

So silent I was. I kept quiet as the boat bumped against a mooring, sat patiently as Evan leaped out to secure the craft, and waited until his strong hand guided me up until I stood on a dock. He steered me forward with his arm around my shoulders—not an unpleasant sensation, though probably unnecessary—until I heard a door scrape open and a bolt shove home behind us. A security something beeped softly.

"May I take this thing off now?"

"In a moment, madam."

I was being led down a dark passageway, right into one room, left into another.

"Now?"

"Not yet."

We walked for about another ten yards and then I heard a voice. "My word!" it croaked. "Have you delivered death to my doorstop yet again, Evan?"

I whipped off the mask and stood staring into the candlelit face of Sir Rupert Fox. He stood before me wrapped in a blanket in the center of what looked to be an empty ballroom—marble floors, mirrored walls, slender pillars, a dark fireplace at one end—all of it lit by electric lanterns as well as candlelight. Though the light seemed inadequate for such an expanse, it didn't take a spotlight to see he was sick. "Rupert! What's wrong with you?"

"Phoebe! Imagine seeing you here...after all... Wasn't the last time just after you...sent us to Tahiti?" He began to cough racking heaves that shook his frame so hard I thought he'd topple over.

Evan and I raced to his side. "You must lie down, sir. To bed with you immediately. You were not supposed to get up while I was away."

"Yes, back to bed now," I seconded, looking around. So where was the bed in this marble wasteland? Surely not that foldout steel-legged mattressy thing set up in the center of the room beside a pillar and a single unlit Tiffany lamp?

But with Evan on one side and me on the other, that's exactly where we steered Rupert, while the whole time I glimpsed the ghost-like reflection of our movements in the wall-to-ceiling mirrors at the far end of the room.

"Where is this place?" I whispered.

"That must remain undisclosed at all costs," Evan answered as he tucked his employer under the covers, made him swallow two ibuprofens with gulps of water, and wiped his forehead with a cloth from a bowl of melting ice. "It is imperative that no one discover our hiding place." And then in a louder voice, he asked: "Have you taken your antibiotics, sir?"

"You gave them to me...before you left...old chap."

"Indeed I did. Just testing. Now, it is absolutely critical that you rest. Ms. Phoebe will only stay a short while—" he shot me a quick glance "—and then I shall deliver her to her accommodation, as planned. What can I get you in the meantime?"

"A doctor, surely?" I said, looking up at Evan.

His green eyes met mine—worried eyes, I realized. "He was seen by a physician earlier today—"

"At an exorbitant price—highway robbery..." Rupert wheezed.

"He charged a reasonable fee considering that we swore him to secrecy," Evan said. "At knifepoint, if I recall." Turning to me, he added: "Sir Rupert was diagnosed as having a probable case of pneumonia following a bad cold that he was fighting in London. We won't know for certain until the test results come back."

"The doctor bled me, Phoebe, *bled* me," Rupert rasped.

"He drew blood for the tests," Evan clarified, almost but not quite rolling his eyes. "You were in no danger of expiring during the procedure."

"Nonsense. For all we know he was a black market quack." Rupert coughed.

"I checked him out thoroughly, I assure you. The good doctor is a very legitimate practitioner, just one inclined to line his pockets with extra money."

"The Italian way," Rupert remarked in his alarming voice.

"Nevertheless, we were grateful for his services." Evan had the patience of a saint—an armed saint, maybe, but nobody's perfect.

"Valid doctor or not, Rupert should be in a hospital," I said.

"Impossible under the circumstances," Evan remarked while Rupert gazed up at me with feverish eyes.

"What circumstances?"

"They would have me...killed," Rupert rasped.

"Who would have you killed?"

"Unfortunately, we may have more than one candidate with possible murderous intentions in this city," Evan responded mildly.

I knew of at least two.

"I am not popular in...Venice," Rupert said.

"Then why did you come?" I looked up toward the tall ceiling with its ornate wooden timbers shrouded in shadows and suppressed a shiver. "And why here?"

"Long story..." Rupert closed his eyes. "No energy left to tell it. Evan, my boy, do fetch us...some tea...if you please. We may be camped out...in this haunted villa...but we needn't live like specters."

"Haunted?" It did feel haunted but then so did most of Venice.

"Tea, Evan," Rupert murmured.

"Tea coming up." Evan caught my eye as if to say *don't tire him* and was gone in an instant, dashing across the vacant room on his long legs and disappearing through an arched door on the far end.

"What is going on?" I pulled up a folding chair and positioned it by the camp bed. His face shined with sweat, his eyes feverish. "Tell me. This... this—" I gazed around, grappling for adjectives "—this moldering heap looks unhealthy, if not dangerous. I can smell mold if not ghosts."

"Ghosts don't smell, Phoebe—" he paused as if considering his words

"—well, maybe they do. This...this is truly a lovely...building but I admit... to never wanting to stay in it...like this. Two murders took place here...and unaccountable misfortunes to the owners. I am here as a...last resort."

"Some resort," I muttered. Obviously it had been a large palazzo of some sort, a once dignified and ornate Renaissance establishment that had, for whatever reason, been left to ruin. "You should be recuperating in a hospital or at one of those luxurious hotels you favor. Really, I never saw you as much of a glamper."

He emitted something like a snort. "A glamper indeed. It makes a perfect...hiding place. The locals...think it's haunted and...avoid it at all costs. It has been...deserted for years." Though he labored with every breath he seemed intent to talk.

"I gathered that but from whom are you hiding exactly and why here?"

He waved a hand at the shadows before letting it drop back to the bed. "At least I own this and so can...stay with some impunity. I bought it decades ago...an investment. I planned to restore it as...my Venetian bolt-hole."

I looked around. "A bolt-hole the size of a palace?"

He took a moment to catch his breath. "But I am persona non grata... in this city, always have been. They have a long memory here...never forgetting so much as...an imagined infraction." He spent a few minutes recovering before continuing. "And I couldn't get workmen...to restore it...quickly."

"All right—" I nodded "—so you shafted someone, probably cheated them out of some priceless piece of art for which they'll never forgive you, plus you tried to marry some man's daughter, which didn't exactly work out —got it—but what brought you to Venice this time? Tell the truth." I just needed him to say it.

"Oh," he rasped, "a fine one to speak of truth, Phoebe...after you sent... us on a wild...goose chase."

I patted his hand. "And how did that feel, Rupert, after the multiple times you've tricked me over the years? I've been on so many wild-goose chases these days, I try to fly in a flock."

He looked at me aghast, almost like he was seeing me for the first time. Then he closed his eyes and emitted a sound like sandpaper against a chalkboard. "What happened...to you, Phoebe? You used to be...so sweet."

"Gullible, you mean. I've grown wiser. You lost nothing by taking a detour to Tahiti except maybe upping your sunburn quotient."

"Nonsense. I'm diligent...with my SPF." At least the old humor was there. "But you are wrong about losing something. I shall explain all as soon as I am able."

"The Rembrandts were all forgeries, compliments of my brother's consummate skill," I continued. "But that's all beside the point now. Let's put it behind us. We have more pressing matters to deal with. Besides, I've missed you and you missed me. Don't deny it."

"I don't...deny it."

"Good—" I squeezed his hand "—so let's get back to being friends and try a dose of honesty while we're at it—honesty as in full disclosure, not your shifty half-truth variety. Why are you really here, Rupert?"

He fixed me with his bleary eyes. "For the sake of Maria Contini."

I pulled my hand away. "I knew it. Damn it, Rupert. You know that Nicolina believes you may be responsible for Maria's death." I wasn't thinking. That was one bomb I shouldn't have dropped in Rupert's weakened state.

"That's preposterous!" He propped himself on his elbows and fumed at me. "Me kill Maria? I loved her once! She always has a place...in my heart!" And then he began to cough and cough.

"Calm down. It's all right, everything is all right." I dashed over to the little foldout table, retrieved what I hoped to be cough medicine, and spooned some down his throat followed by water. "Evan!" I called, but suddenly Evan was speeding into the room while Rupert's face reddened to the point of combustion. For a hideous moment I was afraid he'd expire on my watch.

Evan, wearing an apron and bearing a tray of tea things that he set down with a clatter, rushed to my side. "What happened?"

"I can't get him to stop coughing."

"Sir Rupert, calm yourself at once!" Evan ordered, laying a hand on his forehead. "You are not to get upset. Ms. Phoebe will leave you to rest immediately."

Rupert shook his head and clasped Evan's arm, his eyes nearly bulging from their sockets. "Tell her," he gasped. "Every...thing. Within...reason."

"I don't think that's wise, sir, for her sake or yours."

"Tell her!" Then he took a deep heaving breath and fell back against the pillows, eyes closed, one hand flapping in the air as if waving us away.

Evan caught my eye, lips stern in that chiseled chin. "You have exhausted him, madam."

"He has exhausted himself." I met his gaze steadily, trying to block how devastatingly attractive a muscled man looks wearing an apron and scowling. As if this was the time for such thoughts.

We watched Rupert carefully until the patient appeared to be resting and his face had lost its explosive flush. When I was certain he was dozing, my eyes met Evan's again and I pointed toward the door at the far end of the ballroom and mouthed, *Let's talk*. He nodded and I followed him across the marble floor.

Carrying a battery-operated lantern, he led me through another huge empty room with tall shuttered windows and damp-stained brown wallpaper that might have once been gold silk, down a dark hall, and into a back room lit with various portable lights. One spotlight blazed onto a microwave, hot plate, and a two-burner radiant-heat cooking surface.

I looked around at what appeared to be a kitchen/office space furnished with old-fashioned counters, a central butcher's block commandeered as a desk, and an assortment of blinking lights that may have been battery packs. A stack of books sat neatly on one of the counters, another bookmarked and sitting on the floor beside a chair.

"So not a crack of natural light is allowed in this fortress, right?" I asked, trying to read the book's title in the pocket of gloom.

"I have secured this building with the necessary features, including cameras, remote surveillance, and alarms. However, from the outside, it must still look like an abandoned building, which is admittedly a challenge. Please take a seat." He turned and offered me a chair at a folding table. "The book is on Renaissance art, by the way, history being a bit of a hobby." So he'd caught my curious glance. Well, of course he did: nothing escaped Evan.

In a moment, he whisked away a pile of electronic circuitry and clutter that occupied the surface. Evan was a technical genius but working under these conditions must tax even his abilities. A technical genius who read history and poetry? I caught another title on the spine of a book sitting on the counter at my back: *A Dedication to the Stars: The Universe in Poetry.*

I scraped over the metal chair and settled in, dropping my carpetbag at my feet, and waited for him to join me, which he did with his usual quick efficiency. This would be the first time ever that Evan and I had license to discuss a situation one-to-one without Rupert taking the lead. It was unsettling. Do we now behave as colleagues, friends, what? I knew Evan's deference to be only a veneer that locked down a fascinating and dangerous combination of skills and attributes but the man still unnerved me, especially like this. And I thought the feeling could be mutual.

"Is the Renaissance the historical period that interests you most?" I asked.

"All centuries interest me but I try to soak up as much detail as possible if the period is relevant to my mission."

"So the Renaissance is relevant to this mission?"

"Possibly."

Why was he feeding me these details? Really, I needed to take the lead here and the best defense is a strong offense, as they say. "Okay, Evan," I began, "so tell me what's going on and skip the 'within reason' condition Rupert added. The situation is critical, you must see that, and we have to work together. I know I can help. Nicolina believes Rupert—and you by default—may be in some way involved in Maria Contini's death."

"That's completely untrue," he said, looking mildly annoyed at the thought that he would ever participate in such an act. I waited but that's all he said. Getting information from this man would be like prying barnacles from rocks with a toenail clipper. Presumably he'd been trained to keep his cards plastered to his brawny chest during his MI6 days but still...

"What part's completely untrue—the part about us working together or the bit about you two being involved in Maria's murder?"

"The latter. The former is something we will continue to do, I trust."

And he was always so formal, which was disconcerting in itself. I leaned forward, watching him carefully. He had a little tick by his left eye that twitched almost imperceptibly when he was reining himself in. Maybe Her Majesty's Secret Service ousted him on that fact alone since it gave him away every single time. "Nicolina says that should she learn that Rupert was anywhere near Maria on the night she died, she'll kill him herself." I paused, waiting for a reaction. Something flickered across his chiseled features. "That worries me because she's fully capable of it. Well?"

"Well, what, madam?"

Hell. He was back to the "madam" bit. "Was Rupert—or you, for that matter—anywhere near Maria Contini on the last night of Carnevale?"

Evan fixed me with his gray-green gaze but said nothing. His twitch started twitching and, in this case, a twitch is worth a thousand words.

I flattened my palms against the table and stared at him—hard. He stared back in stony silence. He was a much better starer than I—didn't even blink. "Oh, hell, Evan. I was afraid of that, but why? Tell me there's an explanation."

"Madam—"

"Stop it, just stop it. Call me Miss Phoebe like I'm some character out of *Gone with the Wind* if you must, but stop with the 'madam' bit. It makes me feel like ancient history. Why did Rupert come to see Maria? Tell me."

He sighed, and glanced away before returning his gaze. "I admit that I disagree with Sir Rupert's insistence that you be brought into this situation. It is exceedingly dangerous. You would be far safer if you were to excuse yourself from the countess's company and return home."

I squeezed my eyes shut. "I'm just going to forget you said that. Try speaking to me like I'm an adult and not a child needing protection. Let's begin again: Why did Rupert come to see Maria?"

He kept his eyes fixed on my face. "In London, Sir Rupert received a phone call from Ms. Contini insisting that he visit her in Venice immediately. She said that it was urgent and that she had found something of great interest to them both. Naturally, Sir Rupert caught the next plane and we arrived in Venice on the final day of the festivities."

I waited. "And?"

"He called Ms. Contini upon arrival and arranged to meet the lady at a designated location of her choosing."

"Let me guess: the designated location was somewhere near where Maria's body was found."

He leaped to his feet and, in one swift motion, fetched something from the counter and returned to spread a large sheet of paper across the table. A map of Venice, marked in various places with red circles and perfect hand-labeling here and there, wound its sinuous blue canals before my eyes. "Ms. Contini was to meet Sir Rupert here." He placed a finger over one of the circles hovering beside a ribbon of blue. "He waited for nearly an hour but she failed to appear."

I leaned over to read *C de Cannaregio* typed over the blue. "She was to meet him not far from her own villa?"

"At her family's former weaving facility down the canal, yes. Her body was found here—" he tapped another circle "—floating in the canal."

My eyes met his. "That was the night the painting was stolen from the weaving studio—the Bartolo. There's no way Nicolina will believe Rupert isn't behind this. He looks as guilty as sin."

"We are aware of that. Furthermore, I have just been informed that Ms. Contini's phone records were hacked at 10:25 this evening and, should the hacker be Seraphina Tosci, which I have no doubt to be the case, she now knows that Sir Rupert made the last call that the lady received."

"And the one that drew her outside to her death. This is terrible. We have to convince Nicolina that Rupert isn't behind this." I stared hard at him. "Because he isn't, of course, is he?"

"Of course he isn't. Sir Rupert would never kill anyone and has never instructed me to do so on his behalf. I wouldn't, unless in self-defense. That's not who I am."

It was more information than he had ever previously disclosed about himself and it left me momentarily speechless. I flashed back to Noel killing a Camorra dude in Orvieto when it could have been avoided. "But you are former MI6. Surely killing was part of your job?"

"In self-defense. I was not and have never been an assassin."

Clearly he was a bit touchy on the subject. I let it drop. "I believe you," I said finally. And I did. "Besides, I have never thought Rupert a murderer —a scoundrel, yes, but a murderer, no. I don't know why I'm so convinced about that, considering the nefarious episodes he's involved me in, but there you have it. Nicolina, on the other hand, thinks he's quite capable of murdering her friend."

"Perhaps she judges Sir Rupert by her own proclivities." He tapped the table with one long finger. "Both the countess and her handmaiden are capable of violence with little provocation." Those gray-green eyes never left my face—steady, reliable, true. "We have never trusted the contessa, despite our long association with the lady. Furthermore, we are concerned about the partnership you have developed with her over this last year, an arrangement for which Sir Rupert holds himself responsible since he first introduced you two. However we believe—"

I held up my hand. "Stop right there. If you're about to make some inane statement about poor little Phoebe falling in with the wrong crowd, spare me. I fell in with the wrong crowd the day I was born and have been tangled in the roots of my gnarly family tree ever since. You two are also a result, I remind you, so anything you say that reeks of patriarchy is just going to piss me off."

He pulled back, a little smile playing on his lips. "I certainly wouldn't want to piss you off."

"Damn right you wouldn't, and discussing my relations with the countess is strictly out of bounds. I know what she's capable of. Moreover, I know what you two are capable of, murder excluded." I paused and studied him for a moment as he sat there holding himself in check from something—mirth, perhaps?

Did he really believe that little Phoebe was the same naive woman he had rescued in Turkey, or forgotten that I, in turn, had rescued him on at least one occasion? How quickly the male cranium forgets. Blame fossilized conditioning brewed in testosterone that seems to gum the brain cells together like solidifying tree resin.

More importantly, I wondered how much he and Rupert knew about our art repatriation plan. It wasn't exactly a secret since we were operating in conjunction with Interpol but our enterprise certainly must prick the interests of Sir Rupert Fox and anyone else who operated on the fringes of the law. Maybe my spell of anonymity had ended sooner than expected. "What do you know about 'my relations' with the countess, anyway?" I ventured.

"You just told me that discussing your relations was strictly out-of-bounds."

"It is unless I request it. Consider this a request."

"We know just enough to be concerned," he replied.

"A cautious answer if ever I heard one."

"Let me clarify. We know that you are forming an art repatriation agency—"

"Tentatively called the Agency of the Ancient Lost and Found."

The eyebrows arched as he continued with a little smile. "The Agency of the Ancient Lost and Found in cooperation with Interpol, but we are concerned that the countess may not be operating from the same good intentions as you and Max Baker. We have information that certain artifacts that probably originated from your brother's Jamaican repository have been passing through the black market."

"And you know that how?"

"The black market network is surprisingly tight in some respects and information has a way of getting around if you know where to look. At the very least, it usually has the means to identify which artifacts go missing and correctly identify the perpetrators. Your brother and Mr. Halloran were not discreet and, may I say, even haphazard in the end. Which pieces fell into their hands is more or less common knowledge. The only information that is not widely known now is which pieces are now in the hands of Interpol, which fell to Halloren, and which items are in the keeping of you and the countess."

"And which pieces Rupert missed out on."

"My employer came out of the debacle rather empty-handed, much to his chagrin."

"How that must have rankled."

He smiled. "True. In fact, it may have even compromised his immune system."

I couldn't resist a grin. Still, the only way to identify who has what was to cross-reference the contents of our vault and Nicolina's against Interpol's and thus determine which pieces were outstanding. As if that was going to happen anytime soon. We were still in the organization phase. "You must know that there is no way I'll ever disclose our holdings to you."

He nodded. "At the moment, yes. Perhaps at some point you may be persuaded differently. For now consider this: What if the countess is selling pieces from her repository without your knowledge? Keep that in mind."

"As if I haven't." I'd had my own niggling doubts about Nicolina from the beginning but trouble was literally my friend these days so I regularly walked the line between trust and suspicion.

"May I add that informants have alerted us to the fact that Halloren may be also selling pieces from his haul to fund his operation."

"What operation?" I asked quickly.

"His criminal operation as art thief. He has managed to regroup rather well following the Jamaican debacle."

I sat back, thunderstruck. "But I thought..."

"That perhaps he had mended his criminal ways? On the contrary, it appears that he's only intensified them." Then, after several moments of him watching me and me not speaking, he added: "I'm sorry to drop this on you, seeing that you and Halloren are—"

That did it. "Are what? We are nothing. Let's stay focused on the matter at hand, shall we? Nicolina and Seraphina may attempt to assassinate Rupert while the real perpetuator runs free. That's the issue at the moment. What are *we* going to do about it?"

Something snapped behind his eyes—satisfaction, what? "For the moment *I* intend to do everything in my power to assure that Sir Rupert stays safe. He is my prime concern. Sir Rupert's butler is arriving on an early flight tomorrow morning thus relieving me of nursing duties. As soon as he arrives, I will be free to investigate further."

"Sloane?" For some reason I couldn't imagine Rupert's fastidious butler clanking around this grand hovel.

"Sloane. I will then be free to work more directly on the matter at hand and with you, if you will agree. Meanwhile, Ms. Phoebe, you are in the best position to do the necessary groundwork since you are staying at Ms. Contini's villa and possibly surrounded by suspects or, at the very least, by those who may have pertinent information. I urge you to convince the countess that Sir Rupert was not involved in Ms. Contini's demise and would never harm her."

Just once I wanted to hear him talk like he didn't have half the British Empire stuffed into his mouth. I sat back and crossed my arms. "Oh, that will be a piece of cake. You do realize that I will need to tell her that I've been in contact with you and that she will probably trust me that much less as a result?"

"Unavoidable."

"And since Nicolina is more than willing to believe Rupert is behind Maria's death and the robbery, too, she may not be moved by anything I say. She told me all about the broken engagement and the promised paintings and how Maria crumpled to family pressure on both points. To her, that gives Rupert motive."

Evan leaned forward. "If that alone was motive for both a theft and a murder, it would have happened long ago. Sir Rupert hasn't seen Ms. Contini for over two decades. Why did she suddenly call him and request that he meet her in Venice? That is the question."

I leaned toward him. "How do you know the call was even from Maria? There's another question."

"It was placed from her private line in the villa. The lady did not possess a cell phone. There was a second call that night, which thus far remains untraceable."

"But if Rupert hadn't spoken to Maria for decades, he might not recognize her voice. In other words—"

"Perhaps he's being framed."

"That's not what I was going to say."

"Nevertheless, it could be true."

"Whatever the case, that stolen painting must be behind this somehow."

"So I believe."

"She needed the money, Nicolina says, which the state of her house supports, which is probably why she sold the Crivelli. Maybe she was about to sell the Bartolo, too."

"I thought the same thing."

We stared at one another for a moment. I imagined his thoughts flickering across his features, the strong jaw clamping hard on determination. I pitied anyone who got in this man's path, but if it ever happened to be me, I hoped he'd be wearing that apron. *Crud, Phoebe, stop it.* I had yet to disentangle my heart from one man; I didn't need to be attracted to another.

"Either way," he said finally. "There is something else behind this, something bigger and potentially more deadly."

"Like what?"

"That's what we need to discover."

"*You* must have some idea. I only just dropped into this mess."

"There are possibilities too convoluted to get into now." He checked his watch. "It's 12:15 and best that I deliver you back to the villa immediately. We can resume this as soon as I can manage. In the meantime, I have something for you."

He reached into his pocket and pulled out an iPhone that looked suspiciously like mine, right down to the Anatolian kilim wallpaper.

"Oh, great—you and your phones. What does this one do besides monitor my every move—explode random articles, unfold into an instant gondola, play Vivaldi's *Spring*?"

His brief grin was heart-stopping. I made a mental note to provoke one just like it at the first opportunity. "Something much better. When used correctly, it will enable you to gather information from the surrounding environment. It—"

"We plebes call that spying."

"Spying, yes, but it's more than that. Among other things, it has some handy weaponized features that I'll instruct you on when next we meet. And you'll have me on call. Briefly, if you hold down the lower volume button and walk around a room, it will detect surveillance devices and even pinpoint their exact locations. It can also act as a metal detector with a bar graph illustrating the percentage of metals found when you activate the X-ray app by pushing the eye button. I'm rather pleased with the new X-ray features, but admittedly it's still very much at the development stage. Please take it with you tonight. Should you need me in the meantime, just push the top volume button twice and I'll come."

"The top volume button—cute. Why not use an Evan icon?"

That flash-grin again. Yes, I liked it a lot. "Too obvious. Also, that would require you to be turned on, er, turn on the phone, I mean."

"I don't mind turn-ons." *Hell, Phoebe, just shut up.*

A grin combined with those knowing eyes. Hell. "Nevertheless, this way you only need to press the button twice."

"Still, I want an Evan button. Work on that, please."

His eyes met mine. "You need to give me a little more time for an Evan button."

"Take all the time you need," I said. "I'll be waiting to press your button when necessary." This wasn't the first time we'd played these double entendres but it seemed more dangerous now somehow.

At that moment a little device on the counter began emitting feeble croaks. "Evan..."

I turned and gasped. "A baby monitor?"

"Sometimes the simplest technology does the job." He jumped up and dashed from the room.

"Can you give me a hint about the phone's other features?" I called, following after.

"Later. We will continue this at another time, Ms. Phoebe. Bear with me." I wouldn't mind "baring" with him someday.

We arrived to find Rupert sitting up in bed looking petulant. "My tea, where is my tea?" he rasped.

"Baby monitor is just the thing," I muttered.

"Sir, it is getting very late and I really should get Ms. Phoebe back to her quarters."

"Before I pumpkinize," I added sourly.

Rupert flopped back against the pillow. "Very well. Have you...told her all?"

"As much as we have time for tonight. As soon as Sloane arrives, I will disclose further."

"Very well."

I strode up to the bed and looked down at my rumpled, feverish friend. Seeing him this way made my heart ache for multiple reasons. Here was a man who couldn't bear the sight of a wrinkle on his clothing but who now lay wrapped in a heap of tangled bedsheets. That alone was enough to induce conniptions. "I hear that Sloane is coming to tend you tomorrow. He'll insist you get better so you must get right on that. Besides, we can't have you croaking all over this venerable old ruin, can we?"

"So sympathetic," he wheezed. "You will...visit again, Phoebe?" he asked, attempting to prop himself up again and failing miserably. I adjusted the pillows behind his head.

"Is that better? I'll come back as often as it's safe and when my vaporetto driver there can manage. Obviously I can't come by myself."

He grasped my hand. "You'll need a...disguise."

"Yes, but it won't be the plague doctor again, I can tell you that."

"You will...help find Maria's killer?" he rasped.

"I will. Now, rest and follow the doctor's orders so that the next time I visit you, I can see more of my sartorial friend."

Evan tapped his watch.

"Must go. See you soon." I squeezed his hand. I was halfway across the room when it hit me. "Oh, Rupert, before I forget: Would you happen to have a size five millimeter knitting needle I could borrow?"

8

Nothing about the trip back to the Contini villa encouraged conversation. Being stuffed inside a blackout hood counting the number of right- and left-hand turns was challenging enough. Exhausted by then, I struggled just to stay awake. When we finally arrived, Evan helped me to remove my hood and mask before assisting me up to the dock. I had no idea where we were.

"You only need take the right-hand turn at the end of that bridge," he said, indicating a small *porto* directly ahead, "and then you will be on the Cannaregio. From there, proceed down the canal side until you reach the villa. I will be keeping an eye on you until you are safely inside."

"Don't worry, I'll be fine. A bit of a walk might wake me up."

Evan lightly touched my arm. "I cannot overstate the need for caution, mad—Ms. Phoebe. There is something at work here that even I fail to grasp. It concerns that villa and the Continis, for certain, but beyond that we know so little. Extreme caution is necessary."

"I will be extremely cautious." I remained standing where I was, rather enjoying the feel of his hand on my arm, the man's proximity. He removed his hand and the spell was broken. "Well, then. Take care of Rupert and hopefully I'll see you soon," I said, heading toward the bridge.

I never looked back, never looked around, but kept on heading across the bridge and onto the street that rode the canal. A few people were still about but I had no sense of being stalked or even observed except by Evan's friendly eye. As soon as I crossed the construction area with its temporary steel walkway across the canal, I arrived at Maria Contini's villa. The door flew open before I had the opportunity to touch the knob.

"Phoebe!" Nicolina stood there with Seraphina right behind her. "Where have you been? We have been so worried!"

I stepped inside. "Sorry about that but neither of you were around and I needed a walk. Where have *you* been, by the way?"

I heard the countess sigh as she followed me into the salon where I took a seat and clasped my hands across my knees. Before me sat a silver tray of vino Santo, three glasses, and a dish of small biscotti. My stomach growled ominously. I helped myself to a glass of the sweet liquid and dove into the biscuits, crunching away.

"It was necessary for us to go out. I see you found the jacket. It is lovely, yes?"

"Yes, perfect, thank you—very useful, as was the gun, but I'm afraid I disposed of the spy devices. I hope that doesn't make me appear too ungrateful," I said mildly while pulling out the gun to ensure I'd disengaged the safety—check. I immediately turned my attention back to the wine and munchies.

"Spy devices?" Nicolina asked.

"The ones secreted in the lining of my jacket—surely you knew?" I stole a glance toward her. Apparently she didn't. Nicolina was staring at Seraphina, who uttered something in Italian. A brief exchange followed at which point Seraphina left the room.

"I apologize, Phoebe. Seraphina only seeks to protect you," Nicolina began once she'd left.

"Why does everybody say that?" I said while dusting crumbs from my lap. "I get the gun part but spying on me, too? That sounds more like someone hoped I'd lead them to Rupert."

"Phoebe!" To her credit, she appeared genuinely shocked, but I wasn't buying it for a second.

"Being the suspicious creature that I've become, it occurs to me that getting to Rupert might even be the real reason why you've invited me to

Venice in the first place. You knew he'd contact me, so having me tracked served a dual purpose."

"I assure you that I did not realize Seraphina had you tracked. I apologize. Please believe me. She only wanted to ensure your safety. The gun, the jacket, are all to that purpose. Oh, and the jacket, it comes with a secret pocket inside. May I show you?"

"Yes, of course." I removed the jacket and passed it over, which prompted Nicolina to stand, shake off the crumbs, don the jacket (which looked so much better on her model frame), and reveal the leather sling secreted inside.

"A hidden holster?" I said, slapping my hand over my chewing mouth in the interests of decorum.

"Yes, specially designed. I have had several made and thought you could use one, too."

"Oh, I can. Thanks. Once I removed the tracking devices, I just loved it."

Nicolina returned the jacket and took her seat beside me. "Phoebe, be truthful: Where did you go tonight?"

"Thanks for asking. Truthfulness is always the preferred state between friends, don't you think? But if I have reason to suspect someone is less than truthful with me, I'm going to be less than forthcoming myself." That statement, by the way, contains more syllables than I usually manage after a glass of wine. I bit into another biscuit. "Forgot to eat," I mumbled.

"But you left the villa without telling me. You could have texted," she said.

"You could have also texted," I pointed out. "I'm supposed to be here to help you. You were out looking for Rupert, weren't you?"

"Yes. We have had word that he has been in Venice since the day that Maria was killed but we have yet to find him. There, you see, I have been honest."

I nodded. "Good start, so I will admit that I have seen Rupert tonight." I caught her sharp inhalation. I brushed crumbs off my lap. Really, I didn't belong in a villa with a countess. "But I can't tell you where he is because I simply don't know—I was blindfolded. But I can tell you this: he is not responsible for Maria's death. Absolutely not. He received a call from Maria to come to Venice, and when he had landed, they spoke briefly about where to meet. When he arrived at the designated location, Maria didn't show up. He is being framed."

"And you believe this?" Nicolina said, turning to me with that hard glint in her eyes.

"I absolutely do and I intend to prove it somehow, but try not to assassinate him in the meantime, will you? Look, Nicolina, you don't execute a man before you have proof that he is guilty."

"But I know in my heart that he is guilty."

"When it comes to men, your heart is an unreliable measure. Besides, how can you try to harm a friend? You are basing your suspicions on circumstantial evidence. Don't judge Rupert until you have all the facts, which, I assure you, I'm going to help you get."

"Then at least let him face me and explain his innocence himself, then perhaps I will believe him."

I downed the last of my wine. "That's not possible at the moment. Can't you just take my word for it for now?"

"But, Phoebe, how can you ask that if you have no more proof that he is innocent than I do that he is guilty?"

"Because we are—*were*—all friends, that's why. He's helped you in the past, remember? Doesn't that count for something? Why all of a sudden do you want to execute him for a crime you have no proof he committed? I'm asking that you stay your hand in the name of our friendship—yours and mine—if nothing else. Tomorrow we'll discuss this in more detail and you can tell me everything you haven't yet disclosed about Maria, the paintings —the whole backstory. Because I know there's plenty you haven't told me. Anyway, right now, I'm exhausted." And possibly a little wine-soaked. I stood up and strode toward the door. "So, off to bed I go."

"Phoebe, wait."

I turned.

"Tomorrow, it will be a very busy day and we may not get an opportunity to speak."

"But I'll continue my investigations, regardless. I said that I'd help you find Maria's killer and I will but I'll need full access to the house and Maria's vault in the meantime."

Nicolina stood up. "That will not be possible. The warehouse is a crime scene and the police will not allow access. Besides, this is not my house."

"Actually, it is now, more or less, since you are the beneficiary. Get me a set of keys, which I'll take as a gesture of goodwill. 'Night."

THERE'S A REASON WHY I AVOID VINO. THE NEXT MORNING I SLEPT LATE —too late—oblivious to the stirrings around the house until at least 11:00 a.m. My eyes opened on the new iPhone Evan had given me that I'd left stacked on top of the old one on the inlaid side table. I jolted up. What if Seraphina or Nicolina—anybody, for that matter—had entered the bedroom while I slept and tampered with the phone?

Picking it up, I studied it, puzzled by the green light that flashed across the screen's surface when touched, illuminating bright blue fingerprints. What did that mean? Green meant *go* so that had to be a good thing. Blue probably not so much. Maybe Evan had worked it so that if a stranger touches the phone, the thing displayed the fingerprints? Oh, hell: I needed a phone lesson and fast.

I turned off the old phone and secreted it in my carpetbag's hidden compartment and pocketed the new. Next, I chose a fresh pair of jeans, a black turtleneck, and a multicolored scarf that was bound to dispel any notion that I was into the minimalist look. By the time I poked my head out the door minutes later with my arms full of toiletries and clothing, I could hear the cadence of new voices filling the downstairs space—male voices. The villa had company.

After quick ablutions in a bathroom—I had a sink and a toilet in my room but neither a tub nor a shower—where the pipes whined painfully and the water took forever to warm, I dressed and crept downstairs, pausing outside the salon door where two dark-suited men were speaking to Zara and Nicolina while a uniformed man looked on. The *polizia* already?

"*Signora,*" one of the suited men said, catching sight of me and stepping forward. Nicolina smoothly intercepted, speaking to him in Italian, which caused him to nod curtly at me and turn away.

"We are being interviewed," she said, stepping into the hall. "I have told them that you have nothing to offer since you did not know of Maria until yesterday and are here only as my friend. There is no need for you to be involved in this tedious affair. First, I give my statement, then I must visit the lawyers and the funeral people. It is all very distressing. This may take many hours, Phoebe."

"Have they released the body or determined cause of death yet?"

"Not yet." She lowered her voice. "It's best not to ask such things when the police are around. Please, take breakfast on the patio upstairs without me. I have asked Zara to prepare something."

"Did you ask for a set of keys, too?"

"Yes, you will find them next to the coffee flask but you will find nothing here. We have combed the villa already, as the police are doing now."

I nodded. "But an extra set of eyes always comes in handy. Don't worry about me. I can take care of myself."

Nicolina touched my arm. "Yes, of course you can, but we must talk later. About Rupert, I mean. It is not good that we keep secrets from one another."

"Sure."

She retreated into the salon, clicking the door shut softly behind her, leaving me in the hall, trying to disentangle all the things bothering me, which were plenty. Not for the first time, I desperately wished I could speak Italian, at least enough to know what was being said behind those doors. Yes, I was willing to eavesdrop and, if possible, use one of those surveillance devices on my new phone, providing that I knew how. One way or another, I was being maneuvered by Nicolina, used for some purpose I had yet to discern. It wouldn't be the first time. But I had to get ahead of the game because, as it stood, I was way behind.

However, nothing is possible first thing in the morning without coffee.

I returned to the stairs and climbed three flights, continuing on until reaching a narrow marble stairwell washed in daylight. Moments later, I found myself on a small square rooftop patio with a pair of high trumpet-shaped Renaissance chimneys in one corner and a barricade of stone and canvas screening the drop. The morning breeze was bracing and surprisingly warm. I stepped out, breathed deeply, and looked around.

A Venetian rooftop loggia. I'd glimpsed them from the water countless times, always wondering about those lofty spaces where residents captured a slice of private outdoors in a city where exterior space was at a premium.

This one looked as though it had been well-used for alfresco dining over the centuries with its vine-covered pergola overhanging the little table that now bore three glass-covered platters and a thermos. Beside the thermos sat a ring of keys, which I quickly pocketed, but the view momentarily banished all thoughts of food and coffee. I gazed out at a vista centuries old, a scene of canals dancing in sunshine with boats of commerce and pleasure plying the waterways.

For a moment, I just soaked in the scene, checking out the gondolas transporting tourists down the canal below along with vaporettos and private motorboats. I broke my reverie only long enough to grab a roll, a piece a cheese, a slice of salami, and a mug of strong coffee before returning to the vista. So, Maria Contini's villa stood at the beginning stretch of the Cannaregio close to the Grand Canal? A prime viewing spot with the crossways of the two canals converging.

I had just bitten into the roll and gulped back some coffee when I saw her—or, at least, I thought it was a her—the figure of a dark-haired woman standing on a roof patio much like mine only on the opposite side of the canal. A pair of binoculars was focused on my person. For a moment I thought it must be a tourist gawking at the villas in her line of sight but her position never wavered.

For a second, I tried to appear as though I was studying the view, looking slightly to the left while keeping her in my peripheral vision. She remained fixed to the spot before turning abruptly away. I tossed my half-eaten roll onto the table and scrambled around looking for something that had to be there: a pair of binoculars. Nobody has a roof vista without them and, sure enough, Maria Contini's mother-of-pearl version sat tucked under a shelf of glasses. I grabbed them and ran back to the balcony only to find that of course by then my spectator had disappeared.

So, now I needed to find out about the building across the canal. Maybe she was just a casual viewer but I thought not. I took my roll and a mug of coffee and descended the steps.

On the way down, I bumped into Seraphina heading up.

"*Buongiorno*, Phoebe. The countess asked for me to accompany you to keep you company. Everyone will be very busy today. Ah, good, you have found breakfast."

"Thanks for the offer, Seraphina, but I don't need a tour guide or a companion. I have work to do and I'm sure you do, too."

"The police, they do not have questions for me, only the countess. I am just a servant, you see? I keep you company."

Going solo was not an option, in other words. I wondered how long it would take for the police to learn the extent of Seraphina's services. We carried on to the next landing, the top-most bedroom floor. Turning, I faced her with my back to my door. "I just saw somebody staring at me through binoculars from a roof across the canal."

"Perhaps it was Evan. He is watching you, no?"

"This was a woman."

"Many people are curious about Signora Contini's death, so perhaps it is the press. Either way, it must be stopped. I will go with you."

Like I wanted that. "Fine. I'll meet you downstairs after I brush my teeth." In a second I was back in my room, resolved to shake Seraphina's company as soon as I could without causing suspicion. I'd just have to lose myself, which should be easy enough in Venice. Of course, she hoped I'd lead her to Rupert at some point, which had to be avoided at all costs. But there was another pressing matter that had to be attended to immediately —two, really.

First, I pressed the bottom volume button on my new phone and strolled around the room, ridiculously delighted when the screen flashed red, intensifying as I drew the phone closer to a little knob fastened onto a skeleton clock on the mantel. I plucked off the knob, studied a thing the size of a watch battery, and continued until I found two more. Minutes later I whacked the disks on the floor with the heel of my sneaker and dropped the broken pieces into my pocket. Only when the phone no longer flashed red did I stop.

That done, I fished out my old phone and called Max, who had yet to answer my text from the night before. The call rang and rang. Next, I tried his house phone and even the gallery with the same result. A ping of alarm hit. I was just about to hang up when suddenly a voice answered. "Yo, Peaches here."

"Peaches, hi. Where's Max? I keep trying his numbers but he's not picking up."

"Phoebe? How are you doin', girl?" Something pounded in the background. "Just me and da contractors here at da moment. How's Venice? Always wanted to go to Venice."

I lowered my voice. "Venice is fine, I think, but there's lots going on here and I could use a confab with Max."

"So confab with me. Max and Serena took off for a long weekend in da country. I'm thinking it's a bone-jumping weekend but dey're being plenty zip-lipped about it. Acted like they were looking for antiques—yeah, right."

For a moment I couldn't speak. "A bone-jumping weekend?"

"Yes, you know what I mean by dat: man and woman dig each other, man and woman decide to take off for a little one-on-one—read dat literally—time together, and—"

"I know what you meant, Peaches, but I'm just stunned that we're talking about Max and Serena. Since when did romance bloom between those two?"

"You mean, how'd dat bloom without you knowing? It's been right under your nose da whole time but you've been pretty absorbed with da breakup of you and your hottie, not to mention your brother and all. I get that totally. My bro's in jail, too."

"I know." Why was she repeating all this?

"I knew my bro was a sicko. You found out in one blow. And then your hottie turns out to be involved—gutting."

I was about to protest the use of *hottie* applied to Noel but gave up. I was picking up on signs that Peaches was upset about something—too much time alone, who knows? "How I missed that between Serena and Max is baffling but they've gone away for the weekend together, seriously? Well, that's great and I'm happy that Max finally recognized the good woman right under his nose but surely they don't plan to leave their devices off the whole time?" Knowing Max, maybe he did.

"Why not? Some people do dat. They're crazy."

"Peaches, are you okay? I haven't heard you slip into Jamaicanese since you arrived in London. What's going on back there?"

"Oh, crap. Can't keep Jamaica off my tongue when I get stewed up. It's just that the dudes we hired to do the upstairs floor called to say that they can't start on Monday like they promised. I mean, you kidding me? I said You were contracted to perform a service on a certain date and now you say you're behind on another contract so you can't start ours? It's like they're working on island time and that just doesn't go down here. That's not going to happen, I said. The whole reno gets held up until those floor guys get the job done, see? Think I'm going to let that happen? Hell, no. I told them they better get their butts over here next week or else."

"Or else what, what did you tell them?" Sometimes I forgot that the first time I met Dr. Peaches, she was slinging a machine gun at a bunch of drug runners. Though she was doing a phenomenal job of acclimatizing to her new life, it is a process, as they say.

"Or else there could be violence, I said."

"No, no, no, Peaches, please curb your kick-ass tendencies. You've scared off half the contractors already. If these guys bolt, we'll have to find yet another and that will take ages. Just chill. We can wait a week or two for the floor. We're in no real hurry, right? Who's there now?"

"Just the wall guys. I made them work Saturday to finish the drywalling 'cause we were going to get way behind. They'll bugger off after today while we wait for the floor contractors. Okay, I promise not to threaten them with bodily harm. Not yet, anyway." She inserted a string of colorful curses. "So...are you really okay there in Venice? Sure you don't need a bodyguard or a helping hand or something? Soon there won't be anything for me to do here with the worker dudes gone."

"I'm fine at the moment but I'll let you know if that changes. Please stay put until Serena and Max return on Monday. Don't go off threatening anybody just yet, okay? Take a few days off. Get reacquainted with London, maybe. I have to go now but I'll check in later." I clicked off, my pleasure over Max and Serena's liaison muddied by an anxiety that was building by the minute. Yet, I had more immediate things to worry about just then.

I quickly brushed my teeth and donned my new jacket before slipping from the room. Seconds later, I bounded downstairs to where Seraphina awaited in the hall, her petite form compacted into a buttery brown leather pantsuit and a pair of high-heeled ankle boots. She stood, arms folded, watching me descend, the salon doors still firmly shut behind her and her mouth pulled into a tight little line. I had kept her waiting. "So, you come at last."

I stood looking down at her, grateful for my two-inch height advantage.

"For now, but I require much more information if I am to assist Nicolina with her investigation."

"I will assist the countess with her investigation," she stated.

So, it was like that, was it? Could Seraphina be jealous of my involvement or simply frustrated to have me underfoot? "And so will I in my own way. I presume we can cooperate with one another?"

"But of course."

I broke the standoff and indicated the closed door. "So, the interview continues. This is going to be one exhausting day for Nicolina." I was only making neutral conversation.

"The countess is a strong woman," her assistant said with a nod.

"As are we all—a good thing, considering. Oh, and before I forget, Seraphina, I have something for you." I scraped up the surveillance bits from my pocket and held them out to her. "You might want these back. Maybe you can glue them together and use them again on someone else. By the way, I consider this kind of thing very uncooperative considering I was asked to come but I won't mention this latest violation of my privacy to Nicolina unless you do."

She fixed me with a penetrating gaze best served for staring down pickpockets.

"No hard feelings," I said as I emptied them into her hand. "I'm getting used to spy paraphernalia but that doesn't mean I want it in my face. Why did you put this in my room?"

Her pert, sharp-eyed gaze intensified. "You are in touch with Sir Rupert Fox. I must assure the countess's interests."

"And I must assure *all* my friends' interests, including my own. Do we understand one another?"

"Perfectly," she said between her teeth.

"Excellent. Let's get going."

I had thought that we would walk down the canal to the closest bridge and simply stroll over to the building in question but Seraphina insisted we take the boat. That involved bounding down the basement stairs and helping her place the vessel onto its rails so that we could slide it into the water. That done, I studied the canalscape as she puttered through the narrow tributaries at the helm, transversing the main canal to a dock close by the building. There was no rush—I knew the woman would be long gone—but I could have walked there much sooner. Seraphina must have known that, too.

Moments later, we were on the street opposite the canal standing beside one of the countless little restaurant bars that lined the water, the only defining feature to this one being that it sat almost directly opposite the Continis' villa.

As restaurants go, it was a relatively humble affair with an outside eating area of a few metal tables that hugged the blue-and-white painted front with a sun-bleached striped awning over all. An aproned waiter beckoned us over, pointing to a daily special sign fixed on a sandwich board. Seraphina shook her head and began bantering (or I assumed that was bantering) as I backed up far enough to see past the awning to the upper stories—three floors with presumably a roof patio at the very top.

Seconds later, Seraphina was at my elbow. "Luigi says that this is an apartment building—three flats. He says that he does not personally know those who live there except one old man who has lived on the bottom floor for years and a young man who moved in months ago—an art student, he thinks. But the top flat had been empty until a few weeks ago. He says has seen many different people come and go over the last few days. A woman, she just arrived earlier this morning and left a half an hour ago. Very suspicious."

"Suspicious, why?"

"He has never seen any of them before last week—three men and a lady. None of them appear to stay overnight. Foreigners, he thinks."

Foreigners. I knew locals can always tell a visitor from myriad telltale signs. "Is there any way we can get up there?"

"Of course. You distract, I pick."

It is a testament to my new lifestyle that I immediately went up to Luigi and requested to use the facilities with what I hoped was a desperate look on my face. He frowned as if to say *no buy, no pee* so I ordered an espresso. As he dashed inside to fetch it, I watched Seraphina go to the door to the right of the restaurant, unfold a little wallet of tools, and open the door in seconds. I tossed down a euro on the nearest table and followed her in.

A tall narrow flight of stairs led upward with three metal mailboxes affixed on the wall nearby, each with a grimy doorbell button. The first two floors had names neatly typed in the plastic sleeves but the topmost one remained empty. Seraphina pressed the upper one repeatedly. No answer.

Without a word, we climbed the steep stairway, passing a blue-painted door on the first landing, one with a bike locked outside on the second, and a plain wooden one on the top floor upon which Seraphina knocked imperiously. I'd have loved to know what she would have said had anyone responded since I was too out of breath to do much more than pant at that point.

My companion had the lock picked in seconds and we stepped into a dusty, unfurnished flat smelling faintly of garlic with a single front window overlooking the canal and two smaller back ones facing the rear of another building. We both strolled around, me stepping into the tiny back bedroom and Seraphina into the galley kitchen. My Foxy phone tingled in my pocket.

Turning my back, I slipped the phone from my pocket and read: *Sloane has arrived. Can we meet? E*

I typed back: *With Seraphina now. Where?*

Push lower volume button twice and hold. I'll find you.

I heard Seraphina's footsteps marching in my direction. I dropped the phone back into my pocket.

"No one has lived here for weeks but in Venice flats do not stay vacant for so long."

"I doubt this one is vacant, either. I'm betting that someone's rented it for the sole purpose of surveillance. You'll need to search immediately for the lessee," I said, turning around. "You have amazing skill with that kind of thing, right?"

Seraphina shot me a quick look, possibly surprised that I had made a statement that sounded suspiciously directive. Clearly I needed to go head-to-head in a power struggle with Nicolina's indomitable assistant. "I will do this, yes, and you must not jump to conclusions," she said. "This is probably the press staking out the countess for the next big story. In Italy, we love our big stories."

I narrowed my eyes at her. Why was Seraphina downplaying this? Someone was watching the villa. That couldn't be good, no matter the circumstances. Turning, I strolled to the front window and pointed to the Styrofoam coffee cup loaded with cigarette butts. "It is a stakeout, for sure.

Look at this. Someone has been watching the villa for days, if not weeks. Is the Italian press really so bent on a story that they'd put four people on the job? I always pictured news hunts to be the domain of some lone-wolf paparazzi stalking the unlikely victim. Come, let's check out the roof. I saw the little door to the left of the landing."

I bounded out of the flat and stopped by the door—locked, of course. Seraphina jiggled her little tool into the keyhole and it sprung open in seconds. Moments later we were on top of a shabby little rooftop with a single plastic table and four matching chairs, two of them knocked over. The bottom of the concrete banister was littered with stacked cups of ashes and cigarette butts. "Hmm, messy, and signs of a long, protracted stakeout," I remarked as I stepped up to the railing. "Now why would anyone be that interested in Maria's villa, Seraphina?"

"As I say, probably the press."

I didn't believe that and I bet neither did she but I played along. "So why not plant one of your little surveillance devices up here so we can at least identify the reporters who are violating our privacy? Surely there must be laws against that kind of thing in Italy? You can send the paper responsible a cease and desist order or the Italian equivalent."

I turned to find Seraphina seeming to consider this for a moment, though I guessed she was more likely trying to think up a reason why to counter my suggestion. After a moment, she nodded. "Yes, this I will do."

"Excellent. So while you're doing that, maybe I'll to do a bit of research and you can report back to me later." I made for the exit.

"But there does not need to be such a hurry," she said, dashing after me. "I can do these things later."

"Nonsense," I said, waving my hand dismissively as we descended the stairs. "This must be dealt with now. There's no time to waste."

When we emerged outside, I turned to her and waved goodbye. "See you later."

In moments I was striding down the street, leaving her standing there watching me with her mouth pursed in annoyance. Check one for Phoebe. But, I thought as I clambered over a little bridge, Seraphina did not give up so easily. She had to have another plan.

❧ 9 ❧

It occurred to me as I turned a corner to march down a narrow street edging the water that Seraphina probably expected to track my whereabouts using my tampered phone. No doubt that those blue fingerprints belonged to her. Now what? I pulled out my superphone and tapped out a message to Evan: *I'm free now but I'm sure Seraphina is tracking me.*

The response came back immediately: *She is but to no avail. Don't worry, I have you covered. Keep walking.*

He had me covered—an interesting thought. I strode past churches and other intriguing old buildings until I reached a smaller canal where I took a left-hand turn and continued deeper into the heart of Venice. Somehow I ended up across from the International Gallery of Modern Art, but as tempting as it was to drop in for an eye-feast, I kept on going. I'd look over my shoulder every thousand feet or so expecting to see Evan emerge from behind a building, but nothing—nothing, that is, until a motorboat suddenly came into view zipping toward me.

When the boat slowed and I looked down at Evan at the same time that he looked up at me, our eyes held for seconds too long. I ignored his hand and climbed into the boat without assistance. "Good morning, Ms. Phoebe."

That greeting nearly spoiled the moment. "So," I said in my jauntiest tone, "I see you've ditched the *Phantom of the Opera* meets the *Lone Ranger* look." Today he dressed like himself in a turtleneck under a chocolate-colored leather jacket with jeans and a version of those peaked hats he preferred. The man was very good-looking, if you liked that square-jawed brawny type. Not me, of course. I preferred them lean, swarthy, and perpetually missing in action apparently.

He smiled. "Most conflicting interests already know that Sir Rupert and I are in town and that you and I are colleagues of a sort. Doubtless we have attracted attention, not all of it friendly."

Was that what we were—colleagues? Well, I suppose we were. "I'm beginning to think we may have attracted *significant* interest."

His mouth formed a grim line when I told him about the surveillance on the roof. "Things may have intensified sooner than I anticipated," he remarked.

"What if we're tracked to Rupert's hideout?"

"Sir Rupert is thoroughly fortified in his current location and I have sentries watching from all possible directions. I've also taken precautions regarding Seraphina's tracking devices. The enhanced phone I provided detects interference and records fingerprints."

"I figured out the fingerprints."

He pulled down the throttle and began a slow putter down the canal with a self-satisfied smile on his fine lips. "Please open it now, Ms. Phoebe. I sent you another message explaining the details."

I did exactly that, grimacing at him for the "Ms. Phoebe" bit before skimming the message quickly. I looked over at him. "You sent her to St. Mark's Square?"

"That's where she thinks you've gone. Whether or not she follows you there is left to be seen. Just know that she will be unable to track you using her rudimentary tracking devices and thus you are free to move around Venice at your leisure, at least to roam without her particular scrutiny. Obviously you may have attracted other interests."

I cocked my head at him. "Do I detect a note of pride?"

His lips quirked. "A smidgen, admittedly. Since Seraphina has long been in competition with me so naturally there is a touch of rivalry between us."

"I know that you are former MI6 but is Seraphina a former agent, too?"

"She did belong to the equivalent of the Italian secret service once, out of Rome, I believe."

"I haven't been keeping up with my who's-who of ex-intelligence agents apparently."

And Seraphina seemed as devoted to Nicolina as Evan was to Rupert. The things that money can buy. I wanted to ask him what his life was like in Rupert's employ but now wasn't the time and maybe that time would never come. Evan had always been a very private man, and though the barriers between us were lowering, I didn't want to presume too much. Our colleagueship was only at the beginning, after all. "Are we off to see Rupert now?"

"Not until tonight, mada—Ms. Phoebe—after Sloane has finished attacking the building with his bleach and mousetraps. Every dust bunny appears to him like a dragon lurking in the corners so it's best we don't annoy him further by our presence."

I laughed. "How's Rupert doing, anyway?"

"Much better now that a steady stream of tea and scones have been directed to his bedside. His mood, at least, has improved. I'm afraid I've been much too busy with security duty to attend him in the manner to which he's become accustomed."

Why was he opening up to me like this? He had never shared so much delightful detail or commentary before. He had always acted as a mouth-piece for Rupert with a wall of tedious formality raised like a force field between us. Now he was revealing himself as a person. "What do you have in mind today, then?"

"I suggest we put our heads together to compare the facts we have gathered so far and see if we can work out next steps."

"Sounds good. We'll need a quiet spot for that, preferably one where dust bunnies have already been banished and I can have a decent breakfast."

He grinned. "I have just the place."

And so we zoomed down the waterways under blue sky with me feeling more relaxed than I had in days. I didn't care where we were going at first, content to let him take me there. Still, when we suddenly jetted off across the lagoon, I was intrigued. "Where *are* we going?" I called above the slap of waves against the bow.

"Torcello."

Torcello. I had never heard of it. I knew of Murano and I knew of Burano, where I had gone as part of a tour group long ago. I sat back and waited for Torcello to come into view, which it did twenty minutes later by way of a central tower stabbing the blue sky.

As Evan slowed the boat at our approach, he said: "This island was one of the first to be populated after the Veneti fled the invaders, and in 638, Torcello became the bishop's seat; hence the building of the Cathedral of Santa Maria Assunta and the central tower you see ahead. Impressive Byzantine mosaics are in there and I do wish we had time for a tour. In any case, in the tenth century, it was more important than Venice as a trading center."

"What happened to cause its demise?"

"The plague, malaria, and marshes that eventually devoured the harbor is the short story. Today it's mostly ruins, which has left it with kind of a haunting quality like a dismembered saint—"

And the man had a poetic turn...*a dismembered saint.* "I always find saintly relics sad—the toe, the knuckle, the supposed skull of Saint So-and-so separated from its body to be stared at and revered forevermore. Whole mummified bodies under glass are particularly gruesome."

"And yet, as you know, it is part of Italian Catholic culture and revered as a result. Catholicism leaves a deep, lasting mark on its citizens even among the disbelievers, especially in Italy."

So perhaps he had been raised Catholic? Whatever the case, he appeared to have some strange affinity to this little island. Stranger and stranger.

"For Torcello, sadder still is the way in which the Venetians plundered this island by absconding the stone with which to build their own structures yonder. The island has been picked apart."

We entered a short canal with a wharf at one end and boats tied up along the bank. We secured the boat among others of varying shapes and sizes and strolled down a bush-lined lane as quiet as any country path. Though a few people ambled around, the sense of space was remarkable compared to the press of bodies across the lagoon.

The buildings here were mostly shabby and crumbled with paint-scabbed shutters and mottled terra-cotta walls. Of course, this being Italy, every deteriorating inch was artlessly beautiful. I gazed down at the ground beneath our feet—primarily gravel and beaten earth—making me think that the Venetians had plundered even the cobblestones.

Soon I was gaping at a white granite stone seat positioned like a throne along one of the paths that wandered through the remains of the town when Evan stopped. "They call it Atilla's Throne but it was more likely where the bishop held court and preformed judiciary functions. Pardon me." He took out his phone and tapped a quick message. "Excellent. She is ready for us."

"She?"

"Sophia, my friend. She has agreed to provide us a quiet place to talk and breakfast also. Come, Ms. Phoebe."

Ms. Phoebe followed him to a lovely salmon-colored stucco house with green shutters hanging on by rusting hinges. I'd love to knit or paint that one day but my attention was diverted to the open door. We stepped into a kitchen as humble and charming as anything I have ever seen with an open shutter blowing a warm breeze through lace curtains and an Italian breakfast waiting at a linen-covered table.

An extraordinarily pretty woman greeted us dressed in a sweater and a full patterned skirt. I estimated her to be in her thirties, her face free of makeup and her smile wide and welcoming. "Evan, you have brought your friend. I am Sophia and you must be Phoebe." She grasped both my hands and pulled me toward her for a brief air kiss.

"Hi, Sophia. Thank you for the welcome and the breakfast. I haven't eaten properly in days."

"Oh, that is not good." I caught the look that passed between Evan and Sophia—swift and warm. "Let me take care of that right now. Please sit at the table and I will get the coffee—espresso, Americano?"

Her accent was as musical as a concerto. Everything about her was engaging, in fact. Why couldn't Evan's friend be a rotund middle-aged woman who answered to "Mama" and made heaping pots of spaghetti sauce? What was she to this enigma of a man, anyway, and why should I care?

I took a seat across from Evan and did as I was bid—helped myself to sliced meats, ham, cheese, fruit, and crusty bread. Sophia poured coffee into each of our cups and left a flask. "I will leave you now. Take as much time as you need. I will work in the shop today so no hurry. Giani is keeping watch."

Evan met her eyes again. "Thank you again, Sophia."

"My pleasure." The woman dashed out the door.

"Who is Giani?"

"Sophia's son."

A silence fell across the table while I ate and Evan sipped his coffee reflectively. Had he been anyone else I would have asked about his relationship with Sophia but I could feel the barricade rising around the subject so reined myself in. It wasn't any of my damned business, anyway.

I stirred sugar into my coffee and looked over at him. "Do you have any idea who is watching the villa? They seem to be engaged in a protracted stakeout and one or more smoke too much. Otherwise, I haven't a clue about their identity—a couple of men and a woman. I suspect Seraphina may know who they are but she's not talking. She wants me to think they are the press but I don't believe that for a second."

He leaned forward. "There's evidence that you are under watch by a group of some unknown identity, which she may suspect. Several individuals have been seen lurking about, watching the villa, watching you, Seraphina, and the countess also. I have reason to believe that they may be connected to the murder and the theft."

"But why me? What do I have to do with it?"

"My theory is that they believe that the countess brought you in as an expert to unlock the painting's secrets and thus they require you for that purpose also."

"What? I mean, that's ludicrous. I'm no expert!"

"Consider this from an outside perspective—" he began counting off on those long fingers of his "—you have been involved in several successful antiquities and art operations in conjunction with Interpol over the years; you manage a large textile and ethnographic gallery in London, which is now rumored to be emerging into a lab of some kind; and finally, of equal importance, you are connected to several antiquities elements worldwide. You can, Ms. Phoebe, easily be considered an expert."

I sighed. "I've always said that an expert is only someone who knows slightly more on a given subject than the person naming her as one." I shoved my hair behind one ear. "But I'm really no expert on Renaissance art other than what I learned in university. It's been an interest of mine, certainly, but not in the thorough sense when there are countless true experts out there that could be called in."

"Maybe they have been and found nothing?"

"Then how can I?"

He leaned toward me again. "You underestimate yourself, madam—my apologies, *Ms. Phoebe*. What have you gleaned from the paintings to date? You have seen photographs, I presume?"

I wasn't playing that game without quid quo pro. "You presume correctly, but you show me yours and I'll show you mine. You go first."

His quirked a smile.

"Rupert's seen those works in person and, knowing him, he is not without a theory, not to mention firsthand information," I continued. "Collaborate, Evan, and in the interest of partnership, the first piece of information must come from your side."

That little smile again—partly appreciation, partly amused chagrin. "Very well, though I preface this with the knowledge that Rupert had hoped to share this with you personally. "He and Maria Contini were once engaged—"

"I know all about the broken promises, including the fact that Maria had offered that painting to Rupert as a kind of consolation prize but later withdrew the offer."

"Did you know that part of the reason she wanted Sir Rupert to have those paintings was because he is Jewish?" He could tell by my expression that I did not know that. "She withdrew the offer on the night she told her mother her intent. A great argument ensued, at which point her mother disclosed the fact that the paintings held a valuable secret. Generations of Continis shielded that painting without ever knowing why. Whatever happened, Maria could not give it away, a fact that finally hit home."

"Maria must have known something about their importance prior to that."

"Only that it was essentially hidden in the house for as long as she could remember. The Continis did not want it to be seen; something Ms. Contini hinted had to do with their great value and possibly a religious element."

"Because the bride and groom were from two different religions? But surely that wouldn't have been an issue now?"

Evan grimaced. "Signore Contini was a staunch Catholic and saw marrying into another religion to be a blemish to the family line. He bristled against the possibility of Jewish blood in the Contini veins."

"So he was anti-Semitic as well as a foolish, blindsided pig."

Evan's brows arched at my vehemence but he nodded in agreement. "Aptly put. You don't appear surprised about anything I've disclosed."

This time I leaned forward. "I'm not. You've only confirmed something I've suspected—not about Rupert, of course—I didn't know he was Jewish, but about the Bartolo."

"An exquisite and valuable piece of Renaissance art. I didn't have the opportunity to see it in person, unfortunately—Sir Rupert's affiliation with the Continis being far before my time—but I have seen the photos he keeps."

I plucked out my phone to display the pictures I took of the painting, focusing in on the minute detail of the Bartolo's wedding scene in particular. "The carpets are particularly interesting. Do you see the one beneath their feet?" I pinched open a close-up.

"A prayer rug, correct?"

"Possibly but not one like I've ever seen before. It was probably presented as Anatolian by the look of some of the motifs but those large geometrics are totally out of character. The lantern design is shown upside down for one thing, and though it's not unusual for a Muslim prayer rug to be shown in a church in Renaissance art, there's something off about the whole composition. And the actual knotting of the rug looks Berber. Do you see this twisted key motif right here?" I tapped the phone with my finger as Evan pushed aside the plates to lean forward.

"It looks Chinese."

"It is based on a Chinese phoenix-and-dragon motif and yet those knots linking them form hexagrams, part of a larger one is partially hidden below the bride's feet. That could be the Star of David."

He nodded. "Quite possibly."

"Regardless, that's a mishmash of cultural symbols and has to be significant. Add to that, that the border feature is pure unabashedly Berber."

"Berber as in Morocco?"

"Exactly. I have only ever seen that composition of geometric design in Berber rugs. So why has Bartolo taken the time to visually weave together such diverse elements? The Renaissance embedded layers of messages and symbols into their art, as you know, and this carpet reads like a Renaissance encryption."

Did I see something like appreciation warming his gaze? "Now I see exactly why Nicolina called you into this."

"She asked me to come as a friend for moral support and to help solve Maria's murder. Never once did I think that interpreting Renaissance art might be part of the picture. Frankly, it isn't even my specialty and I'm hardly a cryptographer."

"But you are a carpet expert and evidently those carpets are key. Perhaps the contessa doesn't choose to involve too many outside experts. Perhaps you are the one she hopes will unlock the answers? You do have a certain reputation among the art trade."

"Which would be so nice if she'd deigned to mention it."

"In any case, she did show you the photo. What else have you gleaned?"

I pulled back and sighed. "I'm sure what I see has been seen by others. For instance, if you look carefully at the wedding picture, it appears to take place in a church or cathedral and yet you will see in the background a cluster of people who seem to be raising their hands in dance—odd for a wedding inside a church, don't you think? Also, if you look at the arches over the wedding party they actually form more of an umbrella shape than a true arch, which is just another subtle nod to another culture, probably Eastern. This painting is more than the usual Renaissance contract between two families."

"One that links two religions."

"Yes, Jewish and Christian—something almost unheard of at the time."

"I'll see if I can find out more about this marriage, if there are even records, but there should be something." He said that as mildly as if he would do a quick Google search.

I looked at him. "How? The records would be minimal that far back, wouldn't they?"

"Not in Venice, which is a city that took to recording its every breath long before the fifteenth century. And where there are churches, there will be records, and I suspect this ceremony took place in a church under the guise of a Catholic ceremony, no matter how well-disguised the event. For some unknown reason, the Contini ancestors accepted a Jewish bride into their midst, one who would have been forced to convert and the truth of their union hidden by everyone."

"And a very dangerous thing to do in the 1400s. It would be considered heresy by the Catholic church."

"Indeed, especially as Venice was moving toward segregation. In 1516, Venice would officially segregate its Jewish citizens into a *getti*, the first ghetto in history," he said.

"Oh, my God, what would have compelled a wealthy Venetian family like the Continis to support, even celebrate, such a union?"

He tapped a finger on the table. "That is the question, my dear Watson."

I smiled slowly and said: "Look, I'm Sherlock, you're Watson, and don't you forget it."

He smiled back and beautifully, by the way, but I've said this already. Some things bear repeating. I'd been known to flirt with this man and have him flirt back but that was in the days when my heart belonged to another —safe-distance flirtation, in other words. Now nothing felt safe.

"Let's get back to business, my dear Watson," I said. "It could be love that brought the bride and groom together, though I realize that such emotions hardly served as wedding material back in the day."

He was about to answer when suddenly the door flew open and Sophia rushed in. "I am sorry to disturb but a boat comes! You said to alert you of something suspicious. It is not a tourist boat but carries four people. One appears to have a gun!"

Evan and I exchanged glances and jumped to our feet. "A gun openly displayed?"

"What is this—America?" I exclaimed.

"Giani sees it with his glass thing from the tower. He saw one man open his jacket and the gun was strapped across his body. He just texted."

"Surely they wouldn't try anything here in broad daylight, and what are they after, anyway?" I cried.

"You," Evan said.

"This is crazy. I told you that I'm no expert. I just dust off old things and classify a lot." This wasn't false modesty; I really didn't see myself as being particularly gifted.

"It's not what you know but what they think you know that matters." He grabbed my hand. "Besides, you know more than you give yourself credit for, madam. Come, we'll escape into the church and wait until we can safely bolt for the boat."

Which meant a quick-paced stride across central Torcello straight toward the Cathedral of Santa Maria Assunta, which turned out to be an amazing Byzantine structure with two majestic end walls covered in gilded mosaics. The two flanking walls were whitewashed to enhance the beauty of the two ends. All of this I took in as we race-walked down the aisle.

"Slow down and walk as if you're a devotee," Evan whispered.

I slowed my pace while pulling my wrap up over my head, which probably made me look like some bizarre runaway mushroom. And I did feel a sense of deep respect inside of any religious house, but my presence here felt like an imposition of the worst kind.

The usual mill of tourists wandered around taking pictures of the mosaics, whispering their appreciation, while a handful of those I presumed to be locals lit candles and prayed quietly in the pews or before the image of a golden Christ.

I tugged on Evan's arm to pull his ear down to my level. "They'll be methodical; they'll spread out and comb every inch of this island and are bound to come in here, too."

"I realize that," he whispered back. "Follow me."

So I followed him past the altar and behind a column to where a stone bench sat in shadows against the wall. There we were holding a Bible between us, our heads together as if reading the text together. It was probably one of the strangest moments of my life, to be hiding out in plain sight in that ancient cathedral with Evan, the former MI6 guy. We barely moved as the minutes ticked by and Evan periodically shot cautious glances toward the door.

Eventually a solitary man entered, his eyes darting around the space as if looking for something or someone, neither tourist nor supplicant but a man on a mission. Our heads remained bowed as we waited tensely until he left.

Finally Evan straightened. "They won't leave this island until they find us. We'll have to risk dashing for the boat," he whispered.

"Can the boat outrun them?"

"No. Our best hope is to get a head start."

"But what do they hope to gain?"

"Perhaps to kidnap you. The paintings themselves did not tell the thieves what they wanted to know but they think maybe you can. That may mean that they don't mean to shoot you, at least not at the moment."

"Comforting. They'll just torture me first. And we thought we'd be safe here on this island."

"Torcello was a poor decision on my part for which I deeply regret. I believed it perfect for our meeting, which it was, but it is simultaneously wide open and exposed the way Venice is not. Are you ready to run?"

"Sure."

But before we ran, we walked, casually and hopefully unobtrusively, out the door and across the earthen square. Evan was a big enough man to attract attention for anyone looking for him and I stood out with my red hair and art wrap. Neither one of us wore T-shirts and baseball caps like many of the other day-trippers. Evan removed his peaked hat and tucked it under his jacket, letting his light brown hair blow in the breeze while he gazed about the square as if fascinated by every detail.

When we were halfway down the path heading to the dock, we bolted. In seconds we were untying the boat, but as soon as we jumped in, we saw a man standing three speedboats down talking urgently on his phone.

"We've been seen," Evan said, opening up the throttle. "Hold on."

As if holding on was even necessary. I just sat there, all the way across the marsh toward the open lagoon, the boat racing as fast as it could, which in speedboat terms was like a Smart car struggling to be a Lamborghini.

"I thought you love speed, Evan?"

"I believed this would putter under the radar but, trust me, I have another one more impressive."

It only took minutes to see a speedboat pull away from the island behind us and zoom at our puny wake at a much faster clip. "Do you want me to drive while you shoot?" I called.

"You watch too many spy movies, mada—Ms. Phoebe. Shooting is not wise under the circumstances," Evan called back.

"What circumstance—being chased by a boatload of armed criminals? Sounds like a few shots over the bow as a deterrent just might be the thing."

"Not if they shoot back, which they inevitably will," he shouted over the slap of waves and the putter of the engine.

I gripped the sides, thinking that we could row faster than this. Meanwhile, our pursuers were gaining on us, making me wonder what exactly they had in mind. If it was true that they wanted me, which I still considered ridiculous, then Evan would be seen as an obstacle worth killing in their eyes. And who would see a kidnapping in the middle of the lagoon where boats zip by all the time and a shout or a cry— maybe even a gunshot—probably couldn't be heard? Suddenly I felt frightened.

Evan was talking into his phone between quick glances at the gaining speedboat. Venice was growing closer but not close enough. I imagined scenes where James Bond raced down the canals in his superboat but I doubted we'd even reach the canals let alone zip anywhere in this one.

Our pursuers were so close now that I could make out their features— three tanned men and one woman, all wearing sunglasses, leather, and stony expressions straight out of some thriller movie. They looked like carbon copies of one another. And then Evan was slowing down and another boat was pulling up from the opposite direction—shiny, new, and, I suspected, jet-propelled.

"Quick, jump!" Evan called.

Leaping from one rocking boat to another is not easy even when stopped, especially when carrying a carpetbag. The chop alone set the thing to swaying like crazy even while the driver tried holding the two boats together but I still managed to leap over the side into the other boat.

A little guy with a leathery face and a cigarette between his teeth grinned at me. Evan jumped in behind me, yelled something in Italian, and took the helm while the little man sat back and bared his tobacco-stained teeth in the direction of the approaching speedboat. Our little boat was left to float away by itself.

That left our pursuers arriving just in time to grabble with our wake, the new speedboat being far faster than even theirs as we whipped the water toward Venice. This may have been the fastest boat I'd ever been in, fast enough to leave the bad guys far behind while yelling at our backs.

After that, it took mere minutes to reach Venice, Evan taking diversionary maneuvers by diving into different canals snaking through the city —left, right, left again. Our pursuers disappeared from sight. Once we were slipping down a quiet narrow canal between two buildings, Evan cut the engine. "Do you see that archway to the right, madam?"

"Yes, Evan, I do." I needed some smart-ass name for him.

"Take that alleyway through the buildings, cut across the street to the left, cross a bridge, and within a block you'll come to Cannaregio and the villa down the canal. It's the safest place for you right now as Ricki here informs me that the Contini residence is crawling with police. Go inside and stay there until I contact you. We are going to divert our friends and ensure that they are not on your heels."

"I need to speak to Rupert."

"You will."

I watched the arch draw closer with its time-worn steps leading into the water and in seconds I had jumped out. "Be careful," I called as they pulled away, and within ten minutes I was striding up to the door of the Contini villa without further mishap. My temper, however, was on the boil.

A uniformed carabiniere stood by the door, his back straight but his gaze shifting in all direction. "I am staying here," I said as he moved to block my way.

"Your name, *signora*?"

"Phoebe McCabe."

With that he opened the door to let me pass and I moved directly across the hall to the salon, combing my matted hair with my fingers and fortifying myself for what had to be done.

Inside the room, Nicolina could be seen sitting in tense silence, her hands in her lap, while across from her sat the same suited detective I had seen earlier plus another. On the other side of the room, a white coveralled man was dusting for prints. Everyone stood when I entered.

"Phoebe!" Nicolina cried in a mix of welcome and desperation.

I shoved a lock of fuzzy windblown hair from my brow. "Afternoon, Nicolina, Detective. Excuse me for interrupting but I've just been chased across the lagoon by a boatload of armed thugs who may or may not have been after me because they think me more important than I am. Mind if I join the conversation?"

❧ 10 ❧

Detective Guido Peroni from the Venetian Questura was a thorough man. He had already been stationed at the villa for six hours interviewing every member of the household and returning again and again to grill the weary countess, who assured him that she was doing everything to cooperate. To Nicolina's credit, she did not pull arrogance as a shield in the kind of imperativeness that a countess might well deploy under the circumstances.

I had, however, thrown a proverbial spanner in the works. After I had disclosed to Peroni everything I knew or thought I knew about the painting, it became apparent that Nicolina had not.

"And you believe this painting may be a kind of cipher, Ms. McCabe, and that may be why you are of such interest to your pursuers today?" the detective asked as he sat there with the photo portfolio open on the table before him. He was a thick-set man in a well-tailored suit with a receding hairline and shrewd eyes that glinted in the light washing through the tall windows. Beside him on the couch sat another suited policeman, younger and leaner, taking notes while listening to every word with the diligence of a human lint-catcher. Occasionally he'd interrupt me for clarification of a word or an idea. Though both men's English was excellent, he obviously was ensuring that nothing was lost in translation.

"Possibly," I said, "though I can't imagine why anyone who knows even a little about Renaissance symbology couldn't see the same things. I'm not a Renaissance scholar by any means. I studied art history as a generalist."

Peroni was peering at the Bartolo with a magnifying glass. "Yes, but you are a textile expert, are you not, from a big London gallery? And with affiliations with Interpol and a recent history of involvement with several key finds?"

So he did his homework. I hurried on. "My reputation is exaggerated, but back to the carpets: please understand that my assessments are only guesses and need a lot of research to back them up."

Peroni turned to Nicolina. "Did you request the help of Ms. McCabe because if her expertise?"

"No," Nicolina replied evenly. "I asked her to accompany me for moral support as a friend."

"How fortunate for the countess that you have such an experienced friend." He turned back to me. "Please tell me your assessment of these carpets to the best of your knowledge."

Taking a deep breath, I attempted to pull it all together. "The paintings have an odd combination of cultural motifs that can't be accidental. You know, of course, that Renaissance art often used portraits and paintings to capture a moment of significance, kind of like a pictorial contract," I told him. "This one shows a wedding between two families, two very different families, I might add." I waited for Nicolina to explain more but she appeared locked in some fortress of her own choosing. I sighed and continued, a shield of my own in place by way of my most scholarly tone even though I was in way over my head. "Though Bartolo was not known for embedding secrets in his work the way da Vinci was, I think it's reasonable to assume that he may have been commissioned by one or both of the families to do exactly that."

"Interesting." Peroni was focusing on a detail of the nave. "I am not an art expert," the detective said, looking up at last, "but one does not live in Venice without some knowledge of the subject. Bartolo was from the Sienese School, am I correct?"

I nodded.

"So these families are Sienese?"

"Not necessarily. Renaissance artists often traveled all over Italy on commissions from wealthy patrons. If the families wanted to put a little distance from this contract and their hometown, they might choose a painter from another city. Still, I believe that the motif in the bride's robes are actually from the Continis' own weaving mills, which could mean that one of the parties is from Venice, maybe even from this family. I can't confirm that, though."

Peroni turned to Nicolina. "Is that true, Contessa, that these fabrics may be from a Contini mill, which I understand has stood down the street for at least that many centuries?"

Nicolina's face remained unmoved. "It is true that Maria Contini has many motifs stored in the vault's library and that this may be among them."

The detective did not acknowledge that comment but placed the photo upon the table and drew back. "I see with my humble and unschooled eye a beautifully painted scene of a wedding party, which appears to be taking place inside a church of some wealth and majesty. I know nothing of carpets and motifs but I do know most of the churches and basilicas in this city and this one is not known to me."

"I believe that's because it's actually a composite of two houses of worship—a church and a synagogue—and it's supposed to be a symbolic location rather than a real one." I shot a quick glance at Nicolina, who refused to meet my eye. "The altar and the nave seen to the left are clearly Christian but the dancers behind the bridal party appear to be forming a chuppah with their hands and, if I'm not mistaken, the design under the bride's feet could be the Star of David. That's just a guess, of course, but it does explain a few things. Even the arches in the wall to the right appear to be a blend of two architectural styles—half Gothic arch, half Eastern, which doesn't mean anything by itself but could when combined with the other elements. It is my guess that this painting is the Renaissance equivalent of a contract between two wealthy families—one Christian and one Jewish, an incredibly risky and startling partnership given the age in which it occurred."

Peroni looked at me in surprise while Nicolina's eyes widened with something like fear.

"The clues are recognizable but I doubt they'd be evident to any casual viewer in the past. The painting is probably for the owners' eyes only but a contract nonetheless." I turned toward Nicolina again. "The paintings have never been cataloged or appeared in any exhibitions. The family has kept them private for centuries."

"The Continis have always been very private people," Nicolina said evenly, "and naturally one does not wish to advertise their priceless art."

"And yet someone obviously discovered that they existed and hence it is gone," Peroni said.

"Yes. Anyway, as I said, it would be extremely dangerous for a Jewish girl or boy to marry into a Christian family or vice versa," I continued. "The marriage would have to be hidden, and the reasons for those two families coming together in the first place significant. The wealthy rarely married for love but as an alliance between two families in order to bring together fortunes or titles. In this case, one must have been significant enough to be worth the risk."

The detective was watching me carefully. "What do you think may have prompted this partnership?"

"Since Jews have been persecuted across the ages, that's what puzzles me, too. I don't want to eliminate the possibility of love—the bride and groom do seem happy, it's true. Maybe they wanted to hide themselves under the cover of another family, but why would the Continis agree to such a thing when it would mean risking their lives?"

"And so a secret locked into the carpet, perhaps, something worth killing for?"

I met his deep-set brown eyes. "My guess is a dowry. The bride is standing on the Star of David and the groom is on the edge of the motif. She brought a valuable dowry to a wealthy Christian family, one that for whatever reason was worth the risk both families took to secure it. It had to be protected at all costs."

❧ 11 ❧

Commissario Peroni and his team exited shortly after that, insisting that a guard be placed on the house despite Nicolina's pleas that she didn't need one. Nevertheless, a guard was assigned to the patrol outside the building and Peroni assured us that he would return within the day. I had no doubt they would.

That left Nicolina and me sitting soberly in the salon with so much unsaid between us that I swear it darkened the air. Or maybe that was just dusk.

It was me who broke the silence. "Why didn't you tell me what you knew about that painting, Nicolina?"

"Because I did not know how important it was!" It was as if I'd flipped her switch. She threw up her hands. "I did not know that this family's history was in any way related to the theft! I should have, perhaps, but it is a priceless work of art in its own right, yes? Also, I would have told what I did know once we had time. When have we had time? First the police came and the funeral arrangements had to be made on top of the horror of losing Maria under such circumstances!" She covered her face and wept. She was exhausted, overwrought even, and I knew I was being an insensitive pig.

And she had a point: there hadn't been much time and, admittedly, she had a lot on her shoulders. But I wasn't quite ready to let the matter drop. "Of course, it's been terrible for you. I understand that, but to leave me in the dark while putting Seraphina on to me, too—that I'm having trouble swallowing."

"I was looking out for you," Seraphina said, appearing like a stealth missile into the room.

Like I believed that. "Really? More like you were looking for Rupert."

Seraphina's little face was so pinched it might have been one of those apple dolls. "Yes, we wish to speak with Sir Fox, this is true, but when I saw we were being watched across the way, I knew I must protect you, too."

I got to my feet. "Without telling me, by saying it must be a paparazzi stakeout? Do you think I'm stupid?"

"No!" Seraphina and Nicolina said at once.

I crossed my arms. "Well, something's got to give. I'm not putting up with this. I was asked here to help solve a murder, not be lead around by a leash like a puppy." That's exactly how I felt.

Nicolina had crossed the room to take me by the shoulders. "Forgive me, Phoebe. I am sorry for keeping such secrets. I come from a family of secrets and promised Maria that I would not talk of her family, but now I see I was wrong. Too many things are burying us alive. They killed Maria, whoever they are—Rupert, somebody. It must end; we must find the truth! I will try harder from now on, I promise."

I pulled gently away. "Then let's start with this family history and you can tell me everything you know, but please let's eat first. I haven't had a proper dinner since we arrived. There seem to be a few good restaurants around." It was a peace offering, a chance to regain neutral ground.

Nicolina's swollen eyes widened. "This is terrible! I will rectify this as soon as possible but no restaurant."

Apparently you can tell an Italian that she's been a misguided person but never imply that she hasn't fed you properly. The country's citizens had standards. The countess rang the bell for Zara, and uttered a string of the imperious Italian sentences to the housekeeper, who shot me a hostile glance before exiting the room.

"Zara will prepare dinner for us," Nicolina said. "I have requested fish and local dishes. I have not eaten properly since we arrived, either. I have been a very poor host."

"Thank you. In the meantime, I'll head to my room and freshen up. My hair must look like I've wrestled a Gorgon and lost. We can have that long talk of ours after supper."

Escaping to my room gave me time to think and to truly fix my disheveled self, which revealed near-mythic proportions in the mirror. Medusa had nothing on me, snaky tresses aside. After something like a shower under a sad little trickle of water, I changed into my only non-jeans pants—leather—donned a silk blouse Nicolina had given me the year before, and fastened on a pair of gold hoop earrings. Really, that's about all I could manage in the elegance department but at least I felt moderately presentable.

While I showered, someone had delivered a tray of sweets, bread, and cheese along with wine and water. It was all I could do to keep from devouring the whole lot but, as it was, I ignored the wine and took the edge off my hunger with a bit of cheese and sweets. The Italians ate so late —9:00 p.m. in this case—but that gave me plenty of opportunity to study the painting further.

I also checked my phone—no word from Max but an update from Peaches arrived assuring me that she hadn't threatened any of the construction dudes yet. Then I sent a quick message to Evan to see if I could visit Rupert that night.

The response came back minutes later. *Sir Rupert is finally sleeping soundly. Perhaps I could come to the villa and speak with the contessa and Seraphina tonight instead?*

I'll run it by Nicolina, I answered back. *Somehow you have to enter without being seen by the police guard.*

I left my carpetbag on the chair, shoved my phone into my pocket, and readied myself for dinner with the countess. By the time I descended the stairs, Nicolina was sipping an aperitif in the salon dressed in a long burnt-orange Fortuny gown. She stood when I entered the room, the woman and the gown heart-stoppingly beautiful as she twirled in the candlelight, the silken Delphos folds glimmering in the light. "I wear this in your honor,

Phoebe. Maria gave it to me as a gift long ago and I brought it here to wear for her also."

"Lovely." I touched her silken sleeve reverently.

"She was wearing a stenciled velvet Fortuny coat when she died," Nicolina said, "which says to me that her appointment that night was very important to her. She rarely wore her Fortunies out as they are now too fragile."

I met her eyes. I needed to tell her sometime. "She was going to meet Rupert. She had called him in London and asked him to meet her here in Venice on some important matter. He came as soon as he could but she failed to appear at the appointed time. They were to meet near the warehouse. I believe him, Nicolina."

She turned away to face the fire. "And you did not mention this to either me or the *commissario*?"

I rubbed my neck. "Peroni only asked me about the paintings—that's my excuse. Anyway, Rupert is in hiding—from you, from who knows else— and he's sick besides. What would happen if I added the police to his many Venetian interests? I agree that he needs to step forward and speak to the police himself, which I'm sure he'll do as soon as he is able." Weak, so weak. Why did I defend him? "But, in the meantime, will you raise the white flag long enough for Evan to come and meet with us here? If we're truly going to find Maria's murderer, we need to work together for once."

"Oh, Phoebe," Nicolina said, swinging to face me. "You are so trusting!"

"And you are so trigger-happy!" I said. "Don't we need to at least gather the necessary evidence before reaching conclusions?"

"Ah, that is the lawyer in you talking. Rupert above anyone knows about the painting and that it may hold a secret. Maria's mama had revealed their importance to her during that last horrible argument and Maria went to Rupert in distress to share all before Papa Contini chased him out of town. He should be on the suspect list."

"And he could say the same about you. You are the sole beneficiary, after all."

She froze. "Me, a suspect? But I would never...and I was not in Venice when Maria died."

"You could have hired somebody—Seraphina, maybe—and you can believe that Peroni will have you checked out as a matter of course."

"Yes, you are right," she said finally, rubbing her temples with a manicured hand. "How foolish how that never occurred to me. I have been so preoccupied." She turned back toward the fireplace, her gaze fixed toward the empty place over the mantel.

"So," I said, stepping forward. "Why don't we approach this collaboratively? Let's assume that everybody is innocent until proven guilty and discuss what we know together. Let me see if I can arrange for you to talk to Evan at least, since Rupert is unwell. Maybe tonight?"

"What is wrong with Rupert?" she asked, swinging around.

"Pneumonia. He looks awful, burning up with fever and the whole nine yards. I'm convinced that he's innocent, Nicolina. Whoever murdered Maria and stole that painting is probably connected to those bastards that chased us today, not Rupert. Evan was with me when they chased us out of Torcello, remember."

"Torcello?"

"Evan thought it the safest place for us to have our meeting today."

"Ah." She smiled, nodding. "Perhaps also to give him an opportunity to see his ex and son again."

For a moment I couldn't speak. "Evan has a son?" *Giani.* That explained a lot. In fact, it explained everything except why it bothered me so much.

"You didn't know?"

"No, of course not. I don't know any personal details concerning Rupert's right-hand man. Why would I?" That came out unintentionally cross.

"Seraphina had him checked out years ago. This liaison occurred before MI6, before he even met Rupert. In any case, I agree to speak with him but it must be later tonight since Seraphina and I must go to the warehouse and retrieve some documents immediately following dinner. The police finished with the crime scene only today. Now I am allowed to enter again and there are sensitive documents I must collect immediately."

I nodded, only half listening. "I'll go with you."

"Excellent. We can use the help since I do not want to involve anyone else for the time being."

"Why?" I asked, suddenly paying attention.

"Because I do not trust anyone except maybe you." She stepped up to me and took my hands in hers. "You I see as my friend, though I know I have not behaved as a friend to you. Still, you I trust. But I must ask you to consider that perhaps Rupert did meet Maria as planned and killed her to obtain the keys to the vault."

"The keys?" I asked.

She squeezed my hands. "Just think, Phoebe: if she was meeting Rupert to take him to the vault, Maria would have had the keys with her. She always took them everywhere. She showed them to me once—on an ornate key chain from Murano. The studio's outside door wasn't broken into but the security code was penetrated and only the door to the safe was blown. Someone used the keys to enter the building and they are now missing, taken by Rupert that very night, perhaps."

"No," I said, pulling my hands from hers. "I absolutely don't believe that Rupert had anything to do with this. Promise not to try to assassinate either him or Evan. We need the chance to clear his name, to clear both your names, and find the truth."

"You trust him in everything?" the countess asked me while studying my face intently.

"Of course not! It's pure foolishness to trust Rupert carte blanche but I don't believe him capable of this particular crime. Besides, we still have this gang chasing us. They're the main suspects now."

Nicolina gave a rueful smile. "I would not have killed him, anyway, not like that, and Evan is a formidable opponent, in any case. No, I was just very angry and—what do you say?—venting. I was venting."

I lowered my voice. "What about Zara?"

"Thoroughly investigated by both Seraphina and the police. Her alibi is clear and she has worked for this family forever. She was with her family that night and Seraphina says she is heartbroken by Maria's death."

"That doesn't mean she couldn't have hired somebody."

"But why?" she asked. "And why now?"

"Maybe somebody got to her."

A bell rang down the hall and Nicolina sighed. "We will leave this for now. Let us regain our friendship over dinner."

I wasn't certain how much of our friendship existed but I really did want to trust her eventually. For the time being, I followed her into a spacious formal dining room where a sea-blue damask tablecloth had been spread over the long table set with silver and sparkling crystal. Silk velvet jacquard the hue of deep burnished bronze hung on the windows.

Seraphina did not dine with us, and other than to deliver dishes, Zara stayed out of sight, too.

"They eat together in the kitchen," my hostess remarked. "It is a long-standing custom in Italy that the servants do not eat with the owners of the house, even in this day and age. Of course, Seraphina and I don't follow such rules at home but here, and since we wish to talk, I thought it best. Also, Zara and Seraphina have been friends for many years and prefer to be by themselves also."

"I understand. Besides, I don't think Zara likes me, either," I whispered to her over the basket of rolls. I said it as a joke but it was true.

"I don't think she likes anybody after Maria's passing, except Seraphina, perhaps. Certainly she resents me becoming the new mistress here. She is very angry, it seems. I have shared with her the sum Maria wished to leave her in her will but it brought no consolation. That blouse looks lovely on you—Gucci, correct, the summer 2017 collection?"

"I think so, and thank you for the gift. I keep these pieces for special occasions, which aren't all that frequent." Nicolina loved to shower me with designer clothing, which I both appreciated and treasured but left me feeling as though I was receiving a subtle nudge to dress more appropriately for the world we intersected together—hang out with an Italian countess, dress like a countess, or at least like an Italian. I took a sip of water from a crystal goblet and smiled. "Tell me what you know about the family history, please."

She gazed at me from across the table, a diamond earring catching the light. "I do not know as much as you think, and what I do know I didn't believe important at first. The Continis were wealthy textile merchants in the fifteenth century, exporting silks and woven cloths all over Europe and beyond. It was in the family stories that they had joined with a Jewish family sometime in that same century and that the painting recorded that event. That's all I know."

"Maria didn't mention a cipher?"

"She told me that she believed there may be a secret hidden in the painting but had no idea what."

"Where did the Jewish family come from?"

"It is not known—possibly from someplace East. The Jews were being persecuted all over the world and were constantly on the move so they could have come from anywhere."

"But this family must have amassed great wealth to have a sanctioned union with a wealthy Venetian family despite religious barriers. The bride must have been expected to renounce her faith, or to hide it, at the very least. How common was it for Jews to renounce their faith in order to marry, anyway?"

"No more common than it was for a Catholic to marry a Jew with the blessings of the family, I would think. In Italy, if one marries a Catholic, it is the other religion that must convert. For me even twenty years ago, to be born Catholic in this country was to ban me from marrying a Protestant unless he converted, so imagine a union between a Catholic and a Jew five centuries earlier? But this much I can say: Signore Contini was very anti-Semitic. He became so enraged when Maria wanted to study the Kabbalah that I thought she would leave the house."

"Maria wanted to study the Kabbalah?"

"It interested her greatly. In fact, she had been studying it for several years in secret. She was proud to have Jewish blood in her ancestry."

I sat back. The pieces were falling together but still with enough spaces between them to keep the picture far from my reach. For a while, I focused on eating, especially when the fish arrived to stare me in the face. I covered the head with a bit of risotto while carefully removing the bones. "What about this cousin," I asked at last. "Does she know anything?"

"She is Maria's father's younger deceased brother's daughter and she has never shown the least bit of interest in this family or its history. Maria had only met her once, to the best of my knowledge. She lives in Milan."

"And if she changes her mind and contests the will?"

"She assured me she would not. I explained about Maria's desire for the museum and that I will sell this crumbling villa in order to finance the renovation. She can have all the art inside these walls but for the textiles and the missing painting, should it be located. What need have I for a villa in Venice, anyway? Now that Maria is gone, I will have no desire to visit much except to oversee the museum. As for the other properties—there are two, I believe—a farm in Tuscany and a vacation property somewhere. Those I will sell to finance the warehouse restoration, as well."

Nodding my approval, I dove into the rest of my dinner while trying not to speak with my mouth full. Zara had created a feast of risotto with red wine, fried sardines, pasta, and polenta with not a speck of anything green in sight. It was delicious but I couldn't do it justice.

Nicolina poured a little wine into her glass while I waved away the offer. "As soon as the body—" she hesitated, fortified herself with a sip, and continued "—as soon as we can, the funeral will take place. I have been assured that this can happen within the next few days. I have provided you with something to wear."

I shook my head. "Whenever the funeral is, I'll use that time to explore and research since everyone's attention will be elsewhere."

"I had hoped you would keep me company."

"You won't need my company, Nicolina. You have Seraphina, and I would be very out of place at the funeral of someone I didn't know, despite my feelings of affinity with Maria." Besides which, I couldn't get images of *Don't Look Now* out of my head—the funereal black gondola sailing down the canal. "But thank you for the outfit. I'll return it."

She waved away the thought. "You must keep them."

"Well, thank you again and for ordering this magnificent feast." What I would do with that dramatic black outfit, I had no idea.

Nicolina appeared relieved that I'd accepted her peace offering as she toasted me over the table. "To friendship! *Salute!*" My water goblet and her wineglass clinked over the candles.

Through dessert of gelato and coffee, we spoke of more neutral subjects until the table was cleared.

"So," I began, "are we going to just stroll down the street to enter the warehouse tonight?"

That brought a smile. "No, certainly not. It is best that our activities remain private. I have another way." She rang the little bell on the table and in strode Zara, to whom Nicolina said something directive that caused the housekeeper to scamper away. Seconds later, in came Seraphina.

"Seraphina, tonight we go to the warehouse to collect those files we spoke about and Phoebe will accompany us. Following that, Sir Rupert's man, Evan, will visit us here at the villa to discuss possible suspects." Nicolina waved one hand by way of aborting protests. "We are attempting collaboration."

"Collaboration." Seraphina appeared to ponder the word. "Very well. In that case, I suggest that we take the secret passage to the warehouse so as not to draw attention and that Sir Rupert's man enter the villa through the canal door."

"Good idea." Nicolina nodded.

"Secret passage?" I asked.

"At one time, the Continis owned all the buildings in this block," Nicolina explained, turning to me. "A private passageway—probably no longer in good condition—runs at the back of the buildings at the canal level. Centuries ago it was built to assure the Continis didn't muddy their shoes when traveling back and forth to their place of business. Maria took me through it a couple of times when we were younger, all in fun. Girlish games, you know," she added with a sigh.

"Good. I'll just text Evan and tell him to meet us at the back canal entrance, shall I? What time do you think?"

Nicolina and Seraphina exchanged glances. "Perhaps 10:30?" Nicolina suggested.

"Ten-thirty, it is. I'll just go upstairs and change." Which I proceeded to do, texting Evan along the way: *Success. Come to the villa at 10:30 by boat via the back canal door.*

After I had received *Confirmed* in response, I climbed the stairs, pondering the idea of Evan with a son and an ex, the lovely Sophia. It bothered me at some level but I didn't want to prod too deeply as to why. Maybe because I'd always thought of the mysterious Evan as monkish— probably even preferred to think of him as the attractive unobtainable man, perfectly safe for flirting purposes. After all, didn't he live in a kind of cell of Rupert's choosing waiting on his every need? Now I had to broaden my image of him as a man with the same needs as any other. Well, of course I knew he had *that* need. Our playful flirting had told me that much. Luckily I didn't have time to think too long on the subject.

Since my hands would be full carrying files back and forth through this mysterious tunnel, it made sense to leave my carpetbag behind. To that end I changed into jeans, sneakers, and sweater and shoved my cell phone into my pocket. After donning my new jacket, complete with gun, I was ready for the evening.

When I met Nicolina and Seraphina downstairs minutes later, both had changed into leather jackets and pants complete with sleek little high-heeled booties that left me totally baffled. High heels for stealth missions through mysterious tunnels? Badassed chic totally escaped me. My sneakers, on the other hand, made me feel like a Clydesdale draft horse set off to plod with a pair cantering thoroughbreds. We each carried a plastic carrier bag to add to the effect.

Still, I was thankful for those treads when we stomped down to the cantina moments later, wove through the damp shrouded shapes, and watched as Seraphina pried open a low decrepit-looking door at the end of the cavernous room. The hinges shrieked in protest but eventually cooperated enough to reveal a dark, foul-smelling corridor. All three of us stepped back.

"It is in much worse condition than I thought," Nicolina remarked, holding a tissue to her nose. "Many floods over the decades."

"Mold," Seraphina said ominously. "We will need protection and perhaps to cover our noses. There are coats over there by the door. I will put something together against the mold."

Nicolina and I waited while Seraphina rummaged against the far wall by the boat door.

"Smells moldy, all right." Seemed like a bad time to mention my mold allergy so I just coughed for effect.

"Mold and spiders and all manner of unpleasant things," Nicolina agreed as she lifted a tarp covering a long shape beside us and poked her flashlight underneath. "The family's ceremonial gondola. I wonder whether it will ever sail again? I suppose I must auction it off."

Before I could comment, Seraphina had returned carrying three full carnival masks plus three yellow well-used hooded raincoats. "With the hood and the masks over our faces, this is the best possible protection for in there." Seraphina indicated the corridor with a jerk of the head. "I will go first."

She donned the slicker, pulled up the hood, and slipped a glittery, feather-plumed mask over her face. For a moment she reminded me of some jaunty bank robber with a thing for bling. Nicolina, on the other hand, being a taller and more striking figure all around, appeared utterly bizarre in an old ill-fitting raincoat and a grimace mask straight out of Greek tragedy. As for me, I was just grateful not to be wearing a plague doctor beak for once and thought my silver and golden sequin-encrusted sun/moon mask rather spectacular. Whether it offered much protection for penetrating slick, mold-slimed corridors was left to be seen.

Thus decked out like actors from some Carnevale Meets Freddy Krueger B-movie, we entered the yawning corridor. We had to hunch as our backs scraped against the fungi-encrusted ceiling while trying not to breathe in the stench of mold and whatever dead things putrefied the air. Rats, I thought. Seraphina was ahead, me behind her, and Nicolina bringing up the rear, each of us grasping flashlights along with our bags, and yet it was impossible to see much of anything. It was dark, and we were in full face masks trying not to breathe in too deeply but gasping for breath all the same time. Touching the walls even with the gloves I had the foresight to bring was to be avoided but it was impossible since balancing myself on uneven surfaces was part of the territory.

Our scout wasn't wasting time and seemed intent to traverse this disgusting corridor as quickly as possible. That wasn't the problem so much as my inability to keep up while slipping on the greasy cobbles. The ever sure-footed Nicolina behind me asked: "Phoebe, are you all right?"

"Fine," I croaked, and scrambled on.

Once, a few inches of wall to our right opened to briefly reveal the canal and briny air. The disintegrating brick must have toppled into the canal months or even years before, indicating the fragility of this passage-way. Yet, that single lungful of semifresh air kept me going awhile longer.

The corridor was not only dark and slippery but refused to follow a straight line. It formed a torturous route through a closed-in passageway snaking behind the buildings, including steps in some places. By the time we reached a steep set of stairs rising straight up, Nicolina shone her flash-light over Seraphina's head and claimed: "We are almost there."

Seraphina bounded up the steps and called: "Stay back. I will fight the door." The sound of wood wrestling against stone penetrated the gloom. Splintering noises followed and soon Seraphina called: "It is free."

We climbed up and up, my breath struggling inside the condensation-slicked mask, which I couldn't wait to tear off my face, while my hands braced against the slick walls. In moments we had burst into another dark room, this one as dry and dusty as an abandoned cathedral.

I removed my mask, shrugged off the raincoat, and found myself standing in a huge space, one so expansive I couldn't see the opposite wall from where I stood. More tarps shrouded tall mounds everywhere our flashlights landed.

"This is the main studio, second floor. The first floor is storage, the top the offices. Look, Phoebe." Nicolina flung away a tent-like covering over one of the mounds to reveal an old loom possibly six feet long and still threaded with warps as if the weaver had aborted a project before it began.

"See how many kinds there are?" Nicolina said while removing the covers from several different varieties. "There are looms for silk, looms for velvet, looms for special robes for maybe a queen, yes? This one made golden thread into brocades, Maria said." She stood lost in thought before an old upright loom that still wore the remnants of fraying cloth caught between the silken warp.

"How old?" I asked.

"These are mostly reproductions of much older looms but some have been repaired and still contain the original parts maybe five centuries old. This one, for instance," she said, indicating a long frame loom with a wooden wheel attached to one side. "I think Maria said this was the oldest. The studio wove its last textile in the late 1800s, a bishop's mantle, I believe."

"Nicolina, this place is a treasure," I gasped. "I mean, really!"

"And yet so many see no value in historic textiles."

"Fools!" I said with vehemence. "Textiles clothe us, reveal who we are or who we want to be, and are quite possibly the result of some of the first of humanity's technologies." Okay, so soapbox time but that's how passionately textiles speak to me.

"Yes," she said sadly, "I knew you would understand and now it is my task to preserve it all somehow. Come, let us go upstairs to the vault."

We carried on up another flight of stairs to the third floor, Seraphina leading the way. She switched on the light, presumably because this being an interior room, cracks in the shutters had less chance of giving us away.

She then proceeded to check every corner as if expecting a thief to be still lurking there.

I focused on the vault, a large walk-in structure with a blackened gaping door dominating the space. Nicolina shook her head and muttered in Italian over the debris, the damage to the floor, the papers strewn everywhere, the fingerprint powder dusting every surface.

"Plastic explosives," Seraphina remarked, poking her head in moments later. "It could have been worse."

"But what if the blast damaged the paintings? It is still an explosion," Nicolina fumed.

Seraphina pointed to the interior of the vault where no signs of damage could be seen other than a bulging impression on the inside of the door and the apparent rifling of the papers and files inside. "The blast damaged only the locking mechanism."

Nicolina strode forward. "But they did not take the jewelry box, did not take the cash in the strongbox, just the painting and what else?"

"Maybe they were interrupted," I suggested from the doorway. "The painting was presumably easy to spot but maybe other items not so much. They wouldn't have had much time. Didn't you say that this studio may have once woven the same textile as in the bride's gown?"

"So Maria believed."

"Where might sample fabrics be, do you think?"

"In the library," she remarked, staring at a wad of papers scattered on the floor. "They were looking for something," she remarked. "Peroni thought so, too. We must find the deeds to the properties and any earlier copies of the wills plus a list of possible holdings."

"I'll visit the library in the meantime."

"Yes, do. For now, Seraphina and I must sort through what is left and compare it with the will, a copy if which I have. I doubt that everything in the vault was recorded but I'm thinking jewelry, the properties..."

"What were these properties exactly?" I asked.

Nicolina bent to pick up a leather-bound portfolio. "The Continis owned an olive orchard in Tuscany, I think, and a vacation property somewhere."

"Morocco," Seraphina said, stepping into the vault. "Zara mentioned that the family used to go to Marrakech years ago for sun during the gloomy months. It was where she first met the family decades ago."

"Oh, yes," Nicolina mused as she passed the leather portfolio to her assistant. "I had forgotten that—the riad. Maria never went by herself after her parents died. She said the intense sun did not suit her."

"I believe it's been leased out as an Airbnb now," Seraphina commented as she began collecting the documents and folders. "Maybe we will go sometime."

"More likely I will sell it." Nicolina turned to me. "Phoebe, the library, which you will find interesting, is in the room down the hall if you wish to take a look. Once we collect all these documents, we will come to retrieve you."

I checked my watch: 10:10. Still plenty of time. I turned the corner and strode down the hall to the next room. I just stood in the doorway for a moment flashing my light around. It was a small library with a single wall of tall fat books housed behind glass in what looked to be a humidity-controlled environment.

I stepped forward. A tiny round sensor measured the percentage of moisture inside the shelves and a table stood nearby. I ran my phone light over the dusty table with its study lamp before moving on to the shelves, staring at the books that were unusually thick, like scrapbooks or journals.

The writing on the spines was Italian, of course, but the thickest and the oldest-looking of the leather-bound volumes sat way back at the far end of the shelf with Roman numerals imprinted in gold onto their spines. The first volume caught my attention immediately: *MDXV-MDC.* 1515 to 1600?

My hands were trembling so much when I slid open the glass and lifted the oldest volume onto the table that I thought I'd drop it. Of course I shouldn't be handling such a treasure without gloves in the first place, but since my gloves were so disgusting, I didn't have a choice.

I flashed a quick glance up to the windows. Too long arched windows shuttered against the light and, if my orientation was correct, they looked out over the back canal and not the Cannaregio. That settled it: I risked turning on the lamp. With excruciating care, I opened the cover, letting it fall open on a compendium of line drawings of motifs and patterns. My mouth went dry. I couldn't believe what I was seeing. Could it be that every pattern produced by the house since the establishment began was recorded in these books? Why hadn't anyone mentioned it—had it been forgotten, overlooked, or what?

Nicolina appeared at the door. "Phoebe, we have collected all that is valuable. We must get back if we are to meet with Evan. Are you ready?"

"Nicolina, these are important. If they are what I think they are, they could be a repository for every fabric pattern the Contini house ever produced. It's amazing that such a thing even survived these centuries. Imagine a recording of every bolt of fabric, including who they went to—whether to market, to specific customers—since the studio first began?"

Of course a weaving house like this would record such things. They were like recipes, and other volumes might contain records of dyes and maybe weaving "cartoons," which the weavers used to set their looms. Thousands of patterns are recorded in the safekeeping by the Victoria and Albert Museum alone, but this house has remained in the same Italian family for centuries. One single family. It's incredible.

"Yes, Maria wanted them preserved. This I will do when all is settled."

"But they are at least as valuable as the jewelry and deeds."

"To some, perhaps."

"Maybe we could take a couple of these volumes with us?"

Nicolina shook her head. "They are too heavy and awkward, Phoebe, and they could be damaged in the tunnel, yes? All our bags are full. Tomorrow we will return to retrieve them, but for now, I must study what is needed for the will."

I couldn't refute her logic: dragging those precious volumes through the corridor without protection hardly made sense. "Right. Tomorrow, then." Reluctantly, I returned the one volume to the shelf, closed the glass door, and prepared to make the journey back. With my hood up and the mask secured, I gathered up the bundles, now stuffed into the carrier bags —one per hand—and followed Seraphina down the stairs.

But I could not get those books out of my head.

They stayed on my mind all the way back through the corridor, which was just as unpleasant as expected—worse actually, since my hands were full and I almost dropped my load onto the slimy surface more than once. Luckily, Nicolina was bringing up the rear and her impressive reflexes always seemed to catch me before I fell headfirst into the slime.

Ten minutes later, we broke into the dimly lit cantina and not a second too soon from my perspective. I dropped the bags and ripped off the mask before leaning against the tarp-covered gondola, gasping for breath. Meanwhile, my companions made their way through the shrouded forms toward the stairs, masks still in place.

Suddenly I heard a crash and a man shout something in Italian followed by, "Or I'll shoot!"

🦋 12 🦋

Seraphina was pointing her gun and shouting when I dashed from the shadows, my hands in the air: "Evan, it's me, Phoebe! That's Seraphina and Nicolina. Put down the damn gun!"

The man crouching behind a mound of boxes stood up and lowered his pistol. "Ms. Phoebe? Are you unharmed?"

Nicolina yanked off her sequined mask and flipped back her hood and spoke in her most imperious tone. "What are you doing here? You were asked to come to the back canal door, not break it down!"

I turned. The door to the canal hung open on its hinges, part of it shattered as if hit with a battering ram. And the boat was gone.

"This is how I found it minutes ago," Evan explained, his tone measured. "I called out but there was no answer. Naturally, I was afraid you'd been robbed or worse, and was about to head upstairs when you appeared."

"You are lucky I didn't shoot you," Seraphina muttered, glancing at the ruined door. "Someone has broken into the house."

"More likely I would have shot you," he remarked. "I've given this level a cursory check. They must have escaped with your boat."

"Upstairs immediately!" Nicolina ordered, heading for the steps with her own pistol drawn.

"No, wait, Countess! I will go first," Seraphina cried, dashing after her, but her employer's sleek booties were already up to the kitchen. Evan and I bounded after them, me pulling out my pistol along the way.

Once on the main level, everyone fanned out as if by some unspoken stealth investigation code. I took the main salon and dining area, keeping to the corners and swinging my gun around 360 degrees when entering a new room the way I'd seen television cops do. I'd have felt ridiculous if not for the overwhelming sense of threat. Either intruders were currently in the house or had been recently.

Seraphina could be heard calling to Zara. There was pounding on a door, an answering cry followed by a tense exchange in Italian before everything went silent. I continued with my downstairs investigation, poking into cabinets, peering into closets. Every room was empty but I couldn't tell if anything was missing, once I discounted the obvious, that is.

Minutes later, I met Evan in the hall. "All clear," he told me, "at least in terms of active intruders."

"Same here but what about the police outside?"

Before he could reply, my phone pinged in my pocket. I pulled it out and read a text from Nicolina: *Nothing missing up here. Do not speak of anything important aloud. Come upstairs.*

I turned the phone for Evan to read. He nodded and we proceeded upstairs in silence. Nicolina was waiting at the second-floor landing, one finger to her lips. Behind her down the hall, Zara sat in a chair with one hand over her mouth while Seraphina stood on a chair nearby taking apart a lamp sconce. Nicolina opened her palm to show us a tiny surveillance device that had obviously just been retrieved.

"Common as ants," I muttered until Nicolina shushed me.

Evan picked the thing up between his thumb and index finger, bringing it under a table lamp to study. Though I was no expert in these things, it certainly didn't look like the ones I'd smashed this morning. When he straightened moments later, he shook his head, expression tense. *Don't recognize it*, he mouthed, and pulled out his phone to help Seraphina scan the premises for more.

Nicolina and I stood together watching as her assistant glowered at him when, seconds later, his phone flashed red while passing it over a picture frame she had just investigated. "He is very good," Nicolina said barely audibly. She touched my arm and our eyes met.

"What about the police officer outside?" I whispered.

She whispered back. "Leave him. Come, we must talk." And with that she beckoned me to follow her up the stairs to the roof.

Only when we were standing under the pergola, buffeted by a cool damp breeze, did she speak. "Do not trust anybody."

"But—"

"Phoebe, listen: there has been a spy in this house, someone who has placed those devices. It could be the police when they were here today. There were at least six special agents all over the house. Dirty police happen in Italy, too, yes? Commissario Peroni may not know about it or perhaps he is on—what do you say? *On the take*. Until we know, we cannot take chances."

"But why break down the canal door and steal the boat?"

"I do not know. They were seeking something, maybe they found it. Upstairs in Maria's room, the mannequins are fallen over, the library books tumbled on the floor—all very messy, as if they were in a hurry. They knew when we left the house this evening."

"But nothing is missing?"

"Nothing I can see but I do not know every single item. When Zara recovers, we will have her go through the house to check everything. She is very upset."

"And what about Zara?"

"She can hear nothing without her aid and goes to bed early. They must have known that, too."

"And they probably bugged the salon where I shared my theories with Peroni. They must know everything I suspect by now. They've stolen my ideas!" Such a travesty. My ideas, at least, were mine, *mine*!

I cast a glance across the canal to where I had first seen the watcher in what seemed like years ago. "So they stole the painting thinking that it would lead them to something even more valuable only to discover that they needed additional information, information they may have gotten from me." A sudden chill hit my spine. "But they still need more. Nicolina, I've got to get back to my room."

"We will scan there, too."

"Now," I said, and with that I practically ran downstairs. When I reached my door, I froze. Evan stood in the center of the room with two shattered devices in his hand. His eyes said it all.

"Where?"

He pointed to the bedpost and side table.

"Seriously? But I'm sure I passed your detection device over both of those."

He frowned. "Unless you hold the phone no farther away than three inches from the surface, the sensor may miss the device. This one was tucked inside the lady's mouth." He indicated the carved nymph on the bed who appeared to be blowing kisses.

"That's no lady, that's a nymph," I remarked.

He studied the carving more closely and smiled. "Correct. In any case, I will need to work on improving the device's distance capabilities. The other one I found under the table placed in the back corner."

"And my bag?"

"Other than Seraphina's tracker that I located yesterday, it appears clear."

I relaxed. "Thank God. That thing comes with me everywhere."

"Nevertheless, my device requires more work apparently. I've tested on five kinds of trackers to date but there are more, like these, for example—cheap enough to purchase by the handful."

"Online?"

"Chinese mail-order, yes."

It was disconcerting to think that surveillance devices could be purchased as easily as printer cartridges. "But when would they have found the time to secrete them all over the house?" Despite the reputation of corruption, I didn't believe the police had hidden these. I doubted they used Chinese technology, for one thing.

"That's the question."

"Is the room clear now?"

"I certainly hope so."

I launched myself into a pacing trip around the bedroom, fuming with frustration and angst all the way. Nicolina stepped into the room and indicated for us to follow her back up to the roof. Minutes later, the three of us crowded to the back of the pergola.

"Seraphina has returned to the basement to secure the canal door and then will return to the house to continue the sweep. I will go through the house with Zara to see what may be missing before returning to the task of studying the will against the contents of the vault. The clues may lay there. You may assist me," she said magnanimously, waving a hand to include both Evan and myself.

"Whatever you need," Evan said. "I am here to prove the sincerity of Sir Rupert's efforts to work with you."

"And I no longer hold Rupert responsible for these thefts and Maria's death. Too many things do not add up."

But I was barely paying attention. Something like a collision of seemingly random thoughts was hitting me just then. "If they placed these devices here, they may have done the same thing in the warehouse," I mumbled.

Nicolina shot me a quick look. "But why?"

"They are looking for something and hoping we'll lead them to it." I said nothing more, my mind too busy running over the fact that what could be the most critical clue may yet remain safe. For now. "I have to go back to the warehouse tonight."

I heard Nicolina's breath catch. "Why?"

"I don't want to say. Everything I've said to date has been recorded apparently. How do we know that we're not being eavesdropped on still? I'll go, collect what we need, and come right back. How long would it take —maybe twenty minutes at the most? I know the way. I'll be right back."

"I'll come with you," Evan said.

"You won't fit. It was challenging enough for the three if us to squeeze through that corridor," I said.

"This is true," Nicolina said. "A big man would find it very difficult."

"I will manage. I said," Evan enunciated between his teeth, "I will come with you. It's too dangerous for you go there alone." He was towering over me, using the intimidation of his six foot two of height to hammer home his point.

That was new. I stepped back. "Don't do that, Evan, don't use that male thing on me." I was looking him straight in the eye—not that that was easy in the shadowy light, and being over a foot shorter didn't help. Actually, it was bloody awkward. "If you want to protect me, stay near the tunnel entrance and watch my back. Seraphina kicked that tunnel door open earlier tonight, leaving it compromised, and the canal door gaping, too. I'd feel much safer knowing those two entrances were protected."

He said nothing but I could feel him working it out from all angles.

"That is a very good idea," Nicolina said. "It will be some time before Seraphina can fix the door."

For an instant, it was just Evan and me locked in a moment of tense struggle—powerful, a little sexy—but I was determined to emerge as the woman on top. That was my thing. I tipped the scales by adding what I hoped as just a touch of wry humor: "And I'm Ms. Phoebe to you and don't you forget it."

13

The last thing I wanted was to return to that tunnel under any circumstance but I was so focused on retrieving what I needed, I would have tried walking over hot coals. Evan agreed to play guard dog only on the condition that I remained in contact with him every step of the way.

"If I detect any issues, anything at all, I'll be through there in a shot," he whispered as he fastened the flashlight he'd jiggered together onto my hood, "Ms. Phoebe."

"Right," I said, shrugging the strap of my plastic-wrapped carpetbag into a better position over my shoulder. "And you'd probably get wedged in somewhere along the way. It's a tight squeeze, I said. I'll be fine." I turned to study the opening, which, now that I had a high-powered lamp to penetrate its gloom, looked a lot like a gaping wound.

The phone in my hand vibrated. I swung back to him. He was standing in there thumbing me a text: *What are you after? Tell me.*

He looked up and mouthed, *Ms. Phoebe.*

I put a finger to my lips and mouthed my reply: *Be back soon.* Next, I pocketed the phone and headed for the tunnel, pulling up my mask along the way. Evan had found a rubberized clown mask, which he'd lined with tissue and widened the nose and eyeholes. Though it was no less uncomfortable, I could certainly see and breathe better.

Taking a deep breath, I bent over and dove into the corridor. Having done this twice, I was better prepared. I knew where the most troublesome parts were, where I almost tripped twice, where the mold and rat droppings had slimed the floor to the point of making a gooey mess. By keeping one gloved hand on either side of my body, I could steady myself while proceeding in a bent-over run.

Surprisingly, not having Seraphina ahead of me made it easier. For one thing, I could see better and, if not exactly feeling more confident, at least I knew the path ahead. Sort of. Whatever the case, I managed to scramble to the warehouse steps without a single tumble.

Inside the building minutes later, I removed my mask and raincoat, hanging both on the corner of a loom that jutted out from under a tarp. My text to Evan was brief: *I'm in the warehouse.*

All clear back here, he responded.

I admit that knowing he was watching my back was fortifying. Forget that it was unlikely he could get to me quickly, anyway. Right then, I was focused on being inside a weaving studio alone. It was like standing inside a cathedral, hushed and hallowed with all that I revered. But I had to get to work.

So I hoisted my carpetbag farther up my shoulder, pulled a flashlight from its depths, and strode across the weaving floor to the next set of stairs. My single light didn't provide enough illumination so I used my phone light, too—anything to dispel those shadows crowding in around me. The feel of that empty, abandoned place was something I was determined not to dwell on. I'd return in daylight and take a proper look at those looms, as Nicolina promised.

I traipsed back up the squeaky staircase to the office floor, past the vault room, and around the corner into the library. I couldn't wait to switch on the desk lamp. Crazy, I know, but feeling those shadows crowding in behind me spooked me to no end. "Just an empty building," I whispered, relieved when the little lamp sent a pool of soft light around the small room. Placing my carpetbag on the table, I shot Evan a quick text: *In the library. Not long now.*

Removing the earliest two volumes from the shelves, I wanted desperately to take both but I couldn't carry two. Each volume was nearly two feet by two feet—even taking one wasn't going to be easy—but what if I missed something? I'd take the earliest volume for sure, I decided, since it would more likely hold the clues I wanted, but I'd photograph the second.

With that in mind, I hastily began taking photos of the foxed yellowed pages with my phone, careful not to damage the brittle parchment. This time I wore proper plastic gloves that Evan had conjured—too big but workable—and yet my heart pained at the possibility of tearing a single page.

Totally absorbed in my work, brittle page after brittle page passed by while I took photos and attempted to read the cramped script—a mix of Italian and Latin: forget that—pausing to gape at this magnificent compendium of Renaissance textile design.

The phone pinged a text in my hand: *Taking too long. Are you all right?*

I texted back: *Lost all sense of time. Coming now.*

Damn. Reluctantly, I replaced the second book on the shelf—there was always tomorrow—before carefully wrapping the first in plastic and tucking it under my arm. Any archivist would have a conniption seeing me handle these priceless works that way but hopefully, someday soon, care would be taken with the entire collection. They badly needed a conservation doctor. Switching off the light, I stepped into the hall.

How is it we know something is wrong before our senses provide the evidence? I stood still as death listening to the empty building. The creaks and skittery noises I recognized as settling wood and rodents but something was off. Only when I crept to the top of the stairs did I hear the whispering clearly. I froze. There was no way in hell anybody should be in this building. Evan, maybe? No way. He'd call out or text. I pulled out my gun and released the safety.

When I took my first step down the stairs, I caught a whiff of something noxious like lighter fluid. At the same time a plume of smoke began billowing around the base of the stairs illuminated by my light like a roiling snake. A stab of fear shot through me. The only way out was down. I risked taking several more steps until I was nearly at the bottom, feeling heat on my skin and fear in my gut.

"Who's—" My cry died in my throat. A rolling billow of flame was moving toward me from the end of the room, licking at old wood, devouring scraps of fabric, consuming the entire tinderbox of a studio. I could not see signs of a single human being, just an aggressive expanding fire. Turning, I dashed up the stairs, feeling heat on my back and legs as if the flames were chasing me up. One glimpse behind me filled me with terror.

I panicked. Where could I go, how could I escape? With fumbling fingers, I called Evan, yelling, "Help! Fire!" before dropping the phone back into my bag. Shit! Maybe I could go inside the vault and shut the door? Iron and steel withstood fire, didn't they? How stupid that was, I realized. I'd suffocate or roast long before ever getting rescued. Maybe I heard an alarm, maybe I didn't. I didn't care, I had to escape.

Running back into the library with the flashlight in hand, I slammed the door shut and shoved the table under the windows, dropped my bag and book on top, and climbed up to flick the shutter catch. The shutters released immediately but the casement's mullioned glass frame had a lever so rusted that I doubted it had been opened for decades. Nothing I did made it budge even when I banged it with the butt of my gun. Next, I tried grabbing a knitting needle to lever the thing open. No luck. In pure desperation, I released the safety, aimed the gun, and fired at the catch. It blew apart instantly, allowing the casements to fly open with a shatter of broken glass.

The blast of cool night air that followed was like the kiss of life. By then, fire was lapping at the wood behind me and thick smoke was snaking tentacles under the door. But air also feeds fire. I fumbled with my phone and called Evan again. "At the rear canal window!" I cried before shoving the thing deep into my bag again. No more time for calls.

Flames crawled up the wall and licked at the sill. I balanced on the window ledge with hands grasping the frame until I felt a searing burn on my left hand. Snatching it away, I grasped the edge of broken glass, ignoring the sharp bite into my palm, intent only on what lay below. A straight drop into the canal three stories down. It was nothing. Hadn't I dived from promontories higher than this, and what was the cool depths of a fusty canal next to the churning sea? That didn't bother me. What bothered me was losing my carpetbag and relinquishing my hold on that treasured volume of Renaissance design. It was crazy but since my imminent death by roasting was delayed, all I could think about was what to save.

But what could be rescued by tossing those disintegrating pages into the canal? The inks would run, the paper would pulp, everything of value would be ruined by water as readily as by fire. And now it was too late to save them all, anyway.

Soon the whole room would go up in flames and all the volumes with it. What could I do? And yet I wavered, reluctant to let go. Then I saw the boat zipping toward me down the narrow back canal.

"Jump!" Evan called out. A surge of relief hit me so strongly I could have kissed the man had he been close enough. As it was, he pulled his speedboat under the windows and called for me to jump again. I knew he didn't mean to jump into the boat itself. From this height, I could break a leg or damage the boat or both. He meant for me to jump into the canal.

I pulled inside to grab my carpetbag and the single precious volume, the smoke so thick by now I could barely see. I heard rather than saw the flames devour the other volumes as the glass shattered across the room. Fumbling for the objects while holding my breath, I returned to the window.

"Items coming down. Catch!" I cried. I tossed the priceless volume out the window, which he caught with ease. Such a good catch. Next, I tossed out my carpetbag, which he also caught, and then my jacket and my sneakers one after the other.

"For God's sake, Phoebe, will you just jump!"

Another boat could be heard echoing against the ancient walls. Sirens pealed in the night. With flames making a grab for my legs and the room succumbed by smoke, I held my breath and jumped.

14

The canal was that brutally cold after the heat of the fire that I thought my blood would ice in my veins—punishing cold, colder than time. For a moment I had the uncanny sense that I had plunged straight into Venice's frigid heart and that I'd freeze there until the breath left my body. But the water wasn't that deep because my feet briefly touched bottom.

Still, seconds feel like years in terror-time as I kicked my way up. Breaking the surface, all I saw was black churning water with the roar of boat engines and sirens over all. Waves of water engulfed my mouth and eyes as I gasped for air while spinning around and around trying to orientate myself. There were two boats, I realized, and shouting, lots of shouting, and then a gunshot. Suddenly hands grabbed me from behind and lifted me backward into a boat where I kicked away like some furious tuna. "Damn you!" I cried as I struggled to wipe the water from my eyes.

"It's me! Lie still," Evan called. So I lay still for seconds, coughing up water while the boat pealed down the canal. A bullet pinged somewhere to the right.

"Stay down! The bastards are shooting!"

Like I couldn't tell that. Flipping onto my stomach, I struggled to my knees. "Give me your gun!" I called. I could see it sticking out of his jacket holster as he stood manning the steering wheel, his back exposed to bullets.

"No!" he called back. "I'll outrun them!"

Hell, why didn't men ever listen to me? I assessed the situation in a flash: our boat racing away with the pursuers gaining on us in what appeared to be their own superboat. Evan had whipped us into a main canal while performing various diversionary maneuvers by making one sharp turn after another. But that wouldn't be enough. We had a zero head start and they'd soon be right on top of us.

I was thrown against the side a couple of times before I could reach into my jacket to remove my own gun, safety catch still unreleased, and turn to face our pursuers. They were gaining fast.

Nicolina had provided me with a gun that was more than adequate for what I intended but that hardly mattered when my hands where shaking so badly that I couldn't grip the handle and my left palm hurt like hell. I must have burned it or cut it or something but damn if that would stop me.

"Don't try it! You could get shot!" Evan cried.

Oh, please. A treasure of art and design was burning and I might get shot? I was so furious just then I could take on a boatload of thugs and more. I held the gun with both hands, propped it on the back of the stern seat, and fired at the prow of the approaching boat. And missed. I turned to Evan and called. "Slow down, will you? I need a second to hit the hull full-on."

Understanding crossed his face. He let the boat drift. We ducked, both of us keeping down as the other boat approached. They had cut back on the throttle, too, and now puttered toward us cautiously. I estimated the distance—six, five, four yards until I could read the model name on the prow. I totally ignored the two figures standing behind the water-splashed windshield as I took the first shot below the waterline. Evan did the same thing, firing twice into the hull, but he had the idea to fire a flare at the boat's windshield, too.

"Brilliant!" I cried while the night blazed neon pink. Literally.

"Happy you approve!" he called back as he returned to the wheel to rev into the boat equivalent of warp speed.

I gazed back at the pandemonium. The flare had temporarily blinded our pursuers and, with a little luck, their boat would start taking on water.

Meanwhile, we were zooming down one of the side canals. Just before we turned the corner, I caught a glimpse of the reddened skyline far across the city. The studio in flames! I began shaking so badly I could barely contain myself. Evan leaned over and dropped his jacket over my shoulders, warm with his body heat. I turned my back to him and shrugged off my soaked turtleneck and wrapped myself in his jacket.

"Does Nicolina know the building's on fire?" I called out to him as I poked my arms into his sleeves. He could see my bra—big deal.

"I called. They alerted the authorities," he said, looking over his shoulder at me, one hand on the wheel.

I fumbled into my bag to retrieve my phone. Three messages from Nicolina topped the list. I speed-dialed her.

"Phoebe! Thank God you're all right!" she rasped. I could hear sirens in the background, people shouting. "Phoebe, the studio is gone, Maria's legacy gone!" Nicolina was crying.

"They knew I was going there tonight. They burned the place down, all that history!" I coughed.

"Phoebe, forget that. You could have been killed!"

My hands were numb, my heart number. The phone slipped and fell to the floor. I picked it up again. "Got to go," I said. "Talk later."

"No, Phoebe, wait—"

But I turned the phone off and dropped it into my bag. My hand throbbed, my heart too numb to feel a thing. The boat was proceeding at a nearly sedate pace now but I barely noticed, barely noticed which direction we were taking, either, only that it was circuitous with a lot of turns down dark little canals.

The studio was gone. Centuries worth of priceless design information and weaving artifacts gone. Old looms that had withstood the ages with loving care had been slaughtered, burned alive as their brittle bones went up in flames. Only the ignorant would do such a thing, the kind of ignorance that had once burned witches at the stake, turning their magic and wisdom to ash. I buried my head in my hands and sobbed.

I wasn't sure when we arrived or even where exactly. Evan put his arms around me and lifted me out of the boat. There was somebody else there, too—Sloane, I realized—and lots of instructions being bandied about for the care of this soaked, half-naked woman.

"She needs a hot bath, man!" That was Evan.

"But we don't have working plumbing in this infernal hellhole, Evan, you know that. You will need to rig something up." That was Sloane.

"Then rig it up I will."

"We can use that dreadful marble death chamber upstairs. Sir Rupert refuses to go inside the place."

Marble death chamber?

"Phoebe! Dearest Phoebe! What happened?" croaked Rupert as he shuffled down a long dark hall toward me in furry bedroom slippers and one of his satin robes. He attempted to grab my icy hands in his but I only let him have the good one. "Oh, my dear, what a disaster!"

Evan answered him over my head while still holding me tight. "The bastards set fire to the building, sir. Ms. Phoebe narrowly escaped with her life."

Back to *Ms. Phoebe.* I dimly remember him using my name. "What kind of monsters set fire to centuries of history, let flames ravish priceless information that will be lost to civilization forever?" I wailed. "What kind of bastards do that?"

Rupert gripped my one hand tighter. "The same kind who set fire to a building with you inside, Phoebe. Monsters indeed! Sloane, tea, immediately!"

"Coming up," the butler called back as he dashed down the hall.

"I'm going to fix you a shower, Ms. Phoebe," Evan whispered in my ear, releasing my shoulders and passing me over to Rupert—reluctantly, I thought.

Rupert nodded at him and led me by the arm into the shadowy ballroom. "Come, come, my dear. We shall have tea and place you beside the space heater until you thaw. You are shaking like a leaf! You fell into the canal, I understand. How dreadful!"

"I jumped into the canal," I told him.

"Yes, well, I am missing part of the story, it seems."

"You still sound terrible," I told him, and then I started crying again. Really, I was a mess.

"It's shock, dear Phoebe. All very understandable." He patted my back. "Here, do sit right down."

I was guided into a big blanket-covered chair in front of a modern heating device that looked like a sleek revolving doughnut but which gave off considerable heat. Rupert fussed a bit by tucking a blanket around me until finally he collapsed onto a stool nearby and tried to take my injured hand. I winced and pulled it back inside the oversized sleeve. "Dear Phoebe, I would despair if anything had happened to you. I just don't understand who these bastards are."

"But we know what they want." It wasn't a question.

"That blasted painting! I didn't believe Maria when she told me her suspicions about it long ago—I thought it some fanciful *Indiana Jones* imaginings—" He paused to cough, recovered, and went on. "But the dear woman was apparently right all along."

"But you knew it was valuable." It came out like an accusation. Tea had arrived. With my one good hand, I took the mug Sloane proffered and sipped gratefully.

"Of course I knew it was valuable," Rupert croaked, waving the hovering Sloane away. "It was by Domenico di Bartolo so how could it not be valuable? But to murder and burn to obtain it? It was not *that* valuable, Phoebe, not Raphael or da Vinci valuable. No, it's not, and yet somebody behaves as if it is worth millions of pounds, which must mean that Maria may have been correct all along—" he stopped to steady his breath "—when she told me that the painting held...some kind of secret."

"But she was going to give both paintings to you as a wedding present once—"

"More to keep them with her when she left the family bosom than to give them to me specifically. We were eloping, after all."

"You were eloping?"

"Well, yes, old Father Contini—a male supremest if I ever met one and an anti-Semitic nasty piece of work besides—would never allow his daughter to marry a penniless Jew—not that I was penniless exactly but I was still a little young to have yet amassed my own fortune at twenty-five, wasn't I?"

"I didn't know you were Jewish until recently."

"Yes, I am Jewish, Phoebe—not a practicing Jew but Jewish nonetheless. Does it matter?"

"Of course not but I didn't know."

"Why should you? But that's rather beside the point, isn't it?"

"No, it isn't, considering that the Bartolo commemorates an extraordinary marriage between a Christian and a Jewish family at a time when such high-profile unions could be deadly."

"Well, yes, of course. Maria was very proud of her family's Jewish roots, as thin as the bloodline was after all these centuries. Her papa, however, preferred to keep it under wraps. It was her desire for me to have the Bartolo for that very reason as well as to assuage her guilt, I suppose. I was very bitter following the broken engagement, I admit. She was my first love, you see." More coughing chased down by deep sips of tea. "Ah, yes, what was I saying?"

"You were very bitter and Maria was going to give you the paintings, anyway."

"Yes, until her mother suffered a massive heart attack and died in protest, which ended that idea rather dramatically, don't you think? Her mama wasn't...against our marriage so much as she was against Maria taking those paintings with her. They have been...oh, dear. Give me a minute, please." He breathed quietly for a moment before continuing. "They have been traditionally willed to the female heir of the family, you see...but should a generation pass without progeny, their fate hung in limbo. Maria didn't have children—" he sighed "—so it's all rather tragic, really. Though she assured me...that she would will me the paintings, it didn't matter to me by then. I wanted nothing more to do with them or her...and told her as much after which...I proceeded to leave Venice. I thought—I thought—"

Another coughing fit consumed him, this one bad enough to send Sloane scurrying in with admonishments to stop talking immediately. Rupert was ordered to his bed and me upstairs.

"Evan has rigged up a shower in the master bathroom, Sir Rupert. I will lead her there now."

"That place?" Rupert wheezed from the camp bed. "You cannot allow her to go in unattended, Sloane, not after what happened. It's ghastly."

"That was a long time ago, sir. Besides which, the plumbing is far more ghastly than any sordid tale. The room itself is perfectly usable despite the intolerable cold, which I believe we have somewhat remediated. Regardless, we really must get her out of those wet clothes."

So, I was to be spoken about in the third person. I shrugged off the blanket and got to my feet. "And the book she rescued from the fire, where is that?"

"In the kitchen, madam, and it is quite unharmed after tonight's adventure, I must say."

"That's because Evan is such a good catch," I pointed out.

"So he says, though no woman has managed to catch him yet." Sloane chuckled at his own joke but suddenly sobered at the sight of my hand. "You've suffered a burn, madam, or is that a cut?"

"What, where?" Rupert croaked, sitting up.

"On the left hand, sir. We will steer her into the shower and then attend to it properly." Sloane held my carpetbag in one hand and took my arm with the other.

"I'm quite able to walk, Sloane, thank you," I said, shaking him off. "Now where exactly is this marble death chamber?"

"That is rather a dramatic term for a perfectly lovely marble bathroom on the second floor. Installed in the early nineteenth century," he said, leading me into a long dark hallway, his lamp held high. Once a butler, always a butler apparently. He was a slight middle-aged man who I had only ever seen wearing his tidy green uniform, which he wore even here. "With exquisite detailing, I must say. I'm sure you'll be impressed, at least with the finishing, if not the plumbing."

"And the 'death chamber' part?"

"Apparently a man was shot by his lover there decades ago. Old news, as they say, but Sir Rupert is rather fixated by the lurid tale, that and all the other fates that have befallen the palazzo's previous owners."

I climbed the stairs, my gaze glancing over damp-splotched flocked wallpaper and resting briefly on a chandelier whose crystal droplets glinted like frost in the flashlight. I thought of the ruined warehouse and the light that had burned out in this city tonight.

A glow was coming from an open door halfway down the hall. Evan stepped out. "It's ready for you, Ms. Phoebe."

With the two men following at my heels, I stepped into a large bathroom completely tiled in rosy marble but for a single mirrored wall. Brass fittings gleamed in the lamplight and a large marble-tiled double tub sat between four pillars in the middle of the room. It was both ostentatious and gorgeous all at the same time, yet felt massive with the shadowy light.

"I guess it's as good a place to murder someone as any," I said.

"Easier to tidy up afterward," Sloane remarked. Obviously butlers think on the practical aspects.

Had it been another time, another place, I might have laughed, but as it was, I just wanted to get this done. "So, this is the makeshift shower?" I gazed up at a contraption I took to be of Evan's devising: a large plastic water container suspended over the tub with a cord dangling down.

"Yes, a bit primitive, I'm afraid," Evan explained.

"Not up to your usual standards, you mean?" I remarked.

"Definitely not but hopefully it will function. All you need do is step in and give the cord a tug to release the flow. The water is still hot but I'm afraid it's not likely to stay that way for long."

Sloane peered into the tub. "I scraped away as much as the grime as I could but it's best not to dally, madam. Who knows what's down there. Evan, what is the story on the pipes?"

"I decided to abstain from investigating further after the snake encountered an obstruction. Hopefully the thing will drain of its own accord, which is the best we can hope for."

"Very well, then," Sloane said, stepping back. "Let us permit the lady to get on with it. I've set your bag on the counter, madam, and left a clean towel for your use. Please do take care to wash that hand thoroughly so I can tend to it when you emerge."

"We must tend to that hand" Evan said suddenly.

"It's just a bit of a cut and a burn," I told him, holding my wounded member away from his gaze. "Now, leave me, please. I'm not in the mood for a communal shower."

He almost looked embarrassed as he backed out. "Of course, ma—Ms. Phoebe, but I'll wait outside in case you need me."

Need him, why would I need him? Of course, I could use a little help taking my clothes off but this was hardly the time. I shut the door, stifling a brief bittersweet jolt thinking of Noel as I began the one-handed business of peeling off my damp jeans—trickier than I'd expected. That my hand throbbed seemed irrelevant. All that mattered was the carnage I'd just witnessed and the expanse of despair that had opened up inside me as a result. It was as if the loss of Noel, the imprisonment of my brother, and all the trauma that followed had suddenly hit me anew. And here I thought

I'd managed to shove it all to the back of my mind. The heart is not so resilient, after all.

Leaving my jeans, panties, and bra on the floor and clutching my toiletries with my one good hand, I climbed shivering into the tub, cringing at the cold marble beneath my feet. In a minute, I'd pulled the cord to release a trickle of warm water, blessedly welcome after the dank canal. I tried to whip up a bit of lather from my shampoo but the most I got was a few halfhearted suds while my wounded paw burned.

As the water poured down over me, I closed my eyes and vowed to catch the bastards who killed Maria and sent her legacy up in smoke. I didn't care who they were, they'd pay. I doubted I could trust anyone anymore, not that I ever could. The world was peopled with self-serving, ruthless monsters who counted human life and history as worth nothing if it stood in the way of some kind of monetary gain. Damn them all to hell.

Minutes later, the water stopped trickling and I stood in the lamp-lit bathtub shivering. It had grown unaccountably cold despite the space heater. The one long shuttered window was covered with plastic so there were no drafts coming from that direction and yet I felt a definite breeze.

One glance to the right glimpsed my own naked image reflected palely in the floor-length mirror like a freckled ghost. Damn these Venetians and their creepy mirrors. Something was rumbling beneath my feet. I looked down to find brackish water regurgitating at my feet. Quickly, I climbed out and snatched the towel from the counter.

And it was freezing in there.

Luckily, my carpetbag carried a change of clothes—my carry-on emergency kit. I dressed as quickly as a one-handed woman could, hauling on fresh panties, yanking on a pair of dry jeans, a sweater, and topping it all with one of my art knit cardigans. My bra was damp so I'd go without. Stuffing my damp things into my bag, I tried to fling open the door but it wouldn't budge. I shook the knob and pounded with no success. It was crazy after what I'd been through to feel panic over a stuck door and yet I did.

Hell, was Evan out there? I desperately wanted him to be out there. "Help, I can't get out!"

He was. "Madam, are you turning the knob?"

"Of course I'm turning the knob," I called back. "I didn't lock the door,

I only shut it." But apparently it had locked itself. More likely the wood had swollen shut in the frame, meaning I'd just have to try harder, so I rattled the door with even more vigor. Still the thing wouldn't open. I turned back to the room, freezing now as if I stood in a refrigerator instead of two yards away from a space heater. And the atmosphere had turned as thick as sludge.

Did I believe in ghosts? Sure, I did. Centuries of people can't have got that wrong. But was I afraid of ghosts? Naturally, but right then I was too angry to be frightened of vapors. "Back off!" I yelled into the gloom. "The dead don't have any teeth next to the murderous living! Go to hell!"

And then the door flew open and Evan fell into the room, knocking me against the wall. For a moment he stared down at me, stunned. I stood crushed against his person inches away from the heating element. "Who were you talking to," he whispered.

"The dead," I told him, pushing him gently back. "Let's get out of this place." I grabbed my carpetbag and got out of there as soon as possible.

Minutes later, I was sitting in the kitchen—now spotlessly tidy with all of Evan's paraphernalia apparently banished elsewhere—while the two men inspected my hand under a large spotlight.

"Second degree burn, by the looks of things, plus a rather nasty cut. I suggest a loose bandage to let it breathe." That was Evan speaking.

"Plus the addition of basic antiseptic as we cannot count on it actually remaining sufficiently clean given the countless sources of pestilence seething around this moldering pile," added Sloane.

I looked up. "Gentlemen, thanks for your concern but I'll take both the antiseptic and the bandage for now. Could we get on with it?" Anything to stop a debate. That prompted a small smile from Evan, who quickly tended to my hand with a gentle efficiency while Sloane scuttled off, presumably in pursuit of either germs or tea.

Once I had been bandaged, I returned to the ballroom to where Rupert sat bundled in his chair beside a small table, waiting. "Feel better now, I trust?" he asked, indicating for me to join him where another chair that had been pulled up beside his. Evan disappeared for a moment and returned with a stool for himself.

"I am, and you?"

"Reasonably, though I must take care apparently. Phoebe, we really must talk."

My gaze landed on my rescued book and the two photographs sitting side by side on the table, one of the Bartolo, the other the Civelli. "I agree." I sat down and reached for the Contini pattern compendium, relieved to find that it had held up to the recent adventure better than I. "This is the only one I managed to save," I said. "The others are all gone now."

Rupert leaned over and patted my knee. "There, there—a tragedy, I agree—but I've been thinking of what possible motive these—" he paused to take a deep shaky breath before continuing "—brigands could have for attempting to burn the place down?"

"Are you certain it was arson?" Evan asked.

I looked over at him. "I smelled what I realize now must have been lighter fluid or something similar. Whoever the arsonists were, they entered the building somehow and spread a ring of something highly inflammable around the weaving level before igniting it. They meant to burn me alive apparently. Who knew I was there except Nicolina, Seraphina, and you?"

"That's what I've been asking myself. I've run your phones and all your belongings through my devices as a precaution and found no sign of tampering. I must have missed one back in the Contini home."

"What about the roof? That's the only place we spoke freely."

"Possibly," he said. "I should have checked more thoroughly." The man seemed to have a thing bearing responsibility but he'd had zero time to check every inch of that villa.

"Nicolina suspects the police," I remarked.

"Indeed, but perhaps it is she who is behind all this," Rupert remarked. "But why? Why burn the warehouse and steal what will become her own painting?" I asked.

"To cover her tracks, perhaps, to set loose a school of virtual red herrings to throw the authorities off her trail...in order to get Maria out of the way. I'm only playing devil's advocate here, you understand, and I don't truly believe...that the Nicolina I once knew to be involved...with such a heinous crime as murdering one friend and attempting to burn...another but people do change."

"Maybe," I agreed, "but surely not that much. I don't believe Nicolina did this. No, something or someone else is behind these crimes and it all leads back to that painting." My gaze rested on the two glossy photos sitting on the table before us. "How long have you had these?"

"For ages." Rupert leaned back in his chair, eyes closed. "They have been enlarged from a very poor photo I took eons ago. The detail is very fuzzy, as you can see."

And it was. I peered over at them. "I have clearer images on my phone. So—" I pulled back "—why did the thieves send the studio up in smoke tonight?"

"I postulate that they needed to eliminate anything that might lead to the secret location," Evan replied.

He postulates. Taking a deep breath, I turned to meet his steady gaze, that lovely gray-green almost the color of smoke in the lamplight. "So, you believe the arsonists were trying to burn clues that might lead us to it?"

"Perhaps burn the clues along with the one person who may be able to decipher them," Evan said quietly.

"But if they've taken to burning clues, they must now have a pretty good idea where or what that secret is," I pointed out.

"That's what I'm afraid of."

Rupert was looking from one of us to the other. "Do you mean that these bastards already have the answers and may be trying to eliminate anything or anyone who might stand in their way?"

I didn't answer him. Instead, I wrapped my arms around myself to try to stave off a new wave of shivering. "But why wouldn't they have taken these clues on the same night they stole the painting and murdered Maria?"

"Because they didn't know what they were looking for," Evan said. "Now they do, or at least believe they do. They may have left devices around the place the night they stole the painting."

I nodded. "So they knew when I was there tonight, heard me in the library pouring over that pattern book, even heard Nicolina describe what she planned to do with those files. The whole time we were sending them every possible detail to help them send everything up in smoke." I swung around to Evan. "And now they know where you are holed out, too."

"Yes. We will have to move," he agreed, turning to Rupert. "We have already begun seeking out alternatives, sir. Sloane is on it now. I'd best give him a hand. We may have to leave tonight."

"Really, so soon? Where shall we go?" Rupert croaked.

"Still working on the details, sir. I'll let you know as soon as it's sorted." And with that, he strode from the room.

"I can't say I'm sorry to finally leave this abysmal place but I'd far rather be sitting snug in my country house about now," Rupert commented once Evan had left, "feet up by the fire, maybe a good book in hand. Meanwhile, Phoebe, what else do you remember saying?"

But I wasn't listening. I was thinking, my eyes cast down on the shadowy floor. I got to my feet, picked up the design volume along with the two pictures, and headed out the door. "I'll be right back."

"What? Wait! Where are you going?"

To the kitchen, with its superior light source, oblivious to anything else but chasing a hunch. When I entered, Sloane was across the room speaking on a phone and Evan could be seen sitting in an adjoining room busy on a laptop.

Setting the book on the kitchen table with the painting photos on either side, I fished out my phone and opened up my photos to the close-ups I'd taken. Then I orientated the spotlight so that it blazed over all and began turning the pages to study the earliest entries.

Bartolo had painted the wedding scene in approximately 1441 and the Continis had begun keeping records of their textile designs about a decade earlier. The earliest design recorded was a simple vine and floral motif set against red velvet with a gold embossed ground—all recorded in the journal with paint over ink, illuminated-manuscript-style. A few threads of the original fabric clung to a space next to the illustration. Other samples from the same period showed variations of similar designs in colors predominantly red, gold, and blue, all faded, all lovely, but not particularly extraordinary.

However, when I slipped over several pages to the later mid-1500s, the designs showed a subtle shift. The motifs became more complex—flowers inside of flowers, layers of detail so rich that the thick curving vines had sprouted curlicues with filigreed centers and extraordinary birds cavorting amid the branches. I pulled away to use my phone as a magnifying app and returned to study one particularly detailed motif: a silk cut voided velvet with what looked to be three pile warps and gold brocaded wefts depicting pomegranates and peacocks, the vines forming a knotted design like interlacing stars. A border ran along one side of the illustration depicting blues vivid enough to glow after all these years. The sample piece had apparently been removed. I opened my photos and stared at the Bartolo carpet.

"Where was that place in Morocco that the Continis owned?" I asked no one in particular.

"Why, in Marrakech."

Turning, I found that Rupert had shuffled into the kitchen and plonked himself into a chair.

"Do you know anything about it, like where exactly in Marrakech or how long the family owned it?" I asked.

"Of course," Rupert puffed. "Maria and I were going to bolt there for our honeymoon, since it was virtually uninhabited at the time...but for a couple of caretakers Papa Contini left in situ. We thought we could buy some time...at least until we could decide exactly where we would live for the rest of our lives."

"How long has it been in the family?"

"Oh, forever, I believe. It was very old and tucked away in the medieval part of the medina...and apparently had been in the family for...centuries. The Continis never parted with a thing, you see—not daughters, not paintings, not properties—"

"Do you remember what it was called?" I interrupted.

"Well, no, not exactly. Phoebe, what are you thinking?"

I pointed to the design journal. "At approximately the same time as the Bartolo wedding commemorative was painted, the designs in the Contini factory began to change with the work becoming more complex, the dyes more varied, and with certain reoccurring motifs appearing with interlacing designs, including a few geometric features that have echoes of Berber combined with extraordinary florals such as that one." I tapped the painting of the bride's dress.

Rupert leaned over and peered at my phone. "My word, are you saying what I believe I'm hearing?"

Evan stepped out from the side room. "So, the bride's family came from Marrakech!"

I swung toward him. "And it makes perfect sense. Morocco has a rich textile tradition dating back thousands of years with influences from all over Africa and the East and the Jews were moving all over the continent at the time. That must have included Morocco."

"And aspects of the Moroccan flag actually form a star," Evan pointed out, bringing up the country's flag on his phone.

"Does it?" I marveled. "So supposing that a family living in Marrakech was making exquisite textiles for the sultans at the time but because of religious persecution felt compelled to leave the area?"

"And supposing they managed to strike up a friendship with an Italian merchant trader in the same business as they, one whom, for the exchange of some secret—" Evan added, picking up the story.

"Like the recipes for special dyes or weaving techniques—" I chimed in excitedly.

"—decided to form an extraordinary contract to bind their two houses and businesses?"

"But," I said, striding up to him, "what if the Jewish Moroccan family needed to further seal the deal in the tradition of a dowry, an incredibly rich dowry, considering the risks to the groom's family?"

"Possibly one too valuable to transport by horseback along with the bride, at least not immediately. Morocco was fraught with war at the time, I believe, with factious elements in a power struggle. So if traveling across Europe wasn't dangerous enough, carrying a fortune in some kind of unknown wealth within a country at civil war would be." Evan was at least as caught up with the story as I was.

"So," I said, tapping him on the chest with my one good hand because I couldn't help myself, "the wealthy Moroccan family wrapped the location of this dowry in a cipher and had Bartolo paint it into the commemorative painting to keep it safe until it could be transported to Venice. Both parties knew of the location at the time but agreed not to retrieve it until times were safer."

"But time and life intervened. Perhaps the parties died or for whatever reason it became impossible to retrieve the dowry."

"Maybe because of the plague or smallpox or something?" I suggested.

He grabbed my hand and held it tight. "Or some other calamity befell the parties until all the individuals who could unlock the cipher were dead and the secret lost forever."

"Until now," I whispered, pulling my hand away not because it didn't feel good but because it felt too good. "It's got to be in Morocco, which explains this."

Returning to the table, I picked up Crivelli's *Annunciation*. "All this time I couldn't figure out what the first painting had to do with the Bartolo but now I think I understand: it was meant to be added as another clue but not necessarily related to the marriage painting. If you look in the background to where the landscape rises to meet the blue sky, you'll see something very strange for Italian Renaissance art—palm trees. It's not that they didn't exist in Italy at the time—I think they did—but they rarely appear in ecclesiastical art."

"Also, there is very little else that is green amid the foliage, also atypical for the period since we know how the Renaissance artists loved to ground their work with local flora and fauna," Rupert added, donning a pair of glasses from his pajama pocket. "Look at this and tell me if this doesn't rather look like an abundance of sand?"

I'd already reached the same conclusion. "Sand, yes, and that light seems very desert-like to me, though at first I thought it Tuscan."

"So what else does this tell us besides that this Jewish bride may have come from Morocco?" Rupert peered up at me, his spectacles slipping down his nose.

"That I need to go to Marrakech immediately, obviously," I said.

⬥

THE USUAL FLURRY OF PROTESTS ERUPTED FROM MY SELF-APPOINTED male protection squad. I waited until they subsided before restating my position, even hearing out each of the supposedly logical points that Rupert and Evan posed as if I seriously considered them. Finally. Foxy wheezed himself into a coughing fit.

After he recovered, I began: "Thank you for your concern, gentlemen —really, I mean it—but as you've already pointed out, nobody here is able to go with me. Rupert's too ill; Evan must protect Rupert; and we can't even alert Nicolina and Seraphina to my plans in case it tips off the mole. So, who's left?"

"Ms. Phoebe," Evan began, "I—"

I held up my hand. "Enough. Look, somebody has to go to Marrakech and trace these clues to the source and there's nobody able to do it but me apparently. Who else is there?"

"But it is exceedingly dangerous!" Rupert spewed. "You can't—" (deep shaky breath) "—go alone!"

"I'm not planning on going alone exactly. Is it possible to get me on a flight out of Venice to Marrakech before dawn?" I asked Evan.

"If not before dawn, then possibly first thing in the morning," he said, frowning. "I would suggest you travel under an assumed name, which takes some time to organize—"

"Evan!" Rupert croaked, shooting him a baleful glance.

"What's the riad called?" I asked him. "Seraphina said it was now an Airbnb."

"I don't recall," Rupert gasped, hastily downing an inch of cold tea while Sloane poured him a glass of water from a bottle.

"More like you don't want to tell me," I said. "Do I have to call Nicolina to find out?"

"That wouldn't be wise," Evan said. "We have no idea if we've located all the bugs yet."

"So it would be much safer if Rupert just told me, wouldn't it, Rupert?"

Rupert glowered at me from over his glass. "Phoebe, we will not be there to protect you but if you insist—"

"I do."

"Very well." Rupert sighed. "The riad is called—"

"La Maison Oasis Bleu," Evan intercepted. "I took the liberty of checking it out some days ago. You must try to limit speaking, sir."

"A French name?" I asked.

But Rupert was not a man easily silenced. "I believe that Signore Contini thought a French name more fitting...for the tourist trade considering...that most of the visitors are either British or French, Morocco having..."

"Morocco having once been a French protectorate," Evan finished for him, "but I believe the riad has gone through many manifestations over the centuries."

"Makes sense." I nodded, eager just to get going before I changed my mind.

"I will make your bookings under an assumed name, madam—er, Ms. Phoebe—"

"Try 'Phoebe.' It escaped your lips at least once tonight."

He chose not to acknowledge that remark. "—and arrange your travel documents accordingly. Meanwhile, there is much to do. Excuse me." With that Evan dashed back into his anteroom, which, I had decided, must have been some sort of pantry.

Sloane stepped forward. "Sir, I suggest that you return to your bed immediately. In fact, I must insist. Indeed, you will need to recoup your strength for the long night ahead. I will return to assist you to dress once the arrangements are made."

"Shall I help Rupert back to his bed so you can get to work?" I asked, offering Rupert one arm while tucking the design compendium under the other.

Sloane rewarded me with a slight incline of the head. "Very much appreciated indeed, Ms. Phoebe."

"Come along, Rupe. Your staff have their hands full so it's best to keep out of the way."

Rupert bristled but allowed me to lead him back into the ballroom. "This is so unsettling...so upsetting," he wheezed.

"Yes, I know—to be sick when there's so much going on."

"I was not...referring to that, but yes, I'm usually...more in control than this."

"Of course you are," I soothed, "and you will be again once you've recovered. Everybody gets sick once in a while, Rupert. Why are you so shocked that it happened to you?"

"Poor timing," he sighed. "Just very, very poor timing. I feel that this is—"

"Right. Stop talking."

"—part of my history, my story, perhaps." He took a deep breath. "Maria and I...it was very long ago but it is...part of who I am...yet here I am, too weak to do much."

"Sometimes you just have to allow others to tell parts of our stories for you. Maybe it will be a slightly different perspective, but it's still part of the tale. In the meantime, try to just sit back and let the rest of us take up the reins, all right?"

Once I had him sitting on the edge of the bed, he gazed up at me. "Since when did you become so...*bossy?*"

I wanted to laugh but I couldn't quite pull it off. "It's part of my personal growth continuum. Everybody changes, Rupert. Besides, if we don't change, we may as well be dead."

"Don't say the 'D' word around here, please." He shot a quick glance around the shadows while taking a deep breath through a gurgling chest. "What about Noel? You haven't even...mentioned the lad." He kicked off his slippers and lay back while I covered him with a blanket.

"And I don't intend to except to say that's over," I said briskly.

"You can't...mean that."

"Yes, I can, and I do mean it absolutely. It took a long time for me to figure out what I want in life and to realize that he can't be part of it. You haven't been in contact with him, have you?" I studied his face.

"No, of course not. Since Jamaica, he's disappeared from the radar but..." He closed his eyes. "He used to always...look out for you and...he may be doing so now. You must watch for him."

"I hope he doesn't show, but if he does, I'll be ready for him. Besides, he'd be better off looking after himself. Once Interpol catches up with him, they'll be putting him away for a long, long time. Sparks flew between us, I admit. It wasn't a relationship so much as a string of steamy events under heightened circumstances. That's not what I want."

"I hope you mean that," he rasped.

"I do. Now get some rest."

Wait, there is...something I need to tell you. Should have...told you sooner..."

"Just stop. Rest. You can tell me later."

I left him dozing while I plucked my phone from my bag and in seconds had fired off a couple of quick emails. That didn't mean that I had time to answer any, though I noticed three from Max and two from Serena.

Minutes later, I was sitting across the kitchen table from Evan, listening intently to the details of my emerging escape plan. He had the preliminaries mapped out and now all that was needed was confirmation from a couple of his contacts. I was given a prepaid Visa card and told that someone would meet me at the airport with a package of credentials for my new identity— Penelope Martin, fiction writer, researching for my new book.

"Fiction authors have unlimited scope for investigating unusual and arcane matters," Evan explained. "By the time you arrive in Marrakech, Penelope will have two books in a series for a genre known as romantic historical suspense available on Amazon. The books are bogus, of course, but since they aren't advertised, no one will ever purchase them before they are taken down. They are there only to bolster your disguise in Marrakech."

Ask why this surprised me. "Is that legal?" Stupid question, I know, but it just came out.

His restrained smile was strangely regretful, maybe a little sad that two people who believed they stood for the forces of good—at least one of them did, anyway—now resorted to the tools of the enemy. But that's just my interpretation. He was probably thinking something totally different. "Nothing we are doing here is strictly legal, madam—"

"Phoebe."

"*Ms. Phoebe*, but we employ whatever strategies and tools are available as a means to an end in a world seething in crime and violence."

I couldn't let it go. "But you used to be MI6. Your entire modus operandi was to defend Britain, presumably working as an agent on the right side of the law, and now you work for Rupert, who is...less than honest," I finished limply. For some reason I could not openly call the man before me a crook, not when I saw him as so solidly dependable, incredibly talented, and worthy of a better descriptor.

He studied me in the half-light of the lamp, the little quirk quirking away. What was he thinking, what was he restraining himself from saying? "Perhaps there is more going on here than you know."

"What a shock that would be."

And then he stood up. "Now perhaps we had best return to our preparations. Excuse me. Oh, one more thing: I have written out a set of instructions for working the features on your phone. Please put them safely into your bag."

"Sure," I said. I took the wad of paper from the table and mindlessly stuffed it into my carpetbag. That left me sitting at the table awash in a knot of feelings I couldn't begin to untangle. Meanwhile, I could see

Sloane busy making reservations across the room. Apparently they were putting Rupert up at the Cipriani since they believed the danger to his health more of a threat than any assassination attempt, especially now that Nicolina and Seraphina had called off the hunt. Or had they? At least nobody had attempted to follow us here—yet, anyway.

A boat was to pick me up for a ride to the airport at 5:00 a.m., a bit earlier than necessary considering that my flight left at 7:00, but the household was exiting for the hotel at the same time.

Clearly, I needed rest. At last, I tucked myself into a shadowy corner and pulled on my still-damp bra, gathered all my things together in one spot, and took up Sloane's offer to catch a few z's on a foldout cot. The next thing I knew, the butler was shaking me awake, dosing me with strong coffee, and urging me toward a waiting vaporetto for a flight on Air France to Paris de Gaulle and then on to Marrakech. I agreed that the roundabout route made for a good diversionary tactic in case anyone followed but it also made for a long day. And I was traveling ridiculously light, even for me, and even for what was supposed to be a three-day trip. I tried to take the design compendium along but Evan suggested that I leave that with him, which I reluctantly did.

Rupert, now dressed in one of his dapper traveling suits that hung off him alarmingly, shuffled out to say goodbye. "Do take care, Phoebe. We have no idea whether this gang is on the trail in Marrakech at this very moment, and they appear to be a ruthless lot. I think you going by yourself is a very bad idea, very bad indeed. You could...be walking right into—" A coughing attack hit again.

"It's all right, Rupert. I'll be fine," I said, giving him a hug. "Just take care of yourself and get better, will you?"

"The boat is here, mada—Ms. Phoebe," Evan said. "I will try to come as soon as I am able," he whispered at the villa door after loading my luggage. "I regret to say that we never did have time to go over your phone's capabilities but please study my cursory cheat sheet. I've also taken the liberty of packing a few supplies for your voyage in one of Sir Rupert's spare roller bags." In other words, my gun. "And please keep us updated on what you discover using only the phone provided. My plan is to track down our mysterious interested parties or at least keep them occupied while you're gone."

I nodded and made for the dock, suddenly aware that no effort had been made to keep the villa's location a secret from me this time, which made perfect sense since everyone was leaving. That gave me the opportunity to gaze up at the mysterious palazzo as the boat pulled away, surprised to find it beautiful despite the interior decay and the deep wrap of gloom that shrouded the shuttered windows. Positioned on the edge of two merging canals—I had no idea where since I didn't feel like locating it on my phone just in case—it must have once been a luxurious palace on a quiet but prime location.

Turning my face to the wind, I settled in for the ride across the lagoon, clutching my carpetbag like it was my last friend on earth. Maybe I could have used a little friendly company just then as I watched the dawn struggle to crack light into the darkness. The boat driver nodded at me once but otherwise kept his eyes glued on the water, no doubt struggling to stay awake for such an early-morning trip.

※ 15 ※

The rest of my voyage played out like a blurry rerun of an old spy movie. While sipping coffee in the Venetian airport, a man brushed by me and dropped an envelope into my bag. Inside a washroom stall minutes later, I removed an American passport featuring my face with a false name—Penelope Martin, writer. It was sobering to witness how easily that kind of fraud could be arranged and even more so my willingness to participate in it. All for a worthy cause, I told myself. Regardless, if they ever discovered the gun or my bogus passport, I could be in jail for a long time, despite my Interpol affiliations.

Passing through customs was still a breeze and my basic French helped smooth the way through de Gaulle where I had enough of a layover to purchase a few warm weather tourist-worthy clothes. Otherwise, I slept through the flight to Marrakech, arriving at around two o'clock in the afternoon. Strolling into the airport's arrival area minutes later, I was on my way out the revolving glass doors looking for a cab when someone touched my shoulder.

"Miss Martin?"

I turned to stare blankly at the young man in the long white robe and round blue skull cap holding a sign and grinning at me. "You are Miss Martin, yes? I am Hassan, your driver. I have description." He read from his phone: "Very nice-looking red-haired lady. Not expecting ride so must approach."

Crud. Right. "Yes, yes. I'm Penelope Martin but I wasn't expecting to be picked up, like you said." I might have been had I read all the papers Evan had packed in my bag, which I only did much later. And I might have been had I practiced thinking like Penelope instead of like Phoebe—Penelope the writer, that is. And then it hit me that Evan had described me as "a very nice-looking red-haired lady." That part I liked.

"Sorry, I was just imagining the plot for my next book, which will be set right here in Marrakech," I said, shaking myself from my reverie. Weak, very weak.

"You are a writer. Very exciting. First time here?"

"Yes, first time."

If possible, the young man's grin grew even broader. "I take you to your hotel and give tour along way."

"No tour, thanks. Straight to my hotel."

It was as if he'd never heard me as he took my bags and led me across a parking lot to a plush taxi van. Soon it became clear that I was getting a tour whether I wanted it or not but I decided to relax and enjoy the ride. Being sealed inside a plush air-conditioned vehicle while driving through a panorama of color and image wasn't a bad introduction to a new land. I applied my sunglasses and wondered if I'd brought adequate sunblock.

Wide modern boulevards with sports cars easing up beside camels was only one of the many baffling sights that whizzed by. Impressions of color, sand-colored buildings, old pinkish brick walls, and glimpses down narrow, medieval streets added to the other-worldly sense. For a moment, I forgot to be exhausted.

"Very beautiful mosque," Hassan was saying. "The Koutoubia Mosque built in 1150."

"That early?" I said, staring up at the amazing minaret. So Marrakech had been an established city long before the Italian Renaissance began. "Were there many Jewish families living there back then?"

Hassan seemed taken aback. "Morocco Muslim country, Miss Martin. That is a mosque."

"Yes, of course." *So, skip that line of inquiry, Phoebe.* Suddenly I was exhausted and my hand burned relentlessly. By that time, I had my phone

out and was tracking our progress to La Maison Oasis Bleu on Google
Maps and realizing just how much farther we seemed to be getting from
the destination. "Look, Hassan, thank you for the tour but I'm tired.
Could you just take me to my riad now?"

"Yes, lady. Right away."

But *right away* did not mean directly. The taxi parked outside the
arched gate of an ancient pink stone wall that rose far overhead and looked
as though it dated from the beginnings of the city.

"We walk," he said cheerfully. "Follow me."

Hassan took my roller in hand while I hoisted my carpetbag over my
shoulder and together we strode through the arch into a jumble of
centuries. The souk, I realized as we passed stalls crammed with tiles,
painted plates, copper and brass lamps, and lengths of gorgeous textiles of
every imaginable fabric, many draped over walls. I could be in Istanbul and
the Grand Bazaar, only a more chaotic, rougher, and less pristine version,
though no less magical.

Narrow alleyways crowded with people in both Western clothing and
the traditional djellabas jostled with motorcars and donkeys while the
sound of ringing cell phones and the calls of the waterman filled the dusty
air. Once we pressed against a wall to allow a donkey burdened with
carpets to trot past us in a narrow lane, while the donkey man rang his bell
and called for us to move please in three languages. I caught glimpses of
carpet shops, some hanging their wares outside their doors in a kaleidoscope of pattern and color. It was all I could do not to stop, feeling as I did
as though I had fallen back into time and landed in a pile of pattern and
design.

I'd return to savor it all, I told myself as I followed Hassan deeper into
the medina, not that I had a clue how to return anywhere in this warren of
ancient streets. We passed several places that appeared to be hotels and
even more restaurants, but every time I'd hoped we'd reached our riad,
Hassan kept going.

"Not far now, lady," Hassan called to me as we entered a tiny
malodorous square. No more than a rough gathering of dusty stone buildings with dark little alleys branching off in three directions, the place
seemed populated only by skinny mewing cats—starving cats, I realized. I
stopped to gaze at one particularly pathetic little white kitten while

fighting the overwhelming urge to bring it food. I'd return to feed it as soon as I could.

"This chicken stall," Hassan said, catching my interest and pointing to a shelf set deep into one of the stone walls that appeared to be the source of the smell. "Chickens sold here Wednesday and Friday." He grinned. "Very busy then. Cats like."

So, a merchant would bring live chickens to this stinky little square and slaughter them right here for the waiting customers? That explained the stray feathers I saw embedded into the gravel below my feet. Got it. What we take for granted in our pristine supermarket world, I thought. Welcome to how the rest of the world lives, Phoebe. I mean, *Penelope*.

On the other hand, talk about fresh chicken...

"Please follow, lady. Riad just here."

The riad was nearby? Maybe this was part of the old Jewish quarter years ago, that is if Marrakech even had a Jewish quarter. Admittedly by then, I only longed for something simple and predictable like a chain hotel with clean white sheets, not whatever lay at the end of the short alley that Hassan was leading me down.

At the end of the narrow corridor stood a tall carved door leaning against a deep blushing terra-cotta wall. Since a potted palm sat in a puddle of sun directly before the magnificent portal, I knew it wasn't a working door, yet still I walked toward it, probably on some kind of color-induced autopilot.

"Here, lady."

I turned. Hassan had stopped about halfway down the short alley. Backtracking, I found myself standing before another carved door, this one so low I had to duck to enter as Hassan beckoned me forward. And so I stepped straight into an oasis of calm and beauty so intense it struck me dumb.

"I am Shada," said a young woman in jeans and a silk blouse standing before me. A shy beauty in her late twenties with wide brown eyes and an up-to-the-minute dress sense (shirt half-tucked into her jeans and strappy high-heeled sandals). "Welcome."

"Thank you, Shada," I said, gazing around. "Wow, this is magnificent." Did Maria have a hand in its decoration? I wondered.

A tiled courtyard featuring a gleaming blue pool fringed with lush sun-filtering greenery drew my eye immediately, but soon my gaze skimmed past the gleaming brass lanterns, ornate tiles, textiles on the walls, and chairs gathered around the pool in gestures of comfort. I was led to one of these seats and offered mint tea, water, plus an assortment of little pastries. Only after I had sipped the tea poured by a fez-capped young man named Mohammed did I notice the copper floor lanterns, the filigreed white plasterwork, and the fact that Hassan stood beside me waiting patiently. I looked up.

"Lady, I go now but I arrange tour for you anytime. My cousin, he has van and we could go to Atlas Mountains."

"Thanks, but my research is right here in Marrakech," I said, shaking off my stupor. Actually, I wouldn't mind going to the Atlas Mountains but this wasn't a vacation. Then I realized he was probably waiting for a tip. I didn't have any dirhams, only pounds and euros, but reached into my pocket to offer him a ten-euro note, which he took with a quick bow and disappeared out the door.

Shada stepped forward. "Your room is ready, Ms. Martin. Your bag awaits you," she said in impeccable English. Though gracious and lovely, her demeanor almost seemed apologetic but I couldn't decide why. Soon, I was too busy taking in my environment to care.

The riad was built on three balconied floors that wrapped around an open courtyard with a pool embedded into its bottom floor like a faceted sapphire. Shada lead me to a narrow staircase in the corner that twisted around the stories in white marble and colored tiles. I climbed the stairs behind her, my eyes glomming on to the textiles, mostly Berber with traditional motifs, every one rich and vibrant. Some time I'd study each one but right then I was too tired to pause.

All but one guest room was situated on the two upper balconied levels with a library and lounge leading off the main floor below, Shada told me. And since the doors to every room but one were wide open, I glimpsed cozy interiors, each one unique, luxurious, and intriguing. Arched windows along the hall echoed so much of Venice's Renaissance buildings that it was impossible not to note the connection. That the trade between Venice and the East had been brisk was undeniable. The creative mingling of cultures proved it.

"I'm actually here to research my new novel—I'm a writer. Is there much information about the history of the riad? It looks very old."

"It is very old," Shada said, turning to me. "My brother studies architecture in Paris and he says the building has '*bons os*,' good bones, as they say in French. Do you speak French?"

"A little." Actually, I could read French but my accent was too rusty to mention.

It didn't help when she slipped into French, leaving me struggling to keep up. "You will find whatever we have on the building in the library but most of it will be in Arabic or French," I think she said.

I spoke in English. "Do you sleep here, Shada?"

Taking my cue, she responded in my mother tongue. "No, I live with my parents. Myself and Ingram manage the riad but we don't stay overnight."

"Ingram?"

"You will meet him tomorrow. He does not work this afternoon. This is your room here. You'll find it perfect for writing, I think, but the rooftop is equally good. Very quiet."

"Do you mean that the guests are alone here after 7:00 p.m.?" That alarmed me.

"You will be perfectly safe. The tourist police patrol the medina and the riad is very secure."

Except that the roof was wide open to the elements as well as to anyone who might decide to drop in, plus the tourist police didn't know I was being dogged by murdering thieves. Naturally, Shada didn't run in the same circles I did or know what's possible for the enterprising criminal types. I peered over the balcony at the pool glowing turquoise through the fringing palms. Sky above, pool below, and the chaos of the medina plus the world itself seemed light-years away.

"And do the owners live in Morocco?" I asked, pulling back. I knew the answer but I wanted to see if she did.

"No, the owner lives in Italy." A shadow crossed her lovely features—I guessed that she might have heard about Maria's death—but she recovered quickly. "Breakfast is served on the rooftop terrace from 8:00 to 10:00 every morning," she continued with her customary shy smile. "There is a night number to call for emergencies in your room. Everything is very safe here. No need to worry," she said.

If only she knew. "I'm sure it's very safe. Are there other guests staying?"

"Two others—a couple from America one level down and another lady arrives tomorrow. You will find it very peaceful. Would you like supper tonight?"

Of course I was hungry but staying awake until dinner seemed an unimaginable feat. "What about something light that I could eat in my room? I'm so tired right now that I just want to sleep."

"I will have a cold supper prepared for you and placed in your room's refrigerator," Shada said.

"Just leave it outside the door, please." That way if I did wake up ravenous, I'd have something to gnaw on. "I plan to take a long nap."

After that, I stepped into my room and a narrow, richly decorated space opened up around me like the inside of a jewel box—painted deep ochre with a tiled fireplace, a rug across the tiled floor, brass platters and jugs on the mantel and inlaid tables, deep chairs for reading under colored glass lamps, and a bed tucked into the far end covered in a silken patchwork coverlet. If I were a genie, I'd live right there.

After Shada slipped away, I opened the borrowed roller bag, dug through the clothing Evan had packed as a decoy—a men's silk dressing robe plus a white dress shirt still in its laundry package—sorted through my recently purchased clothes, and removed the gun secreted in the bottom level. That thing would go with me everywhere, as would my phone and anything else I needed. I wasn't taking chances, not here, not anywhere.

In fact, I took the roller, carpetbag complete with phones, and jacket into the bathroom with me, leaning the roller against the door, jiggered in such a way that if anyone tried to enter, the clatter of a brass soap dish would give warning. All the knots loosened in my neck and shoulders when minutes later I stepped into the tiled shower and let hot water pour down over me for as long as I needed. As for my hand, I gingerly unsealed the bandage, cursing softly all the way. I'd leave that open to the elements now to help it heal but the water felt like torture on my wounded flesh.

About forty minutes later, wrapped in a towel and refreshed, I stepped into the room and realized that someone had entered long enough to turn down the bed, sprinkle pink rose petals over the covers, and leave a chocolate on my pillow. Lovely. Unsettling. There was even a covered plate in the small fridge along with several varieties of juice and bottled water. Excellent service though it was, easy access to my room did not feel like a good thing.

I sipped a bottle of orange juice while checking the door—flimsy ornamental wood latched by a simple bolt. That wouldn't do. After hanging a Do Not Disturb sign on the knob outside, I dragged the roller bag into active duty again, this time balancing a brass platter from over the mantel against the door. If it fell to the tiled floor, it should wake the whole riad.

Next, I scanned my phone messages. Evan's received the first response: *Here now. Weather's fine.*

He came back immediately: *Same here. All settled. BTW: code is not necessary on this phone. It is secure.*

Really?

Seriously.

Right. Leaving that thread, I finally responded to Max's frantic demands for updates by explaining in code that it wasn't safe to describe anything right now. *They speak French and Arabic here*, I wrote. Referring to other languages was our way of saying that we couldn't write or speak freely. I added that the weather was fine since weather references indicated the safety factor and I didn't want him worrying.

He must have been waiting for a message from me and responded right away by letting me know that *The weather is clear in London but sunshine will be moving out that day*. Got it: reinforcement was heading my way. And I badly needed it. Forget this business of Phoebe rushing off to single-handedly rescue some unknown treasure on foreign soil. I knew I couldn't do this alone and, right then, I didn't want to try. I'd lost all the adrenaline that had propelled me to Marrakech. Now, all I felt was the chill of fear.

There were messages from Nicolina, too, but I'd let Evan keep her informed on my behalf. Presumably he could better figure out how to communicate with her without alerting the spy network.

Relieved, I shoved the gun and phone under my pillow, left the bathroom light on, and dropped over the velvet cliff into a deep sleep.

And awoke with a start, leaping from the bed with no idea where I was, my heart pounding. It took a few seconds to orientate myself. My watch said 12:33 a.m. Once my brain activated, I retrieved my gun and phone in seconds. Flicking on a lamp, I saw that nothing had disturbed my brass platter security system, yet something had obviously disturbed me—a loud noise, maybe. In my dream I recalled what could have been tapping sounds but now everything was quiet.

I grabbed the closest clothing on hand—my jeans, T-shirt, and jacket still draped over one of the chairs where they'd been tossed. With my bare feet shoved into sneakers, the gun in my bag slung over my shoulder, I carefully disengaged my alarm system and cracked open the door.

Outside it was surprisingly cool, the desert air descending in a frigid pall over the balcony. I crept to the railing and peered over. Below, the pool and the night-lights glowed but otherwise everything appeared deceptively peaceful.

As I crept down the tiled corridor, the full impact of being alone in a foreign land in an unsecured building hit. It's one thing to know this by the preternaturally bright desert light of day and quite another to have it settle around you in the dead of an Arabian night. Yet, by the time I'd padded downstairs to the bottom level, the seductive lighting and hushed beauty of the place calmed most of my fears. Almost. So what if a sound woke me up? Abrupt noises startled me from sleep in London all the time so why not in Marrakech? Anyway, there was another couple staying here some-where so it's not like I was alone. Maybe they just returned from a late dinner out.

My hand was throbbing and there was no way I could get back to sleep right away. Instead, I dashed back up to my room, retrieved the plated food, and returned to the bottom level, leaving my bedroom door locked with its useless ornate iron key. Seconds later, I had tucked myself into a back table slightly hidden behind a pillar facing the pool to devour my supper—a cold meat pie that looked vaguely like a Cornish pastie wrapped in phyllo with a side of fresh fruit. The whole thing was gone in minutes, finished off with a bottle of guava juice.

As I ate, I mused: What was I hoping to find in this building that hundreds of others before me may have sought and left empty-handed? There were only so many materials that consistently held value in centuries past and they were the same items that held value now: gold and jewels. What else would a wealthy family consider to be a worthy dowry, anyway?

On the other hand, how could any family hide something of such value for centuries in what may have once been the family home? But then again, where else would they hide it, considering that they lived in a world constantly threatening to annihilate them? If not their home, where? I couldn't imagine this long-ago Jewish family, obviously wealthy and maybe now catching the notice of a less tolerant sultan, risking burying it any place else. And *bury* had to be the operative word.

And it had remained in the Contini family for centuries and been transferred through the generations. That, too, was unusual. A Christian family owning property during uprisings in Morocco was almost as strange as Jews owning property under those same circumstances. On the other hand, Morocco had a history of being a tolerant Muslim country, a reputation of acceptance and coexistence, with the exception of occasional blips of religious persecution. Was it so far a stretch to believe that somehow alliances forged either through business or friendship had somehow helped to preserve this property and its secrets through the centuries intact?

That was the question. My gut said the story unfolded this way and that was all I had to go on at the moment. Following the union of the two families—the two religions—the Continis had been unable to return to Morocco to claim the dowry and had eventually forgotten the codes to finding it. If they'd tried in the last few centuries, they'd obviously been unsuccessful. Maria had tried, I was sure of that.

A chill ran over me. Supposing the ruthless gang knew about the riad and suspected that it may be here all along? What if they'd been here and tried to find it, were trying still? What if they thought they needed me? My throbbing hand testified to the lengths they'd go to retrieve it.

One way or the other, somewhere in this filigreed building, one that must have been renovated countless times before, lay a long-lost fortune that nobody had a clue where to find.

Leaving my plate on the table and with my phone in hand as a flashlight, I took myself on a reconnaissance mission around the lower floor. The little night-lights tucked under little brass wall sconces and in the alcoves everywhere made the extra light unnecessary but I didn't care. My phone was my security blanket even if it might track me and probably knew my very thoughts. Had Evan managed that trick yet?

Stepping into the first room off the courtyard brought me to the library. Well, now... I flashed my phone across the shelves of books, the paintings of desert scenes with the camels and sunsets, the smoldering fireplace, and realized that it would take hours to study this room alone.

Since there was no adjoining room, I stepped back into the courtyard and around the corner into another, this one with leather chairs and etched brass platter tables everywhere—the lounge? Back out again, I padded down the tiles to a door labeled Office— locked—and then through a pair of double spring doors beside it that led to a kitchen, all in a mix of marble and stainless complete with microwave and bake oven. Backing out, I next followed the entire perimeter of the pool, discovering that the rooms were only on one side of the building with the other consisting of a long wall decorated by textiles and panels of carved wood.

At the very back wall, an open door beckoned me on, a door that lead into a smaller roofed courtyard with a basin-sized marble fountain set into the center of an elaborate mosaic-tiled zellige of triangles and starbursts. I stepped up to the basin floating with rose petals and noticed two bowls sitting side by side on the blue tiles with a fat white cat busy lapping from one. The diner left its dish immediately to brush across my legs in a plume of soft fur. I sat down on the edge of the fountain and allowed myself a cat moment, indulging in the purring friendliness, oblivious to anything else except to vaguely note another room in front of me—door open, the final guest room.

Sometimes cats are better than men, I thought, deep in the comfort zone. "What's hidden here, kitty?" I mumbled into its fur. And then I heard a sharp crack that jolted me to my feet and the cat to the floor with an indignant mew. The sound came from overhead. Yes, definitely overhead because now I heard a deliberate chink-chink somewhere far above.

I bolted into the pool courtyard and all the way up the stairs. When I reached the top level of what I presumed to be the roof, the door was locked. Maybe I would have tried picking it if I knew how. On the other hand, if some unauthorized person was up there chipping away at something, did I really want to surprise them? My hand fell from the knob. No,

I didn't, even if armed. I was still feeling the heat after being nearly roasted alive.

Moments later, I was back in my room, tucked into bed with my clang-activated alarm in place, my gun under my pillow, and my phone on charge. I'd have pulled the covers over my head if I wouldn't have felt like a kid.

For some reason, I couldn't distinguish the line between brave and stupid just then.

❧ 16 ❧

The next morning I read my texts while huddled under the shade of one of the roof's potted palms.

Nicolina had sent the first:

Phoebe, I know where you are. You should not be there alone but we cannot help right now. The warehouse has burned, maybe too much to be restored, and tomorrow the funeral for Maria goes forward. All so devastating! And for you very dangerous. These people are monsters! Be careful, my friend. Evan says it is safe to text you. Please respond. I worry. XXX. N

I typed back a quick response: *So sorry, Nicolina. Too many losses!*

Then I went on to read Evan's: *No sign of bad weather. I'm hoping it hasn't all blown your way.*

Shit. I looked up from my screen and gazed out across the medina. Was the gang keeping a low profile after the arson stint or had they followed me here? I had the sickening feeling that they knew exactly where I was and why.

"Yoohoo! You know what they say about those people who spend all their vacays stuck to their phones."

I looked up at the bright blur of orange waving at me from the other side of the roof. Pocketing my phone, I applied a smile to my face along with my sunglasses and strode over to join her by the railing. June and Joe

Meredith from Vancouver were apparently thrilled to have someone to talk to since the riad had been mostly empty for days. They wanted to adopt me, it seems. "But I'm not on 'vacay,' June. Like I said, I'm working."

"Working? You're a writer, aren't you? It's not like a real job with a boss or something. Look, we're thinking of taking one of those camel trains into the desert tomorrow and staying overnight in a tent—" June was gazing out toward the Sahara "—and we'd love you to come with us as our guest. Joe could nab us the tickets."

"Sure thing, honey," Joe called. The paunchy middle-aged man with the air of perpetual resignation toasted us with a tiny cup of Arabic coffee from a mound of pillows.

"Joe thinks he's a sultan." June laughed. "Look at him there. Sit up, darling. You'll dribble all over your Ralph Lauren," she called.

"Thanks but no thanks." I smiled. "I mean, I appreciate the offer but I have research to do right here."

"Oh, come on. Wouldn't a voyage on an authentic camel train to meet with a genuine Berber tribe be just the thing? You could write a book about that."

A tourist camel ride to a Berber camp set up especially for show—how thrillingly authentic. "Actually, I'm well into my book now and what I really need is to settle down and do the research right here. My novel is set in a riad, you see. It's historic verisimilitude I'm after."

"Historic verisimilitude?" she said, verging on but not quite hitting a note of derision. Her smile was wide, her earrings—some kind of etched silver and dark wood dangles that I couldn't take my eyes from—shone below her short blond bob. The bright pink and orange of her silken pantsuit struck me as perfect for the climate but hard on the eyes. Attractive, probably in her early fifties, I almost liked her but at the same time couldn't wait for her to leave. "Look, Penny, there's the fascinating medina out there, you know? Surely you're not going to stay cooped up here all day and let it pass you by? At least come with us to the square this morning and take a look around."

"No, really," I said, my fixed smile making my cheeks ache. "I'm here to research and that's what I'll do. Thanks, though, really, but I'll be working."

Blowing a gusty sigh, she swung around. "Okay, Joe, I can't talk sense into this one. Let's get going."

"Let me finish my coffee first." Mohammed, the lean young man who slipped ghost-like around the riad taking care of our every need, was just refreshing Joe's cup.

"It's, like, your third dose already. Leave it and let's go."

Yes, please do. Returning to my chair, I picked up my teacup—a glass set into a filigreed brass holder—and returned to skimming *The Complete History of Marrakech* written by Pierre M. Maison in 1826. Only a writer of that age could believe that history could be complete instead of a single perspective frozen within the amber of time, understanding, and circumstances. What made Pierre's perspective interesting, however, was his line sketches of the city almost two centuries earlier. And, I thought, comparing his map of the medina with the modern tourist version, it didn't look as though it had changed all that much in some quarters.

Keeping my head down fixed on the book seemed to seal the deal with the Merediths. A reading person must seem so dull to them. In any case, they finally left, after which I got up and prowled the roof looking for signs of whatever had awoken me the night before. Something like chipped tiles or a pile of crumbled stucco shoved into a corner would do nicely but nothing appeared amiss. No obvious signs of chiseling or hammering anywhere, either. If someone had been up here banging away last night, they'd tidied up after themselves.

"Miss Martin?"

I looked up from inspecting the grout around one of the beautiful blue tiles to see Shada standing nearby. "Call me Penny. I just love these tiles," I said, getting to my feet. "Are they very old?"

"I don't believe so, maybe a few decades."

"When was the riad last renovated?"

"I am not certain but not since I've been here. Penny, forgive me but I noticed your hand." She stepped forward, pointing to my wounded member, which I had laid bare to the elements the night before.

Looking down at my reddened flesh, I realized that the swelling had increased. "I cut myself—careless, really."

"Pardon me for interfering but I think you need to have that tended. Wounds like that can easily get infected here. Perhaps a salve and to keep it wrapped would be better? There are pharmacies in the medina or I could ask someone to come here. It is no trouble."

She seemed genuinely concerned. "Thank you, Shada. I promise that if it's not better by this afternoon, I'll take you up on your offer." She nodded and slipped away.

Meanwhile, I studied the wound in the sunlight, noticing a bit of festering around the edges. Not good.

But I chose to shove it out of my mind for the rest of the morning and part of the afternoon in order to dive into the library's resources, most of which didn't exceed a couple of centuries old but which still made fascinating reading. Besides, it was comfortable in the library with its plush chairs, shelves of books, and endless supply of mint tea. The noticeable absence of bad guys wanting to roast me alive was a definite plus.

After plenty of tea sipped from filigreed cups and a perfect lunch of soup and salad served in the pool area, my hand gave up on throbbing and launched a brutal stabbing campaign. I checked my watch: 2:25. Where was my reinforcement?

Meanwhile, I met Ingram, a bearded young man with merry eyes and an obvious appreciation of pastry who bowed slightly when Shada introduced us and said he would be happy to take me to the medina along with some version of my every wish being his command.

"I'll wait, thanks."

Ingram and Shada exchanged worried glances. And then, at 3:10, my waiting was over. A bell rang and soon a very tall black woman dressed in a startling bright turquoise belted robe with a backpack slung over her shoulder stepped into the riad.

It was all I could do not to shout my delight, but through some unspoken agreement, we pretended not to know one another. She grinned in my direction. "Hi ya."

"This is Miss Penelope Martin," Ingram introduced us, "an author, and this is Miss Peaches Williams." There was no way I wanted to correct him for the "Miss" thing.

Peaches eyebrows arched. "An author, wow, just wow. I've never met a real author before."

"Hi, call me Penny."

"So call me Peaches. My real name is Penelope, too. What a coincidence, hey? Peaches is the nickname my daddy gave me."

"Cute." I wasn't certain whether she was playing wide-eyed innocent or what, but Shada, obviously overwhelmed by the sight of a six-foot-tall black woman dressed in a caftan, seemed eager to take her new guest on the tour even before the welcoming tea had been served.

"I will show you the riad. Please follow me."

"Right on," Peaches said agreeably.

Remaining at pool level, I listened to Peaches's enthusiastic and knowledgeable commentary all along the route, her melodious voice echoing over the balconies and from even inside the library and lounges. "Wow, like, the *moucharabieh* screens are just out of this world—so intricate! And the gebs are, like, fantastic!" Well, buildings were her thing.

"Yes, thank you. The owners put every care into the details," I heard Shada say. "I'm afraid I don't recognize the word *geb*, though."

"That's the trim—all that gingerbread in the corners."

"Gingerbread?"

"Stuff they make in England with spices, a sweet bread, you know? I'm from Jamaica myself, though you wouldn't know it to see me. Thought I was from Sweden—ha, ha. We love gingerbread, too. I can make it for you sometime." A deep laugh followed, one that seemed to provoke a giggle from Shada.

They were moving up to the next levels now. "And here is your room," Shada said. Once they stepped inside, the conversation grew muffled.

"Nice but I prefer the one opposite the fountain in the little courtyard," Peaches said, emerging minutes later. "That okay? I'm shy, see, and like my privacy."

Yeah, right.

"Certainly. You may stay in any unoccupied room you want," I heard Shada say.

"Fantabulous. I'm just going to settle in, you know?"

"Certainly. We want you to be as comfortable as if this was your own home."

It was like listening to a radio play, ridiculously entertaining to me in part because I knew the protagonist was actually playing an enhanced version of herself.

I sent Ingram to fetch Mohammad for mint tea all around and settled down to a poolside table to wait. By the time Peaches had been registered and joined me, Shada was wrapped in a headscarf with a robe over her

Western clothes ready to exit. I realized then that she had been in a hurry to leave all along. Maybe it was a cultural misstep for a man to show a lady her room so she had to stay long enough for that.

"I do not work this afternoon but Ingram and Mohammed will take care of you." And with that she bowed and left. Mohammed, in the meantime, was slipping into the kitchen to fetch us a tray of pastries while Ingram had disappeared into the office.

Peaches sat down in the chair beside me and whispered: "So what the hell is going on?"

"I'll tell you later," I said. "What took you so long? I've waited for you all day."

"What took me so long? I went shopping in the medina and its friggin' fabulous, for one thing. Have you been? Like, I get the cabdriver to drop me off—he tried to take me to his uncle's carpet shop but I wasn't having that—and found this store that sells robes of every color you can imagine. I bought five! Serena told me there was no way I should come to Morocco in my stretchies. This being a Muslim country, I get that, but I can tell you, I've seen plenty of tourists in short-shorts that would make my threads look sedate. Don't people have respect?"

Stretchies was her word for the spandex and the leather body-hugging outfits she preferred. I leaned over. "You still don't exactly blend."

She grinned. "Think you do with your screaming red locks? Besides, I never blend, sister. Hey," she said, looking up, "here comes tea."

As Mohammed served the steamy mint brew, Ingram appeared with a map. "I have marked the place in the medina where the pharmacy is located, Miss Martin. Not very far. I have called to say you are coming. Ask for Shadiz. He will take care of your hand."

"Hand? What's wrong with your hand?" Peaches asked, whipping her attention from Mohammed's adroit tea-pouring techniques to my wounded member resting now out of sight on my lap.

"I burned it. On a stove," I added, bringing it into view. My injury looked far too severe for any minor household accident.

Peaches hissed. "So, like, I'll take her, Ingram. Pass me the map."

Ingram looked from one of us to the other. "I would be happy to—"

"No, no. I passed that place a short time ago—like something out of *Harry Potter*, right?"

The young man beamed. "Yes, miss, exactly!" Obviously the beloved wizard had reached even North Africa.

"Right. Come on, Penny. Let's get you some help," Peaches said, lifting from the chair by one elbow.

I insisted on at least changing from my jeans to loose trousers and a tunic top first (and to ensure my gun was packed deep in my bag) before allowing myself to be mustered out the door, through the alley, and into the malodorous courtyard. Peaches continued steering me by the elbow.

"I need a hat," I said.

"Forget the hat for now. What the hell happened?" she said the moment we were well away from the riad.

I provided my summary as briefly as possible, ending with my belief that the riad held the hidden dowry. "It's much more complex and serious than I ever anticipated. These bastards murdered Maria Contini and tried to kill me, too. Whatever it is, it must be valuable."

"Holy shit!" she exclaimed, slapping a hand over her mouth when a passerby cast her a sharp look. "You needed me before this. I told you I'd be your bodyguard, woman."

"I didn't think I'd need a bodyguard when I went to Venice," I protested as she steered me along. "Besides, I mostly have the skills to take care of myself. I'm just no match for a gang." The last one I dealt with were the Willies, of which her own brother had been the head. That we helped put both our criminal brothers behind bars might not have been the traditional bond of sisterhood but it worked for us.

"What were you doing going into that building alone, anyway?"

We were in an alley now, treading the winding path among tourists interspersed with robed locals and plenty of zipping mopeds. I hated those things. They were the auditory equivalent of motorized flies and made it damned hard to see if we were being followed. One zipped too close to me, this one of the expensive motorcycle variety, forcing me against a wall and putting me further on edge. I could have sworn that same red T-shirted guy had passed us at least twice before and that at least one helmeted motorcyclist made a couple of drive-bys, too. "I wasn't alone. Evan was waiting for me by the entrance. We were in touch every second. How'd I know they planned to torch the place?"

"So why didn't Muscle Man go in there with you? What kind of body-guard is he?"

"He didn't fit in the corridor," I said, "and neither would you, and he's not my 'bodyguard.' We're on the same side of this particular scenario, that's all."

"Well, I'm your bodyguard from here on in, got that? No foolin' around. Her Majesty has one, Sir Rupe has one, and now you have one." Her Majesty referred to Nicolina, not the queen.

"Sure but you are also our engineer and head contractor," I reminded her.

She snorted. "Multitasking is my game. As soon as the labor force gets their lazy butts back to work, I'll get back to the other job. I'm also part of our new enterprise so let me feel useful, will you? I don't know shit about art except that my brother traded drugs for the stuff. For now, I watch your back, sister. And maybe your hand, too." She had me by the wrist now, tugging me through the medina like a naughty child and I almost didn't mind. In these vulnerable moments, I was willing to temporarily take the back seat. "You're lucky you didn't get burned to a crisp and what's with trying to protect a book of fabric scraps—you crazy, woman?"

"It was a very valuable historic compendium of everything the Continis had produced, not 'fabric scraps.' I—"

"Wait, I think this is it." She dropped my hand and took out the map.

We both stared at the building before us, a partially open-air shop painted bright blue with jars and unidentifiable bottled things lining the front. Strange objects dangled in the breeze—gourds, calabashes, and at least one rare cat pelt. "That's a pharmacy? It looks like a Chinese medi-cine shop crossed with something right out of *Harry Potter*, like you said."

"Yeah," Peaches said. "The North African Harry Potter magic shop—a Berber pharmacy. I've seen different pharmacies all over Africa but I've only just heard of the Moroccan ones. How cool is that?" While Peaches had been studying engineering in London, she had taken several trips to the southern African continent in search of her roots. Her face broke into a wide grin. "Let's go."

"I think I'd prefer a Boots about now."

"You nuts? These guys are like one of the oldest pharmacies on earth. Half of the pharmaceutical stuff is based on these potions. They're like medicine men and they can certainly tend to a wounded paw like yours. Come along, Phoebe."

"Penny," I reminded her, stepping forward.

"Penelope's my real name, too, remember?"

"I didn't choose it, Evan did."

"I got to meet this Evan guy. Sounds like a piece of work."

Inside, the shop was a fascinating blend of the cosmetic, the medicinal, the magical, and everything in between. Cones of colored powders caught my attention right away and for a moment I was oblivious to the beautiful woman with the perfect skin who stepped before me describing the benefits of argan and rose oil, a jar held in each hand. "Sure, I'll take both," I mumbled, heading for the color wall.

"Penelope," Peaches called. "Bring your paw here to meet Shadiz."

I turned. Peaches was standing beside a man in a kind of turban and a white robe, one arm slung over his shoulder. Both were beaming as if they'd just encountered a long-lost friend.

"Shadiz, thank you for seeing me," I said moments later as we were ushered into a back room and to what could have been an examining table had it not been covered in some kind of dust. Shadiz spent a few moments cleaning up, Peaches assisting as if it were the most natural thing in the world. I was instructed to rest my hand on a length of clean white cloth while Shadiz inspected it, muttering to himself in Arabic all the while.

"I think he's saying it's not good," Peaches remarked.

"Not good but not deadly. Shadiz fix," the man assured me with an encouraging smile. "This happened how?"

"I burned it on the stove."

"But there is a deep cut there also," he said, studying my hand intently.

"I'm a mess in the kitchen," I said. "I cut myself with a knife, too."

"Tell him truth. We need friends here, Phoeb, and Shadiz is a friend." Peaches was staring at me—I mean, seriously staring.

"I will do you no harm," he said, placing a hand over his heart. "It is my pledge to Allah. Speak the truth and I will help you. Healing is in my hands."

Try arguing against that. "Fine. I have a ruthless gang of thieves following me who have already killed one person. They think I may lead them to something important and maybe I already have—or close, anyway. Now it seems they want me dead, too."

Shadiz straightened. "You have my protection." In a moment, he stepped out, returning moments later with a basin of fragrant water, the lovely cosmetics saleswoman with him carrying a tray of implements and unguents.

"While I work, please read the wall and Fatima will translate."

I gazed up at the wall to my right, realizing for the first time that there was writing in gold script above the shelves. Fatima began translating.

"O mankind! There has come to you a good advice from your Lord, and a healing for that which is in your hearts. And We send down from the Quran that which is a healing and a mercy to those who believe."

And while she read, Shadiz drained the infection from my wound with a quick stab of something I hoped was sterilized—I didn't look—and bathed my hand in a dish of warm, fragrant water. Next, he applied a pungent ointment and wrapped my hand in a length of gauze. Yes, it hurt like hell and yet it felt soothing at the same time. Unaccountable, I know, but there you have it. When he was finished, my hand felt much better and I believed it would heal at last. Magic, belief, a higher power—who knew?

"Thank you, Shadiz. What do I owe you?" I asked.

"When I do God's work, I do not take payment." Then he bowed.

Unable to thank him in any other way, I went shopping in the main store, purchasing pots of dye powder, argan oil and rosewater bath oils, herbs, a package of real saffron, eucalyptus rubs, and an assortment of frankincense, jasmine flower, and musk, avoiding the dried hedgehog and chameleon bits. I was probably overcharged for the whole lot but I didn't care. When I finished paying for my treasures, Peaches had disappeared.

"In back room with Shadiz. Everything okay," Fatima assured me as she turned to help the two Swedish backpackers looking for a snoring aid. That left me to further explore the shop of wonders, marveling at some things, wincing at others, until I stopped dead by the front door. The man leaning against the parked moped outside was definitely the same one who'd streaked past us on our way over—swarthy skin, a red sports shirt worn over jeans, a skim of a beard. To me he looked exactly of the same ilk as those who had terrorized me in Venice. I ducked back into the shop.

"Fatima, where's Peaches?"

She pointed toward the back of the store. Dropping my parcels on the counter, I dashed through multiple rooms and through a beaded curtain until I found Peaches and Shadiz head-to-head in some kind of intense negotiation.

"Penny," Peaches said, obviously delighted with something. "Shadiz will get me a knife."

"A knife? What good's a knife?"

"Yeah, that's what I said but he doesn't deal in AK-47s or guns of any kind. A knife will have to do. I'm pretty good with one actually." Then she caught my look of alarm and added: "Kidding, just kidding, about the guns, anyway!"

"Forget the guns! There's a guy out front who followed us all the way from the riad. He's waiting for us to come out now. Tell me what good a knife's going to do us there? We can't go outside and stab him!" Admittedly, I was overreacting. Blame the trauma of the last few days. I turned to Shadiz. "Is there a back way out?"

"You expect us to run?" Peaches's expression had turned murderous. She spun around and strode through the curtain, Shadiz and I scrambling after her. We practically had to run to catch up, which we couldn't do until she was out the door, across the alley, and had taken some little man by the scruff of the neck. Only not the right little man, as it turned out. That one had disappeared.

"That's not him!" I cried.

The little man was squealing and crying out in Arabic at this tall Amazon who had suddenly accosted him. Peaches released him and he fell to the dust. In seconds, he was on his feet and scurrying down the alley.

"I know that man. He delivers packages for me." Shadiz shook his head sadly. "This will not be good."

"Damn," Peaches muttered. "I planned to just scare him, you know?"

"And here comes the cavalry," I said.

There were two uniformed men marching down the street toward us with the delivery man beside them pointing at Peaches. While we stood waiting for an encounter, Shadiz stepped forward, hands raised, laughing. He spoke to the officers as if it was all a big joke, a huge misunderstanding —ha, ha. The officers appeared unconvinced. Probably had the attacker been anyone but a very tall black woman, the matter would have been smoothed over more quickly. As it was, Shadiz had to do a lot if talking while apparently appeasing his delivery driver.

"Morocco is one of the few countries in Africa with serious racist issues against darker skins," Peaches said under her breath. "But not so bad here in Marrakech, I hope. And me being female and stronger than most of these guys doesn't help. That's two counts against me. A couple of dudes called out 'Obama' when I was walking by on my way over."

"That's a compliment, isn't it?"

"I doubt they meant it that way."

We fell silent when Shadiz returned with his arm over the shoulders of the trembling delivery man. "Kamal, please meet my friends, Peaches and Penny. They were attacked by a bad man earlier and you look just like him. Isn't that amusing? I am sure Peaches is sorry to have frightened you."

"Yes, I am, Kamal. Very sorry," Peaches said, bowing as if trying to shrink to the man's height. "Will you forgive me?"

Kamal squirmed in Shadiz's embrace but his employer gripped him tight. "We forgive, yes, my friend? Allah wishes us to forgive so all is forgiven."

One of the officers spoke in rapid Arabic, obviously unamused, but finally Kamal threw up his hands mumbling something in Arabic and suddenly the party was over. Shadiz ushered us back into the shop and called for tea, which was served in yet another back room. Then he left us alone.

Which suited me because I was shaken. "They know where I am."

"I thought it was a case of mistaken identity?" Peaches asked, sipping her tea. "Think I'm going to love this stuff eventually. Hell, that was close. Did you see how armed those cops were?"

"You tried to throttle the wrong man but the guy I saw earlier was definitely one of them. I never really got a good look at any of them except to notice that the three guys looked so much alike they could have been brothers. They all had the same wiry build and short hair. That was one of them, I'm sure if it."

"Yet he took off."

"Probably saw me from the window. Look, let's get back to the riad. We have work to do."

"We have to come back later and pick up the knife. Shadiz has to have it brought in tonight after dark but he's open until 9:00."

"What do you need a knife for?"

"Protection obviously."

"But I have a gun."

"Good for you but that still leaves your bodyguard defenseless. No, I'm getting me a knife."

We thanked Shadiz, gathered our bundles, and left. This time my bodyguard kept surveying every passerby our entire way back through the medina but neither cyclist made another appearance. Still, any little thing made me uneasy now. They were in Marrakech, I was sure of it, and every robed man, every veiled woman, could be one of them. What would they do next?

"They must know where we're staying," I whispered as we crossed the stinky chicken courtyard heading for the riad. "That may be one of them I heard chinking away last night."

"Yeah, maybe. From what you've told me, they must know you're here if your stuff was bugged and everything. We just have to make sure they don't get to the booty before us."

Which wasn't going to be easy. Back at the riad, Ingram met us at the door, relieved to see my bandaged hand and that we'd had such a good shopping episode. Though we insisted that we were just going to relax indoors for the rest of the afternoon, he and Mohammed were so attentive that it was challenging getting down to serious investigation without being observed. And then there was the housekeeping staff busy mopping the tiles and cleaning the rooms.

Finally, we resolved on a room-by-room assessment with at least one of us posted at the door at all times. "We'll make like we're playing chess together or something, you know, new best buds," Peaches said. "Let me go have a shower and change into my stretchies. Then we can get down to work."

"We should start upstairs and work down," I whispered.

"I know you heard chipping up there last night but nobody in their right mind is going to hide something for seven hundred years on a roof," Peaches pointed out. "That thing would have been repaired and then repaired some more, as in multiple times. Whatever's hidden here has to be on the floor level. That's why I chose the lower bedroom."

I saw her logic. "Fine, we'll start in the library." I held my phone before her eyes. "See this? No ordinary phone, this. Evan provided a cheat sheet for all its special features and I'm sure he mentioned something about an X-ray app."

"Are you kidding me?" she said, plucking it from my hands. "Never saw an X-ray app on iTunes."

"And you won't. The man's a genius. He invents all these fabulous effects in his spare time, when he's not protecting Rupert and reading, that is. Anyway, meet me back in the library once you've freshened up."

I retrieved my phone and took off to my bedroom to read the cheat sheet. I stared at the pages and pages of tiny print script, totally befuddled. Where I expected bullets and point form, there were paragraphs and diagrams. I shook my head, stuffing the pages back into my bag until later. Next, I started to unpack my treasures and was applying an argan cream to my parched skin when my phone pinged. Nicolina. *I found something important in the documents. Having it couriered to the riad today.*

Found what? I texted back. When the answer didn't come immediately, I dashed downstairs, meeting Ingram on his way up. "Would you like to have supper prepared here, Miss Martin?"

"Yes, sure. Ingram, how often do couriers come to the riad?"

"As often as necessary, miss. Are you expecting something?"

"A parcel from Venice but it's already almost 5:00 p.m. How late will they deliver?"

"That depends on the sender, miss. I've known them to come very late at night."

"But what if you're not here and the riad is locked up for the evening?"

"Then the courier will ring the bell. Maybe he delivers it tomorrow." He spread his hands.

"That won't do. I need it tonight. It could be very important."

"I will leave a sign on the door if it is after 7:00 and say to ring bell. Excuse me, I will go tell the kitchen to prepare supper now. Maybe a chicken tagine, miss?"

"Sure, sure—anything is fine." I was too stirred up to worry about mere food. Moments later I was knocking on Peaches's door. For a moment, I inhaled the rose fragrance wafting up from the tinkling fountain and tried to just breathe. Empty bowls sat nearby but the cat had disappeared.

The door opened and there stood Peaches enveloped in a white bathrobe with her face smeared in cream and a cat in her arms. "Meet Fadwa, the house cat. I'm giving this argan stuff a try. Apparently it's made from the undigested nut droppings of tree-climbing goats. Can't beat that for a selling point, hey? What's up?"

I stepped inside a room much like mine only wider and, if possible, even more luxurious, the Moroccan version of the presidential suite. "Nicolina texted me to say that she's couriering me something from Venice. It's supposed to arrive tonight."

"Well, that's good, isn't it? Let me wash this stuff off. Here, you take Fadwa. Keep talking. I can hear you from the bathroom."

"It's good that she found something, yes, but what if the courier's intercepted?" I leaned against the bathroom door stroking the cat. "I mean, that guy tailed us this morning, which must mean they're watching the riad. Supposing the courier comes to deliver the parcel and the thugs jump him and steal whatever it is?"

"Wow, you're, like, one step ahead of me and halfway down the road." She stepped out of the bathroom wiping her face. "So, like, we'll have to watch for him, won't we? Give me a sec to change and we'll get to work."

Peaches didn't do secs, she did ages.

Fadwa took off and I spent the time studying the paperbacks Peaches had left scattered on her bedspread—three of them, each with a bare-chested man on the cover. From there I went on to answering Max's latest weather-related text, assuring him that the sky was still clear—how often would that change in Morocco?—and that a high had blown in just today. If he were to suspect even half of what had happened, he'd hop a plane in a shot, which would only complicate things. As far as my texts to him were concerned, the weather would remain grand. Finally, I pulled out Evan's sheets and strained my eyes looking for descriptions of an X-ray app.

"Apparently it's activated by pressing on an eye icon," I told Peaches when she finally emerged from the bathroom.

"Cool."

Minutes later, I watched as she strolled around the little courtyard, studying the foundations intently in her black bodysuit with a loose silk overblouse, no doubt in courtesy to Muslim modesty. "This part of the riad's original," she remarked just seconds before the five o'clock call to prayer sounded.

"How do you know?" I said after the call had finished.

"There's no indication that the foundations have been significantly disturbed in centuries, see? Before I came, I dug up this article on traditional riad construction and they all had a big central courtyard where the pool is now and often smaller ones of washing or housing animals like this. Also, take a look at those timbers up there."

Craning my neck, I gazed overhead. "Old."

"Very. These desert climates can preserve wood for centuries. Looks like parts have been repaired like that strut over there but basically she's the same."

"Ladies, supper will be served at 7:00 by the pool."

We turned to find Ingram standing there smiling. So far the man seemed oblivious to any undercurrents between his guests, probably just delighted that we were getting along so swimmingly.

"We'll be ready," I told him. He nodded and backed out.

That left us almost two hours to search, beginning with the lounge, which came up solid with no false walls. Next, we moved to the library where Peaches paced out the perimeters with my X-ray app in hand while I tapped on the walls behind the books.

"I'm seeing nothing suspicious, either. How sensitive is dis thing, anyway?" Peaches asked.

"I have no idea." I unfolded Evan's cheat sheet to study the instructions again. "He says it will detect metal in stone and concrete within a distance of three feet."

"So, not all that ground-penetrating." Peaches was running my phone up and down every wall in a kind of grid pattern. "Dis man must be some kind of wonder."

"You're lapsing into dialect again."

She straightened, shook back her cornrows, and grinned. "Yeah, I am. Tell me about this Evan."

"There's nothing to say. He's been Rupert's bodyguard and right-hand man for as long as I've known him—ex-MI6. Ridiculously talented."

"Single?"

"I guess."

"Good-looking."

"I suppose."

"And a genius, too, you said." Then Peaches slapped her thigh and roared with laughter, waving the phone in the air with her other hand. "Nothing to say about him, right? Woman, you crack me up!"

"Why?" Truly, I didn't get it. I was just stating facts.

"Well, what's going on here? Did we miss a party?"

We turned, stunned to find June and Joe standing in the doorway, the library looking as though it had been hit by an investigation squad. Whole shelves of books sat on the chairs while I stood in the center of the room holding the cheat sheet.

Peaches flipped a wave at them from the fireplace. "Hi ya. I'm Peaches Williams. You must be the Merediths."

"Yes, June and Joe." June stepped forward, looking around.

"What have you girls been up to in here?" Joe asked.

"Waiting to grow into women, I guess," Peaches quipped.

"Checking the structure," I said quickly. "Peaches is an engineer and we got to talking about authentic riad construction and decided to check it out." I hated feeling defensive but crud.

"Seriously?" June was gazing at Peaches with undisguised suspicion. "You're an engineer? Where do you work?"

"London. Where do you work?" Peaches pocketed the phone and strode toward her, still smiling but wearing an undeniable look of challenge.

June backed up, applying a grin brighter than her lipstick. "I'm retired. Sorry if I sounded confrontational. You just startled us, that's all. We were just coming in for a rest before going to dinner tonight. Maybe you'd both like to join us? We're going to a restaurant right off the Djamaa el Fna. Be our guests, why don't you?"

"We can't," I said, entering the fray. "We've already arranged for supper here at the riad. Some other time, perhaps."

Peaches swung around and began replacing the books, Joe helping. "Yeah, some other time."

After the Merediths had taken off for the evening and we'd devoured the chicken tagine with warm flatbread served with an orange almond salad, we began investigating the rest of the lower rooms. The staff were cleaning up after supper in the kitchen, which left us more freedom to work.

"I don't think we can find anything this way," I said, frustrated after we had run the X-ray app over the lounge and nearly the whole parameter of the lower floor. "Maybe it isn't hidden behind the walls, after all?"

"Where else would it be?" Peaches said, looking up from where she crouched on the floor. "It has to be somewhere near the foundations or in the floor itself. No place else makes sense."

"We need that envelope Nicolina sent. Where's that courier?"

"Did Her Majesty say anything more on what's coming?"

"No, except to say it was an envelope and very important."

I stepped out into the pool courtyard, now lit in candlelight and fili-greed lanterns, and strode to the door as I had at least five times over the past couple of hours. Now that dark had fallen, it was less likely that a courier could reach the riad safely. Cracking open the door, I peered outside. Quiet, the overhead motion lights briefly flicking on to illuminate the narrow alley. Damn.

When I returned to the courtyard moments later, Ingram was waiting for me dressed in his jacket. "Miss, will you be needing anything else?"

"Just that courier."

"I will check the main roads on my way home but I am certain it will come tomorrow morning for sure. Do not worry."

And I was equally sure that it would not come in the morning and that I should damn well worry. If it didn't arrive that night, it meant someone had intercepted it. "Thank you, Ingram."

Moments later, Peaches and I were alone in the riad. She bounded into the courtyard with her arm draped in fabric.

"I'm going to make a dash for Shadiz's and get me that knife. Are you coming?" She was shrugging on her long robe and wrapping a scarf around her head, fastening part of the fabric over her mouth like a veil. "A guy in the souk showed me this. I'll show you, too. I bought you one on the way here." Out came a scarf a lovely shade of green shot with iridescence—not my style but gorgeous. "Cactus silk, they called it, if you can believe that. Hold still while I wrap it on your head. There."

"You look very mysterious," I said through my veil.

"You, too. That's the idea. These Muslim women are on to something. Come with me tonight."

"No way. I've got to wait here for that courier. Do you need my gun?" I asked, lowering the mouth covering.

"Keep it. I'll scare the bejesus out of any of these mini dudes that might try to jump me. Would you jump me dressed like this?"

"A six-foot veiled Wonder Woman? No way."

"Right on. Be back within the hour."

I couldn't talk her out of leaving but watched her stride down the alley with a pit of nails in my gut. "Be careful!" I hissed.

"You be careful!" she called back.

But I wasn't the one stepping outside the safety of the riad. Back inside, it was just me alone inside the building. I returned to my room, admired my scarfed self in the mirror, and decided to wear it for now. I changed into jeans and my jacket complete with the gun loaded with a fresh round of bullets, pocketed my phone, and returned to the courtyard to wait and work. At least my hand had stopped throbbing, my stomach was full, and I almost felt fortified.

The desert night had chilled so much that unless I stood beside a heating pillar or remained inside one of the rooms, it was freezing. The staff had lit the fireplaces in the library and lounge areas but I continued to stride the perimeters of the central pool, now glittering like a jewel with its candlelit reflected water, using my phone app as a detecting device. Nothing but earth and maybe the occasional lost coin or buried earring revealed itself in ghost outlines under the tiles but maybe I'd missed something. I was distracted. Twice I went to the door to check the alley. Twice I saw nothing.

I was midway along my second round when I heard a cry. My head jerked up and I listened, fear prickling my spine. It came from outside the riad—not a cat sound this time but definitely human. Drawing my gun, I ran to the door and poked my head out. At the end if the alley a motorcycle lay with its back wheel spinning up the dust.

With the safety off and my gun raised, I crept to the end of the alley, peering out from behind the wall at what looked to be a deserted courtyard lit by one streetlamp and a moon far above. No humans in sight but that had to be the courier's motorcycle with the saddlebag carriers lying there.

The locals drove mopeds, not that expensive bit of machinery abandoned in the dust. Then I heard a thump followed by a mew of pain.

I took a step farther into the courtyard. Only then did I see the second motorcycle on its kickstand and a man sprawled facedown in the dirt. Another man stood over him, a knife gleaming in one hand and a large brown envelope in the other—my envelope!

He caught sight of me and sprung forward, the knife raised. I caught a flash of a dark scar across his face and an angry twisted mouth.

"Like hell!" I aimed the gun and fired at his leg, the impact causing him to spin around in a wail of shock and pain, dropping the knife in the process. "Give me that envelope, you murderous bastard!" I said, lunging forward, but he recovered enough to spring at me, giving my face such a wallop that it sent me sprawling onto the ground.

Seconds later, he had retrieved the knife and was hopping on his bike, zooming down the road as I stumbled over to the fallen driver. I didn't need to feel a pulse to know that sightless stare meant death. Damned if I was going to let that brute get away with that!

🟊 17 🟊

Nothing infuriates me more than violence inflicted on the innocent—that courier, Maria, me—let alone murdering, thieving bastards in general. And I damn well wanted that envelope back! I was too angry to sit quaking like a leaf inside the riad. When my temper detonates, I'm all in.

Only I wasn't some hotshot bike rider. I knew enough to get around on open roads but driving down a winding medina congested by stalls and people while following a moving target? Not in my skill set. I didn't even know where the headlight was at first. And the medina was alive with foot traffic, at least as busy in the evening as during the daylight hours with clusters of pedestrians clogging every path. Luckily, this pursuit wasn't about speed so much as keeping that bastard in sight. Which wasn't easy. I'd pulled up my mouth veil so at least the wild woman driving through the streets was somewhat incognito.

My bullet must have done plenty of damage because he seemed slower than I expected and unnecessarily reckless. Blood splattered the dirt as I wound through the paths, a trickle I could follow Gretel-style in some conditions. Pedestrians congesting the lanes meant I could never get close. Once, I saw him wobble into a stall of dates far ahead, sending mounds of dried fruit into the path and people screaming in all directions. I was blocked by a donkey hauling barrels and could only scream for the people ahead to be careful, that the man was dangerous. Whether they heard or not, I have no idea, but soon he was back on the bike, yelling at the stall owner and shooting a quick vicious glance over his shoulder before zipping off.

When I lost sight of him again, I panicked. Straddling the bike in a crossroads, I peered up the shadowy paths one by one, struggling to see a moving bike among the surge of evening shoppers. The stall lights illuminated only the faces of bystanders directly facing the shops. Everything else seemed like a heaving mass of shapes. To add to my distress, my jaw began to ache and my hand throb and I realized he'd hit me hard enough to cut my cheek.

For a moment, I struggled with uncertainty, a few seconds of dark night of the soul. Maybe I wasn't cut out for this badass stuff? Maybe I should just crawl back to the riad and call the cops? Who the hell did I think I was?

Then I heard a man shouting in Arabic with a group of elderly women in hijabs waving their hands in one of the lanes ahead. The women screamed, one of them swinging her shopping bag around as I zoomed up the lane in that direction. Forget uncertainty: I was going to get that bastard.

By the time I maneuvered through the shoppers, he was already well ahead and the press of buildings had opened into a huge square alive with flames, lights, and crowds—the Djamaa el Fna square, the original night circus in all its glory. Never in a million years did I expect to find myself hurling on a motorcycle in that crowded arena of wonders, glimpses of fire eaters and snake charmers whizzing past as I maneuvered around stalls and performers. He was trying to shake me by weaving in and out of the wagons and it was all I could do to stay upright in this raucous milling space. And people were shouting at me. "Slow down, lady!"—the only call I understood. Slow down? I was trying to speed up!

If it weren't for the women on the blankets, I would have lost him completely. I was just maneuvering between a snake charmer and a stall of candied oranges when I saw him far across the square being pulled from his bike by three women. I was too busy keeping one eye on the cobra rising from the basket on my right side to see exactly what was going on at first. It looked like the women, all in veils and hijabs, were trying to help him. No, wait, maybe not because the killer began shouting and trying to push them away—brute.

By the time I'd zoomed closer, I could see them pointing at his bloody leg and saw him kicking at the collection of little pots on their blankets. Henna artists! The struggle reached a pitch by the time I was within yards of them but by then the churlish idiot had seen me and was pushing the women away so fiercely that one stumbled back on her blanket. The others, now enraged, began screaming and pounding him with their fists. *Yeah, you give it to him, sisters.*

I eased closer, moving the bike with my feet. If I could only get them to hold him down while I grabbed the envelope... But suddenly he flung them off and pulled out that still-bloodied knife. The women backed up, circling around him as he climbed back on his bike, the knife still glinting in his hand, and his fierce gaze fixed on me.

By now we'd drawn a crowd.

I pulled down the mouth veil and yelled: "That man's a killer! He just murdered a man and he tried to kill me! Stop him, somebody!"

But the circle was widening, leaving the killer all the space he needed to take off, scattering the bystanders like bowling pins. Shit. That meant I had to chase him again. This time we wove around the last of the square traffic and burst onto an open rode.

An open road was preferable, maybe. At least I knew the basic rules of paved roads with cars and traffic, not that we followed any rules. The killer was swerving onto sidewalks or sandy shoulders any time the traffic backed up, which meant I had to do the same. I would have loved to blow out his back tire but who says you can shoot a gun while riding a bike?

At some point, he took off across a park along paved paths lined with rose borders and tall palms before diving back onto the road. He traveled at a good clip now, me following close behind, but his driving was crazy— nearly hitting a bench and ramming into a tree later. Once we dove through a date grove, which almost unseated me as we bumped along. He knew where he was going, I didn't, but the streetlights helped. I was so intent on keeping up that I was barely paying attention to anything else until we broke out onto a highway again.

We must have traveled straight for another ten minutes, which gave me plenty of time to figure out what I'd do if I caught him. He was failing, I could tell that much by his erratic driving. How long would it take for him to pass out? Maybe I'd wait until he was forced to stop and then take the envelope. Really, that's all I had, which didn't seem like much.

Now the traffic, the boulevards, the groves of oranges and dates, all looked the same until suddenly I realized that they had fallen away except for the occasional orchard. We were zipping on a highway straight into the desert. Don't ask me why that scared me. Hell, I was chasing a brutal killer so what was a little sand and nothingness? Maybe it had something to do with the fact that my fuel gauge had settled on empty. I was literally running out of gas.

Now what? Though there were occasional cars on the highway, a grove or two, I saw no gas stations and I could hardly pull over for a fill, and to make matters worse, I realized I'd picked up a tail. Another motorcyclist, this one in a helmet, was rapidly picking up speed. Maybe it was one of them and I was like a victim sandwich wedged between two killers. Shit!

Meanwhile, bastard number one had veered off the road into an orange grove, this one of the unlit variety. Determined not to lose him, I followed him in. It was dark and the ground uneven and soon I realized that I could no longer see his taillights, which meant he was probably off his bike and trying to trap me. Either that or had finally bitten the dust. And now the light of that other bike was bouncing through the grove right for me.

I came to a screeching halt, my heart stomping wildly as I jumped off the bike and dashed toward the trees, pulling out my gun along the way. I knew that the first guy would be waiting for me somewhere ahead, if he was still alert, while the second probably planned to block my escape. I had no intention of falling into either trap. Turning slowly around, I tried listening for the first bastard but that damn second motorcyclist was making too much racket. Slipping behind the shadowy trees, I crouched and waited.

Cyclist number two zoomed in behind my bike, jumped off his own, and made his way into the grove. That's when the shadow of the first guy staggered out from behind the palms and stumbled down the path toward him. If the first guy saw the second, he didn't show it, but then he was so bent over he could barely stand. How hard would it be to kick that bastard to the ground and retrieve my envelope? Only now I had to contend with the second biker, who had pulled out a gun. So I'd wait until the armed cyclist got close enough for me to shoot him in the knee, wait until he was disabled, and then retrieve my envelope from the first guy.

Or that was the plan. My attention fixed on the second cyclist, I watched as he strode closer to the stumbling man. The wounded guy spied him at last and lurched to a halt. I fully expected the two to greet one another other but instead the guy in the helmet lifted his gun and shot. I watched in horror as the wounded guy crumpled to the ground. The killer flung off his helmet and called out my name.

Damn, damn, damn! I jumped up and cried, "What the hell did you do that for, Noel?"

"Phoebe, are you hurt?"

"No, I'm not hurt, damn you! Did you kill him?" I ran up to the fallen man sprawled in the dust and felt his neck for a pulse. Dead. "Of course you killed him. You always do. Why do you always kill people?" I turned on him, waving my bandaged hand in his direction. "Why couldn't you have just wounded him like I did? You don't need to kill them dead every time, Noel."

He stared at me, stunned. "Hell, I should have invited him out for a beer, then—my bad. You kill them dead the first time, Phoebe. How many times have I told you that? If you just wound them, they'll come back for you, madder than ever, like this one did. Are you responsible for that mess of his leg?"

"I'm a crack shot now, and yeah, I nailed him in the leg, but you got him right between the eyes, I see." A clean shot. Hardly any blood. I wanted to upchuck into the bushes but kept it together.

"Always shoot to kill, Phoebe," he said between his teeth.

"Never!" I cried. "That's where we differ, on that and a million other things apparently. I will never shoot to kill unless I have to, got that? Even if they're murdering, brutal bottom-feeders trying to roast me alive like this one did."

"He tried to roast you alive? In that case, I'd kill him all over again, if I could." He spoke softly now. "Okay, so this isn't quite the welcome I'd expected from you. Good to see you again, too, Phoebe. What the hell is going on?"

"What's going on?" Okay, so I admit I wasn't exactly keeping it together just then. "You're supposed to be thousands of miles away on the run, as usual, not here stalking me, messing with my plans, not to mention my head. I had this under control, Noel. Who invited you to the party?"

He tossed down his helmet. "Are you kidding me? That guy had a knife in his hand. I probably saved your life."

"Look at him." I pointed to the corpse. "Does he seriously look like he could have done me any harm? He was maybe five minutes away from collapsing. Now I can't even question him, damn you. Did Rupert tell you where I was?"

"Rupert hasn't made contact with me since Jamaica. I always keep an eye on you, Phoebe. I told you I would."

"A tail on me, you mean. That has to end, Noel. I don't want you or some hireling stalking me."

He'd stopped, searching my face. "What's wrong? Look, Phoebe, I forgive you for setting Interpol after me, okay? I knew you had to do something about Toby and I accept that it meant I'd get snarled up as collateral damage."

"You weren't just collateral damage. I told you in Jamaica that either you turned yourself in and let me cut you a deal or they'd drag you to prison with my blessings."

His brows arched. "You seriously thought I'd agree to go to jail just so we could live some boring life together in the future?"

A knife couldn't stab deeper. "That was the choice, yes: live on the run or spend a dreary future with me."

"I didn't mean it that way."

"Yeah, you did. So you made your choice and I made mine."

"Look, woman, I've risked my bloody neck for you again and again but I will never willingly be caged up like some goddamn animal!"

"Got it. I also get that you've fallen way beyond the Robin Hood of the Art World crap and landed squarely in the midden heap of cheapo-sleazo art thieves."

"Cheapo-sleazo?" He swore with vehemence. "Haven't improved the adjectives, I see."

"It fits. Do you think I haven't figured out that you made off with the most valuable pieces in Jamaica, including the genuine Raphael? Do you think I don't know that you've become a crook of the worst kind, maybe *the* worst kind?"

"Since when did you become so damn self-righteous?"

"Since I realized what I really stood for and what I won't stand for any longer."

"Well, hell, aren't you the fierce little Pollyanna? I heard you were working with Interpol now. What are you doing for them, anyway—some kind of elite Barbie Doll agent chasing killers into the desert by yourself? I mean, seriously, are you kidding me? How dumb-ass is that? And what happened to your cheek?"

I swallowed hard, fighting back tears. There he was, my first real love, standing before me with his sharp-boned face tight with emotion and his eyes roiling pain, hurling insults at me. Even so, I knew it came from hurt and anger so I vowed to take the punches. "Forget the cheek. I want you to go away and never see me again. It's over, do you understand? We're not on the same side anymore. Don't come tracking me down unless you want me to call Interpol on you all over again."

"Whoa!" He lifted his hands. How I loved those hands once. Still did, maybe. Had to get over it. "Since when were we ever on the same side? We were just lovers caught in the line of fire, that's all, but in the big picture, I'll always be on your side, no matter what you say. Furthermore, we're kind of related, remember, my father being your godfather? I'll never be out of your life, so live with it."

Now the tears were rolling down my face in earnest. "If you ever see Max again when I'm anywhere near, we'll make like distant relatives. Otherwise, it's over, believe me, though how can it be over when we never really started? You'd just drop into my life long enough for us to fall into one another's arms—the once a year passion extravaganza—and then be gone. Talk about messing with my head. I'd stay longing for you for months afterward, hanging on for a postcard or a tip that you were off stealing something somewhere or at least still alive. That's a relationship? That's hell! When I said it was over, I meant it." And then because I couldn't just stand there blubbering, I added: "I was managing this by myself, by the way. Barbie's learned to handle a gun, defend herself in martial arts, and kick ass when she needs to, starting with yours. Get with the times, bozo."

He laughed, if you can call it that. "Bozo—got to love it. And how many degrees do you have, Miss Word Virtuoso?"

We stood facing each other, a dead man and a thousand light-years between us, while orange blossoms punched fragrance into the air and two motorcycles beamed light into the darkness. He looked haggard and pained. I felt broken and bruised. Emotion was draining from me faster than the dead man's blood, leaving me cold and brutally alone.

I wiped my eyes on my sleeve. "I need to get something off him. He knifed a courier and stole it from me. That's why I chased him."

Crouching, I felt under the dead guy's shirt where I could see the outline of an envelope. Pulling it out, I stuffed it under my own shirt. "Thank God it's intact."

"What is it?"

"I'm not sure. Nicolina couriered it from Venice."

"Ah, yes, the killer countess. Do you want to go back to my place and check it out?"

"Your place? Do you have a flat around here or something?" My arms encompassed the desert, the grove.

He grinned. "Not exactly, but I do have a tent strapped to the back of the bike. That's where I've been staying while here, which is why I look so ungroomed, in case you haven't noticed. Haven't had a shower in days."

I was trying not to notice anything more about him than I had to. "I'm not going into a tent with you, Noel. I have to get back to the riad as soon as possible. Peaches will be frantic. Oh, hell, I've got to text her that I'm okay."

I dug my phone out of my pocket and stared at the screen's upper right-hand corner in dismay. "No signal!"

"We're in a desert, remember?"

"This should be a satellite phone!"

"So maybe the satellite's busy or something."

I looked over at him as he wiped down my bike. "What are you doing?"

"Eliminating your fingerprints with bleach. I carry it everywhere in desert climes. That knife of his is probably covered in the courier's blood, right?"

I nodded.

"So, I'll leave that and wipe the courier's bike clean, leave the killer's. How many people saw you riding tonight?"

"Probably half of the Djamaa el Fna square but I had my scarf up." Or part of the time.

"Clever. They'll never clue in that a Westerner with a strand of flaming red hair sticking out might be you. At least they won't find the bikes or the body until morning. Let them figure out what happened. With luck, you'll be gone by then. Do you know who these guys are?"

"No, only that they've been tracking me since Venice—four of them, three men and a woman, now two men and a woman. I'm positive they killed Maria Contini."

"I found some things out for you that you might find useful: turns out they're all part of the same family with close ties here in Marrakech. Whatever they're after, they've been hunting it for decades and, make no mistake, they think it's rightfully theirs."

"How much do you about this, anyway?"

"Enough. Where's the courier's body?"

"Outside the riad. If Peaches comes back and finds it, there will be trouble. She was going back into the medina to buy a knife and they already think she's an anomaly."

"If they find her with that knife, they'll probably throw her in jail."

"You were the second cyclist tailing me today."

"Just watching your back, Phoebe. Come, we'd better get you to the riad. Climb on."

Like I wanted to be that close to him after all that was said but I was beyond arguing. Instead, I fastened on his spare helmet and climbed on behind him, half sitting on the mound of his tent duffel, and wrapped my arms around his waist.

"I knew I'd get your arms around me tonight somehow," he said as we zoomed off toward the highway.

✤ 18 ✤

I t was a good thing that he couldn't see my tears as we zipped toward Marrakech. If hearts were weighted, mine would have dragged that damned bike to a halt. And the man I wrapped my arms around was a lot thinner than I remembered. What had he been through during these months since he broke with his partner in crime—my brother—and escaped from Jamaica leaving all possibility of a decent life and the woman he supposedly loved behind? Whatever, he'd made his choice. Now all that was left for me was to heal the gaping wound after I'd made mine.

Twenty minutes later, the bike slowed as we approached the chicken courtyard. It was nearly eleven o'clock and at last the traffic was thinning around the city, leaving an unnerving quiet. I expected to see police cars hemming the lanes around the riad, anything except this deadly stillness.

At the end of the lane, deep in the shadows, he cut the engine and I dismounted.

"No body," I whispered.

"Did you think they'd just leave it in the dust for people to walk around?" He climbed off and wheeled the bike behind a broken wall.

"Of course not." I watched him unfasten his duffel and toss it over his shoulder. "I expected to see crime tape or something but there's no indication that there was ever a murder here. What are you planning to do—pitch your tent in the courtyard?"

He grinned that devilish grin of his. "Of course not. I intend to go around to the back streets and scale the walls to your riad's roof like I've been doing for the last two nights. It's a four-foot climb from a tassel shop and then over a few tiled houses to the riad's wall—damn simple. It's worked out rather well as long as I go to roost after the staff closes up for the night."

"That was you I heard up there?"

"I was trying to open a can of beans. Look, let me into your room long enough to take a shower tonight, will you? I promise not to threaten your virtue. Like you say, it's over. No worries."

"No worries—seriously? What if somebody sees you?"

"So? Is the place crawling with morality police or something? Tell them you picked up a local for a night of fun. I don't care. I can pass as Moroccan. Doesn't matter since I'll be gone by dawn."

I thought over all the possible reasons not to oblige him but anything I came up with didn't work. I'd really rather not have his tempting freshly steamed body anywhere near mine but all he wanted was a shower.

"Besides," he added, "I'm there to keep an eye on you, and if you think you've beaten these guys because one's down, you're kidding yourself. They're out there still and I'm guessing mad as hell. They want whatever's hidden inside this place and obviously whatever's up your shirt—I wouldn't mind having some of that myself, but hands off, I get it. Trouble's just begun."

He did have a point. "Wait for me on the roof and I'll come up as soon as the coast is clear. Can you unlock the door from the outside?"

He grinned. "Of course I can. I can pick anything open except maybe your rusted heart."

So that was how it was going to be now—sniping quips? Well, fine. I pushed past him, relieved that he kept watching me right up until I had inserted the key and tapped in the code. Minutes later, I was inside the courtyard facing Peaches and the Merediths.

"Where were you, Ms. Martin? We've been worried to distraction!" June rounded on me and all I could see were those pink nails sailing through the air as if to squeeze my shoulder or pat my cheeks or stab my eyes out, take your pick. I stepped back. "We almost called the police." She stopped. "What happened to your face?"

Peaches stepped between us. "We were worried. You hadn't mentioned going out anywhere." Her eyes were searching mine and I was trying to say that I'd explain all when I could. What must I look like—the tears, the filthy face, the bruised cheek?

I looked up at her. "I decided to take off on a bit of research."

"Alone?" Joe said from behind her.

"Yes, alone." I stepped away, heading for the stairs. "I'm not a kid. Anyway, I got mugged on my way back from the square. I'm fine, though." I touched my cheek gingerly.

"Mugged!" June squealed. "And you are not fine! Look at that cheek. Come with me and I'll clean you up."

"I'm perfectly able to wash my own face. Sorry for worrying you but I'm fine, I said. Just a bruise but I gave as good as I took, I can tell you."

"Did he steal anything from you?" June called.

"No, because I didn't take anything of value with me. Now, please, all of you, go to bed." And with that, I dashed up the stairs to my room, latching the door behind me. Sanctuary at last. All I wanted to do was bawl my eyes out but I didn't have the luxury of that at the moment.

The first thing I did was pull out my phone and scan my messages. Evan's came up first. *About to board the plane to Marrakech. Should be there by 11:30.* That info sent a flurry of mixed emotions through me, the most bizarre of which was thoughts of Evan encountering Noel. That wouldn't be a love-fest but he'd be gone by then, I reminded myself.

Next came Nicolina's text: *Did the envelope arrive? The police want to know where you are. Investigation on the fire continues. Stay safe. N*

And one from Max: *Hope you have lots of sunshine. Come back refreshed. Love, Max*

And one from Serena: *Hope you're having a wonderful time. Have something to tell you when you get home. Rena*

I didn't have time to answer any of them but I posted a quick text to Interpol in London with my coordinates. If the answer didn't come back within the hour, maybe I'd place a call, but Agent Walker always reacted to my texts even if he didn't send a reply. He'd come and to hell with the consequences of that one.

I tossed the phone to the bed and I tugged out the envelope to spread the contents. Vellum, no less, and very creased and very old, too. My fingers trembled. A map, no a diagram, maybe, but the strangest one I'd ever seen. It was like miniature weaver's cartoons for multiple carpets, one on top of the other, with overlaying symbols and designs so closely packed that it was almost impossible to distinguish anything.

Somebody knocked on the door. I carefully refolded the diagram and slipped it under my pillow. "Give me a minute." Only after I had splashed water on my face did I answer it, finding Peaches, arms crossed, standing outside.

"Took you long enough," she whispered, and then more loudly: "Hi, Penny. Thought I just check to see if you were okay."

"I'm fine. Come in." I shut the door behind her.

"What the hell really happened?" she whispered once I'd dragged her into the bathroom to ensure privacy.

I gave her the short version, ending with my showdown with Noel in the orange grove. "So I told him that it was over," I finished.

She whistled. "So, he's here and you ended it with him. Hell. How'd Lover Boy take it?" Peaches technically used to work for Noel and my brother when they were fighting her brother's rival gang back in Jamaica. She probably knew him better than I did. Yeah, it's that complicated.

"Badly but there's no gentle way to break up with a man like that. He's a born renegade and I was too blind to see it before. Life as a criminal seems to be his manifesto and life as a fool seems to be mine."

"Don't be so hard on yourself. You loved him, didn't you? We all do dumb-assed things for love. Anyway, I could have told you what he was really like long ago, woman. There were plenty of times I wasn't sure who was running the Jamaican operation—your brother or him. Finally, I decided it had to be him. Seemed that Toby had lost his marbles and Noel was taking full advantage of the situation."

I stared at her. "Why didn't you say something?"

"Hell, honey, do you think you were ready to hear that from me? Besides, it didn't matter since we blew up the whole operation and put our two masterminding bros in jail. Too bad we let the worst one get away."

I rubbed my eyes. "Anyway, now he's been hiding on the riad roof."

Her eyes widened. "Holy shit. He's up there now?"

"Apparently." I put my finger to my lips. "Keep it down."

"But why is he even here?" she hissed.

"He swears he's taking care of me, my self-appointed guard dog or something. He's pulled this trick before, ghosting my heels whenever I'm in danger. I'm trying to sever the leash but it's not happening fast enough."

"You buying that?"

"It fits his pattern. He always seems to show up at critical moments. I'm going to let him in to take a shower like he requested once the Merediths go to bed. Then maybe he'll leave. Where are they now, anyway?"

"In the lounge 'calming their nerves—'" she inserted air commas "—with a bottle of Scotch they dug up somewhere. What a pair. Damn near drove me nuts."

I clutched her arm. "What happened to the body?"

"What body?"

"The courier's. When I left, he was sprawled in the dust after that guy knifed him."

Peaches held her breath, eyes fixed on mine. "I came back, like, maybe forty minutes after I'd left and there was no body outside, no blood, nothing."

"But a body can't just up and disappear. When did the Merediths return?"

"At about 9:30, long after I did."

We stared at one another. "They're watching this place, whoever they are. Noel thinks it's a family matter," I told her, "a family that believes whatever's here belongs to them. Maybe they were the ones who cleaned up the evidence so as not to draw the police?"

"Makes sense," Peaches said, "but if that's the case, they know you've got the diagram and will be wanting it back, like soon." And then she added, "And maybe revenge their brother or cousin or whoever while they're at it."

"Thanks for reminding me. They were vicious enough before one of their own got killed. Anyway, Evan's on his way, thank God. He says that a storm's coming in from Venice."

"Muscle Man's coming here with Hottie on the roof?"

"Will you stop calling him that? He doesn't feel hot to me when he shoots a guy point-blank in the head. Anyway, we could use the extra manpower if the gang breaks in tonight."

"Shit, do you really think they'll do that?"

"How else will they get to the diagram or what it's hiding? There's one more thing: I've alerted Interpol."

"Well, hell." I watched her thinking out the complications. "Yeah, we're supposed to be working with them, aren't we, but what about him?" She stabbed a finger at the ceiling.

I shrugged. "I'm going to tell him that I called them. That way, if he wants to escape sooner, he can leave."

"And if he stays?"

"His choice. Maybe Interpol will get him this time. Either way, they have to be involved since anything buried on Moroccan soil over a few centuries old belongs to Morocco and now there's a vested interest through Italy with Nicolina. That means a long drawn-out court battle and it's not our problem. We work with Interpol now so all we get to worry about is keeping on the right side of international law."

"Still getting used to new loyalties but yeah. Think I'll go downstairs and check on the Merediths."

Once she'd left, I pulled out the folded vellum again, spread it out under the table lamp, and tried to study it but everything from the labeling to the images were too cramped to distinguish with its jumble of geometrics and Latin. Using my phone, I pinched open the camera screen to enlarge aspects but nothing I saw in that scramble made any sense. It was as if some long-ago designer had taken multiple drawings of carpets or geometric shapes and applied them onto the surface, one on top of the other. I pulled away to gaze at it from a distance but that perspective improved nothing. Eventually, I just took a few pictures.

Carefully refolding the vellum, I tucked it into my bag and crept out to the balcony. Everything was so still out there, all the open bedrooms within my line of vision gaping dark. In moments I had dashed downstairs to find Peaches leaning against a pillar with her arms folded.

"They just went up," she whispered. "It took everything I had short of threatening her to keep Mrs. Busybody from knocking on your door to see if you were all right. Nosy beast. Mom has a word for those that test her Christian values. I'd give it a few more minutes before they get to sleep."

"I can't wait," I said. "I've got to let Noel know about Interpol."

"I'll keep watch in case she comes out." She stepped over to the other side of the pool and fixed her gaze on the second-story end unit, and for the first time I noticed a hilt of something sticking under her belt.

"Is that the knife? Subtle, very subtle."

She grinned. "Yeah, I told June that it was an ornamental dagger that I use as a toothpick. Hard to hide, though. They used to wear them either attached to their belts or strapped to their legs. This one's handle is real silver and sharp enough to slice a hair."

"Wonderful," I said, gazing at the thing uneasily. "See you in a few minutes." With that, I made for the stairs.

Seconds later I was tapping on the roof door. It flew open in an instant.

"What took you so long?" he asked.

"If one more person asks me that... Look, I've called my Interpol contact in London so I'd advise you to skip the ablutions and get out of here."

"Seriously, Phoebe? You've called the cops on me already?" He stood there grinning at me, all shadows and wolfishness, as if my calling Interpol was some kind of joke.

"It's not about you, Noel. I called Interpol because I work with them now. It's too bad if you're on their most wanted list, but, oh, well. Still, I wouldn't stick around here if I were you."

"They probably won't be here until dawn. I'll still take that shower, if you don't mind."

"You can take your shower but then I want you to go, and if you plan on hanging around to steal something, forget it."

"Ouch."

The door clicked shut behind him and we crept down the stairs to my floor where I indicated for him to enter my room. "I'll come back in thirty minutes, which should give you a chance to shower or shave or whatever," I whispered. "Make sure you're gone by then."

"You're crazy, woman. Before this night's over, all hell is going to break loose. You need my help. Ask me to stay, why don't you?"

"Not this time, Noel. Never again." I turned to leave.

"Answer me one thing." He was taking off his clothes right in the doorway, tossing his jacket aside and pulling his shirt up over his torso. "Is there another man?"

I looked away. "Does it matter?"

"Probably not. Want to come in and scrub my back for old times' sake? I promise I can make a clean dirty woman out of you yet."

But I turned on my heels and bounded back down the stairs without comment.

Peaches was waiting for me. "The light's gone off in the Merediths' room finally. Is he leaving?"

"At the moment he's taking a shower. You know how he likes to play close to the edge. Forget about him. Let's try to figure out this diagram or whatever it is."

"Let's use my room."

So we retreated to her back room, shut the door, and stared down at the vellum sheet together. For a few moments neither of us said a word.

"So, what is that?" she said finally. "Looks like one of those stencil drawings where the outline of, like, twenty others have been printed on top," she said.

"That's what I thought, too. Vellum was often scraped off so that new writing could be applied but usually the previous script was pretty much erased first. This looks like layer upon layer was deliberately applied. Vellum, by the way, is an expensive surface and had pretty much given way to the cheaper parchment after the 1100s."

"If you say so."

"The point is, somebody wanted this to last. It's meant to be a cipher."

Peaches strode to the other side of the bed and stood back again. "There doesn't appear to be any right-side-up."

"That's what I thought."

"I was hoping for a blueprint. Blueprints I can read. This looks more like—"

"A mandala, maybe?"

"But that's Buddhist or Hindu, not Christian or Jewish, right?" she asked.

"I'm beginning to think that maybe that painting contains every religious element for a reason. It celebrates God and love, regardless of dogma. It's a brave manifest for all that's right in the world instead of everything that isn't by celebrating an unusual marriage inside a house of worship."

She gazed at me and whistled through her teeth. "What are you getting at?"

I straightened and faced her. "This is my gut talking so take it or leave it."

"I respect your gut so maybe I'll take it."

"All right, then. I believe that the bride and groom in the Bartolo married for love in a dangerous time and that their families supported the extraordinary union for their own reasons. Yes, wealth was involved but something else besides. It's as if two families from two great religions chose to come together in the name of the similarities between their religions rather than all the differences. After all, Judaism is the foundation of Christianity—their roots are the same and love reigns true in both."

"So does plenty of negative aspects, like the horrors of religious persecution and the narrow-minded adherence to religious norms."

"All interpreted by man—and I mean that in the general sense—who in my opinion has never proved himself to be an unbiased translator."

She nodded. "Yeah, that's true enough. Blame all the religious wars regardless of the denomination on man using religion for his own purposes. No religion is exempt from that travesty."

"But what if two enlightened families saw beyond all that and that whatever we're seeking is symbolic of a religion beyond dogma? A religion truly based on love, on what connects us not divides us?"

Peaches shook her head. "Yeah, well, wow. Talk about an incredible find. Something like that is a message for the world and the timing couldn't be better. The answer has to be here somewhere."

"Yes, but where do we look?" I pulled out my phone and thumbed through until I reached the Bartolo painting and passed it over. "Do you see any similarities in the painting to anything you see in the diagram?"

Peaches peered down at the screen, pinching it here and there. "Maybe. I mean, there's lots of triangles and elements that could be easily shifted about to form iconology but it doesn't look anything like that." She indicated the vellum with a nod of her head.

I touched my cheek. Ouch. "Let's leave it for now and come back to it. I'd better check on Noel. I'll catch up with you in a few minutes."

She folded up the vellum and passed it over with my phone, which I shoved deep into my pocket. "I'm going to take a walk around, see if I get any bright ideas."

The riad was filled with a hushed quiet when I retraced my steps back to my room moments later. The Merediths' door was still shut and the night-lights had come on—some kind of automatic timer, I guess.

I knocked on my bedroom door. When nobody answered, I opened it a crack and peered in. Damp towels tangled on the floor but there was no sign of Noel. I stepped inside. So he'd used every one of my towels unnecessarily, really?

I gazed around at the mess he'd made, more determined than ever to end whatever had been between us. He might be gone from my room but I needed him gone from my heart and head, too, and everything he had done that night was helping. I'd just check out the roof to hurry him along.

Backing out of the room, I swung my carpetbag over my shoulder and strode for the stairs. If nothing else, I had to ensure that the roof door was locked. Noel had picked it open so maybe now it wouldn't lock properly. We couldn't leave that door unsecured when the gang might be on their way—three of them left, not including Noel.

I reached the top of the stairs and froze. The door hung wide open. I stood staring as a chill breeze cooled my cheeks. Surely not even Noel would do that? He might be behaving spitefully but would he deliberately endanger all of us? Besides, I'd watched him pull that shut behind him before we went to my room. Did he go back up but leave it open? Pulling my gun from its holster, I released the safety and stepped out.

Above, the stars spangled the sky, visible even here amid the medina's illumination. With gun in hand, I swung around 360 degrees. The terrace was still, night-lights illuminating enough to see that there were no pitched tents, duffels, or any other sign of obvious habitation. At the same time, it was impossible to see behind every deck lounger, table, or pile of pillows.

"Noel, are you here?" I whispered.

No response. I crept forward, keeping close to the stairhousing wall and heading toward the potted palm at the terrace's far perimeter. The air was cool. I was trembling but my hand gripped the pistol as if it were the handlebar of a bike hurling down a mountainside. Every nerve tingled.

Ducking into the shadow of the palm with my back to the wall, I stared out. Here I felt less exposed but I was picking up on something beyond my senses, something on this roof that didn't feel friendly, somebody hiding, somebody waiting.

I heard what sounded like a door clicking shut. What? Stepping out with my gun raised, I could see the stair door now closed on the other side. Maybe the wind had blown it shut. Maybe it was spring-loaded and I'd somehow tripped the mechanism. Maybe I didn't know what had closed it but I sure as hell didn't want to be locked up on that roof.

I sprung for the door—locked! I gripped the handle and shook it but it refused to budge. I'd call Peaches to let me out. I'd— Then something metal-sounding flicked behind my back, sending me spinning around. I couldn't see anything at first, only the mounds of furniture and pillows. Then something moved on my right as a shadow leaped out on me, knocking the gun from my hand and throwing me to the ground.

Deep-set eyes drilled into my skull as I lay on my back, a man on top, straddling me with his hands around my throat. "You will do as I say," he hissed, pressing on my windpipe. "Or I kill you."

I tried to nod, struggling to speak. He loosened his grip. Now there was a woman standing over us who picked up my gun and spoke to her companion in Arabic, maybe. The man climbed off me and together they hoisted me to my feet.

"You will do what we say," she said, pointing my gun on me. Great— two armed people. Where was the third? "Give me the bag," she demanded.

"My carpetbag? You want the diagram, don't you? Well, good luck with that. It's inscrutable," I said.

I could tell they didn't grasp my meaning. "Inscrutable: unreadable, useless!" I clarified.

"You will tell us meaning or we kill you," the man snarled. He stepped forward as if to strike me but the woman stayed his hand.

"No. We want her to think, Omar," she warned. "The bag!" She wrenched it off my shoulder and I could do nothing but watch as she dumped the contents onto the tiles. In a moment she had the vellum unfolded and was staring at it in the half-light. "What is the meaning?"

"Who are you?" I asked.

"Shut up. What is the meaning?"

"I don't know, I said."

"But you know." She was fixing me with her drilled-deep eyes. They looked so much alike, the two of them, like flip sides of a gender coin. Same tanned skin, same bony faces and thick black curly hair.

"No, I don't," I said. "I can't figure it out."

"You will tell us or you die," she said, waving the pistol at me.

"Where is our brother? What did you do with Yousef?" the man demanded, threatening me with every inch of his wiry frame.

"Yousef? Is that the guy who killed the courier? He's your brother? I don't know where he is. I shot him in the leg but he got away on his bike."

"You lie. He called, said he got diagram," Omar said, poking the air before my nose with his finger. "You chased him! You got diagram back!" He so wanted to hit me, I could tell.

Three could play at this. "Okay, so I did chase him, straight into an orange grove off the highway. He was losing a lot of blood and fell off his bike so I took the diagram back. That's where I left him. You'd better go make sure he's okay instead of wasting time with me."

Not a good idea mentioning the blood part. The two of them exchanged glances, which was all the time I needed to knock the gun out of the woman's hand with a sharp uplift while shoving Omar against the door with my shoulder. His shot rang wild, aiming for the stars, as I scrambled off.

Five seconds or less was all I had as I snatched up the diagram. No time to wrestle a gun, too. Seconds only to get myself out of the range of fire and away, which meant only one thing: I had to jump, this time right over the edge of the terrace roof.

❧ 19 ❧

I bolted to the side of the stairwell housing to where the air-conditioning unit hugged a low wall and flung myself over it as full of prayer as I ever had been in my life and I mean multidenominational prayer. I had no idea what was on the other side except that it wasn't the street. And like an idiot I closed my eyes and held my breath as if I were diving, the diagram gripped between my fingers.

But I ended landing on my feet no more than four feet down. And took off in a mad scrabble across the tiles, tucking the vellum into my shirt on the run. Noel had mentioned his route from the street to the roof but all I cared about was the reverse path. Since the riad backed up against a maze of buildings crammed together, I knew this one had to be the route he'd taken.

All I wanted was to get away from the killer duo and warn Peaches as soon as I could risk pulling out my phone. That meant I had to get off the roofs to a safe place but had no idea which direction to take. Noel hadn't exactly drawn me a map. Twice I tripped over a cable and pitched flat on a corrugated surface and once I banged into one of the satellite dishes that sprouted out from the roofs like slanted mushrooms. It was a crazy, uneven surface and the moonlight and starshine only baffled me with shadows.

Once, out of breath and dizzy after a stumble, I turned to see the figure of a man balancing with a gun in hand silhouetted against the deep azure sky maybe fifty feet away. I hauled myself to my feet and launched in a crouching run beside a low wall, keeping deep in the shadows. My best hope was to lose him in this maze of broken concrete and misshapen mounds. If I arrived at a drop too deep to jump, I'd scuttle off in another direction, maybe duck behind a chimney, or under a tent, or up a low promontory. People used these roofs, I realized. Signs of daytime occupation were evident in the laundry lines, the chairs pulled up inside little concrete terraces, the rooftop grills.

I kept going like this for maybe fifteen minutes until I noticed that the roofscape had changed from rough-scrabble to newer, more decorative and upscale materials. Now I appeared to be on some sprawling multilevel roof complex with white decorative trim. This must be the air-conditioning and ventilation area for some big building. With no signs of Omar, I figured I must have shaken him at last so I took a moment to slump behind an ornate chimney and speed-dial Peaches.

"Where the hell are you!" she hissed.

"Somewhere over the medina being chased by one of the killers," I whispered. "They attacked me on the roof. Have you seen them? One, maybe both, must still be at the riad. The important thing is that I escaped with the diagram."

"Well, shit, woman, don't you have all the fun? All I get to do is babysit the Merediths. Evan just arrived and the doorbell woke them up. He's calming them down now with more charm than I've seen from a man. Hell, and I thought my daddy could lay it on. He's telling him he's your boyfriend."

"Seriously?"

"Yeah, seriously. Speaking of boyfriends, is Noel with you?"

I peeked out from behind the chimney, quickly pulling myself back. "Noel's gone somewhere. Where is he when he might actually be useful? So far I'm fine, thanks for asking. The others have to be somewhere in the riad. Watch out. There's two left out there that we know of, remember, not counting the one chasing me. Got to go."

"Wait, Evan wants to talk to you."

There was a muffle and then: "Phoebe? Where are you exactly?"

He said my name. Crazy what a little thing like that will do. "I don't know," I said. "I just took off across the roofs after they tackled me."

"Text me the coordinates from your phone and I'll find you."

"No!" I whispered. "Don't leave Peaches and the Merediths alone."

"The killers are only interested in you. Text me the coordinates, I said. Never mind, I'll track you." Then he clicked off.

He'll track me, shit. Shoving the phone back into my pocket, I crept up to the wall. I needed to find my way down to the street somehow. I peered down three stories seeing nothing but handfuls of people strolling along a well-lit boulevard. There was a guy in a fez wearing some kind of uniform directly underneath me, maybe the doorman of this establishment. No way down that way.

I turned. Behind me stood a small square building that I was beginning to recognize as an enclosure for the top of a stairwell. They were all over the roofs of the medina. Some led to sunning terraces, others to technical equipment like air-conditioning and ventilation units. Each one had a door and every door I'd tried that night had been locked. This one was no exception.

Now what? I'd arrived at a dead end of sorts, and unless I felt like climbing up and balancing along a partition that separated the business end of the building from whatever lay on the other side, I'd have to retrace my steps. Hoisting myself up onto a ventilation housing, I peered over the wall that ran deep across the complex. It was like gazing down on a fantasy palace straight out of *Ali Baba*. This must be a hotel designed like a monstrous riad, all the varying terraces lit like some magical playground for the very rich.

Below was a small pool set in what seemed to be a cozy terrace area with a little bar tucked into a copse of flowering trees. To my left, a filigreed border of arches separated a much larger pool dropped into the center of a spacious balconied courtyard. Yet another small raised terrace sat under an awning in the corner to my right. The whole place wafted money along with the scent of jasmine and orange blossoms but nobody stirred that I could see. Music played from speakers tucked out of sight. Gorgeous or not, there was no easy way down and I had no doubt that security would be tight. Nothing obvious like barbed wire but alarms had to be everywhere.

A sound behind me made me turn. Light-blinded, I couldn't see anything at first but I could hear heavy breathing and something like a curse in another language. I'd been found.

I watched as the shadow man approached while I considered my options. Tackling him in armed combat could only be a last resort. I wasn't good enough to risk it unless I had to. Escaping was preferable. I swung back to the wall—a long lantern-lit crenellated border of concrete with drops to various levels, none I wanted to think about jumping. My best chance was to head to the right where the raised dais with its cushions and awning promised a soft landing. At least it was a ten-foot drop there instead of a thirty to fifty one—my best chance to keep limbs intact.

Omar lunged forward while I sprung for the wall. It was easy to hoist myself up but hellishly hard to stay upright once I got there. Maybe a foot wide with the lantern crenellations positioned every two feet, balancing on that surface would be fine if I didn't need to lift one leg periodically to cross a lamp. As for speed, forget it. Omar, on the other hand, was damn good at this while I got hit by vertigo within seconds.

I had no choice but to try stoop-crawling next, which worked long enough for me to scramble across the steepest part of the drop. Completely focused on maneuvering the obstacles, I didn't pay attention to anything else until I heard Omar speak only a few yards away. "Stop, Phoebe McCabe, or I shoot," he hissed.

"No, you won't," I called back. "You need me alive."

"Alive, yes, not whole. You hurt brother, I hurt you."

A quick look over my shoulder saw him watching me with a calculating look, his gun pointed right at me. Shit! I jumped up and made a running leap over the next few lanterns, propelled more by fear than sense. A shot cracked out and hit a lantern near my left foot. Somebody screamed as I jumped down into the awning.

And kept falling deeper into folds of some kind of striped silk that completely covered me as the tent ripped off its tethers and sent me falling into a mound of pillows. I heard cries and shouts as I struggled to release myself from my silken cocoon. It took me seconds to realize I was the one doing the screaming.

Somebody arrived to me to help me unwrap. After the last fold of silk had been pulled away, I saw a startled-looking woman standing there with a bougainvillea flower tucked behind her ear. "Are you okay?" American accent. "My boyfriend and I were at the bar and then I heard you scream," she said while untangling the rest of the fabric from my feet.

"I'm okay, just shaken up, thanks. He tried to rob me." I turned to see Omar struggling with two fez-hatted men—waiters, maybe. "Him!" I pointed. "He attacked me! I was sitting here and he jumped on me and wanted to steal my cash!"

"She lies!" Omar cried, but the gun that had fallen to the tiles didn't add to his credibility. Suddenly two security guards came dashing onto the terrace, one speaking into his walkie-talkie, the other rushing to pick up the gun. A man in a suit arrived, brass name tag fastened to his shiny blue bolero chest.

I went into wronged damsel mode. "What's the meaning of this? I come up here to relax and suddenly this...this creature attacks me! What kind of hotel is this where security is so lax?"

"Madam, madam, we are very sorry," the suited man said, hands open. He spoke rapidly to the security team in Arabic and they tackled the protesting Omar to the ground. "We endeavor to keep our guests safe. This is very unusual, very rare. We are so very sorry. What can we do to make it up to you?"

"I'm going to my room. You can talk to me later."

"Wait, lady, the police are on their way. You must tell them what happened," the manager called.

I was halfway to the door. "You can see what happened," I said over my shoulder. "An armed man broke into your hotel and tried to rob a guest. Now, I need to rest. I'll talk to the police when they come."

Which was soon by the sounds of the sirens pealing from somewhere outside. The last thing I needed was for someone to figure out that the tent had encompassed me from the outside in, not the other way around or that I wasn't even registered at the hotel. No, I needed to get away and fast.

The lobby was akin to a long carpeted portico with the oasis-like pool area gleaming through the arches. I bounded downstairs but soon forced myself into a nonchalant stride. Guests were standing around talking excit-edly about something that had happened on the roof. News travels fast.

I sailed straight past them all, through the whispering automatic doors, and onto the street. In seconds I was striding away from the sirens and pulling out my phone to figure out where I was exactly.

A man strode up behind me. "Just keep walking, Phoebe," he said, linking my arm with his.

20

"Make like we're a couple," Evan whispered, pulling me close as we strode rapidly down the street arm-in-arm. "The police will be all over here in a minute. Are you hurt?"

"I'm fine," I said, "but Omar is going to jail."

"Omar is one of the gang, I take it. How did you escape this time?"

I gave my summary, assuring him that much was pure luck.

"Did you use the phone's taser feature?" he asked, looking down at me at last.

"What taser feature?"

"The one where you hold down the home button and the volume button simultaneously, which signals the phone to temporarily emit a taser-like shock—very handy for disabling attackers. It's hot off the desk, so to speak. I've yet to see it tried out on a living thing."

"You don't test on animals, do you?"

He looked shocked. "Absolutely not! I only test on deserving humans."

"Good, but no, I did not use the taser feature since I didn't know about it," I hissed.

"The directions are very clear on the cheat sheet," he said with mock chagrin.

"Do you mean that lengthy tome you printed up? That is not a cheat sheet, Evan, that is an instruction booklet minus an index. I suggest that you master the point form."

He grinned. "My apologies, madam. I note that I must deploy brief teaching videos in the future."

"Yeah, you do that. Put it right up there with the Evan call button."

He smiled as we continued rapidly along, him steering me into a little path between the crush of buildings. "This way. So, I understand that Halloren arrived," he said, his tone suddenly serious.

"Unfortunately, yes. He claims that he's been keeping an eye out for me. Apparently he's been camped out on the riad roof since we arrived. He's gone now."

"Don't believe it. He's here for a reason and it's not about you, no matter what he claims."

I pulled my arm from his. "Forget Noel. He's the least of our problems considering that, whoever this gang is, there are two more left out there—a woman and another brother we have yet to see. Both have to be nearby. Two down, two to go, in other words. How are we supposed to decipher this diagram with them waiting to pounce?"

"I doubt that they'll pounce until we've uncovered the hidden dowry. Why not let us do all the work? But we'll be ready for them by then. If my hunch is correct, they've been anticipating that moment since you arrived and are probably growing a bit impatient about now. That's probably why that guy accosted you tonight."

"Only, Omar was also itching for payback because I shot his brother. Forget that Yousef killed a courier and snatched away that diagram in the first place. If the sister hadn't intervened, I'd have more than a bruised cheek."

"You killed him?" he asked sharply.

"No, I didn't kill him. I shoot to disable, never to kill, contrary to the assassins' creed or whatever. Noel killed him."

"Just his style. Is the diagram still in good condition? I saw it before the contessa packed it away to the courier service."

"As safe as a seven-hundred-year-old piece of lambskin can be after a few wild dashes onto the desert air." I stopped and looked around. "I recognize this lane."

"The riad is just ahead."

"And Noel's motorcycle was parked right over here." I strode up to the broken wall and peeked over. "And it's gone."

"And the man with it, I trust."

Somehow I doubted that. A part of me still hoped he'd be waiting in the wings ready to help at the last minute.

We crossed the courtyard and dashed down the alley, Evan watching our backs as I inserted the key card and pushed open the door.

"There you are!" June was on me as soon as I stepped into the courtyard. "What is the meaning of this, Penny, waking us up with your gentlemen callers and causing a commotion in general? Have you no consideration for your fellow guests?"

Peaches rolled her eyes behind her.

"June, sorry for the disruptions. I—"

"Disruptions? Is that what you call it when someone spends a fortune to ensure a delightful Moroccan holiday only to have a single disrespectful guest disturb her peace again and again?" She was standing in front of me with her arms crossed over her magenta bathrobe, eyes flaming indignation. For some reason, I noticed her earrings. She slept wearing dangles? "First thing in the morning, you can be sure I will be lodging my complaint. What kind of guest goes out at all times of the night and requires a man to fly in and bring her home? Disgusting." She turned on her gold-tooled Moroccan slippers and marched toward the stairs. "Come along, Joe."

Joe had been staring at Evan as if he'd just manifested out of a genie bottle but now scurried after her like an obedient puppy.

"Well, that was strange." I looked from Peaches to Evan once the couple had retreated. "Fly in to bring her home—really?"

Peaches swore. "You'd think you had been out prowling the streets picking up stray men or something. What were you doing?"

"I'll tell you later. Is everything clear around here?" I asked her.

"If you mean did I find anyone lurking in the shadows, no. I did my rounds floor-by-floor while you were gone and the roof is latched from the inside now. Nothing looked out of place up there besides your stuff all over the terrace," she told me. "I gathered it up and put it back in your carpetbag, by the way. It's on your bed."

"Oh, thanks. And nobody tried to jump you?"

"Hell, no. I'd hoped they would so I'd get my swinging arm back in use but I'm not interesting enough apparently."

"So, no signs of anyone else besides the Merediths?" Evan asked, stepping forward, his bag in hand, and gazing around at the balconied levels.

"Nada," Peaches said. "I gave all the rooms a cursory check but they looked empty."

"But I'm sure they're here. I'm working on a device that will pick up body heat signatures in rooms of a limited size but I didn't have the right equipment with me in Venice," Evan told her.

She looked at him in amazement. "Seriously, you can do that?"

"That and more," I said, "but don't let it go to his head. Maybe we should check all the rooms again just in case." I was looking up at the balconies, every room but mine and the Merediths' wide open. Each were dark, which made for perfect hiding places unless thoroughly checked. "There still could be somebody hiding up there."

"Smoking them out would take too long and require more person power than we can spare at the moment, given our time restraints," Evan said. "We need to find this thing before the staff returns in the morning. We'll deal with problems when the time comes. Let's get right to work. Where can we go that has a blank white wall?" he asked.

Blank white anything was notably absent in this pattern upon pattern environment but we led him into the smaller courtyard where the back wall had managed to remain undecorated. Following his directions, we busied helping him set up his laptop on a table dragged from Peaches's room while he fiddled with his equipment. I had no idea what he was up to.

"You didn't mention he was gorgeous in his list of attributes," Peaches whispered when we were inside her room bringing out chairs for the evening's operations.

"Will you stop," I said, my exasperation playful but my point firm. "He's Rupert's assistant, remember, not one of your man-chest heroes."

"But I bet he's got one just like that." She pointed to one of her paperbacks tossed on the bed—a bare muscled chest holding a puppy dog. She went through those things like vitamin pills.

"He's here to help us prove that neither Rupert nor Nicolina are responsible for Maria Contini's death because she was killed to get to whatever's buried here. We find whatever it is and hopefully put that and the killers where they belong. Forget the romantic fiction."

"I'm only interested for aesthetic reasons."

"He's not my type," I hissed, grabbing a chair by the rail back.

"Oh, yeah, what type is that—short, fat, and bald?" She grinned.

"Lean, murderous, and wolfish apparently. Look at Noel. Anyway, I'm just exorcising one man from my heart so the last thing I need is another, chest or no."

"That's exactly what you need, sister, and that guy's got the goods, that's all I'm saying."

We differed on the fundamentals of romance. "Let's get to work. Anyway, what's wrong with short, fat, and bald? I've met guys like that who would melt your socks off."

"Wouldn't know. I've only just started seriously wearing socks."

Back in the courtyard the two of us stood gazing in wonder as an image projected onto the wall. Hovering as if in midair, the lines and angles took a second to focus.

"Is that the diagram up there?" Peaches gazed from the laptop to the projected image.

"That's the diagram Nicolina sent, yes," I said.

I stepped forward. Evan, standing in a white shirt with his sleeves rolled up over his substantial biceps, turned and explained. "Before Nicolina sent the diagram, I photographed it in sections using a program that has the capacity to break down levels of any geometrical design, enabling one to study it from multiple angles in 3-D. Watch."

He touched the keyboard and sections of the diagram fell apart into separate areas like a folding screen. Touching the keyboard again raised the images up as if we were gazing at them sideways. Each time he tapped, the triangles, rectangles, and spheres realigned to create a new design, each as incredibly complex and beautiful as the last, like kaleidoscope mosaics.

"Like sacred geometry?" I whispered.

He smiled. "'There is geometry in the humming of the strings, there is music spacing of the spheres.'"

"And he quotes Pythagoras, too," Peaches marveled. She reached out a hand as if to touch the image. "Cathedrals were built on the principles of sacred geometry. It's everywhere in ancient architecture hidden in such plain sight. The universe is engineered on geometry."

"It is," Evan agreed.

"Can you spread the sections apart on a flat level?" I asked.

He tapped the keyboard. "Done."

As the sections rearranged themselves, Peaches stepped closer. "Bring the top square over here and move that rectangle there."

"Here, you do it." Evan stepped aside. "Move the sections around with your fingers. The screen is touch-enabled, all drag and drop." She did as he asked, moving each section around with her fingers until they formed a series of connected rectangles, large and small. Now we were looking at a schematic that looked surprisingly like a blueprint with triangles littering the top of the screen as if waiting to be placed. "This is the riad," Peaches said. "See, the central courtyard is this large rectangle here and this smaller courtyard is where we stand. If I rearrange these blocks around, it forms the other rooms, only I don't get what to do with those triangles up there."

My mouth had gone dry. "Triangles combine to make stars. Look." I dragged each of the triangles down, squeezing the images to reduce them in size and placing two overlapping equilateral triangles in the center. "A hexagram." I brought out my phone and thumbed to the Bartolo picture. "And the bride is standing on a hexagram. If we can find this geometric configuration somewhere in this riad, we might find the dowry."

"Even though the hexagram wasn't claimed as the Star of David until two hundred years later?" Evan asked.

"It wasn't acknowledged as such until the seventeenth century but it appeared all over the ancient world long before then. The star has always been a symbol of power and hope." My eyes met his.

"It must be hidden in the mosaics," Peaches said, "but the original tile work must have been replaced long ago."

"Or covered over," Evan suggested, turning away to stride across the courtyard. "It's far less expensive to tile over something than to dig it up and start fresh."

Together we gazed at the tiled floor. "It must be beneath these tiles somewhere. But we ran the detector app across every inch of tile and found nothing," I said.

"So it must be buried someplace the scan can't reach," Evan pointed out.

"The center of the riad." Peaches turned to the door, her excitement mounting. "These buildings were always built around a central courtyard from which everything else radiated outward. So where's the center of this one? The pool!"

We followed her out into the central courtyard where the three of us stood gazing deep into the blue water. "Impossible," she whispered. "They wouldn't have built a pool this deep back in the 1500s. Water was scarce —*is* scarce—in the desert. If there was anything buried here, it would have been found when they excavated for the pool in the last couple of decades."

"Water has always been sacred to desert communities and seen as cleansing, purifying, and ultimately preparing the faithful for worship," I pointed out.

"And there are two courtyards here," Evan said quietly, "one much less public than this but no less important to a family centuries ago. It is where they would have washed and prayed before meals."

Turning, we dashed back into the smaller courtyard and stood by the fountain, staring. It was a small fountain set in a basin no bigger than a birdbath. "So, it must be underneath here," I said. "A fountain of one form or another probably existed in this spot centuries ago and the latest electrical addition could have been installed without significantly disturbing anything below it. I'm betting that if we dug here, we'd uncover an old mosaic featuring a hexagram much like what we see in the Bartolo."

"Underneath which lays our missing dowry," Evan added. "Let's start. First, I'll disengage the fountain by lifting it up—no need to damage anything. The electricians would have rigged it for easy repair. Then I'll start removing the top layer of tiles. The biggest issue will be draining the basin but I think I've got that worked out."

"I bet you have." Peaches nodded.

"We'll help," I said.

"It's better if I do the digging while you two search the riad for stowaways. Now's the time," Evan said without looking up from the fountain. He seemed deep into calculation mode. "The sound of digging will draw them out so we'd better be ready for interruptions."

That made sense.

"Do you even have a shovel?" Peaches asked, always the practical one.

Now he was lifting up a long narrow bag strapped to his valise and zipping back the cover. "Of course. I always come prepared." Out came a fold-out shovel. "If I change the head, it turns into a rudimentary pickax but I doubt I'll need that." He looked up. "Do either of you have a gun?"

"I have a knife." Peaches pulled out her gleaming blade.

"The wicked sister took mine," I told him, spreading my hands, "but apparently I have a taser."

"Take mine." He pulled a pistol from his holster and passed it over, butt-first. I took it, finding it heavy, made for bigger hands. Still, I nodded and thanked him. "But while you're digging, you'll be exposed to anyone sneaking up behind you if Peaches and I are in another part of the riad," I pointed out.

He quirked a smile, holding up his phone. "A motion detector. If I activate that feature and place it in the floor behind me, it will pick up movement coming through the door up to a distance of ten yards. That's enough to send a warning."

Peaches whistled between her teeth. "Let's get to it, then," she said, turning to me. "Any suggestions on where to start?"

"At the top floor. You guard the stairs while I check each of the rooms. Between the two of us, we should be able to catch a rat if it bolts."

"Sounds perfect except that we have a bathroom issue and I don't mean that kind. While you check each bathroom, you'll be out of my sight for seconds and your back exposed to being jumped from behind." She had more commando experience than I did and it showed.

"Yeah, I see. Let me figure that one out," I told her.

We left Evan straddling the fountain while twisting it from its pedestal, his phone pulsing a blue light in the center of the floor.

I wasn't nervous about checking each of the rooms, though I probably should have been. With Peaches watching from the top of the stairs with her phone light beaming down the corridor (we still hadn't located the master light switch) and her knife at the ready, she had my back. That left me to grip the gun in one hand and my phone in the other, theoretically. Practically, the gun was too heavy for me to manage comfortably while holding the phone in my wounded hand but that's exactly what I tried to do.

First, I worked out a sequence. I approached the first room with confidence, flicking on the bedroom light and striding forward like I knew what I was doing. Slipping my hand in around the darkened bathroom wall, I switched on the light with the back of my hand while still holding the phone. Satisfied that the bright jolt of patterned color jumping out at my eyes was totally of the tile variety, I next gave the shower stall a sweep before backing out. On my way out of the room, I checked under the bed but it turned out that the mattresses sat on platforms with no space beneath. Next, I opened the wardrobe. Every room had a carved wood variety requiring me to swing open the door and wave my gun inside at anybody who might be lurking within. After the first sequence, I vowed that checking the wardrobe first made more sense.

All the empty rooms on that floor received the same treatment, my own getting extra care seeing as Noel had recently been there. It's like I felt his presence imprinted in the space he'd left behind and the thought stabbed me in the heart. A quick glance in the bathroom mirror at my own reflection was enough to bring me back down to earth. I looked like parboiled hell with a bruised cheek and hollow eyes. Wincing, I turned away and returned to my task, following the same sequence three times more on the top level. Tiptoeing past the Merediths' room, I was relieved to see the lights out under the door and that all seemed peaceful.

"All clear. On to the next level," I whispered when I met Peaches at the stairs minutes later.

She held up her hand. "Listen."

All I could hear at first was the deep chunk-chunk of Evan digging before a second sound came through, something like a chair scraping across the floor on the main level. Then we heard a clatter on the level directly beneath us. "That's deliberate," I whispered. "They're trying to separate us."

"Well, it's going to work, isn't it? We can't leave them to run all over this place. You get the one below and leave the one on the bottom floor to me." She made it sound like we were sharing treats. I watched as she bounded downstairs with her knife in hand, leaving me with no choice but to continue down to the second floor without her.

None of the rooms were booked on this level and now I had no one to watch my back, either. Why did that bother me? Maybe because my gun arm was tiring and my other hand had begun to throb. Had I the choice, I'd wimp out in a nanosecond but choice was not optional. Shoving my phone into my pocket, I gripped the pistol with both hands and prowled the floor. This time I flicked on each of the lights closest to the doors but made no move to go inside. If my hunch was right, someone was waiting for me and my task was to stay out of their clutches.

I was halfway down the row when a clang came from the room at the end of the hall—brass banging against brass. Someone wanted me to know where they were or think that. All right, then, I'd just go as far as the door and maybe shoot a warning shot to the ceiling, see if I could flush them out. Or that was the plan. By the time I'd heard the footfalls behind me, it was too late to even turn around.

I was pushed to the ground face-first, the force hard enough to throw me but not heavy enough to keep me down. The gun fell from my grasp. I bucked, which shifted my attacker to the left, giving me time to shove her off, regain the gun while scrambling to my knees. She was just as fast but no trained fighter and now we were facing each other on our knees, both of our guns pointed at the other's chest.

Petite with dark curly hair with a fierce yet delicate face, she stared at me with angry eyes. Maybe forty years old, she looked as though she'd been dragged through life by the scruff of the neck. "You think you escape us, Phoebe McCabe," she said, "but you don't escape. We are here now and will claim what is ours." I had the sense that she wanted to sound fiercer than she was. Her hand trembled.

"Who are you? What do you want?" I asked.

"You know what we want," she said.

"No, I don't. Tell me." I had to get that gun away from her without getting shot. She must know that we were close to locating the dowry so she'd have no reason to keep me alive. "Why did you burn that building down while I was in it? Why did you kill Maria Contini?"

"That was accident! We did not want to kill! My brothers, they struggled to get key and she fell, hit her head."

"Wow—what, four of you against one woman?"

Pain crossed her eyes. Not the first time, I guessed. "So you struggled to get the key to the warehouse, and when she wouldn't just let you have it, you killed her."

"By accident, I said."

"Oh, really? Killing must have been your intention all along; if not yours, then your brothers'. They have anger management issues written all over them."

"Not me!" she protested. So I was correct.

"Your brothers, then. And was trying to burn me alive an accident, too?"

"We thought building deserted! We wanted only to find old deed and burn any secrets to take back what is ours. This riad is ours."

That surprised me. "But it's belonged to the Continis continuously for centuries."

"Not true!" She practically spat the words. "It was sold to our family in 1986 and then stolen back six months later because of secret buried. All their money, they used to bribe. Now we have nothing."

I stared at her, dumbfounded. "What?"

"My aunt Zara came to work for Continis when young girl. She worked here in riad first and she went to Italy with them—like all big family. Many years pass. Signora Contini likes my aunt, wants to give her good life because her family—us—very poor, so she sell riad to her for family here at low price. Every dirham we had, we put to buy house. My aunt, she had savings. There was deed, all legal, and then—" she snapped her fingers "—gone."

Both our pistols were lowering now. Weird as it was, we were kneeling there having a conversation. "Gone? But how can that happen if you'd legally bought the riad?"

"Signore Contini made deals." She jerked her head toward the medina as if crooks were lurking behind every wall. "He discovered secret, wanted riad back to find treasure because his money now gone. Papers were signed. Said our deed illegal. My brothers were given money but it was nothing, a cheat!"

"These are the elder Continis you're talking about, not Maria," I protested, slowly climbing to my feet. She did the same.

"Not Maria, no, but she knew. Her parents die but still she not give riad back to my aunt. She promised money in will. We don't want money, we want what is ours!"

There was a sound below us in the courtyard. We stilled, listening, but continued after a few seconds. I wet my lips. "So you thought you could find it by stealing the painting?"

She nodded. "Maria Contini would not will riad to Aunt Zara. She told her this. Many times we hear Continis say that secret must lie in painting but we could see nothing even after we steal it."

"So your aunt was behind this from the very beginning?"

"No!" she said, cutting the air with her free hand. "She knows nothing! We bug her things, the house. We hear everything. She is just old woman—very sad, my aunt. Do not blame her. I moved to Venice and visit Aunt Zara with my brothers many times when Maria Contini left house. We placed the devices."

Theirs must have been the rudimentary ones Seraphina scoffed at. "And you made the call to Maria that night?"

"On burner phone, yes. I said I must talk about my aunt. She agreed. She said she had meeting with someone after but would meet with me first."

"But you and your brothers were waiting instead."

"Yes. My brothers very angry. She would not give us the key. It was accident."

I saw it all play out in my imagination. "No, it wasn't. You don't just meet with someone at night to politely ask them to pass over property possibly hiding a family fortune and expect it to all go smoothly. Of course she didn't agree; of course there was a struggle, and you and your brothers are responsible for what happened next."

Though her expression remained defiant, I caught the pain running there. Still, though she may have participated, she was not the orchestrator of this tragedy. And Zara had inadvertently been providing access to her niece and nephews spying all along. I knew she had to have factored in this somewhere. "But you still didn't know exactly where the secret lay until you heard me discussing it with Nicolina? That's why you wanted me because you think I'm an expert, which I'm not."

A smile touched her lips. "You have led us back to here. You read the symbols in the painting. Now your man digs for treasure."

"Look—what's your name, anyway?"

"Amira."

"Look, Amira, first of all, he's not 'my man,' and secondly, I have no vested interest in whatever might be hidden here, do you understand? I like the puzzle part, I like the challenge, but neither I nor any of my friends are here to steal anything from anyone."

"But you work for her, that Nicolina who now owns all."

"I don't work for her. She asked me to help find out who killed Maria Contini and now I know—you apparently."

She stepped toward me, gun still pointed at my chest. "Not me, my brothers—very dangerous men. I want only what is right and to give my aunt the life she deserves."

"What's hidden here may not only be valuable but a symbolic message to all the warring religions worldwide—Islam, Judaism, Christianity, even Hindu."

She spat. "Allah only true god. Where is Omar and Youssef? What have you done with my brothers?"

"Omar got arrested for chasing me through a hotel and Youssef—" I hesitated. Telling her that one brother was dead might enrage her.

"And Youssef?" she pressed.

But a noise drew our attention to the courtyard again. This time the sounds of a scuffle were unmistakable. Those few seconds of inattention were all I needed to knock the gun from her hand and retrieve the thing in a flash. Now I held both guns.

"You would not shoot me," she said.

"Not to kill, no, but I wouldn't let you shoot me, either. Come on, Amira, there's been enough bloodshed already. You can't help your aunt if you are all in jail or dead. Let's go down and meet my friends."

She seemed to agree with that much.

We were almost on the bottom level when a cry ripped the air. "Phoebe!"

21

I couldn't tell where the sounds were coming from at first.

"There." Amira pointed, running to the other side of the pool to where two figures struggled in the half-light.

Peaches had a man facedown on the floor behind a table with his hands wrenched behind his back. "Quick, give me something to tie him up with!" she called.

"Can't, got my hands full at the moment." I lifted the two guns to prove it. "Let him up and take my other gun. Amira, stand against the wall."

Amira did as I said, shouting Arabic at the man straining to break Peaches's hold.

"Does he speak English?" I asked her.

"No English," she said. "Don't hurt him."

"Then tell him to stop fighting or I'll shoot him in the leg like I did Youssef," I said.

"Abdul does not listen to me." But she said something that made him still at once. Peaches pulled him to his feet by the scruff of the neck and he —almost a carbon copy of the other two guys—threw me a vicious look as he regained his footing.

"They're all siblings," I told Peaches, "here to take what they see as their property and to compensate for their aunt's hard work, broken promises, and a swindled deal. That's the story in a nutshell, anyway."

"Lost property?"

I leaned forward to pass Peaches the other gun. "The family bought the riad years ago from the Continis, sold to them at a bargain price in thanks to their employee's—Zara's—work apparently. She'd been employed by the family for nearly forty years. Then the elder Contini swindled it back from the family when he finally started believing that a treasure was buried here."

"That explains almost everything." Evan was striding across the tiles toward us. "Here, let's tie them up. I've brought the rope."

He wrenched Abdul around and bound his hands together while speaking to him in Arabic as I held the gun.

"What did you say to him?" I asked.

"I said that it was over, that the police will arrive by morning to arrest them all."

Abdul spat something back.

"What did he say?"

"He quoted the Quran, something about wealth being like a poisonous snake unless you take care of your family, or something to that effect."

"This riad is ours," Amira cried while Peaches bound her hands. "Anything you find belongs to my family!"

"That might have been true had you told the authorities and let the court handle your property complaint." But the words stuck in my throat. I knew damned well how the poor fared against the wealthy in situations like this but that didn't justify murder and destruction.

Once bound, the siblings were marched back into the smaller courtyard where Peaches forced them to the floor against a wall and proceeded to tie their feet.

"How close are you to finding it, do you think?" I asked Evan after he'd assisted with the roping and returned to the digging site.

"Close, hopefully. I've chipped down at least a foot to the original flooring," he said, gazing down at the pile of broken tiles scattering the floor. A ragged hole now gaped where the basin had been while the fountain itself sat a few feet away with its electrical cord snaking away across the floor.

I leaned over and peered down, seeing the outline of much older mosaic revealing itself beneath the rubble. In a minute, I was on my knees prying up the top layer of loosened tiles with my fingers. The first piece— blue against white with inlays of deep carnelian red—had not faded across the centuries and seemed to form part of a triangle. I brushed away more to reveal almost a foot of beautiful, intricate mosaic.

I looked up at Evan as he leaned on his pickax. "It's the Bartolo carpet in mosaic."

"Yes," he said quietly.

"But we can't just destroy it." Tears stung my eyes. I couldn't believe I was willingly participating in the destruction of ancient art.

"We must if we are going to retrieve the dowry. I'm hoping to preserve enough that it can be reconstructed."

"These tiles are inlaid with lapis, carnelian, and other precious materials. It's a work of art in itself. How could anyone just cover it up in the first place?"

"Either politics or religion," he remarked, "the two most destructive forces in history."

"Yes, but this mosaic may say something even more explosive, especially if it celebrates all religions, which could be seen as heresy to all. And the fact that it's not a Moroccan design in itself could have compelled the renovators to bury it." I stood up.

"Do you truly believe this mosaic celebrates omnism?"

"Yes, the same way the Bartolo carpet does. It's a message, a powerful message. Is there any way to preserve it?"

"Sadly not. This should be an archaeological site and protected accordingly, I admit, but if we want to preserve what's hidden here, we need to work quickly."

"It's a travesty."

"Agreed."

I wiped my eyes on my arm. "So, how can we help?"

"Stand back and let me get back to it, if you don't mind. I'm afraid that extra help will only get in my way. I'm trying to preserve what I can."

"Right." I stepped away. I couldn't bear to watch those tiles be destroyed, in any case. I checked my phone, finding that Agent Walker hadn't responded to my midnight text and that all my other contacts in

London were obviously asleep. I strolled over to Peaches, who stood staring at the siblings where they sat bound on the floor.

"How long do you think those ropes will hold them?" I asked.

"As long as necessary," Peaches said. "I can tie a mean knot and Evan a better one apparently. "Where did you find him again?"

"In London, sort of. Anyway, that's the last of the siblings," I said, gazing at Amira. Her brother leaned against the wall with his eyes closed but her gaze remained fixed on every move I made.

"You killed him," she said at last. "My brother is dead?"

"Yes, he is gone. I'm sorry, Amira, but I did not kill him," I told her truthfully. "Somebody else pulled the trigger."

"Noel?" Peaches asked.

"Of course Noel," I whispered.

"Who is this Noel? Why did he kill my brother?" Amira cried, straining against the ropes.

"He thought he was protecting me. Your brother shouldn't have stolen that document or knifed the courier trying to deliver it to me."

But Amira had begun wailing a high-pitched keen, a sound so much like pure pain that it nearly broke my heart.

Peaches covered her ears. "Will you stop?"

Evan paused his digging. "I think I've hit something," he called.

Peaches and I were at the dig in seconds, staring down past the shattered tiles at a square shape just visible under a crumble of earth. "A chest?" I asked.

"I believe so," Evan said. "Who wants to do the honors?"

"You go." Peaches nudged me. "You're why we're here in the first place."

Evan chunked away a bit of earth around either side of the box—rusted iron, at first glance—and let me try to lift it out. It wouldn't budge.

"Here, allow me." In seconds he had hoisted a small chest of about two feet wide and a foot deep from the earth and carried it over to the table.

For a moment, all we could do was stare at the badly damaged metal box that hadn't seen the light of day for over seven hundred years. Encrusted with earth, it appeared as though the fountain may have been slowly leaking onto the metal for decades, maybe centuries. Most of the outer casing had nearly rusted away and the padlock securing it hung from the ring like a

broken jaw.

"I hope what's inside isn't damaged, too," I said.

"Go on, open it." Peaches nudged me again.

Evan gave the lock a final whack with his ax handle and the rest of the lock crumbled to the floor. I stepped forward, touching the lid, trembling with anticipation for that moment in time when a person from one age gazes into another...

"What is the meaning of this?" a shrill voice demanded.

I swung around, my arm still outstretched toward the chest. June was striding through the door, Joe scampering at her heels. For a second, I viewed the scene through her eyes—a ruined floor, three people obviously involved in a search, and two more bound up against the wall. If you could paint a scene for nefarious, we'd nailed it.

"Pardon?" I said, scrambling for an explanation and finding none.

"I said, what is the meaning of this?" June's gaze swung from the siblings to the three of us and back again.

It was such a stereotypical question that I countered with a stereotypical answer. "I can explain everything." My arm dropped to my side.

"Oh, really?" She was pulling a phone from the pocket of her pink robe. "It's time I called the police, something I should have done long ago. There!" She held the phone up as she pressed a number in her contacts, too far away for anyone to see the details. She had the Moroccan police on speed dial? She said something I couldn't catch into the cell followed by a loud: "Come at once!"

"This isn't what it appears," Evan whispered beside me, and then: "Mrs. Meredith, don't do this," he said. "It won't unfold how you expect it to, I promise you that. Don't interfere." He stepped forward as if to intercept her while Peaches slid in front of the chest to hide it from view. "Just leave the room now."

"Are you kidding me—three people demolishing private property? Are you going to tell me that you're just repairing the fountain or something? Come now, Mr. Ashton, do you take me for a fool? What is that on the table?"

"We work with Interpol," I said, stepping forward, "and we're here on official business investigating a murder that has led back to here." That wasn't quite true, and if Walker didn't contact the Moroccan branch soon, we were going to end up in the local jail, regardless. "Obviously, we couldn't inform the staff or guests what we were up to."

"I bet," June said, inching forward. "So you're going to tell me you're detectives now, are you?"

"More like agents for the ancient lost and found. That's what we call ourselves." I was willing to say anything at that point. "My friend actually owns this riad." That wasn't quite true since the ownership of the riad may not have been officially passed into Nicolina's hands yet.

"Though we are not actual detectives," Evan said, striking his most officious tone, "we are indeed working with the authorities to locate buried or hidden artworks. I assure you our actions are quite legitimate, despite the appearance."

If he was trying to distract her with assurances, she wasn't buying it, not that I blamed her. Her look of self-righteous alarm had shifted to something more smug. "Real Indiana Joneses, are you? Why don't you just open the box before the curtain falls?" She met my eyes. "Well, go on."

I turned, reluctant to pollute this treasured moment with June Meredith and her cowed husband looking on but seeing no choice. While everyone watched, I lifted the badly rusted lid and gazed down at what looked to be a bundle of dark red rags that might once have been velvet. As I lifted the bundle from the box and set it on the table, the disintegrating fabric fell away. All we could do was gasp.

Green fire shot from the surface as Evan ran his phone light across the four sides of the box.

"Oh, my sweet Jesus!" Peaches exclaimed. "Is that what I think it is?"

I touched the surface reverently. "A box made of sheets of carved solid emerald? Yes, it totally is." Staring at the ornate, jewel-and-pearl-encrusted lid with its omnistic symbols, I fought the urge to cry—so much beauty with such a powerful message. "And it celebrates the god in all religions, a universal symbol of religious unity."

"Open it."

That was June's voice but I didn't look up, couldn't tear my gaze away from that casket for a single moment—none of us could. I lifted the lid while Evan beamed light into the interior, illuminating the gem surface from the inside out like some surreal jungle mystery. "It's filled with jewels," I whispered, scooping a fistful of precious gems into my hand—sapphires, diamonds, rubies, all sparkling like crazy.

"Holy shit," Peaches whispered, gazing down at a palm full of gems. "I never really got why people would kill for a bundle of shiny rocks but, like, I'm changing my mind."

"This is worth a fortune in any century and is a simply magnificent find," Evan said, while holding a faceted diamond up to the light. "Flawless."

My tears released, blurring in the light of so much beauty. After a few moments of reverent gaping, I shook away the spell. "What's taking Interpol so long? This is going to need an armed guard to safely transport it anywhere."

"Step away now." June again but I ignored her, so intent was I on this amazing discovery.

Amira was shouting from behind me.

"I said step away or I'll shoot."

That caught my attention. I turned to June, who now held a gun pointed right at me.

22

I should have seen it coming. Maybe at some level I had but refused to pay attention.

"Don't looked so shocked, Phoebe. Do you think you're the only one who can make a booking under an assumed name?"

June stood with a gun trained on us, Joe behind her holding a pistol of his own. The three of us were unarmed. I'd left the two guns I'd been carrying near the fountain, and since one of them was Evan's, that left him defenseless, too. Peaches's knife was firmly shoved into her scabbard but that didn't do much good under the circumstances. One move and she'd be shot.

"Who are you?" Evan asked, pitching his voice over Amira's keening. He, at least, did not seem surprised.

"Let's just say we're an interested party. Joe, shut her up."

Joe marched to the wall where our prisoners sat and whacked Amira across the face with the back of his hand. When her brother started shouting at him, he was slugged on the head with the butt of his gun—some distorted sense of chivalry. The brother slumped against the wall unconscious while Amira fell silent.

"There, much better," June remarked.

Now we knew what we were up against. "Who *are* you?" I demanded.

"Call me June—that part is correct. Otherwise, we work for someone with vested interests—not them obviously," she said, indicating the siblings. "You—Peaches or whatever the hell your name is—bring us the box. Joe, get the bag ready."

Joe strode over and I realized that he had a backpack slung over his shoulders. Keeping his gun on Peaches while June leveled hers on the rest of us with a kind of periodic wide-angled swing, he slipped the bag off, one shoulder at a time while still gripping the gun. Peaches cast Evan and me a quick look as she proceeded to lift the chest.

"You were ready for this, weren't you? Just waiting for us to lead you right to the treasure. How did you get to the riad before us?" I asked. I had to keep her talking, maybe distract her.

June smiled a rictus of self-satisfaction. "We've had you bugged for months, listening in to your every thought, even way back in London. We've been tracking your every move, darling. And my, oh my, you have lived a very boring life these past few months, haven't you? At least until recently. As soon as you hit Venice, things picked up but we had no idea you'd lead us to such a bounty as this—emerald and jewels, well, well."

"Bugged her how?" Evan snapped.

"Oh, yes, the gizmo whiz. My employer uses a nifty new technology that, once inserted into an item—let's say the inner seam of a carpetbag—is virtually undetectable even by you. And she carries that old thing everywhere, don't you, Phoebe?"

My traitorous bag was still in my room. How long had it been listening in on my life? At least I didn't need to ask who had put the device there. That much I'd already figured out. I felt sick. "When is he coming?" I asked.

June pulled her lips from her teeth. "Oh, you guessed—bright girl. He's on his way."

"Who's on his way?" Peaches asked standing with the chest in both hands.

"Noel Halloren," Evan said under his breath.

Peaches swore. "You work for that bastard? But how? I mean, we blew that operation up in Jamaica, and when he took off we figured he'd have nothing left."

"Halloran has been pocketing loot for months before that while building his own operation on the side," Evan said. "We've long suspected it but lacked proof."

June smiled, so obviously enjoying this. "Well, he does have a policy: follow Phoebe McCabe and she'll take you to the goods every time. He calls you his lucky charm, sweetheart."

I swore viciously.

"Everyone is being spied on these days, you just more intimately than most," June said. "What, don't tell me you thought he was smitten by your charms alone when he followed you here?"

I didn't actually, but it hardly mattered just then. It would be enough if I kept myself together when I saw him next. What I did before and after was all that mattered.

"Joe, put that thing in the bag, and you, Peaches, if you do anything stupid, I'll blow your brains out. You two, stay where you are," June ordered. She held the gun like she meant every word but even she must have known that she was outnumbered. Besides, I had the sense that she was hired more for her disposition than her skill.

Joe stepped forward with the bag open while Peaches went to meet him carrying the casket, mere seconds when Joe literally had his hands full. And seconds was all it took. Peaches tossed the casket at Joe while Evan and I both launched at June, Evan aiming for her legs, me at her gun arm. The gun went off, hitting the ceiling and sending June back against the tiles screaming, Evan on top of her. I raced to help Peaches, who was rolling around the floor with Joe trying to wrest the knife from her grasp. I lifted the casket and brought it down on his head, sending him to the floor in a heap and scattering jewels everywhere.

"Damn, we're good!" Peaches exclaimed as she pushed his limp body off her. "You'd think we orchestrated that but I would have had him in a few more seconds."

Meanwhile, Evan had June on her feet with her arm twisted behind her back. "We'll tie her up," he said.

"I should have shot you when I had the chance," June snarled as she attempted to kick out at him. "Big MI6 guy, are you? You're nothing but a well-packaged hunk of shit!"

Evan wrenched her arm a little harder. "Now, don't go hurting my feelings, June, if that's your name. We'll just put you over here with the other two."

While he and Peaches bound her up and dragged Joe over to the wall, I busied myself picking up the scattered gems. The casket was undamaged, the emerald sides impervious to even Joe's skull. Still, I was ashamed of myself for using a priceless work of art as a bludgeon. The things we do in desperation.

When I next looked up, Peaches and Evan had both Joe and June tied up beside the other two and were turning back to pick up the firearms. I had just lifted the casket from the floor and set it on the table, Joe's gun tucked into my belt, when a gunshot ripped the air. I saw Evan spin around gripping his shoulder while Peaches lunged toward the door, both stopping short at the sight of Noel's gun.

"Don't make me shoot you, Peaches—we used to be friends once—but you, Ashton, you I wouldn't hesitate to shoot again in a minute." He lifted the gun as if to do exactly that, his eyes flashing a cold light.

"No, Noel, don't!" I cried, throwing myself in front of Evan.

"Phoebe, get behind me," Evan hissed, trying to shove me back. Blood oozed between the fingers gripping his shoulder. He'd try reaching for his gun next and Noel would kill him. That couldn't happen.

"No!" I ran to within three feet of Noel and stopped. "Don't do it, Noel, don't hurt them, please."

"You know my policy on that, Phoebe. Step out of the way and you, Ashton, lay the gun on the floor—now!"

But Evan wasn't moving and I could imagine him calculating possible next steps, none of which would end well. I kept inching toward Noel, my hands in the air. "Don't do this, Noel, don't turn into one of those bastards we used to talk about, the ones who'd inflict violence on anybody for greed. Don't tell me you've turned into one of them!"

"Get the fuck out of the way!" Noel cried, lunging to the left to level another shot at Evan.

Peaches was diving for her knife and June was yelling obscenities as I rammed into Noel, sending his shot wide. But then he had me whipped around with one arm, gripping me across the chest, and the gun shoved into my temple. Everybody froze.

I watched as Evan slowly lowered the gun to the floor.

"Kick it toward me," Noel ordered.

"Don't do it, Evan! He wouldn't hurt me!" I cried.

The arm bracing me tightened. "Are you so sure about that, my love?" Noel whispered into my ear. I wasn't sure of anything anymore. Evan clearly wasn't, either, since he kicked the gun toward him.

"Back off, both of you. Peaches, take that knife of yours and cut the ropes on June here." Joe was still unconscious.

"You tink I'll do what for you, Noel? Do you tink I'm still your little worker bee or something?" Peaches snarled.

In answer, Noel lifted the gun higher on my temple. "Or I'll shoot her, I said."

She hesitated, maybe moments too long, but then picked up the knife to do as he asked. In minutes June was back on her feet holding her hand out for the knife, which Peaches reluctantly relinquished. June then leaned over and plucked my gun from inside my waistband.

"Now, this is what's going to happen," Noel said. "June, you're going to gather up those guns and then proceed to pack that casket into the back-pack and then pass the bag to me. If anybody moves in the meantime, shoot them, got that? Don't hesitate. It's simple, really: if you have to shoot one of them, I'll shoot Phoebe and everybody loses."

"Don't worry," June said, picking up one of the guns. "I would gladly shoot all these pains in the asses without hesitation."

"What in the hell happened to you, Noel?" I whispered as June went about her work. "The man I knew would never do anything this maniacally devious." Maybe I was crying, maybe not.

"Oh, really? How well did you know me really, Phoebe, baby? I'm the same man I've always been only you wanted me to be something better. I never pretended to be anything else."

"Oh, yeah? What about that Robin Hood of the black market crap you sold me on?" I asked.

"That was all Toby. Your dear brother really thought he could rescue stolen art and return it to the original owners beneath the legal radar—that is, until he spun out on drugs and got lost in his own madness. I never bought into that shit."

"Halloren has been skimming the goods for years, Phoebe," Evan added, watching him closely. "He's been the real villain all along."

"Why didn't you say something?" I asked him, straining against Noel's hold. Noel just held me tighter.

"I couldn't," Evan said, pain clouding his eyes.

"He couldn't because he's undercover Interpol, Phoebe—haven't you figured that out yet?" Noel said. "He and Foxy have been tracking you to get to me for years. It took the Jamaica heist for me to figure that out, too."

"Is that true?" I demanded.

Evan met my eyes without flinching. "Phoebe, I deeply regret all of that, believe me."

"And the chauffeuring and bodyguarding bit with Foxy?" I asked.

"All part of our cover."

"*Our* cover? You mean you and Foxy have been playing me for a fool all along?" I swore.

"Not a fool," he said earnestly, "but a valuable connection to a crime family who has been stealing art for years. Rupert and I are both very fond of you. Nothing there was a lie. You must believe me."

"Want me to shoot him for you, Phoebe?" Noel said. "My pleasure, believe me. June, what's taking so long—hurry up, will you?" Noel called.

June scurried back with the bag in her hand, the gun still trained on Peaches. "Here you go, boss. I took two diamonds as part of our payment. It's not like you pay us enough or anything."

But I couldn't take my eyes off Evan.

"Yeah, sure, sure. You do this right and I'll wire you a bonus. Put it on my shoulder and watch the rest of them while we take off."

"Even her?" She indicated me with a flick of the gun.

"No, not her. She's coming with me. As for the others: if Peaches moves, shoot her."

That snapped my attention back. "Me coming with you? Are you crazy? I'm not going to be your hostage."

But then everything happened so fast. Noel fired his gun and Evan collapsed to the floor. Peaches screamed and June yelled at her to be quiet while I was being steered out the door by Noel. And I went, anger and panic burning so deep that all I could think of was how to get this bastard. Play along.

"Okay, Noel, I'm coming with you," I told him as he marched me out the front door of the riad and down the narrow street. "I'm not fighting you so stop twisting my arm."

He released me but kept the gun pressed into my back as he hurried me along. Dawn was just pushing a sharp band of light into the sky over the medina and the air felt heartbreakingly chill. We carried on without speaking until we turned another corner to a narrow street where one of the parked cars winked its lights in greeting.

I didn't know what to expect but not this. "A getaway car? Are you serious?"

"Just get in, Phoebe," he said.

He opened the door and shoved me into the passenger seat, dropping the bag on my lap. "If you don't do as I say, June will shoot Peaches—that's the deal. It's you or her." He pitched his voice louder. "June, you hear me?"

"Coming in loud and clear, boss," June's voice crackled from somewhere under his jacket. A wire.

"Keep the gun on Peaches. If I say shoot her, shoot."

"Got it, boss."

I looked up at his shadowed face. "Bastard! I'll come with you, I said."

"Good, so no attempts to jump out or try anything more creative. I know how creative you can be."

"Ask her how Evan's doing," I asked.

"How's Evan doing, June?"

Crackle. Crackle. "Losing a lot of blood. Should bleed out soon."

"Why did you have to shoot him?" I cried.

"Why do you think, Phoebe?" he said while climbing into the driver's seat and pealing us down the street, narrowly missing a mule piled with carpets. "Shoot them while you have the chance or they'll come after you every time. Once I found out he was undercover Interpol, I wished I'd shot him sooner. Foxy will be next. You should thank me. They've been using you to get to Toby and me for years."

"Damn you all to hell!"

"That's my girl. Fasten your seat belt now. We have a long ride ahead of us."

All I could do was swear at him at first while churning away inside. Admittedly, my brain was not functioning optimally.

"Oh, come on now, Phoebe, not that tired old expletive. You can do better than that."

The thought of Evan dying when all I wanted was to scream at the man for hoodwinking me for so long was one thing, but being in the company of Noel again was something else. My heart was a mess, my mind worse. "You goddamn hunk of stinking twisted assholean chicken shit!"

"Assholean chicken shit—almost has an Oxfordian flare. Better, but not up to your usual standards. Just so you know, you were absolutely right back there: I would never harm a hair on your head. Never have, never will. I don't care if you believe it or not but I love you."

"You call kidnapping me, shooting my friends, stealing a treasure you know I went to a lot of trauma to retrieve all while spying on me...*love?*"

"Oh, Phoebe, come on. Your friends are all working against my enterprise—fair's fair. You are, too, but you my heart puts in protective custody. Come on, admit you still love me just a little. I'm still the lovable rogue you fell for years ago."

"I hate you," I spat.

"Flip side of the love/hate continuum—better than ambivalence any day. I'll take it."

More expletives followed on my part. It seemed as though my ability to communicate in full sentences had gone. It took several miles of driving into a brilliant desert sunrise before I calmed down. "Where are you taking me and why in hell do you expect to get away with this?" I said as I sat slumped back in the seat, numb with pain. "Do you really think I'm going to play your mol and go dashing off on the run with you?"

He squinted into the rising sun and flipped down the visor. "Forgot my bloody sunnies. No, I'm not going to try dragging you on the run with me, don't worry. You'd only slow me down, and cause me a piss-load of trouble besides. No, Phoebe, my love, I'm taking you only as far as I need to get away from Interpol before the troops come flying in this morning. You were my ticket out of the riad without having to shoot Peaches. I've got my getaway all planned, don't worry. My organization is far more extensive than anything I had established with Toby. Even you'd be impressed, methinks. Also, I don't want it to end like this between us. Cutting me loose has left me gutted. I'd hoped we could end things on a brighter note."

"What do you mean I cut you loose? You've been loose from the day we met. I've been your lead to the next heist all along, you (insert colorful expletive) butt-licking bastard!"

He whistled between his teeth. "Now, that was an interesting one, but for the record, I did follow you as much to keep you safe as anything else. That's how it began, honestly. I wanted to see you again, hold you in my arms, kiss you and more—always more. Our mores were something else, weren't they? We've had some—hell, makes me hot just thinking about it—wild times. Remember that night on the roof in Cappadocia? Anyway, I was late grappling on to the value of what you were after. When I saw the Moroccan family tailing you in Venice, I realized the stakes must be higher than I thought so I began to dig around."

"And you discovered that there was a valuable hoard buried inside the riad."

"Thanks to you, yes, exactly. The Moroccan family got in my way once or twice, but shit, they were such amateurs that you and Peaches easily took care of them—nice work, by the way. And then I spent a few days digging around Marrakech and discovered that a sultan, Abu Abd Allah al-Burtuquali Muhammad, ruler of the Wattasid dynasty, struck up some kind of an alliance with a wealthy Jewish Berber family back in the day, the details of which are obscured by time."

"It may even have been an enlightened union of individuals from three religions."

"You always were a romanticist, Phoebe; it's one of the many things I love about you. Whatever the case, something empowered the Jews to the secrete the sultan's riches against political upheaval—who knows? Those guys had enemies like you wouldn't believe. It's all wrapped up in folklore locally and well worth listening to if you ever get the chance. Anyway, how exactly a sultan's hoard gets buried under the floor of a Jewish family's home may never be fully known, but thanks to you, the treasure itself has been retrieved."

I gazed down at the backpack. "And is about to be lost to the world again. This is significant, Noel, important far beyond the monetary value of its contents. This casket is embedded with symbols celebrating unity among religions instead of the bloody divisions. Doesn't that mean anything to you? It needs protecting! The world needs to see treasures like this for what they are—humanity's attempt to rise above the bloodshed and worship universal good!" Okay, so I was crying again.

"You really care about that stuff, don't you?"

"I thought you did, too. I thought we understood one another, fought for the same things! What about the archaeologist's creed?"

He grinned. "You don't seriously think there is such a thing, do you? Besides, I haven't worked as an archaeologist in over a decade. No, the only creed I follow is my own, and though it pains me to see something with so much history and passion behind it fade into the woodwork, in the end that casket will fetch a fortune on the underground market and those jewels will keep me going for a long time."

"You're contemptible. What is your creed now: take what you want and screw everybody else?" Ahead a ragged bite of mountain cut a sharp silhouette against the horizon and sliced my wounded heart all over again.

"Pardon me for being crude but I'd love to screw you one more time."

"Very funny. You're taking us to the Atlas
Mountains?"

"Mountains are a great place to hide. I only need a few days before the dust dies down with a lot of places to hole up in the meantime. Morocco isn't a rich country. They don't have the resources to chase me for long."

A few cars passed us on the highway, a few saddled mules and camels plodding along on the sandy shoulders, too, but otherwise the road was empty. I thought about trying to jump out but he had the child minder lock on. I considered trying to wrest the steering wheel from him but I didn't see how that would end well. For one thing, his gun was in his other pocket and I doubted I'd be fast enough to get it from him. Instead, I sat still, scheming and furious, feeling the press of my phone in my pants pocket. Would anyone track me and who was left standing to do it, anyway?

Recrimination burned deeply. Why was I so trusting? Did love make me blind and stupid, too? I should have never let him into the riad, not that that made a difference in the end. If I was being brutally honest with myself, I still gave Noel too many ins—ins to my heart, ins the riad, ins to my life. Always had. Love was like a squatter: once it set up house, it was hell getting it evicted. My mind said one thing, my heart another. I was so done with this. I needed to change my tact.

"I can't bear to think we're going to end this way, Noel, not after all the years we've sort of been together," I said softly.

The sun had broken through the mountains to pour bloodred light down on us both. "Yeah, Phoebe. It hurts me, too. It's always been you and me, no matter what you think, despite all our differences. What we had together was real but I couldn't just turn myself in and go to jail."

"I could have negotiated a lighter sentence if you had." Having been an almost lawyer, I had connections.

"I'd have died in there, you know that, and besides, do you really see me as living some kind of ordinary life? What would that look like, anyway? Me coming home from work at six every night and watching TV while you knit?"

I snorted. "As if that spells out everything worth living in an ordinary life, and by the way, that sounds pretty damn appealing to me. Life isn't all adrenaline and breathless moments, Noel. There's comfort in having someone you care about nearby on cold nights, someone to hold you when you're hurt and afraid, someone to make supper with on a Friday night plus all those little moments in between. Love breathes life into the ordinary things."

"Sounds like you want a puppy, not a man."

I clenched my teeth after that. We drove for another five minutes until we were at the foot of the mountains with nothing but expanses of scrabbled earth and spotty palm trees all around. He pulled off the road and bumped over the earth to a copse of palms with a flat sandy area nearby and cut the engine.

"This is my rendezvous point and where we part. You can take the car and drive back to Marrakech once my ride arrives. No hard feelings, all right?"

He was gazing at me, one brown arm on the steering wheel, his dark eyes warm and that mouth of his exactly as I remembered so fondly. I leaned over and kissed him. He hesitated only seconds before kissing me back, one hand grabbing mine in case I lunged for his gun. All the passion between us ignited as if all the years and pain didn't exist. He pulled away, breathless. "One more time for old times' sake, my love?" he asked.

"One more time," I whispered.

We were out of the car in seconds, he tossing his gun in the back seat in case I tried to grab it and then locking the door. No one was around but the car shielded us from the road just in case. He furled his jacket on the sand, Sir Walter Raleigh–style, and beckoned me to lie down.

I smiled and shook my head. "You first."

"You always were my woman-on-top kinda girl," he murmured into my hair as he embraced me.

"And don't you forget it." My hands were under his shirt and exploring, a familiar electricity hitting my vitals as I touched him in all those secret places. In moments he was on the ground with me on top of him, our kisses wild and fevered, nothing forced, nothing feigned. I had his pants down and mine half-off when I pulled my phone from my pocket, held the home button down along with the volume button, and pressed the phone against his bare skin. I whispered into his ear: "Thank you for making this so easy for me."

A jolt of real electricity zapped beneath my fingers as the man beneath me flopped still.

23

Tall, dark and tasered was a good look on him. Lying there bare-chested with a rectangular burn below his heart, he'd never looked so fetching or so dead. For a moment, I thought I'd killed him, but no, he still had a weak pulse. I dropped the blistered chunk of phone into the dust beside him. The taser app worked fine but destroyed the phone, seared my good palm, and nearly killed the victim, too. I had to remind Evan to tweak that feature. If there even was an Evan. Shit! *If there even was an Evan!*

I buttoned my shirt and snatched the keys from Noel's pocket, ripping off the wire from inside his jacket while I was at it. I took his phone and wallet, too, and then started up the car before returning to try dragging the limp man into the back seat. Though lean, he was still heavy, and with both hands injured, I lacked my usual leverage. And then I heard the unmistakable sound of a helicopter far in the distance.

Shielding my eyes, a speck like a faraway bug could clearly be seen heading my way. I had expected a car for the rendezvous, not a bloody helicopter! In seconds, I was behind the wheel, forced to leave Noel and take off while I could. I doubted I could outrun a car, but I knew I couldn't outrun a helicopter. And then there was the little matter of the loot in the front seat. Once they found Noel dishabille and the bag missing, presumably they'd come gunning after me. I also had to factor in the fact that by taking Noel's phone, I may have made it easier for them to track.

I pushed down the window and reluctantly tossed the phone. Damn. I'd hoped to use it to call the police. If lucky, maybe I'd get a half hour head start before Noel's team realized what had happen.

Turns out, I got less. Fifteen minutes after I'd started zipping down the highway, that helicopter was trailing behind me. The traffic had picked up. What would they do, shoot the car full of holes like they do in the movies and not care what collateral damage they caused along the way? Maybe they'd try to run me off the road, then drop down and pick the loot out of the wreckage. What did I know? There were plenty of places for a helicopter to land in this desert flatland.

Quick decision time. I whipped off the highway into the parking lot of a gas station complex. The possibility that the car was identifiable or trackable was too high a risk. I dashed into the adjoining leather shop and bought a tooled and beaded camel-skin bag from the money in Noel's wallet. Moments later I had the casket transferred into the bag and left Joe's backpack in the bathroom.

In the truck stop minutes later, first I tried to use the phone. No problem except I had no idea of local area codes or even who to call exactly and my efforts to communicate with the attendant too fraught. What if I called the regular police, then what? Imagining the questions I'd answer while carrying a fortune in my bag and leaving a tasered man by the side of the road didn't bear thinking about. Next, I tried negotiating a ride to Marrakech with a tractor-trailer driver. Whether the language barrier was to blame or some company policy, none of the guys smoking cigarettes and drinking coffee would give me a lift at first, at least until I flashed a few American dollars. Then I was overwhelmed with offers. I finally settled on a delivery guy packing a trailer load of dates to the city.

By the time I'd hurried Salim out the door, the helicopter was in the distance heading back toward us with two more far in the distance. If Salim thought it odd that I leaped into the truck's cab without so much as a hoist up or an official invitation, he didn't say. Besides, he didn't speak English and I didn't speak Arabic. That left a long ride back to Marrakech in a cab full of smoke and Moroccan pop music. I kept the window down, so tense I thought I'd snap in two. Forty-five minutes later, I thanked Salim as he dropped me off near the square and I jogged my way through the medina to the riad.

This time, armed uniformed men packing machine guns surrounded the riad. When I identified myself and held up the bag to prove I was who I said, the bag was whipped from my hands and I was promptly marched inside at gunpoint. All that mattered was Peaches and Evan. By then I didn't care about anything else, not the treasure, nothing.

"Phoebe!" Peaches cried when she laid eyes on me. "My God! I thought he'd dragged you off somewhere!"

"He did. We managed one last tender moment before I tasered him." We hugged, her squeezing the breath out of me. "Thank God, you're okay. What about Evan?"

Agent Walker stepped out from the tangle of uniformed men. "Phoebe McCabe, you never cease to amaze me."

"What about Evan?" I repeated.

Sam Walker gazed at me with his cool blue eyes. "He's been taken to the hospital with two bullet holes and a lot of blood loss. I'm waiting for an update but the last I heard he was still alive, that's the main thing. Otherwise, there's one woman down, two men with a head injury, and another two on their way into headquarters for questioning."

Over his shoulder I saw Mohammed and one of the other riad helpers mopping up the tiles.

"And Noel Halloren is by the side of the highway unconscious, I hope half-dead," I said.

"We've got helicopters out there now. If he's there, we'll get the bastard. Peaches filled me in on what happened."

"I shot June," Peaches said, "and Amira helped by tripping the bitch. Didn't kill her, though. My bad."

I nodded, part of me too numb to take any more in.

BACK IN VENICE DAYS LATER, THE WORLD HAD TAKEN ON A DIFFERENT cast. It had become a noticeably colder universe for me, slightly less infused with the exuberance in which I had previously viewed it. The colors were still clear in my retina but how I saw them had shifted—darker, deeper, richer. But no, just for the record, I was nowhere near depressed, just sadder and wiser.

"Phoebe, thank you again for all you have done," Nicolina was saying. "If it were not for you, we may never have known why Maria was killed or by whom," she continued.

We were sitting in the Contini villa salon with the Bartolo hanging in pride of place over the mantel. The police had located the missing painting tucked into a closet at Amira Alaoui's shabby apartment and now it hung triumphant and undamaged. I could not take my eyes off it, specifically at the hexagram outlined in what must have been knotted gold silk beneath the bride's feet.

"If it were not for you, we may never have known many things," Nicolina continued, looking up at the painting. Those things were too numerous to outline yet again, thankfully—Evan Ashton and Sir Rupert Fox's true roles, Noel Halloren's modus operandi, Zara's unwitting duplicity, and it went on and on. All of it was more than I could process right then. All I wanted to do was crawl inside some quiet place and pull the covers over my head but I had the feeling that the world would always find me anywhere I went.

"I will give the Bartolo to a museum here in Venice, possibly the Galleria dell'Accademia. It memorializes a marriage in Venice and should return to Venice," Nicolina said, but I was hardly paying attention.

"There are lots of things we might never have known without my Phoebe," Max said from the couch beside me. He had flown in the day before and our conversations had been intense ever since. Try telling a man that you tasered his son in a moment of passion. The fact that the son was a bastard was borderline irrelevant; the fact that he still managed to get away with his crimes may have been a comfort to Max but not to me. Noel's helicopter team must have picked him up and whisked him off to safety. My only consolation was that he'd bear a phone-sized brand below his heart for life, a permanent reminder of just how hot Phoebe McCabe can get.

"Look," I said, getting to my feet. "I just have to get out for a walk, do you mind?"

Nicolina and Max erupted at once. "Phoebe, are you all right?" "Shall we come with you?" I don't know who said what.

"No, thank you. I just need to be alone for a bit. Stay here, both of you. Please."

After all, it had been three full days of interrogation, first with the Moroccan authorities and then with Peroni, plus all the endless, convoluted discussions with Sam Walker and my friends in between. And then there was the treasure, a hotly contested item that would be tied up in international courts for a long time—found on Moroccan soil on property owned by an Italian estate. Untangle that one, if you can. At least it was in "public" hands, whatever its ultimate destination, and I had my photos and my convictions. There was a story there that needed to be released to the world, not that I believed for a moment that it alone could change the world. Still, every story of hope counted.

I just needed to leave it all behind and blow some fresh air into my thinking.

"Sure, darlin'," Max said, rising. Nicolina stood, too, both of them casting worried looks at me with the two bandaged hands and what they believed to be my broken heart. If they could see through my shirt, they'd discover that the heart in question hadn't broken so much as hardened to a tensile strength.

I left them standing there and strode into the hall, snatching up my carpetbag where I'd dropped it by the door. The thing was in rough shape, its seams slit and the battered Ottoman kilim textile carefully cut away to reveal the leather interior. There was a metaphor to be had there. Carrying it under the arm was the only possibility now that the handle had been sliced off.

I passed Seraphina in the hall but barely acknowledged her presence. Her friend Zara might yet be charged as there were unanswered questions about how much the family retainer had suspected about her niece and nephews' actions. By default, Seraphina herself might have in some way obstructed justice by not disclosing her own suspicions earlier. She'd had them, I was sure of that. Not my problem either way. Let somebody else figure it out.

In the spring sunshine, moments later, I inhaled deeply and took a left-hand turn outside the villa to avoid again seeing the smoldering and heart-breaking remains of the warehouse in the other direction. Thinking too long on everything that had been lost was more than I could bear.

"Phoebe, wait up!" I turned. Peaches was striding down the street toward me carrying a package. She had taken off on a shopping expedition that morning, determined to update her look, Italian-style. "I've commissioned a leather pantsuit like you wouldn't believe—made to measure, since that's the only way I'd ever get something to fit my booty. What, is everybody size two in this country? They'll even ship it to London for me. Whoa! What's wrong?"

Did my face reveal that much? "I decided to get out of the villa for a while. Max and Nicolina are still there chewing things over but I'd had enough." I continued walking.

"Don't blame you. Would you rather be alone?"

"No, join me if you want. Just don't talk about what happened. I'm done."

"Yeah, okay." She fell into pace beside me, which meant shortening her steps considerably. "May I ask where we're going?"

"I'm not sure exactly but I'll know when I get there."

"Yeah, sure."

We carried along aimlessly, enjoying the warmth and sunshine, the brilliant sense that a fresh new season could override all the pain of the months before. We paused by shop windows to admire a piece of Murano glass or maybe an interesting hat or just anything that caught our eye. Eventually we stopped at a café to order cappuccinos even though the Italians didn't believe in drinking milky coffee that late in the morning.

Sitting there gazing out at the Grand Canal, Peaches tapped my hand. "Mind if I ask one question?"

I caught her eye. "I know what it is."

"No, you don't."

"Yes, I do. It's about Evan, right?"

She sat back and frowned. "Yeah, right. So when are you going to talk to him?"

I sighed, looking away. "I haven't decided. So far, I've just sent him an email to say 'get well soon,' which I thought suitably banal."

"Yes, really. If he knows you at all, he'll know that you reserve such heartfelt messages for houseplants or something."

I laughed. "I'm hoping he'll translate it to mean that I need time to think things through. As for Foxy—can I even call him that now that I know he's been acting in the interests of the law? Anyway, *Sir Rupert Fox* has sent me endless texts with updates, even though I have yet to respond to a single one. It seems that Evan has been recovering reasonably well in a London hospital where they airlifted him a couple of days ago. That's all I know."

"You're not really mad at him, are you? I mean, seriously, if he was undercover he couldn't exactly tell you what he was up to."

"I thought we weren't going to talk about this? But no, I understand perfectly why he did what he did. It all makes sense."

"And yet? Why do I hear a 'yet'?"

And then my phone rang. Pulling it from my pocket I stared down at the call identifier. "Sir Rupert Fox. Again."

"Are you going to answer it this time?" Peaches asked.

I pushed the end button. "I think not. When we get back to London tomorrow I'll have that conversation. Today I'm not ready and right now I have something left to do." Getting to my feet, I shoved the phone back into my pocket.

Peaches moved to stand but I waved her back. "Finish your cappuccino, my friend. I'll just be a minute."

I had caught sight of what I needed while passing along the canal a few minutes earlier and now it was time to do the deed.

The big steel box piled with garbage bags was positioned beside the canal waiting for pickup and, like any malodorous trash heap, worth avoiding. However, I walked straight toward it. If there really was such a thing as an agency for the ancient lost and found, it most certainly needed a virtual dumpster for the letting go part. We all needed one and it didn't matter where.

Pulling my mangled carpetbag from under my arm, I silently thanked it for keeping me company through so many adventures. It had been my amulet, my comfort through all my travels, as much a physical bolster as an imaginary friend. *Release what no longer serves you* applies equally to people or objects. Both can hold you back when you need to move forward. Without a backward glance, I tossed my battered companion of a decade into the dumpster and walked away, strains of *Time to Say Goodbye* streaming on autorewind in my head.

I was halfway down the street when my phone buzzed again.

Pulling it from my pocket, I read Foxy's text:

Phoebe, this silence on your part is extremely distressing (angry emoji). We must talk in person. Please come to see me at once when you arrive in London. We have work to do, and do it together we must. Already I have been presented with a lead for our efforts in the ancient lost and found department. This cannot wait.

Your colleague and, I trust, friend still, Rupert

I smiled and turned off my phone.

THE END

AFTERWORD

Like many works of fiction, this novel names real historical personages without recounting actual historical facts. The painter Domenico di Bartolo was a Sienese painter most noted for his fresco *The Marriage of the Foundlings* upon which the painting described in this book is based. However, I took license with the details of the painting as well as with the backstory described.

One thing that is verifiably true, however, is that both Bartolo and the celebrated artist Carlo Crivelli painted detailed carpets into some of their works and it is this point that inspired *The Carpet Cipher*. Everything else is unapologetically fiction.

JOIN MY NEWSLETTER

So many of my readers love art and textiles as I do and that prompts me to share what I've learned, add background detail to my books, and generally enrich or embellish your reading pleasure. Also, of course I want you to know when my next book is published and occasionally hare sample chapters. Please join the *Agency of the Ancient Lost & Found* newsletter. I promise never to SPAM and I absolutely will not sell your address to third-party interests.

Join here:

The Agency of the Ancient Lost & Found newsletter

Made in the USA
Monee, IL
11 June 2021